Duel with the devil

"HAVE YOU ANY idea, Antoine, how much you disgust me?" Antoine Rolande turned to face Roger Bernard.

"See here now, Roger, we are old friends, and—"

"We were never friends, Antoine. You will see that I have taken the liberty of placing your exquisite pair of duelling pistols on the desk. They will say anything else that need be said between us."

Antoine looked towards the desk—sure enough, his silver-handled pistols lay there, nearly aligned. He moved over to the desk.

"Roger, you jest! You would fight me to the death over a harmless flirtation with a village girl?"

"I'm not jesting, Antoine."

Antoine felt the sweat begin to drip from his pores. He knew that in a duel with Roger he would certainly lose his life. His mind raced, and he felt trapped like some wild animal. He would have to make his move first.

"Well then, Roger, if there is no dissuading you, come take your pick of weapons, and we'll be off into the garden."

As Roger took a first step toward the desk, Antoine sprang. Grabbing the pistol nearest to him, he swung it up and aimed quickly. The gun barked, and Antoine watched through the little curl of smoke for Roger to drop. But the man kept on coming.

"Still the cheat, eh, Antoine?" Roger reached out and grabbed his rival around the throat with a large, calloused hand. He began to squeeze, to twist. The fingers were like grappling hooks as they sunk pitilessly into Antoine's neck.

The Making of America Series

THE CAJUNS

Lee Davis Willoughby

A DELL/BRYANS BOOK

Published by
Dell Publishing Co., Inc.
1 Dag Hammarskjold Plaza
New York, New York 10017

Dell ® TM 681510, Dell Publishing Co., Inc.

ISBN: 0-440-01321-6

Printed in the United States of America

First printing—December 1981

PART ONE

1

A SOUR REEK of smoke hung on the summer air, crawling up the low forested hill where the men lay concealed. Beyond and below their meager screen of underbrush, visible scraps of the Missaguash River glinted steel-grey in the harsh Nova Scotia sunlight. On the far bank, the low outline of what had been their own Fort Beauséjour, until the British took it and renamed it Fort Cumberland, hulked sullen and apparently deserted.

His British Majesty's soldiers were not lolling there in enjoyment of a recent easy victory. On its heels, they had been sent out to set the torch to every innocent Acadian farm dwelling and outbuilding to be found in the surrounding country.

One gathered, watching, that they relished their

assignment. Distant scarlet uniforms had scattered across the landscape in all directions, reduced by the distance to scurrying colonies of ants. The ants were about their grim business with a vengeance, falling upon each outlying target with the earnest purpose typical of their insect prototypes when demolishing a conquered grasshopper.

From where young Roger Bernard stretched flat on his belly, at least a dozen fires could be discerned—some close at hand, some as distant as the mist-blurred horizon. His jaw was set square with anger. His normally blue eyes had gone almost as grey as the river. Under the tanned leather of his face a taut muscle twitched and flickered.

"Bastards!" It was more a growl than a word.

Lying next to him thigh to thigh, his companion grunted agreement. Antoine Rolande's lean length topped Roger's by at least two inches. His red-blonde thatch, thick and curly and an inheritance from a Celtic grandmother, was reminiscent of the dotted flames across the valley which they and their companions watched so grimly. Hate-filled, his eyes were as green as unset emeralds, and gleamed as hard.

"All down the province, they're doing this. Burning. Turning peaceful people out of their homes. They'll get around to our own Grand Pré before the month's out."

"What did we ever do to His Majesty George II of England that we're punished by having a Governor like Charles Lawrence put over us?" Roger muttered.

"We were born to people with French blood in them," answered Antoine. "Isn't that crime enough, to the English? Even though we've never raised a hand against them?"

Every man in the prone line must be thinking similar thoughts, and both Roger and Antoine were well aware of it. They were all Acadians, raised in the same mold of obedience to law and authority; farmers and fishermen so unwarlike that even France's English foes often dubbed them "the French Neutrals." They had bowed in submission to every oppressive edict proclaimed by their sadistic English overlord. Still the persecution continued.

"I don't think it's just that we're French-descended," Roger pondered. "It's because we're Catholics, too. With a priest like The Otter to stand up for us."

The Otter was in truth Abbé Le Loutre, sent over from the Church in Paris, who had arrived in Acadia at about the same time as Charles Lawrence and ever since had been a thorn in the cold-eyed Governor's side. He was in hiding now, perhaps concealed by Indians, always more partial to the French than to the English who had driven them out of Canada. Unlike his native flock, the Abbé believed in fighting back. It was even whispered that he had told many converted tribes that the English had crucified Christ.

Where they waited now for their leader, Joseph Broussard, to appear and give orders, the concealed band on the thickly treed hilltop could look down upon the fort which once had been French. It was foolhardy to imagine a small force of scantily armed civilians could do much against the drilled English garrison; but Broussard's call to the Bay of Fundy villages had gathered desperate young men together for at least one gesture of protest. His Excellency might just possibly be touched by such an effort, where meek compliance only fed his scorn.

"Three peace-loving generations," Antoine snarled, "and now this for thanks!"

"There may yet be some way to convince the Governor we don't menace him."

"And it's also possible, Roger, that the moon is made of green cheese."

Roger inched over slightly, until instead of contemplating crude vegetation he could fix a troubled gaze upon enamel-blue patches of sky beyond overhanging tree limbs.

"Where's Broussard? Have you seen him this morning, Antoine?"

"Not yet. But he'll be somewhere nearby. Waiting for the moment."

They were from the same home village, Roger and Antoine. Grand Pré had spawned them both, cradled them, added the inches to their somewhat varying heights. As small fry surrounded by their fathers' farm fields and learning the Abenaki arts of weir-fishing and canoe-building, they had once been inseparable friends.

Of late, though, that closeness had somewhat diminished. A new family, Despres by name, had moved into the little community from Port Royal, further seaward on the Bay of Fundy. Jules Despres had a daughter.

Her name was Rosalie. She had a voice as soft as a meadow breeze, and her dark hair shimmered like rare satin when she ran through the pastures with it flying loose, and her eyes were the rich brown of a pair of polished chestnuts, and there wasn't a youth in Grand Pré who failed to pivot and stare after her when she passed.

Of them all, Roger and Antoine had been the two

who followed most determinedly wherever she might lead. Neither one had much appreciated the dogged, insistent omnipresence of the other. Comradeship had cooled to mere politeness. Politeness had become controlled irritation.

Either one of them cut a figure which might have caught the eye of even such a budding beauty as was Rosalie Despres: Roger so muscular and with such a fund of laughter always in his blue eyes, Antoine so tall and panther-graceful and so well stocked with the sort of easy compliments well gauged to turn a female head.

But it had been Roger who was her choice, almost from the first Sunday they met on the church steps of St. Charles de Grand Pré. It was Roger, the thoughtful one, the teacher for her. Scant weeks ago, their banns had been read. Rosalie had given him, in token, the only bit of jewelry she had brought with her from Port Royal—a silver fleur-de-lys, hung on a chain so fragile that it was almost invisible. Since the first day she entrusted it to him, Roger had worn it against the skin directly above his heart.

He reached inside his open-collared flax shirt to finger it now, scarcely aware that Antoine's gaze was nailed to the gesture. "We'll be headed home to Grand Pré by sunset, if Broussard finds no opportunity to strike at them."

"He's brave enough," Antoine said, "but he's prudent, too. We're outnumbered ten to one, and the guns are with them. The Governor made every Acadian turn in his firearms months since, as which of us has forgotten? And without cause. We did not threaten him."

"Nor have we ever. We've obeyed every new British edict to the letter."

"Save only the latest one." Antoine plucked a blade of grass, sucked it between his strong white teeth and chewed on it. "The oath he demands that we vow to fight against our own fellow Frenchmen whenever he orders it. That we are known to desire neutrality, that there isn't a soldier among us, that all we want is to lead our quiet lives in peace—all that means nothing to his Lordship."

"His eye is on London," sighed Roger. "Blown great with ambition, is the Governor. He'd burn every man of us at the stake, to catch a nod from King George."

"Burn indeed. Fire seems to be the favorite toy in his nursery."

Flattened close together, they peered out as one man upon the thin haze drifting over the shallow valley below. The acrid reek of it made their nostrils twitch. At this moment the two seemed much as they had been a dozen years earlier: thinking the same thought simultaneously, reacting to it with the same reaction. *Burn.* . . . A dozen scattered blazes contributed to that lazy, almost motionless greyness stinging the air.

Around a crooked jut that gave the hill the semblance of a hunchback came a band of six uniformed soldiers. The tramp of their marching rang loud on the forest quietness. Red coats passed so close beneath them that each gilt button on each trim sleeve cast its separate wink of reflected sunlight. They were laughing among themselves, the British sons of Satan. They were mouthing jokes about some old woman whose decrepit shack was the last they'd fired—and how, once setting it aflame, they'd penned her inside

with their bayonet points until her very rags were
burning on her. Her screams had delighted them.

Listening to every syllable, the men in the copse
lay as though dead—save for one, far down the line
who had to clap a hand hard over his mouth to stifle
the pollen-aggravated sneeze which might have betrayed them all.

A dove broke from the greenery overhead and
streaked across the soundless sunlight. Two of the
soldiers whipped up their guns and banged away at
it. The bird sailed on, unscathed. Rum had been encountered somewhere on the soldiers' morning's round
of destruction. It coarsened their laughter. It ruined
their aim.

The tramp-tramp-tramp of British boots receded.
All along the ruffle of undergrowth margining the
timber stand, taut forms relaxed. A new volley of mar-
tial merriment, more distant than before, rolled back
to them as though it shoved its way through the thin,
insubstantial veil of valley smoke.

"They're headed for the church," Antoine grated.
"Christ cork their bungholes, they mean to torch the
church. That's all they've left of the hamlet!"

"Not even Britishers would burn the house of God."

But in this opinion Roger apparently was in error.
The sextet who just had passed them at close range
were indeed veering onto a path which cut through
carpets of modest wildflowers directly toward the
serene steeple close by the river's hook. Seemingly
this maneuver was but part of some prearrangement;
for along the bank a second English party, somewhat
larger, was likewise approaching. Yet a third, nine
men in this one, had moved into view from somewhere
out of vision to the north.

"What now?" Roger grated. "If we don't even try to stop them—"

As if Merlin's wand had evoked him from thin air, the group's leader was suddenly among them. Joseph Broussard had materialized more silent than any conceivable ghost. But suddenly he was there, a bulky shadow against the dim green light of the trees, gesturing for them to rise.

"There'll be no better chance to warn them that 'neutrality' stubs its foot on the steps to the holy sanctuary, lads. Has each of you whatever he could fetch along?"

There was a whispered sound of common assent. Out of the scrubby stand of fern and bayberry, sumac and ground pine, hands hoisted what few would have readily recognized as weapons: axes designed for the felling of trees, scythes meant for harvesting, hammers which in better days had erected peaceful dwellings, even a garden hoe or two. The Governor had commandeered the very rifles they'd kept to hunt the small game vital to their households in winter. Yet their despoiled owners were not quite empty-handed.

Without another spoken syllable, Broussard motioned the way they were to go. Roger shouldered his sharpened axe. Antoine coiled the long leather thongs of his ox whip about one arm, much as Cleopatra might have coiled her asp. They fell rigidly into a moving line together. No man need be warned to maintain silence. Surprise was the one small advantage they might possess. In full daylight, it was pitiably little.

Down the hip of the hill, their copse straggled almost half the distance to the undefended church. It afforded them only a modicum of cover. Glancing back, any one of their recently passing sixsome might spot them. Looking uphill, any soldier in either of the two other converging parties might sound a warning.

They were men accustomed to forest hunting, the Acadians. They could move like shadows. In this art, their friendly Indian neighbors had coached them well over three generations. The French had clung to seaside fishing and to farming the rich tidal fields reclaimed through their dykes. Unlike the ruthless English, they offered no threat to Indian hunting grounds further inland. Moreover, they paid honest prices for furs their redskin friends trapped. So the Indians had been willing tutors. The Acadians had learned well.

Moving along at Antoine's familiar side, Roger once more fingered Rosalie's silver talisman with the hand the axe left unburdened. His heart, so full of her image, seemed to have risen into his throat. He was no coward, yet his fingers shook as they caressed the fleur-de-lys. To him, as to most men in the moving line, an act of war was utterly strange. Peace and obedience to lawful dictates had been bred into their bones. But burning and looting carried things too far.

By a miracle, no eye in the bands below had yet discerned them. No, not truthfully by miracle. There was good human reason for it. On the steps of the simple edifice which stood alone amid surrounding smoking ruins, a lone figure had appeared.

If she had come through the church door, Roger had been too otherwise occupied to notice. Perhaps she had been nearby in the wildflower field and had run to intercept them. At any rate, she stood there now: a simple novice nun, garb all white, arms quietly folded, statue-silent as she watched the soldiery advancing.

They had sighted her, all of them in all three parties. Almost visible to the other silent men descending through the trees, a ripple like a sea wave seemed to wash over the uniformed figures. Not a ripple of uncertainty, but of excitement.

If she herself grew aware of this, the young nun gave no sign. The hill breeze found her habit's folds and stirred them gently, but otherwise she might have been a holy statue moved out from the dim places behind her to stand in the sun. Eyes fixed on those advancing lines unwaveringly, she merely waited.

One of the party who had passed so near the copse shouted something to his comrades. That it was an obscenity was made obvious by the mocking hoots of the others. Waving the burning brand he carried, the soldier started forward at a quickened dog trot.

Men in the other two converging parties sensed what sport was afoot and likewise quickened their separate approaches to the church. It was obvious that a race to reach her was in the making. New alarm spurting through him, Roger hurried his own steps. His grip on the axe he toted clenched tight, sweat rendering it slippery.

The leader of the band from the riverbank reached the bottom church step first. Still above him, the nun made no motion to retreat. But now she spoke out, clearly.

"*Perdu toute hante!*" Scorn edged her young voice. "*Fi donc!*"

The soldier on the bottom step found humor in her stern reproach. He laughed, the bark of an animal, and made a grab for her. She flung off the groping paw and spread her own arms wide, as if by the gesture she expected to halt them.

Vain intention, if indeed she ever had entertained it! The man merely grabbed again, imprisoning her arm this time, bending it up behind her, forcing her down against him. His free hand caught her flowing skirts in a ruthless fist. He ripped them aside as he flung her back against the stone ledge and plunged on top of her.

Brave though she was, the nun was in the end human. Protection she had devoutly anticipated, perhaps from the cross high over their heads, had failed her. Now, pinned beneath her assailant as she was, belated terror swept away her confidence. She struggled weakly. Almost as one body, the outraged Acadians on the upper trail sprang from cover.

The soldier on the steps was too deep into his ugly business to be aware, at first, of what was happening behind him. But the others, several of them already lining up for their own turns with the nun, were less occupied. Startled shouts still tore their throats as the Acadians reached them, closing in so fast that rifles could not readily be positioned. A lofted hoe crashed down, biting deep into a targeted shoulder, ripping uniform cloth, replacing one red with a different spurting liquid red. A descending hammer met an unwary skull. A sweeping scythe became a sidewise guillotine.

Roger's thought was of the nun: the girl who might, if this were Grand Pré, have been his own Rosalie. Axe aloft, he made direct for the church steps where the soldier atop the writhing female figure was ruthlessly taking his pleasure. Sounds of sudden battle had perhaps added a new frenzy to his excitement. He made no effort to desist or to protect himself. Lust was a fire in him.

As he found the bottom step, Roger realized that

someone else had reached the goal ahead of him. Antoine's ox whip was uncoiled and whistling through the dazzle reflected from the white church wall.

Its lash lined dead across the Britisher's wide shoulders, rending material, biting deep. The animal it punished still seemed unaware. Antoine whipped it back and struck again, more mercilessly. This time, pain mastered the animal hunger defiling the steps. The soldier half-arose, half-turned. The whip caught him anew, dead across the snarling face, severing flesh, fountaining blood.

Then the leader of the sixsome from the hill—he who had sighted the nun first, but then had been robbed of his sport—went into vengeful action. So close its flame singed in transit, the man's torch whistled by, past the church's open door. Wood it struck there was old and dry. With a roar like an angry bull's, flame caught and fed.

Barely in time to sidestep the lunge of a British bayonet swinging tardily into action, Roger pivoted. There was a face behind the bayonet, bearded, bleary with hatred. These were the Governor's hirelings, not proper disciplined troops. They fought like bandits attacking in an alley. Spittle flaked the man's lower lip, his harsh curse seeming to be streaked by it.

Roger ducked swiftly, and the descending spearpoint carried ripping flaxcloth with it as it went on its way. Thrown slightly off-base by the failure of his drive, the soldier tottered for an instant. Roger needed no more time. Upward cut the axe he had lowered to avoid the curling tongue of Antoine's whip. It struck home midway of the bearded chin. Bone shattered. Lacerated ribbons of tongue uncoiled between the slobbering lips. The raging eyes went blank. The soldier buckled.

As Roger swerved back, the roar of the holocaust caught him full blast. In just those few seconds, the little church had become a pillar of flame, from house of worship to inferno in what to him seemed literally no time at all. Stunned, he gaped at the horror.

The creature who had mounted the nun was crawling from her now, recoiling from the hot fury of the blazing wall. Clutching what was left of her white habit about her bared body, the nun rose slowly to her feet. Her eyes seemed entirely empty as they stared down the bruised length of her violated body. Except for a slight trembling of her lips, there was no expression whatever on her young face. None that Roger could identify.

"Sister, you—" he began as he started toward her.

But she had not heard him speak; at least, he didn't believe she had. She turned from him as if he did not exist. In her horror-blighted world, perhaps he indeed did not. One upward step took her level with the open church door, now spewing flame as though it were a devil's maw. Another step, solid, deliberate, carried her closer to—

"No, Sister! Dear God! Please! Please!"

She was past the barrier of fire before he could finish, before he could move. The white rags fluttering about her became living crimson banners. A great red flower bloomed suddenly before his dazed eyes, tossing its wild petals, flaunting its woman-outline, darkening. Roger dropped his axe and bent dazedly above the steps, fire heat at his shoulders. He vomited.

All around him the fierce battle was raging. Several

of the Acadians had wrested guns from their British
owners by now. A sporadic tattoo of shots made counterpoint for the steadier howl and crackle of the
burning. Soldiers stumbled, went down. An Acadian
Roger only half recognized—from Halifax, he thought
—lay motionless and staring Heavenward, a bayonet
spiking from his gut like a banderilla. Roger stumbled
against the prone figure, groping to retrieve his axe.
Figures in red coats were fleeing.

"No way to save the church!" Broussard's familiar
authoritative voice shouted above the general confusion. "Scatter, lads! We've delivered our message!"

The command which had won him his frequent
sobriquet of "Beausoleil" among fellow Acadians rang
now unmistakable on the brief order. He was a man to
be obeyed, and his small force obeyed him. Running
back up the slope toward the copse, Roger found himself suddenly all but alone in the meadow of flowers.
As to what directions the others had taken, where they
had vanished, he had no conception. They were
merely . . . gone.

Who was this beside him now, catching up, drawing
abreast? Oh, Antoine. . . .

"What happened to your axe, Roger?" The voice
sounded breathless, winded. But whether that resulted
from their swift climb or from the unleashed fury of
Antoine's assault with his whip remained moot. Had
the nun's attacker died under the lash? Possibly.
Probably. He had looked broken, crawling away.

"Axe? Oh . . . Axe, Antoine . . . Yes, gone . . .
dropped, I think."

"Rosalie's fleur-de-lys? Did you lose the fleur-de-
lys, too?"

"No. Never. That's quite safe still."

They were nearing the crest.

"How do we find our way home to Grand Pré, Antoine? They'll be after us. Should we hole up here until it's dark? Or should we use what headstart we have, even in daylight?"

"Neither," said Antoine. Roger had a vague notion his friend had bent down as he spoke. A bootlace must have worked loose as they fled together.

He tried to make sense of Antoine's word. He half turned, puzzling. "Neither?"

Antoine stood there beside him, tall, calm, hair a pale flame. In his hand he held what he had bent over to pick up out of the meadow grass. A large, jagged rock.

"Neither," said Antoine. "You aren't going back to Grand Pré at all, *mon ami.*"

Too late, Roger began to move. But Antoine's arm moved even faster. The rock hit with a stunning force, muscle behind it. Roger felt a blinding instant of excruciating pain. Then blackness swooped and there was no pain at all. There was nothing.

2

By LATE SUMMER, the Acadian village of Grand Pré lay in a sort of numb suspension which might have resulted from some prolonged heat wave. Yet the weather had not been oppressive. Crops coming to maturity in the surrounding fields had suffered no period of scorch, nor any lack of sufficient rain. The harvest looked promising.

It was the people who made a difference between this first week of September and any other that the oldest *maman* in the clustered cottages could remember. New oppressions from their British Governor in Halifax made them feel, still more than previously, the weight of a bootheel on their throats. For some reason as yet unknown, their priests had been arrested in every settlement throughout all Nova Scotia. And where the good fathers had been taken no one seemed able to say.

In addition to the firearms already seized, soldiery lately had commandeered those stout little boats which made their fishing possible. Men worked the farms with puzzled frowns of foreboding, although their unspoken dread of coming troubles was still uncrystallized. Women gossiped less on their doorsteps, but sat at their looms listlessly and preoccupied. They were a law-abiding people. They had done little to provoke displeasure in the Governor. Why, then, this mounting ruthlessness?

What had His Excellency in mind, off yonder in Halifax?

Walking slowly along a path which passed St. Charles de Grand Pré, Rosalie Despres felt some of the weight of this general puzzlement. Apprehension pressed down even upon her slender young shoulders.

Mere weeks ago, she had been a symbol of gaiety among the young women in the community: always first to incite her comrades to laughter, always first on the dance floor when the fiddles started squealing, always ready with a rewarding kiss for whatever man shucked the red ear at a corn-husking. No longer. These September days she seemed to feel a lead weight anchoring her one-time exuberance. Her feet would no longer have known a reel from a funeral procession. High spirits had gone off somewhere, abandoning her.

As had Roger. Where was Roger? Why had he not returned, all this while, from the mysterious overnight mission he had departed on, at Joseph Broussard's summons, weeks ago? And why, for the matter of that, was his good friend Antoine Rolande also still missing?

It would have been entirely unfitting for her to put into spoken words the sharp ache of loneliness which Roger's prolonged absence instilled in her.

The boldest hussy in the colony would scarcely admit a longing such as she felt for Roger. She had dreamed of him every night this past long August; and her dreams were of a sort that brought a hot flush to her cheeks just in remembering them. There had been nothing maidenly about her thoughts. True, as soon as he returned they were to be wed. Still, respectable Jules Depres's daughter must at heart be no better than a harlot. She wanted Roger naked in her arms. She wanted Roger naked in her bed. She wanted, wanted *wanted* . . .

Yet he had not come back. He had sent no word.

The four-square simplicity of Grand Pré's beloved church lay a little distance behind her now as she moved along her listless way. What could be detaining the menfolk in there, she could not imagine. Every male of an age to shave had been commanded to attend this meeting and hear some new edict of repression the Governor had concocted. His Excellency's deputy, Colonel John Winslow, coming to instruct them, had brought with him some document (so one heard) bearing the seal of King George II himself.

So be it. Whatever new demand was laid upon the peaceful citizens, they would comply with it, although what more might be expected it was difficult to imagine. Herself, she would, like the others, surrender anything the stern new laws ordained. Anything but Roger.

The day carried with it some unspoken threat which she found it quite impossible to decipher. Why had Winslow's soldiers taken up sentry posts all around the building, pacing there like marionettes with their guns at the ready? Why had the church shutters been closed and bolted, despite the ripe heat of this summerish day? It was absurd to think it, but somehow the dear church had taken on the nimbus of a prison. *Sottise!* Presently, the doors would pop open. The men would pour out into afternoon sunlight, mumbling together about whatever new law Colonel Winslow had imparted.

She reached a point in her restless stroll where the land rose to a low knoll from which the harbor beyond lay tranquilly visible. As often on solitary walks these past several weeks, Rosalie paused now to stare waterward. Roger had not left Grand Pré by vessel. Nor had she the slightest reason to expect that he might return to her aboard one. Still, curiously increased activities of the waterfront these past many days had inspired an equally curious hope in her. Roger might come from that direction. Ships never before seen hereabouts—craft from Boston, from New York, from Philadelphia, from all manner of distant ports in His Majesty's colonies—had been dropping anchor in the Minas Basin since summer passed its turning point. And many had reasonlessly remained here, too, riding the great flux of the Fundy tides like waterfowl reluctant to resume interrupted autumn pilgrimages.

From where she stood, three new ones were in view this day. They were all commercial hulls, with large cargo holds beneath decks. Yet if they brought new consignments of goods with them, none of her neighbors seemed to have caught word of it. No crates or kegs or barrels were being rowed ashore. And—

"Rosalie!"

Her name, so softly spoken, startled her into turning. At first she could glimpse no one who might have spoken. The path stretching back toward the church where the men were foregathered stretched empty. The village green drowsed peacefully. The only moving objects, if one deducted a wedge of southbound geese crossing the sky overhead like some hurled boomerang, were those now-distant military sentries who paced off the churchyard so oddly.

Had the voice really come from much nearer at hand? Or had she imagined it? In the very act of turning back to her idle contemplation of those new masts swaying gently out across the water, she stiffened. Surely a branch of the close-by clump of lilacs had stirred, more positively than a shorebound breeze could explain?

"Rosalie?" It came again.

And this time, careful to keep the bloomless lilacs between himself and any eye behind a shuttered church window, a speaker did ease into her view Tall, and moving with that grace which womenfolk followed when he stepped out onto the floor at a barn sociable. Tall, and that mop of hair gleaming like gold-threaded orange silk. Tall, and fixing her with emerald eyes even as he eased toward her.

"Antoine! Why, you're *back*!"

"Else we could not be speaking. Rosalie, it's so long since I've seen you. I didn't even stop at my father's place, I was so eager to find you."

In his voice there was something husky and only half-controlled, some note of hunger that he might hate to reveal too openly, yet could not quite conceal. She half detected it, accepting it without much question as an echo of days when she had not yet made it obvious to the village that Roger Bernard was the only man for her, ever.

Antoine was only her friend now, no longer a swain; and Antoine knew it.

"Where have you been all these weeks? Why weren't you and Roger both back long ago?"

He still was looking down into her face as if his purpose were to memorize each line of it, perhaps in preparation for drawing a portrait.

"I would have come. I wouldn't want you worried. But I couldn't."

"What happened to detain you? We've had no news at all."

"That's the work of our great-hearted Governor. He wanted no advance news of what's been happening inland to reach the shore settlements prematurely. Soldiers are posted along every trail. Refugees have been turned back, searched, jailed."

The totally unexpected word jarred her. "Refugees?"

"Folk from villages out Fort Cumberland way. Farm folk from around Beabassin. The countryside's been put to the torch, Rosalie. With Joseph Broussard to lead us, we were able to strike one small return blow. But it was a drop in the bucket."

She could see, now, that the handsome man beside her was bone weary. His face, always before a veritable copy of Apollo, was thinner now. Twin lines of bitterness etched it from nostrils to lip corners. Shadows blurred the emerald eyes.

"We've heard very little here, Antoine. That the priests had vanished, yes. We understood that. Abbé Le Loutre incurred the Governor's hatred. But what would explain burning quiet farms or settlements?"

"Or empty churches? One such was the focus of our single opportunity to strike back, Rosalie. Only one lone nun was left to watch over the place when they reached it. Yet they—they—"

His hands came out, seeking her own as if by blind instinct. Rosalie let him cling to her thus for several seconds before she gently freed her fingertips. "They even arrested a nun, Antoine? After the priest had been taken away?"

He shook his bright head heavily. "They didn't arrest her."

"So she's safe, at least. That much is a mercy."

"They didn't arrest her. They raped her, Rosalie. They flung her down on the steps of her church, after they'd set fire to it. One of them ripped away her clothes and—and right there on the steps, with his fellows looking on and cheering, ready to do likewise, he defiled her. That was what sparked our attack."

"You couldn't prevent them? Nor quench the fire? Nor do *anything*?"

"They hate us because we're French. Because we're Catholics. I don't know what boils in their British minds. But they hate us enough to be merciless. I had to get back to Grand Pré and sound a warning, however tightly the inland trails are patrolled. It will happen here, too, when His Excellency is ready. You'll be helpless, like the nun."

Suddenly, a truth was borne in upon Rosalie's consciousness. Pronouns. Each time Antoine spoke, he spoke of "I." What did he mean by "I"?

"Roger hasn't come with you?"

"No," Antoine said. His voice sounded heavy as a stone.

"But why? Why would Roger stay behind? He'd be even more concerned than you."

One of the hands which recently had caught hers close now fumbled toward Antoine's jacket pocket. The groping progress reminded her of a sightless old man who'd lived near the former Despres home in Port Royal. She had so often gone to guide him across their mutual street, so that he might sit in the clear sunlight on a park bench. As he had moved, awkwardly, uncertainly, so Antoine's hand moved now.

When they appeared again from the pocket, something silvery twined between the trail-soiled fingers. It stirred elusively, like a sardine amid a school of comrades. When Antoine held it out to her, she stared down at it, uncomprehendingly, at first.

The silver chain was almost as fine as a strand of silk. The dangling fleur-de-lys—

Her eyes lifted quickly, horror in them. *"Where is Roger, Antoine?"*

"Dead," he answered without expression.

What was roaring in her ears was not the thunder of incoming tide as it lashed against rocks only a short distance below. It was the tumult of a whole world, crumbling, crashing about her, its structure disintegrating, its support timbers cracking.

Yet the roar was an utter silence, holding her tight.

"Do you want me to tell you about it?" Antoine asked, from a million miles away.

Rosalie was not even sure she answered his query with a mute nod. He needed an answer? Didn't he know that she no longer existed? That he stood there watching while she ceased to be? Dead? Who? Not Roger alone.

"It happened at the burning church." The words went on, coming no closer. "The soldier was still straddling the nun when we reached the steps. I got to him first. All I could see ahead of me was those grinding buttocks, and under them white flesh, struggling. I began to lash him with my ox whip. Others closed in. The general fighting commenced."

"And someone—Roger?" Whose voice? Her voice?

"Not right away. The whip did its work. After a little, Rosalie, the beast rolled off her and began to crawl away. Roger moved to help her up. But she only rose under her own power, turning back into the church. It was blazing like a beacon by then. There was a look in her eyes. Dead. Frozen."

"And Roger?"

"Before he could reach her, she had taken the extra step that carried her to what was left of the door. The church was a flaming oven. Like someone walking into the sea to drown herself, she kept on moving. He ran after her, shouting for her to wait. I don't believe she heard him at all."

"He—he followed? Into the fire?"

"He reached her, started to drag her back. There was a grinding noise. The whole frame of the building crashed on them. I saw the fire take them."

"If I'd been there—if only I'd been there—"

"Rosalie, there was nothing you could do. Nor I. Nothing at all."

Silence fell between them there on the knoll. If memories not in tandem with the story he just had told troubled Antoine's mind, no reflection of it showed on his chiseled face. The memories stirring Rosalie stemmed from times further back, times when she had so often clung in Roger's arms—fire of such a different sort flaming in them both. Those memories had nothing to do with Antoine.

When he spoke again, it was of a different matter. "The village seems deserted. As I rowed downcoast under last night's darkness, close in to avoid detection with those stranger ships in the basin, there were shore lights aplenty."

"People were gathering at neighbor cottages then, to discuss the order for today's meeting. All the men are attending it now, in the church. It's at Governor Lawrence's command."

"Meeting?" Antoine glanced toward the church. "What's its purpose?"

"Some new law. That's general opinion, anyhow. There's no real knowledge of details. Colonel Winslow, the Governor's right hand, remains tightmouthed."

"They're in there now? Inside the church?"

"Every man in the settlement." Rosalie's dazed thoughts lay still so far away that her reply was mechanical. "It's gone on now for hours."

"And why are those military sentries yonder posted?"

"Who knows why? Colonel Winslow means to impress us with his great authority, no doubt. Soldiery must be one of the Governor's stern trimmings."

"There'd be no need for soldiers at a gathering of Acadians." A sudden note of alarm underrode Antoine's words, coloring them with an uneasy menace like that of distant thunder's rumblings. "We're peaceful. We're law-abiding. What we're told to do, we bow to the yoke and do. The English have never had to coerce us, never since they won us from France."

"I know," she nodded. "Roger often says—" *Roger.* Her numbed heart split.

Antoine's gaze remained fixed upon the shuttered church. Clearly, he was no longer thinking of lost comrades. "This is no coincidence. It's happening, what I just now prophesied. It fits too well with what's already been afoot at Pisiquid."

The Pisiquid settlement lay not many miles inland, straddling the trail between Grand Pré and Lawrence's capital at Halifax. Ordinarily, local news swam back and forth between the two villages like fish in an open stream. Contact had dried up, these past several weeks. But venerable elders in Grand Pré had taken little alarm at that.

Patrols along the trails were known to exist, in a general way. Doubtless, the Governor wished to keep each farmer in his own fields as harvest time approached. Governmental restrictions were to be obeyed, not questioned.

"Pisiquid?" Rosalie struggled to heed him. "What of Pisiquid?"

"You've had no word of that, hereabouts?"

"Since early August, we've had little gossip from inland."

He spoke slowly. "All males there were summoned to a meeting, just like the one you've described. It was held at Fort Edward. Once all were inside the trap, they were imprisoned—no warning whatever—within the stockade."

"*Imprisoned!* But, Antoine!"

"Word leaked out to Cobequid, just down the bay. Folk there had scant time to flee across the isthmus to Ile St. Jean. British mercenaries arrived at Cobequid on their heels and reduced the abandoned hamlet to ashes."

The horror story, delineating the fate of close neighbors, was sufficient to jar Rosalie even from her private cocoon of anguish. Dark eyes met his, sick with disbelief.

"Why would the British burn out innocent citizens?"

"They mean to uproot us," Antoine intoned. "Because we once were French, they hate us. I told you that before. When we begged to be left neutrals, exempt from bearing arms against France and England alike, that sealed our fate in Halifax. All our bowing to their every law means nothing. Now our own citizens are cooped up in the church like geese in market crates."

"Can Grand Pré do nothing? Nothing at all?"

"What plea could be useful? His Excellency in Halifax has a stone for a heart."

Moments back, Rosalie would have believed that no further disaster could befall her small personal world. But now. . . . "Antoine! My *father's* in there with all the rest!"

"That's to be expected. Jules never lifts a hand against the bastards. He'd meekly follow any Judas goat straight into their abattoir."

"No one protested. No one foresaw treachery. They're *all* in there. What can His Excellency be planning against us? Taking our farms? Taking our livestock?"

"Satan alone knows." Antoine ground out the words. "He'd be the only one in Lawrence's confidence. *Le Bon Dieu* must have exiled that devil from Eden long ago."

Silence again. But this time, their separate thoughts ran along identical channels. From the knoll, they stared back at the ominously silent church with twin dreads.

The brace of burly figures in lobster-scarlet coats who just had climbed their rise from the waterfront were not even on the fringes of Rosalie's or Antoine's awareness. An almost guttural voice, speaking behind them, was a first warning.

"What have we here, then? An Acadian who's defied the Governor's order?"

As one, they turned where they stood.

The soldiers both carried pistols. The weapons had been slipped out quietly in the moment before one of them had announced their presence. Two dark muzzleholes concentrated upon Antoine like a pair of mortician's eyes measuring him for a coffin.

"You were commanded to be at yon church gathering, Acadian."

"I was away in Annapolis Royal these two weeks past. On business for my father. I'm just now returned. I've heard nothing of a meeting."

The spokesman for the pair sneered. "The wench told you nothing? Likely yarn!"

"Doubtless she would have. But we'd just now met, you see, after our separation. We had personal matters to discuss."

"So she's your doxie, eh? I thought as much, watching you together." Eyes which reminded Rosalie of bits of oyster, almost colorless, swerved toward her. "A likely one, too. You'd be a true beauty, girl, were you a smitch better garbed."

Face to face with that leering visage—pocked, fleshy, unshaven—Rosalie thought suddenly, sickeningly, of the nun, Roger's nun. Revulsion shook her;

fear, too, rising in her so abruptly that she had the taste of bile in her dry mouth.

Her slantwise glance caught a clenching of Antoine's fists. But no fist could match a firearm. If Antoine lunged to her defense despite all odds. . . .

The moment teetered between surrender and disaster like a circus bear on a high wire, then resolved itself. The soldier knew his duty. Pleasure was put in check.

"What's your name, farmer? Where do you belong?"

Antoine answered quietly. "I'm Antoine Rolande. My father, Henri Rolande, owns land outside the village. We do not farm it. Our income is from holdings elsewhere."

"A gentleman, then, not a peasant? Well, *gentleman*, you're expected over yon. If he's Acadian and dwells here, your father will be waiting for you with the rest."

"What's this about?" Antoine protested. "Why are you arresting me?"

"Daddy will explain it all when you're reunited. He knows by now." The gun made a gesture. "Since Grand Pré's to be home no longer, you've little interest in that."

"Home no longer?" And that voice was Rosalie's, not Antoine's.

"It's all writ in what the Colonel's been reading to them. Every French inhabitant of this district is to be removed. Vessels are provided to accomplish the same. You're to be shipped south to other colonies, a few here, another bit of you there. Folk more loyal to King George will be taking your places in Nova Scotia. No more Frenchie insubordination."

The gun made its unmistakable gesture once more. For an instant, hard green eyes met Rosalie's suddenly blurred dark ones. Then Antoine turned his back on her and started toward the churchyard, the two with their weapons falling into line behind him.

Left alone on the knoll, Rosalie began to sob.

3

It was quiet in the forest, the sort of quiet composed of stirring leaves and the little rustlings of small secret animals and the occasional beat of a passing bird-wing, which was not really quiet at all, but rather a congress of minute nature noises.

This worried him sometimes. Lying here, he occasionally found himself possessed by the oddest and most inexplicable panic. Because there *ought* to be noises, other noises. The shouts of fighting men. The crackling flames of some big fire run amok. Noises like that. Not noises one might relish, no. Still, they should be there. They belonged.

Just why they should belong, he could never explain to himself. Day after day, night after night, he had struggled doggedly to master the riddle. All it brought him was a thundering headache.

Those headaches themselves, they were another puzzlement. He seldom used to have headaches, or so he somehow believed, even though he could not really say how anything had been for him before the forest. All he knew for certain was that he had not always lain here in this shelter which was half cave, half tent, and which Dawn Dove had created for them.

He had not always had Dawn Dove taking care of him, either: pressing damp, cool rags to his throbbing forehead, spooning him broth of her own concoction, protesting sternly whenever he sought to quit this sanctum and venture out into the beyond-world. She herself made frequent brief trips there, to come back with the berries and herbs and nuts which sustained them.

He was not even sure why he thought of her as Dawn Dove. That was not the sort of name that ought really to belong to her. She was of the Micmac tribe, she had told him. He felt fairly positive that Micmac women had different sorts of names: harsher, less poetic. Puzzles again. Why would he know things like that about Micmac Indians?

What bothered him almost most of all was that she reminded him so much of someone else. Some other woman. Some gentle woman, with dark hair and dark eyes and sun-golden skin, who laughed with a sound like music.

When she laughed, this other woman—who might not really exist at all—made him think odd things. He must have watched her mouth a great deal, somewhere else. Because he did remember (or did imagine) the shape of that mouth very clearly. To think of it had

strange effects on him. His breath would begin to
choke as if he had been running a long distance. His
palms would sweat. His groin would ache.

Or was she a dream? His companion seemed to know
nothing about her. He often asked.

"No one," Dawn Dove would murmur reassuringly.
"Only you and flowers in meadow."

Apparently, a meadowful of flowers was where she
had found him. He had no recollection of such a place,
but Dawn Dove sometimes spoke of it, when he
pressed her to tell him everything there was to tell.
The story, as she related it, was simple, yet in so many
ways, tantalizingly mysterious.

She had quit her own native village one night almost
a year ago, slipping away into darkness to put as many
miles as possible between herself and her kinfolk.
Harsh pressure was being put on her to marry an
aging local nabob. But his very touch disgusted her.
She would have preferred death to lying under him in
his wigwam of bent saplings and bulrushes. Far better
even to have been sold to the *wendigo*, that dread
monster of the north woods who was a fabled embodi-
ment of the hunger and starvation always nipping at
a Micmac's heels.

Wandering, she had come at last to this place of
trees where she chanced upon their shallow cave and
settled into it. Since then, seasons had fled by. There
were farms scattered through the nearby valley, even
a fort the French palefaces called Beauséjour. If one
were fleet as a deer, silent as a dove in flight, food was
easy to steal from them.

Perhaps her story was what had begun him thinking
of her as Dawn Dove. But another word in her saga
was becoming increasingly troublesome. *Beauséjour.*

He was positive he had heard that name somewhere, long before he ever knew the Indian girl. And another name, *Cumberland,* was linked with it in this hooded memory that would not quite turn around to face him. No matter how hard he struggled, it would not come clear.

As for his own part in the tale? She simply had come upon him one twilight lying face down, covered with dried blood, among the wildflowers. She had thought him dead at first. But he was not. Some deep impulse had prompted her to help him. When his blue eyes opened and she discovered he was able to stand (with her beside him for support) she had gotten him to her cave, stripped and bathed him, nursed him through weeks of fever. He must have suffered some serious fall to wreak such havoc on his battered head.

Beauséjour . . . Cumberland . . . Beauséjour . . . That litany kept on repeating inside his skull, somewhere just beyond reach. Lying in the cave, rolled up in a motheaten blanket she had stolen for him, mere inches from where her own was spread upon the rocky floor, he had pressed for new details.

She had but few. "Bad hurt. Like dead in meadow. Then I bring you here."

"I must have come from somewhere. How did I get to the meadow?"

"You are Frenchman."

"Perhaps. It's possible, yes." Certainly he was no Indian. "But that's no reason why—"

"When summer begin, Englishmen come with it. Burn. Sometimes kill. Last thing they set on fire was church. Some Frenchmen come, try to stop. Maybe you one. That when you get hurt, eh?"

He couldn't remember anything like this. At least, not clearly.

Yet a feeling that there had been battle shouts and a great blaze persisted. Her other suggestion—that he had fallen in some treacherous steep place and roamed here with his head wound—seemed less probable. There was no hint whatever of any steep place lingering amid those shadows which tantalizingly surrounded him.

His fever abated. But the grim ferocity with which he struggled to force back some memory which taunted and eluded him brought it back recurrently.

At such times, Dawn Dove went to the brook close by and doused some of her rags to wash away the sweat. For this his blanket had to be opened. It was when her fluttering hands moved about their business that strange feelings stirred inside him most determinedly. Moving over his bared body, touch light as the merest breeze, her fingertips seemed to caress him as well as cleanse him. Her eyes were always softly fixed on his, so perhaps she took no notice of certain embarrassing physical phenomena that he could not control.

Most of all, it was her lips that riveted him.

Whose lips? If only he could remember! He had wanted those other lips. He had burned with wanting them, worse than any fever. His wife? His sweetheart? Or only a mirage, a fantasy? Someone who did not really exist at all?

The summer days grew perceptibly shorter.

Strength returned to him, hastened probably by the foods she prepared for him and the herbs she gathered to stew with her squirrels and rabbits. He would have taken on the task of hunting for them both, but this she forbade with tender sternness. At first, he believed she did not consider him yet sufficiently recovered from his head wound. But slowly he began to realize that there was a different reason.

Outside, beyond their cave and their trees, lay a world occupied by enemy Englishmen, although it once had been a French world, friendly. Her fears for him centered upon this. Hostile soldiers overran their valley.

"I can't stay with you forever, Dawn Dove. I must find out who I am."

"Not go. Safer here."

"I likely have family somewhere. Parents. A wife. Even children."

"No wife! No wife! Parents happier you safe than if take risks to seek them. If children, your parents take good care. *Grandpère. Grandmère.* Children get good care."

"Like the care you've given me these past weeks, Dawn Dove. I know. But if I'm a father, a husband, a son, I have to know. You say there's been burning. There may be no roof over their heads. Even food—"

"Nobody starve. Plenty fish. Plenty meat. Is not season of hunger. Winter far away."

"Dawn Dove, how do I convince you? I'll have to leave. Very soon."

"You leave me, where you go? Where you start look for them?"

"I don't know. Just move from place to place, I suppose, until someone somewhere recognizes me and calls my name."

"You gave me new name. I give you name, too. What name you like? Bold Eagle?"

"My *French* name. Am I really a Frenchman? I'm

sure I must be. I seem to speak the language, even to
think in it. You use French words with me when we
talk together."

"Micmac people speak French. Not strange. Learn
from men buy furs we trap."

As the days passed, he began to form definite plans,
plans he knew Dawn Dove would bitterly protest if
she suspected them. Despite her disapproval, he began
to take brief excursions from the cave's vicinity, sometimes as far as the edge of the woods.

There, screened by the last stand of trees, one
could look out across a wide slope and far into the
distance. Blackened ruins of farm buildings made ugly
scars here and there against the tranquility of the
scene he studied. Green was beginning to creep back
across recently scorched fields. He understood about
these signs of misfortune. The English. Dawn Dove
had told him what had happened here.

The violence had receded, though, drained from
the valley like an ebb tide. The soldiers must have
headed elsewhere. In whichever direction he might
look, little alive was stirring. No wagons on the wind-
ing roads. No livestock grazing, save for a loner here
or there overlooked when the herds were driven off.
No people returning to gutted homesteads. He felt as
if the world had gone off somewhere, leaving him behind—whoever he was.

A great loneliness surged over him. But for what
was he lonely? For whom? Why did he feel this urgency about catching up with them, wherever they had
gone without him? Before it was too late. Before the
dreaded thing happened. What thing? Nothing, perhaps.

"I could head south," he thought. "That way over

yonder must be south. I saw a wedge of geese fly over yesterday. That was the way they headed. Geese fly south at the end of summer. Don't they? I remember knowing once that's what they do."

South didn't seem quite right, some way.

He wished he could see water from here. He couldn't say why, but a landscape didn't look right and proper without water in it. Oh, the river flowed down below of course. But what was a river? Water should be spread wide, wider even than these flower-spangled meadows where nobody seemed to come any more. A river could be pretty, like a silvery sash. But it wasn't *real* water.

"Rivers hunt for oceans."

He felt little doubt of that. They flowed downward, downward, rivers did, seeking lower ground, seeking those glittering seas for which he felt now a gnawing homesickness. Suddenly it made sense. He must have come from the sea, then. He was a sailor, perhaps. He felt uneasy because there was no deck stirring under him.

"I know what I must do. Follow the river. It will lead somewhere. Rivers all lead somewhere. It will get me to the sea. But I'll be careful. I'll hide by day and make progress all by dark. Dawn Dove says there's danger. She must be right."

This unexpected surge of definite purpose excited him.

He turned back from the forest rim, half running as he made his way back toward the cave. When he thrust aside the scrap of canvas at its entrance, she was not inside. The rough rock walls, the ceiling so low he had to bend to accommodate it, enfolded only a stillness with which he had come to feel familiar as the weeks passed. She could not be far away, though. He must tell her he would be leaving. To leave after all her kindness without even a word—

The light splash of the stream where she had dampened her poultice rags sounded off to the right as he left the cave again. He knew already how it flickered and raced among the ferns and green weeds, on its way to the valley. Above the cave there was a small waterfall, and just below the waterfall a pool that caught its rushing gilt ribbons. That was where she would be, scrubbing his worn flax shirt clean again. The forest moss marks that stained his cloth were Dawn Dove's constant worry. Yet she seemed actually to take pleasure in tending to his clothing.

He came through the trees and drew up against the white birches at the pool's lip.

She was here, but she was not playing laundress. Naked in the slanted sunlight which hit the water as if it were scattering coins, she was frolicking by herself in the foam which made lace where it hit the pool's quivering surface. She rolled and ducked and dove and somersaulted, deft as a fish in the shimmering water.

The stream seemed to chuckle, applauding.

Immobilized by the sheer joy of her, he stood where he was, unmoving. She went down again, her long dark hair spread out on the pool's matching darkness like some exotic black blossom opening. She came up, spitting stream water, laughing.

And she saw him there.

For an instant she froze, eyes on his, happiness beginning to break through. Now she was smiling. Very slowly, as if casting off a garment, she began to stand erect. Her skin was copper satin, jeweled with the drops of water which clung to her. Her young breasts lifted toward him proudly. The pool was shallow where she stood. It reached up only half the length of her curved calves.

"Bold Eagle come home early," she said. Her soft voice scarcely carried above the merry rondelet of hurrying water.

"Because I must leave again. Today. Tonight."

Yet he felt that ache, that hunger, looking at her. He wanted to strip off his own tattered trousers, the only garment he wore, and wade into the stream after her. He wanted to know how her sleek flesh would feel, cool from the pool's caressing. He wanted to . . . but *was* it Dawn Dove he wanted?

That persistent shadow of another woman reined him in sharply.

She seemed to comprehend his hesitation. She held up her arms to him, the invitation unmistakable. "No go. No leave. Not ever."

He turned away abruptly, well aware that all control of contrary urgings was held on a leash which might snap at any instant. With long strides he began to lunge down the vine-choked incline back to the cave. She called after him, something in the Algonquian tongue of her Micmac ancestors, but he did not let it check him. She must not weaken his intention now. With first dark, he would be off to follow the river.

When he crept into their hollow place sliced back into the hillside, he found that he was short of wind. He told himself that it was because of the speed of that return from the pool. He then told himself that he was a liar. He was too strong to be winded by any race of a mere twenty yards, a race against himself, at that. Speed had not left him breathless. No.

He began, very carefully, to roll up the remnant of blanket on his side of the cave. Dawn Dove would not resent his taking it. It was her gift to him, and on the river trail, in the daylight hours when he must not travel, it would be useful. Banded with his leather belt, it would make a small parcel; one with scarcely any weight at all.

Even before she reached the entrance he could hear her coming, hurrying, slipping on the small loose stones, thrashing through the fern fronds. She appeared against the mellow light beyond, eyes glaring, hastily clad slimness as taut as a wildcat's.

"You not go!"

He cinched the belt thong through its buckle and pivoted to face her.

"You know I have to go, Dawn Dove. I've told you so, often. And today, it came to me about the river. If I follow the river it should guide me home."

She flung herself at him. She clung. "Here is home. With me is home."

"I'm from somewhere else. People are waiting there for me to come back."

"Who are these people?" she spat. "Where is this place?"

"You know I can't remember. But I must reach them. You've warned me about troubles. If anything's wrong, I can't leave folk who depend on me facing it alone."

"And me? What of me, alone?"

"You'd been alone for a long time before you found me in the meadow. That's why you ran away from your village. To be alone, where no one could master you."

"But now, no. Now all is different!"

There were tears on her cheeks now, trembling like the water diamonds which had studded her bare body back there at the pool. It occurred to him that he never had seen Indian tears before. Once he had believed them impossible. Where had he thought this? Where had the mistaken notion become a part of his thinking?

She drew back from him slowly, almost as if the movement could be accomplished only by ripping skin from her body and leaving it glued to his.

"Then . . . you go. You are strong. I am weak. I cannot prevent."

"Don't hate me, Dawn Dove. Don't grieve for me. This is something I must do. If only I knew why, I would explain it. Then you'd see how much I'll miss you."

Her voice had become practical, almost businesslike. It was no voice she had ever used with him before, except perhaps to keep him still when the fevers tormented him. "You cannot go until dark falls. It could be suicide. You must rest until dark."

Once firm in his decision, he wanted to be on his way. What if that other woman had wept on his shoulder? How would he have answered then? Could she have held him back? But then she was very possibly no more than a dream, that woman, and waited for him nowhere, no matter if he followed all the rivers in creation.

Only one recognizable certainty was involved. Dawn Dove was right when she said that daylight on a trail through what he recognized as enemy territory might very well indeed be suicide.

"I'll wait then. But only until the sun goes down."

"Use blanket roll as pillow," she murmured. "Sleep. If you are to travel all night, sleep now." She gestured for him to stretch out in his usual place.

"You'll wake me up as soon as the light fades? Can I trust you for that?"

"You can trust."

She settled down on her slender haunches near the cave's mouth, faced outward toward the trees. Her back made a childlike line of desolation. Studying it, he felt a pang of misgiving. But that was unworthy. After all she had done for him, he had no right to mistrust her. He closed his eyes.

Somewhere in the bowels of restless sleep, confused half-dreams began to take form again. They came as they had come on many earlier nights, flicking at him like a whip's end, recoiling before he could snatch at them, then snaking out again to tease him. He knew more bits of the truth now. There had been a battle. There had been a towering fire. Had his other woman walked into the blaze, empty-eyed, unhearing, although he shouted after her? Such a picture danced before him. Then it was gone, splintering at a touch.

Only the touch was real.

Hands, real hands, were cautiously at work on the remnants that were his only clothing. They were tugging the ruptured cloth down along his sprawled legs, easing him free of them, taking them . . . where? *Thief!* His eyes flew open.

The cave was almost dark now, although a faint glow still lingered in the frame of the low entrance. She was crouched over him, his purloined garment dangling in her hand. And she was as naked as ever she had been in the forest pool. Her breasts dangled an inch above his staring eyes, heaving slightly to match the rasp of her breathing.

"Dawn Dove! What the devil?"

"No pants, cannot go. I promise to wake. I wake. But I not promise you have pants."

"Give me those back! What kind of a crazy joke—"

"You more pretty with no pants, anyway. With no pants I like better."

He tried to struggle toward a sitting position. With surprising force, she pushed him back. Suddenly she was straddling him, one leg at either hip, her slight weight pinioning him. The warm smoothness of her pressed hard against him. He felt her soft breasts flatten against his own tensed pectorals, nipple to nipple.

She laughed softly.

"No pants. No can stand up. But I make stand up where makes happy."

To his stunned alarm, he felt her hand reaching behind her and down. It traced the hard curve of his own belly. It found what it was seeking already rising to meet it. Soft as the undersides of rose petals, her fingertips began to stroke.

"Dawn Dove! Woman! Stop, now! You mustn't!"

"You not really want to go. See how nice? See how good?"

She squirmed backward abruptly and positioned herself above him, hanging suspended in that crouched position for a breath of time and then descending. Her own thighs were wide apart now. With one quick swoop she surrounded his erection, embedded it in warm wetness.

Beyond thought, beyond reason, he found his own hips surging, meeting, withdrawing, meeting. He was taking her in frenzy. And suddenly he screamed the name.

"*ROSALIE!*"

It was as if a barred door had been battered open. Out from behind it came pouring all the past. The dam in his skull splintered, crumbled, was gone. He remembered Antoine. The held rock. "*You aren't going back to Grand Pré at all, mon ami.*" And Rosalie ... Rosalie ... Rosalie ...

He groped instinctively at his muscular throat. A thin silver chain should dangle there. It was there no longer. It was gone. Dawn Dove was no robber. He hadn't a doubt who had taken it. Until this instant, he had felt no loss of the fleur-de-lys. Now hot fury shook him.

Surging upward, he flung Dawn Dove's childlike weight from him as if it did not exist. She landed hard on the cave floor, rolled over, screamed to match his own earlier shout which seemed still to bounce back at them from the vaulted roof. "*Ro-sa-le-ee-e ...*"

He caught her arm before she could stir again, hand closing on it like a vise.

"Give me my clothes, girl. My God, how long has it been? With Rosalie wondering?"

She made some pitiful attempt to cling to the garment she so recently had eased under his buttocks. He twisted relentlessly. She sobbed and relaxed her hold. He snatched the torn cloth from her and was eeling into it while she still protested. Now the flax shirt, snatched from the propped twig where it had hung drying. And now the blanket roll.

"Not go!" she was whimpering, the fight draining from her. "More happy here."

Roger stood staring down at her where she spread-eagled. "Get out of my way."

"I be your Rosalie. You see how good. Rosalie you forget."

"I didn't really forget her, even when I couldn't really remember. I won't forget you, either, or all you've done for me. I'll always be grateful. Good-bye, Dawn Dove."

He was out the cave's low entrance before she could catch at his leg as he stepped over her. All the way to the edge of the trees he was afraid she might still come after him. But she did not. As he strode across the sloping meadow, dark now under the stars so that he would have seemed only a shadow to any watching eye, he thought of that final sobbing plea of hers. He did not turn back. He did not even slow his pace.

Below, and drawing closer now, coiled the serpent that was the river.

4

CHILL HUNG on the late October air like death's own breath. It rode the wind cutting in across the Fundy waves, where after long delays the fleet assembled by Governor Lawrence at last rode at restless anchor. Twenty-four vessels in all, they had come one by one up the long coastline from colonies further southward—Massachusetts, Connecticut, even Maryland. Each captain had been personally retained by His Excellency himself, and promised a generous reward when he carted away his allotted cargo of unwanted Acadians.

The long dreaded day had come at last.

Penned up like cattle in the guarded church, the men of Grand Pré had finally been permitted outdoors to exercise—but still under the gun muzzles of the soldiery.

In small groups, and still guarded, some had been permitted visits home for long enough to make final arrangements with stunned families before being marched back to virtual prison. If this was what King George considered liberty for subjects who never had raised a hand against him, then liberty took on a strange definition.

With the others, Antoine Rolande endured what must be endured. But he burned with a silent self-fury it was well his jailors could not detect.

Fool, fool, that was what he was! To have returned to Grand Pré as he had done, all because a slim girl named Rosalie would now (granting her a proper while of mourning for a lover who would never return) be available—that was the act of an *imbecile*. Yet he had not been able to wipe her from his thoughts, all the summer weeks he had been making his tortuous return from Beauséjour.

Various willing farm girls he had bedded on his way—more in the nature of repayment for hiding him in their fathers' haystacks than because their bovine charms appealed to him—had in no way quenched the throb he felt between his legs whenever he thought of Rosalie. He had wanted Jules Despres's daughter too ardently to check the yearning. He had killed a one-time friend only to open a channel to her.

But a man who was not besotten would have taken greater thought of the risks.

All down the peninsula he had encountered ample evidences of what the British were up to. The business at Pisiquid was only a single instance. The devastation surrounding their newly renamed Fort Cumberland, just over the New Brunswick border, had been enough proof of British purpose for anyone who had witnessed it, as had he. Lawrence meant to leave no trace of the former French in the conquered colony. An Acadian of decent sense would act accordingly.

Why had he not turned westward after killing Roger? For the most part, the Indians on beyond had proved friendlier to Paris than to London. With their help, and taking whatever time was necessary, he could have made his way to the headwaters of the majestic river La Salle had explored. Far south, where it spilled into the Gulf of Mexico, a whole unconquered French civilization lay waiting.

New Orleans was rumored to be the most sophisticated and entertaining city in the whole of America. Safety would have awaited him there. And women. Not Rosalie; but a hundred other women, a thousand.

Antoine had small doubt of his ability to seduce almost any of those unknown beauties at will. There were mirrors aplenty in his father's comfortable *habitation* at Grand Pré. He had admired himself in those glasses often enough to have a clear notion of what it was women saw when they studied him. The tall, graceful body. Face so flawless that, save for its virility, one might term it beautiful. Thick, curling, copper-gold hair. Jade eyes which could light convincingly with admiration, even with adoration, when that was the message he instructed them to relay.

A wench a night New Orleans might have provided, were that his fancy. Or a proper lady, give him slightly longer to assail the citadel. A lady to his liking, and one who would also be wealthy.

Yet here he was, back in rural Grand Pré and a prisoner: all because of a girl with dark eyes and a certain smile, a girl with whom he had been so callowly engrossed that he was totally unaware of British soldiers closing quietly in. Before he could do more than offer her proof that Roger was dead, they had hustled him into this captivity.

Naturally, he found it to his advantage to explain his return to his equally constrained father in somewhat different terms; the terms of a dutiful heir rather than of an ardent lecher. Henri Rolande had been both delighted and dismayed at the guarded church when his captors first turned Antoine in.

"Son! You were away so long your mother and I began to fear—"

"No reason for that, Papa. A Rolande can still outwit the English when necessary."

"Apparently not, *mon fils.* For here they have us, under lock and key."

"What of *Maman?* Is she safe, without you?"

"I think they will not molest our women. Their officers fancy themselves gentlemen, although God knows Lawrence himself has clawed up every ladder-rung out of the sewers. Does Thaïs know you're here?"

"One trusts rumor will reach her. The instant I was aware you were held here, sir, of course I made it my business to join you. The thought of you alone was insupportable."

"Alone? Scarcely alone, Antoine." Henri's gesture encompassed their surroundings.

St. Charles de Grand Pré was no cathedral. It measured some hundred feet in length by forty broad. With the whole male population packed into it, there was scant room for all to stretch out at night. Both pewtops and the floor space under them were called into use. Not a remembered neighbor face was absent. Antoine clamped his jaw hard in disgust.

In one far corner he glimpsed Jules Despres,

huddled like a forlorn stray dog. The very portrait of personified abjection! How so spineless a creature could have fathered Rosalie it was difficult for Antoine to imagine. He must eventually pay feigned respects in that direction. Jules might someday be of value in swaying Rosalie's affections. But the little toad was so contemptibly docile. One felt more inclined to piss on him.

For the moment Antoine remained at his father's side. Rolande with Rolande. Papa was the closest thing to aristocracy Grand Pré could claim, and certainly the closest thing to wealth. Trade in Indian furs had built him a comfortable fortune, most of it now wisely banked far away in Marseilles. Antoine (how luckily!) was his only child.

Henri was no beauty, rather resembling an intelligent and immaculately turned-out monkey. It was by his mother that Antoine had been presented with his looks. Thais de Veaux had been the undisputed belle of Quebec before her marriage, much as Rosalie was now the belle of Grand Pré in far more countrified fashion. There was still a kind of shimmer about *Maman*; a something Antoine felt confident he had inherited. Heads turned whenever she entered a room. It would be like that for her son, one day.

But along with her radiance there was need for the Rolande money. His arm fell dutifully across his father's shoulders. "We are together, *cher Papa*. Whatever may come."

And now the wheel of time had turned and it was October. The awaited ships were in harbor, ready. The Great Removal so thoroughly planned by the British Governor was at hand. Facing that grim reality, even Antoine found himself shaken. Grand

Pré was not the world. But it was the corner of that world where he had grown to manhood. He was angered at having to leave it in the hands of upstart enemies.

The day seemed to grow colder rather than warmer as a beaten-metal sun climbed toward its zenith. The grey Fundy waters were trimmed with brawling white under the lash of the wind. What lay ahead would be unpleasant, even for a Rolande.

Word was out that more passengers than could be fit aboard were to be put into the cargo hold of each ominous commercial craft. The holds between decks were built so low that only a child could stand erect in one. Supplies were said to be minimal; bread, flour, water, little more. Scurvy was certain to break out, and perhaps contagious illnesses far more deadly.

Antoine tried to estimate the sailing time southward, but he came up with no very accurate approximation. Time was perhaps the only feature of the outrage that might work in their favor, for certainly the captains would be eager to reach port with as little delay as possible, their payment gold awaiting them there.

Port. But what port?

One heard that each of the colonial governors had received notification from Lawrence that certain numbers of—yes, "convicts" was the word used—would be dumped presently upon his undelighted shores. The edict Colonel Winslow had read to the farmers, that first day of imprisonment, had soothingly assured the Acadians that families would be kept together. Another British lie. Now truth was out. They were to be systematically and widely separated, one from another, so any feeble effort at retaliation could be aborted.

Well, whatever was to come, Antoine Rolande would survive it. The weak would doubtless die. There would be mass burials at sea. But he would not be one of the many thus fed to the fishes. He felt a certain worry for beautiful *Maman*, of whom he was genuinely fond. But the Veaux clan were a hardy lot. Her prospects of survival should be excellent.

As for Papa, well, if Henri Rolande failed to outlast this gruelling trial, then eventually funds safely on deposit in Europe would fall into the hands of his sole legal successor. Or if Papa, resembling a monkey in toughness as well as in other respects, did decant from their floating *bastille* in sound condition, inheritance was even so only a matter of waiting.

He, Antoine, could have accepted a less biting breeze, though. The British were not allowing them sufficient garments for a sea voyage which might extend well into November. Nor was Nova Scotia weather blessing persecuted Acadians as they said *Adieu*. But he was young. He was strong. His chief worry this morning was for Rosalie.

When the appointed hour struck, Colonel Winslow commanded all the village men to fall into parade formation. For the first time, some of the Acadians showed signs of stubborn opposition. But Lawrence's deputy had anticipated trouble. He had his troops already in double line from churchyard to waterfront, every soldier shouldering rifle and bayonet. The prisoners were to file between them, down to the waiting ferry barges.

"No!" voices protested. "We refuse, Colonel!"

"There are our homes!"

"No!"

Winslow faced the rabble contemptuously. "Refuse is a word I do not know. The King's command is absolute. It must be absolutely obeyed."

"Our fathers have lived here!"

"Our grandfather's, too!"

"What has any of us done to deserve this treatment, Colonel?"

"I do not love the use of harsh means, understand. But time does not allow for parleys or delays. The ships are waiting. Move your lines!"

When still further rumbles of protest arose among the bitter, frightened Acadians, Winslow wasted no further argument. He swung on his heel to face his waiting soldiery.

"Fix bayonets! Advance upon these wretched rebels! Move them, no price how!"

As the soldiers snapped to an instant, even grinning, obedience, cowed Acadians indeed began to stumble forward in the direction of the waterfront. Those who were slow about it were urged on with brutal shoves and the feints of sharp, shining bayonets. Few dared hesitate even for a backward glance at the village that had been their birthplace. Red coats formed a pitiless double barrier, and between the lines they were forced along as if they were running a gauntlet.

Behind that military human hedge, to either side, the anguished women and children of the settlement watched them go. Most of them were down on their knees, praying and wailing. For the most part, they always had been religious folk. But cracked hearts could see no work of God in this horror which had overwhelmed them. The prayers were sad fragments.

Walking with the others, gold-headed cane support-ing him across rough ground, Henri Rolande partly comprehended the utter desolation to which old friends and colleagues had surrendered. The quality which had brought him to dominance in the fur trade took over. Stamping the rhythm with every jab of his cane ferrule, he began to sing an old harvest hymn, one which had greeted the gathering of the crops on many a Grand Pré Sunday, in years long gone. His voice was not particularly musical, but it was loud and it was steady. It rang out undiminished on the sharp October air.

For an incredulous moment, his paean was a solo. Then someone else in the huddled crowd faltered and joined in, and someone else, and someone else. Even a few of the weeping, kneeling women lifted their heads and added their own ragged cadences. It was by no means a general outpouring. Many of the exiles-to-be still shed helpless tears, past courage or defiance. But the hymn took them all down the hill, still stiff-backed, to the waiting barges.

Among them, Antoine was one of the firmest singers. After a single startled glance as his father's voice first rang out, he saw clearly on which side his future bread was likely to be buttered. Henri would expect a certain behavior of a Rolande, and would forgive no less. Besides, Rosalie was almost certain to be watch-ing. She would remember.

He meant to have her yet.

On the knoll where the lilacs grew, their foliage already brittle with coming winter, Rosalie indeed was watching.

In these weeks since Antoine's homecoming, she had

begun to reconcile herself a little to the devastating news he had brought her. She still recoiled, weakly no doubt, from any thought of Roger's brave though fruitless end. But gradually she had managed to discipline herself against those first frantic inner protests that it could not be true. In life, harsh life, such blows were more often true than not.

Witness the tragedy which was befalling all her neighbors today. They might cry out against it; wail that it would only be a nightmare, a phantasmagoria. Yet before her eyes it was happening.

Early on, once she comprehended that the actual fate of Grand Pré was to be no less than total ruin, she had made a simple plan for herself. Like the nameless nun, although perhaps with a rather more rational awareness of what she was doing, she would put an end to this futile business of living. She could see no ultimate purpose to enduring one degrading day after another. She was not afraid of death, not as she once had been. Roger had accepted it. She could accept it, too.

From the sidewise leers many of the passing soldiers cast in her direction, she had formed a very clear notion of her chances once the menfolk were safely stowed aboard their waiting cargo ships. It would be a genuine pleasure to cheat them of their intentions. Swim out into the icy Fundy one dark night, then, further than strength and the drag of saturated clothing would allow her to swim back. It would soon be over.

And, oh, in that last instant before nothingness closed in, perhaps Roger's spirit, his soul, his lovingness, would find her. Or perhaps he was waiting somewhere for her to come; perched on some fence beside a road in Paradise, whistling their favorite tune to hurry her along until she reached him. It was a possibility well worth exploring.

What turned her from that resolution was her father. Very simply, she could not turn her back on him and leave him with no one.

Since her mother's death, she had seen how it went with him. A poet, a dreamer, a romantic who was never more than fair-to-medium as a farmer, Jules Despres would merely have faded away into a mist man if he'd had no daughter to urge him into picking up the reins again. Whatever he had already done to struggle back into some sort of half-life, he had done because of her. Were he to lose her, too, and Grand Pré as well, what would become of him? He was not a very brave man. He could not contemplate any such decision as she had made for herself. He would merely . . . linger.

So she had not, in the end, gone for that solitary midnight swim.

Where the British meant to send them, she could not even hazard a guess. But with someone who cared for him at her father's elbow, the destination could be of no great moment. She was known for an excellent houseworker. Their cottage, modest though it be, was among the most spotless in the village; as clean, even, as the far handsomer Rolande *habitation*, and Madame Rolande had the luxury of a servant girl. On whatever shore she and her father might be washed up, there was bound to be some need of good domestic help. And she could cook, too. Jules Despres always had been proud to invite a friend for dinner; and Roger

said of her stews . . . Roger *used* to say of her
stews . . . So the thing was, one need have no dread
of the future. One would make out.

Whatever his moral flaws—and they were many, for
honesty was a total stranger to him—their Colonel Winslow saw to it that his men did not rampage in the
village once its natural guards were safely stowed
aboard the vessels. The Colonel kept a tight rein on his
troops. Doubtless they called him a martinet, but never
to his face. Army to the marrow, Winslow would not
have suffered the merest pinch of relaxed discipline.

Once the menfolk were stowed, women and children
were next in line. Allowed to tote only modest bundles
of personal belongings with them, they too were
herded down to the waterfront. Ill-cleansed of the
vomit of despairing sons and brothers and husbands
who had preceded them, the barges were waiting.

Looking back toward the village as the rowing to
the cargo ships began, one could perhaps understand
what had brought on the fate of Lot's wife in the
Bible, frozen to a pillar of salt for the sin of a glance
across her shoulder. Many of the abandoned cottages
had been put to the torch already, even a decent post-
ponement denied their grieving owners. Smoke eddied
across the empty green like a Fundy fog creeping in;
but it was fog with a rancid odor alien to sea salt and
bracken. One might have thought the clumps of flame
blossoming along the shore were the cookfires of an
encampment, if one did not know better.

Yet worse was still to come.

Arrived at each designated transport, the women
had to crawl up a dangling Jacob's ladder, clutching
their goods and babies as best they might. And few
had been many minutes aboard before new shrieks of

terror began. Not many had really believed rumors that even Charles Lawrence could intend the rupturing of family ties. Yet this was the case. Arrived at a ship, one was to learn that one's nearest and dearest were being shipped elsewhere.

With the others, Rosalie reeled before the dawning of this knowledge. What of her poor, feckless father now? The sacrifice she had made for his sake became an ugly mockery. Where would he be taken? What would become of him without her?

She spun back desperately to the ladder she had only just mounted, a babble of pleas and protests foaming on her lips like the spew which had gagged poor wretches preceding them on the barges. She expected no pity, not from His Excellency's minions. She had little to offer in the way of bribery, little of any real value save the silver chain with its fleur-de-lys which had been warmed between her breasts since the hour Antoine returned it to her. But somewhere in this brute crew there must be someone greedy enough to be persuaded by silver.

"Just take me to whatever ship has Jules Despres aboard it," she would beg whoever looked bribeable. "Just smuggle me aboard there. Come dark, it will be safe. Whoever could know?"

But if she picked the wrong target, the game would be up. She'd lose her treasured silver charm, no question of that, and be laughed at for her trouble.

It came to her that she was not a very seasoned judge of character. In Grand Pré, one felt no uncertainty at all when expecting the best of anyone, or at least the kind of honesty which made no bones about offering the worst. These bearded, unwashed, uncouth seafarers were doubtless the dregs of a civilization far better schooled in cunning. Whom dared she trust?

Despairingly, she began to study faces in the crowd all about her. The deck seemed aswarm. Faces. But in which could one read avarice? In which lay warning of an uncompromising devotion to duty which could destroy her? Which might hold some glimmer of the combination she needed now—an honest dishonesty, greed coupled with principle?

Swinging over the low rail from which the Jacob's ladder dangled, a young sailor came carrying a mite of a baby and a bandana bundle. He put down both on the deck and turned back at once to assist a woman who had climbed behind him. Her sheer bulk showed her to be well advanced in another pregnancy. The sailor guided her with kindness.

More even than this, he bore some vague resemblance to Roger. Feature for feature, they were markedly unalike. But he had blue eyes. His hair was twisted into a seafaring pigtail, yet it was brown hair and not of a very different shade. She could not by the wildest stretch of imagination fancy Roger betraying her. Was there a chance that this man too . . . ?

Thinking it (if what went on in her head could be said to be thinking), she took a first hesitant step toward him. And another. "Sir, I do beg pardon, but—"

From behind, a hand closed on her arm. Its pressure held her back. Close in her ear a whisper stirred, all but lost in the busy din. "Daughter! Rosalie!"

Half-convinced that the day's long tragedy had separated her from the last of her wits, Rosalie turned as the hand was urging. Either she was staring into Jules Despres's own countenance or she had indeed gone mad. She could do little but keep on staring.

"It's really me," he nodded, glancing back over his own shoulder nervously.

"But how? I was told they'd put you on another vessel. They wouldn't tell me which."

"At the church, that first day," he answered hastily, "we were promised that families would be kept together. But then, as time passed, we began to recognize what they were really up to. I began to make a plan."

It came to her that he was whispering, like a badly frightened man or one bent upon peddling illegal goods in a back alley. "What's wrong, Father? Has someone hurt you?"

"No, no. But no one must see us talking together, not until the boat's well out to sea. After that, it will be too late. The captain would never put back for one such small matter. He's too eager to be rid of us, and speedily. All of them are."

"You're right, I suppose. But I must know one thing. How did you manage it?"

"First, I found a young farmhand from Ile Royale they'd scooped up in their net and quartered in with us. He's an orphan boy, with no kin to care about or to care about him. For what little money I had in my pocket, he was agreeable to a swap of identities. He became Jules Despres. I became Démocède Sherrard."

"And they didn't suspect, the British?"

"How could they? Those keeping us under watch are strangers to Nova Scotia. An old man from Grand Pré, a youth from somewhere else, how could they separate one stupid Acadian from another? The rest was more tricky business. I had to learn on what passenger list your name appeared. Then I had to make sure Démocède Sherrard was billeted aboard it, too."

"Both feats being impossibilities. Tell me, tell me!"

But he shook his greying head hurriedly. "No time now. Too dangerous. Later. At sea."

He scurried away, fleet as a chipmunk, losing himself in the close-packed deck throng before she could make any move to follow. But she made no such effort. He was right. Their being seen together too soon could breed a whole nestful of vipers.

It astonished her to realize how cleverly—yes, how daringly—her mild father had handled the situation. Her own method might well have precipitated instant disaster. Who was looking after whom in this insane holocaust already wiping out the only world they knew?

5

THE *Pembroke* WADDLED awkwardly once she left the semi-protection of the Basin and hit wilder Fundy water.

Her hundred and thirty-nine tons rode low in the waves, weighted down exhaustingly by the two hundred and thirty-odd passengers cramped aboard her in addition to her normal crew. She was old and she was tired, the antithesis of a stout new schooner. In Charleston, her home port, old tars had grumbled at the news that she meant to put to sea at all. One good storm and her seams would open like those of a midget's jacket worn by a giant. Bottom of the Atlantic, that's where she'd be headed.

Still, where the money was right anything could be made to happen. Evidently that Governor fellow far

up the coast in Nova Scotia didn't give a rap what
condition of a wreck his official purse was leasing, nor
what scum had been scraped up from sinkhole floors
to man her. The day the *Pembroke* had put out on
her mission, bets had run ten to one along the waterfront that she'd never make it to Canada.

Prone on the half a bunk alloted to him, Roger
Bernard now was thinking much the same concerning
her return voyage. It would be a true astonishment if
he and the other Acadians herded up her gangplank,
for delivery to the Carolinas, ever again set foot on
solid land. The old tub was already moaning like some
monster in its death throes. And they had not even
reached open ocean. He wondered if the lifeboats
were any sounder than their mother.

Staring up at timbers low above his head, he thought
of that far off cave where Dawn Dove had nursed him
back to life. Even that rocky roof had not bent a man
double when he tried to stand erect beneath it. In
almost every way, their forest retreat had been an
Eden by comparison. Yes, even to its water sounds.
He would have traded the greedy slap of sea against
rotting timbers any time for the splash of a waterfall.

Yet he did not altogether regret his decision to
resume the real life to which he had returned. His
many weeks in the forest had been less brutal, no denying that, but they had been wrapped in a grey mist of
wondering, of tormenting partial glimpses of events
he struggled futilely to recall. Given a choice of
agonies, he would opt still for these present ones. At
least he knew who he was. He knew what ill fate had
befallen the folk who were his lifelong friends and
neighbors. He knew whose lovely shrouded face

peered out at him from behind the tantalizing veil that had pitilessly obscured it.

That face came as clear to him now as though he had been kissing her only yesterday. He remembered everything he ever had known about her, and cherished each memory. The bitter fact that they were carried by separate ships to doubtlessly separate destinations, that months and even years might drag away before he could find her again, was well offset by the other fact that he could say her name again and feel at second hand the glad yielding of her lips under his. If only her talisman on its thin chain were still about his neck, a touch of it ready at hand, Rosalie would seem almost here with him.

He felt certain that he knew what had happened to the missing fleur-de-lys. Once back in focus, his memory of that instant before the rock had crashed against his head was as vivid as a painted picture. Had Antoine taken it only because it was part of Rosalie? Had his dour resentment because she chose his friend never ebbed? So joyous at his own success with her, had he, Roger, masked the loser's hatred? Yes. Yes on all counts. He had a score to settle with Antoine. Yet on another level, he could pity the man.

A brain could go mad lying idle with such thoughts through the weary sea months still to come—always provided the *Pembroke* did not founder and bring all pondering to a salty end. Instinctively reaching for the fleur-de-lys again, and again finding it missing, Roger crawled from his bunk ledge and, still stooped over, made a tortuous trek to the companion-way. Up on deck, conditions were still overcrowded but at least less stifling.

The wind was colder than it had seemed ashore, a few days earlier. Working his way down river, following his plan to travel by night and seek cover by day, Roger had not at first been too discomforted by a hint of an early-coming Nova Scotia winter. But progress had been exasperatingly slow. British patrols seemed everywhere. Sometimes he had not made a mile a night. Did the devils in their red coats never sleep?

Yet it never had occurred to him to abandon his hegira or alter his objective. The vision of Grand Pré revived in his restored mind always drew him on, a magnet too powerful to oppose. Grand Pré was home. Home was Rosalie. His family, too; but mostly Rosalie. What other world was there?

During that long and wearisome foot march, well as he came to understand the British troops who overran the peninsula, it never had occurred to him that at the end of the trail there might be no world left. Not until the final night, when he took refuge among the branches of a tall oak overlooking his home field, did he have an inkling. He had seen isolated farms burning before, all along his way. But the image of Grand Pré as he always had known it remained solid in his mind. Against odds, he had believed that once he was home the essence of things would be waiting for him there as it always had been.

From that treetop, he had learned the Acadian lesson.

Not a light shone anywhere, not a lamp, not a candle. This alone had pricked him with a thorn of alarm. Concerned, he had urged the moon to rise so that well-known slopes would emerge from darkness. He would be able then to make out familiar outlines.

Out of the east the moon did come at last. A moon

with a great sidewise slice of it missing, as if some Englishman had been using it for sabre practice. A pale illumination washed the countryside. But the black tracery of rooftops he had been awaiting was not there.

At first, the space they always had occupied seemed totally empty. But gradually he made out stunted fragments of silhouettes, far closer to the ground than they should have been. A lintel, topping no door. A bit of wall, framing a gaping window square. A pile of collapsed timbers fallen at all angles like discarded black bones. He knew what had happened, then. The knowledge flung itself together into one awful question.

"Rosalie?"

The very word that had burst from him in the cave as realization returned now was torn sickly from him again as he scrambled down from limb to limb, hit earth, began to run.

The way to the Despres cottage was so familiar that he did not even have to think where he headed. Stumbling feet carried him along quite independently. When he reached the spot, it was exactly as horror had created it for him. Charred logs which once had been walls. Shattered glass that once had been windowpanes. A copper cookpot, lying on its side in the scorched threshold grass. The blackened frame of a chair, obscenely still erect and with a remnant of dress calico flapping from its armrest like a broken wing.

He stood frozen, beyond thought, staring at the ruin.

Behind him, the enemy he had evaded all the long way from Beauséjour spoke mockingly. "Hoho! Another straggler, is it? Come back to hunt for pickings?"

There were four of them, every man armed. But in that terrible moment, now he looked back on it, Roger doubted they had needed their guns. If he made any movement at all, it was no more than a despairing shrug of his shoulders. He scarcely felt the rough, triumphant hands which seized his arm at either side and hustled him along.

He had been shipped off to Annapolis Royal, where a laggard old vessel still waited to accommodate ragtag brought in from the surrounding countryside. And now the all-but-derelict *Pembroke* was off for the Carolinas, with himself aboard. His long escape had ended as he should have known it would. Satan Lawrence was undefeatable. Evil was everywhere. Had it not waited to tempt even Christ himself in the wilderness?

But Christ had not succumbed to it.

As he leaned against the splintery aft rail of the coastal tramp that thought struck Roger with a sudden stirring novelty. Not because he fancied any similarity between his own sinner's career and that of One Who Was Spotless, no. The priest at St. Charles de Grand Pré would have permitted such sacreligious vanity in none of his flock. Like all their Catholic village, the offspring of Marius Bernard had been raised with a healthy recognition of spiritual truth. Although they might be in the one sense God's children, they were still far from being His Son. That was abundantly clear.

Yet the same Satan had tempted them all. Satan took many forms while about his unsavory business. Sometimes a demon in the desert. Sometimes a human

likeness such as His Excellency here in Acadia. And
both should be struggled against. Did they not both
represent Wrong?

It surprised him, leaning there against the rail, that
this view of matters never had presented itself to
him before. He and his neighbors all had been raised
in too humble a tradition of submission. Because over-
lords trampled them in the name of authority, they
meekly accepted the bullying. *Engrais!* In Hades, what
was the Devil but an overlord?

A slow grin began to tug at Roger's previously tight
mouth as he pondered all this. After digesting it somewhat longer, after chewing on a latent point or two
until he felt quite sure he had it right, he straightened
slowly. Along the deck a little distance his father's
rugged friend Vespasien Le Clerc stood staring
bleakly at the churning wake of the vessel and the
shrieking gulls circling over it.

"Good evening to you, Vespasien," Roger nodded.

The older man scarcely glanced up, his gaze still
fixed astern as doubtless his thoughts were fixed upon
a lost land in the same direction. "There's little good
about it, lad. Not for us."

"Something has occurred to me, Vespasien. I'd like
to talk it over with you."

It took two full days for the word to be spread, man
to man, mouth to mouth, always with the greatest caution that no passing sailor caught a whispered syllable.
At the outset, many of the Acadians were incredulous.
The temerity of the suggestion overwhelmed them. For
so long, they had stood meekly aside while Authority
had its rough-shod way.

But the two who seemed to be the leaders, grizzled Le Clerc and that capable Bernard boy, kept at them with facts it was hard to deny.

A very great difference indeed separated a well-equipped soldier force on its own land from a small commercial cargo ship on a lonely bay. Colonel Winslow's troops at Grand Pré had been numerous and armed to the teeth. This crew manning the decrepit *Pembroke* was relatively few, and possessed of little more lethal than a few outmoded blunderbusses and a scattering of belaying pins. Moreover, the soldiers had been a disciplined war machine. The outhouse leavings of this ship's company were scarecrows, little more, and most of them half-drunk on grog within hours of sunrise.

Listening, the hesitant Acadians scarcely could prevent plain logic from seeping in. As their floating prison wallowed further down Fundy, disconsolately shaking heads were slowly replaced by eyes lit with a desperate purpose. Only those Roger and Vespasien could fully trust had been let in on the project. One two-faced traitor in on their intention and the lot of them would finish their voyage in irons.

"As near St. John's as we dare wait, that's how to time the strike."

"But it will be December closing in. If the snows begin—"

"We've seen none yet. The weather may hold. And from St. John's the waterways run deep inland. We could get halfway across New Brunswick, granting our luck."

"Indians? What of the Indians? We'd be at their mercy."

"It's New Brunswick we talk of, man. Is there an

Indian in New Brunswick who ever fought alongside
the English? We French were their friends from the
beginning."

"How fast could word get back to Halifax? How
long before the Governor's after us?"

"We'll put the crew in dorries close to shore, but
they'll have only their feet to carry them toward civilization. And another thing, Lawrence's boats are all
at sea by now. He'll have to supply new ones before
he can start ferreting out where we are."

These councils of war included only a hand-picked
handful. They were invariably convened on an open
deck, and after midnight. To discuss details in the
jam-packed cargo holds, where any ear overhearing
the talk might prove unfriendly, would be to court disaster. It was table-top plain to all what sort their
captain was, with his weasel face and his eyes that
never quite dropped anchor. Any treacherous little
pipsqueak with a story to barter for personal freedom
would know where a likely deal was to be made.

Essential care required extended time. December
was none too laggard a date. Although deferring to his
elder whenever possible, Roger had no intention of
allowing the plan essentially his own to go astray. And
when the day came, he was ready.

He was the one who, at Vespasien's carefully timed
hand wave, opened the hatch to let waiting Acadians
swarm the deck like a plague of attacking rats, jumping
startled sailors in every ship section before the dazed
louts knew what was afoot. And it was he who swung
up to the quarter-deck, having first wrenched a billy
from the grasp of a tar attempting to wield it, and
jammed the crude weapon into the Captain's ribcage
before the unwarned shipmaster could rally. It made

a fair facsimile, the billy, of a pistol—for a man unable to turn his head and inspect it.

"Now, then, *mon Capitaine!* One false move and the gulls eat your guts."

Sweat gleamed on pocked jowls before him. "Don't shoot, you imp of Perdition!"

"A bit of politeness, please, *cher Capitaine*. Signal surrender to all hands below."

"We're no warriors. We're peaceable men on a peaceable commercial venture."

"The goods you laded for Charleston have their own ideas about peace. The signal, man! We've decided we prefer a port well further north."

Within the half-hour of its start, the mutiny was over. Such an amateur uprising might have been crushed without mercy aboard a proper English warship. On a chartered sea bum like the *Pembroke*, it was close to being child's play. Five days before Christmas—and yes, the weather had preceded them, it mounded snow hip-deep on the St. John's landing—the random-assorted company from Annapolis Royal saw their last of the hulk from the Carolinas. It scarcely needed their minimal assistance, but virtually scuttled itself.

Cursing and whining, the crew had been put ashore to find its own way wherever it might elect to head. Now, shivering but safe, the Acadians themselves were on the beach and facing whatever must come next. Like bewildered children, they turned instinctively to the men who had led them to this admittedly precarious freedom.

"We'd die, heading inland while snows block every trail and there's ice hands thick on the waterways,"

Vespasien decided. "So out with your axes. Unfurl your hammers. We'll throw up cabins here and stand off the weather. We can't be followed until Spring."

Immediate ancestors of almost every man in the party had built new towns well before now along the seafront of Nova Scotia. There was little grumbling as these refugees complied. Within days, the first log walls were rising. Axes rang doggedly in the surrounding woods. Trees crashed and were stripped.

Under Vespasien's capable direction, the men worked well. At night, impromptu snow igloos sheltered them. Hunt parties brought in supportive, if not sufficient, game to eke out maggoty stores of grain brought ashore from the *Pembroke* while she still remained afloat. Life in the commune at St. John's was rugged, demanding much and giving little. But they were free men. They were no longer helpless prisoners.

"We'll toughen them up for Spring," Valerian assured Roger, well-satisfied. "Then, when we do have to move, they'll be ready for the trail. I've heard there's a goodly number of Acadian refugees already dwelling in New Brunswick, kindness of the redskins. God granting it, we'll make contact and join up with them."

"A good plan," agreed Roger politely. "But I'll not be a part of it."

"Eh? How's that, lad? What better notion are you cossetting?"

"One for me only, sir. A personal one. Once the camp is in order here and I'm no longer useful, I'll be heading south. I can manage alone. I've had some Indian training lately."

"Have you indeed? I hadn't heard of that. Why south, young one? It was to keep clear from likely slave markets in the Carolinas and Georgia and Santo Domingo that we dug in our heels at what the *Pembroke* spelled for us. Yet you now *want* the south?"

"Not half so far south as all that, sir. The port I have in mind is Boston."

"God's eyes, Boston? In the Puritan colony of Massachusetts? I've heard they skin Catholics alive there and fry 'em for breakfast bacon. Are you mad, Roger?"

"I think not, Vespasien. I have reasons for wanting to go there."

"Which are what? You tell me 'em, blast it, and I'll whittle 'em down to size for you."

"The rumor, sir, is that Boston's where Lawrence's first shiploads of Acadians will be taken. It's possible a—a friend may be among them."

"What brand of friendship justifies a fellow taking on those endless leagues you'd have to travel? You'd be a man my age before you ever found the city."

"In any case, I'll have to try it. This is a very special friend."

In these parts, so someone once had told him, they called it the January thaw. At any rate, the snows did diminish and then cease altogether and a period of warmer temperatures succeeded them. Roughly following the rocky coastline, Roger often made better trail time than he had dared hope for. Which was not to say that the going was easy.

Every skill that Dawn Dove had taught him came into play. He had some notion which berries on the wind-scoured shrubs would be edible, and which were poison. He knew how to set small twig traps for rabbits and other small game, thus hoarding his meager ammunition for the English rifle Vespasien had agreed he might take with him. He even brought into play the old Indian art she had explained to him of winter fishing through a hole in the ice.

Still, he lost weight on the diet. It fell far short of the physical demands of the wintery route he was charting with the aid of nighttime stars. He had studied old area maps at Marius Bernard's fireside years ago, not so much with specific intention of ever using them as because he had a thirst for knowledge in general. Now that boyhood preoccupation stood him in good stead. He could shut his eyes and almost see before him the elaborate convolutions of the shore of Maine, its bays, its coves, its myriad islands. Quite often, coming upon some outstanding curiosity of nature the maps had mentioned, he was able to tell himself almost precisely how far he had progressed and what still lay on ahead.

By February—he thought it must by now be February—he had reached that section of the colony, still far to the north, which was homeland to the Passamaquoddies. One night, before locating a sheltering thicket where he could unlash his blanketroll, he set a twig trap in hope of breakfast. As often when that meal came to mind, he remembered Vespasien's wry commentary on Bostonians and drifted off to sleep still chuckling.

He awoke to find the trap split open. But blood on the snow assured him that game had been taken during the dark hours. And prints alongside the crimson droplets—man prints, moccasin prints—further told him that no larger wild beast had been the robber. He was still looking about, angry and cheated, when the Indian stepped from behind a pine clump.

He was not a tall man, but he had the muscles of an

ox. They showed impressively even beneath the bits
of stitched hide which made up his defense against
the cold. His eyes, like bits of black glass, held no expression. Warily cradled against one arm, he carried
a rifle.

Friend or foe? Roger was thinking quickly.

It was the rifle that decided him. He began to speak
unhurriedly, calmly, his words sometimes in French
but interlarded with scraps of the Algonquinian argot
Dawn Dove had taught him. Micmac was closely
allied to all other native tongues hereabouts.

After only a moment, the other man's grasp of his
rifle relaxed visibly. Obviously, enough of what was
being said was making a favorable impression. Roger's
guess had been close on target, then. He smiled. The
Indian nodded back.

"Passamaquoddy?" Roger pointed, the gesture itself
an inquiry.

His opposite number nodded again, duplicating the
finger thrust. "Frenchman?"

And now the essential courtesies were completed.
They were, if not bosom comrades, at any rate com-
patible. Roger had deduced this when he studied the
weapon. These northern tribes of the loose Abnaki
confederacy—Micmac, Malecite, Penobscot, Passamaquoddy—had warmly welcomed the arrival of Europeans on their shores. The Europeans had here been
French, and had seen no reason to deny their new
hosts the blessings of firearms. The firearms, in turn,
had given the Abnaki at least a short-term advantage
over their hated enemies, the Iroquois, further to the
west. Also, the blossoming French-Indian friendship
had opened the avenue to brisk sales of furs and to
what seemed soaring prosperity.

So it was in a spirit of friendship that his chance trail acquaintance led Roger home to his village. After three days there, during which stay he never did properly learn the name of his hospitable host, he was taken on as a member of a fleet of fishing canoes headed south to slightly warmer waters.

Well down-coast his guardians turned him over to new hosts among their allies and friends, the Penobscot. Here, Roger first saw the remarkable deer masks which he was to remember the rest of his life. Skinned heads of actual deer, horns and all, had been equipped with thongs so that Penobscot braves might wear them as headpieces—their dark eyes alive and glistening behind empty sockets once so useful to their prey. Originally, his new guides told him, these masks had been decoys to lure new stags from cover. But now they were religious objects, used to assure success in the hunt.

And this not far from Holy Boston, where because of their advanced stage of civilization the citizens ate Catholics for breakfast! The quirks of mankind were indeed fascinating. Had the driving purpose which kept him moving not pressed so hard, Roger would have been happy to dally and absorb knowledge. His schooling in Grand Pré had not been extensive. A thirst to increase it explained such things as his love for maps.

But the knowledge he most needed now lay not in coastal forests but in Boston Harbor. Ships headed down from Fundy would have far outstripped the speed he could make ashore through winter-choked pine forests. Not to mention the fact that they had set out weeks before the *Pembroke* assembled its stragglers and hoisted anchor.

Had there been storms at sea? Had those other craft leased by Lawrence been ocean-worthy? Had Rosalie been part of the Expulsion list on any one of them? Had she been shipped further to the south, even to the West Indies? No amount of study could provide a man with answers to questions such as these.

And he had to know.

6

GROUPED SQUARE, almost in the fashion of opposite partners in a country dance, the four bedraggled vessels from Nova Scotia limped into Baltimore harbor. Word of their coming had preceded them. Townfolk were gathered along the quays to witness the arrival, and beyond them the rooftops of the city mounted one upon another rather like amorous dogs. Above the rest church spires thrust Heavenward, a cross surmounting every one.

"Why, they're waving hats and kerchiefs to greet us!" Rosalie murmured, only half believing it. "Papa, there's a look of kindness about them!"

After the ill-concealed hostility of the *Katie O's* sullen crew, all the long way down the continental coast, a welcome of any sort was more than she had dared anticipate. At sea, the cargo of deportees had been treated at best like so many heads of cattle; pushed this way, ordered that way, cramped into below-decks space fit to hold only half their number, ill fed, in want of the most basic living accommodations. Winter winds had cut to the marrow of Acadians permitted to bring with them only garments suited to summer. Pneumonia had claimed many of the party, and the pox still others. Wherever they died, they had been unceremoniously heaved overside with only the prayers of their fellow sufferers to accompany them.

But this crowd stretched out all along the waterfront was exhibiting all the signs of actual friendliness. One plump woman Rosalie particularly noticed as the *Katie O* dropped anchor was holding up her baby for a better view, smiling and pointing as she did so. Not far from the mother, a youth in his early teens was showing off by turning cartwheels. Even the gentry seemed on hand for the event, for carriages were lined up behind the little crowd of folk afoot. From the high seats ladies in plumed bonnets were waving their parasols.

"Papa," she breathed, suddenly hopeful. "Why, they don't appear to hate us at all! And yet their colony is solid British, so I've been given to believe."

"Solid Catholic at its inception," Jules Despres murmured in explanation. "Pure Catholic, in Lord Calvert's day. These people know what it means to be persecuted. Later on, when Cromwell drove the Stuarts from England's throne, Puritans poured into Maryland to take over. Harsh laws against the Catholics were promulgated. Under that regime, those of our faith were even denied the franchise. They were forbidden to hold services of worship in public."

"Can it still be so, Papa?"

"No longer, no longer. Their heaviest cross today is their long, bitter dispute with Pennsylvania over just where the mutual boundary line lies. Land replaces God as the vortex of bloodshed. But they remember. They will be good to us."

During the interminable voyage, Rosalie had developed a new admiration for her seemingly ineffectual parent. His knowledge on a wide variety of subjects continued to astound her. In Grand Pré meekness and mute grieving for Mama had obscured what she now appreciated as an intellectual brilliance. Among their sturdy farm neighbors he had been a fish out of water. Aside from carefully tending to his physical well-being, she had not paid Jules Despres nearly sufficient attention. There was always one callow swain or another knocking at the cottage door to demand her thoughts. And later, there was Roger.

Papa's scheme to keep them together, revealed to her cautiously after the *Katie O* lay well clear of Fundy, was a typical example. Once having traded identities with this young herdsman, Démocède Sherrard—of whom she had until now never heard—he had worked in his own mild, inconspicuous fashion to achieve the rest.

Picking a guard whose veined red nose proclaimed him a tippler, he had day after day gone about currying the fellow's friendship. He had then told his beguiled jailer the hiding place of the bottle of rum kept for visitors behind the Despres cottage chimney, and offered the man a free gift of the cache. In return, his uniformed crony had given him a few moments alone with the embarkment rolls, kept under key in the St. Charles de Grand Pré sanctuary.

"Though what matters it which ship takes you, Démocède, that's beyond me."

"To me it makes no matter. But I have a young niece. I'd like to wave an *adieu* to her."

"Well, take your peek then. But don't be too long about it."

There had been pen and ink in the sanctuary. Locating his daughter among those detailed to the *Katie O*, inserting the name Démocède Sherrard in the roll had been no feat at all—not for a man who in his youth had been a public letter-writer on the Cherbourg docks. Oh, Papa, Papa! And once she had believed he would fade away if she were not beside him!

But now, here was Baltimore. And, friendly or no, Baltimore might prove to be a very different kettle of *bouillabaisse*. As Rosalie joined the Acadian line filing down the *Katie O*'s lowered gangplank, worldly goods weighting the single satchel she carried and Jules marching ahead with a pride she found new in him, she lifted her chin. She must manage at least a counterfeit of confidence.

Grand Pré was gone forever. Roger was gone, although never the dear memory of him. But a new life of some sort lay ahead of her. She'd have to make the best of it.

The Santo Domingo sun blasted down on Antoine Rolande like fire spilled from a crucible. Sweat crawled through his red-blond hair, slithered down the handsome angles of his cheeks, dripped off the deep cleft in his chin. Pausing to mop away enough wetness so his light-seared eyes were not entirely blinded, he stared about him.

His fellows on the labor gang still bent to their picks

and shovels. A lone exception was one now inert at the roadside, who had dropped to his knees and crawled off under a low-growing bush. He had died there and sprawled staring up at the livid sky, his wasted chest no longer rising and falling. They'd let him lie, unburied until dogs found him.

The arriving deportees had been set to construct a new fortification for the authorities in power. They were being treated like peons, like peasants. They worked, so they were told, in exchange for the generous bounty of the government.

Bounty? Antoine's lip curled. He was fed swill in a filthy kitchen. He was housed in barracks a pig might scorn. But he could grasp the government's reasoning. The island's great plantations owned armies of black slaves. Violent hatred of their masters showed in every bent back in every cane field, every mahogany forest. Worse, those in the cane were armed. They swung murderous-looking machetes.

Trouble was coming. When it arrived, the powers meant to be ready, if it meant slaughtering ten thousand blacks. Cannon would be turned upon each sullen rioter who, until now, was kept in line by an overseer's whip.

It gave Antoine grim pleasure to think of the night of the explosion. Surely that was not far away. A good portion of these plantation-owning *grands blancs* were certain to be butchered in their silk beds, hacked to stew meat by the very knives now toiling to fill the masters' coffers. He would give a year of his life to be on hand to witness it.

His narrowed eyes surveyed the scene about him. Piles of crushed rock for paving the intended parade ground of this sub-fort heaped high at every turn.

Sledges swung by unpaid workers kept reducing more of the rocky hillside to building-stone size. All to keep the lucky few in their seats of the mighty.

Granted, if the Rolande family were among those nabobs Antoine might have felt differently about it all. But fate had ruled otherwise. Henri was wasting his business skills at someone else's clerking desk in the town. Madame Thais was huddled over exquisite needle work that would become another woman's adornment. He, Antoine, was a blond nigger on a road gang. He hated every *grand blanc* on the island. He would have relished personally swinging the machete that might soon disembowel every separate one. Twelve thousand of them sipping their champagne, and four hundred thousand blacks seething to rise up out of the plantation fields. What a rare day *that* would be!

Off to one side of the road as he mopped his forehead he saw the woman again, fat but elegant in her velvet riding habit. She sat sidesaddle on a black horse that looked to be pure-blooded Arabian. She had been here before today, watching him closely.

He let his glance lock with her for a telling instant, then looked away. But he could feel her unblinking gaze upon him still, running up and down his lean length, savoring the muscles of his naked back and arms, measuring his long legs, lingering at the region where they joined.

After a moment, the dainty Arab brought her forward at a canter.

"Your name is Rolande," she said, reining in again so close to him he felt the horse's body heat. "You are one of the refugees from Canada."

He looked up at her, taking his time. "Correct on both scores, Madame."

"And I, Rolande, am—"

"Zöe Levi-Strauss." He finished the sentence for her. "Madame Levi-Strauss, the widow who owns Siberie Plantation near the far end of the island. I know who you are."

"You're surprisingly acquainted with Santo Domingo, for an Acadian."

The final word was contemptuous, a deliberate cut. Antoine itched to slap the silk flank of the Arab and set it rearing. It might unseat her. It might crack her fat bitch neck on the litter of broken rock carpeting the area. Damn her!

Instead, he smiled lazily.

"Only a stupid man would fail to make inquiries when a handsome woman displayed interest in him, Madame. You have been here before."

"Insolence! How dare you suggest I have . . . displayed interest?"

"It's your third ride past this spot in as many days, is it not? Each time, you've loitered to examine me. Wondering, I think, how I look completely naked."

Her breath sucked in. Her eyes darkened with fury. But then, tossing back her head, she laughed boisterously.

"I doubt that you really know my position, after all. I could have my friend, the Governor-General, order you flogged for saying that."

"In that case, Madame, my body would be far less attractive. I doubt you would relish blood-stains on your sheets. One imagines they are of fine satin."

"They are, indeed. Which you will have to take on faith, Señor Acadian."

"One must always regret insufficient knowledge, Madame. As perhaps I shall."

Madame Levi-Strauss stirred in her saddle. The sapphire velvet twitched. It was an ill-choice of color for a woman with carrot-dyed red hair. Had she any notion how much she resembled a Mardi Gras clown, with that flagrant mane and those painted cheeks and that black stuff smeared around her little muskrat eyes?

"I stopped only to speak to you on a business matter, Rolande."

"It's hard to talk business when a man's thoughts are elsewhere." Antoine let his green eyes say several things he had no intention of making his lips say.

"Your thoughts should not be elsewhere. My suggestion can profit you."

"We Acadians—we *mere* Acadians—always like a profit. And so, Madame?"

"I need a proper secretary at Siberie. You strike me as intelligent. I spoke about you to the Governor-General. He agrees. It's already arranged, if you agree, too."

"Not even a fool could prefer these rocks to an employer like you."

Her wide mouth curved smugly. "A carriage will collect you within the hour."

"Ah, now, I wonder. In these stained clothes? Unbathed and *sans* cologne?"

"There'll be more suitable garments at Siberie. Be ready, Rolande."

As the Arab danced off along the construction trail, Antoine stood hands on hips and let his eyes follow her. It was well she did not glance back to catch the expression in them. Although he made no sound at all, he was laughing.

Presently he dropped his shovel and left it where it landed. He sauntered to the road's shoulder and sat down in a patch of shade to wait. He knew quite well that the foreman would no longer dare to call him to task.

Madame Zöe was punctual; that, or impatient. Somewhat short of her hour, Antoine found himself sprawled on the rear seat of a handsome plantation phaeton. A uniformed negro sat rigid on the box to handle a currycombed pair, as they rolled up the wide private avenue which led from Siberie's gates to the great house itself. From the look of what he had left his widow to enjoy, Andre Levi-Strauss must have been a very sucessful planter.

She stood ready to receive him in what had been her husband's library. Walls of handsomely bound volumes. Panelling of pale, lovingly polished exotic woods. Heavy furniture upholstered in sleek leathers, red or black or fern-grotto green. Chandeliers that glittered like diamonds. Nothing met Antoine's appraising eyes that did not please him—nothing except the dumpy female in absurdly young lace negligee and hair-ribbons who waited for a butler to show in her new secretary and then discreetly withdraw.

"Welcome." Sometime since their last meeting, her voice had grown husky. "Welcome to Siberie."

"The house befits its mistress. I haven't seen its like since . . . Paris." He had never been to Paris, or anywhere else in Europe. Yet the line was spoken convincingly.

"I hope you will be happy here, Rolande. Very, *very* happy."

"My name is Antoine. At the construction site, Zöe, we spoke of finding less crude wardrobe for me. Shall we estimate the necessary measurements?"

The half-smile on his beautiful mouth was reflected in his lazy green eyes as he began, very slowly, to undo the fastenings of his trousers. When the garment dropped, he kicked it aside. Standing before her Adam-bare, he let her stare for a full dazed moment.

"Well, Zöe? Are you satisfied?"

She seemed not to be *religieuse*. Yet her answer could befit one. "My God!"

"Everything's real, you know. Touch it and make sure."

She managed an oddly shy and unsteady step toward him. Antoine took care of the rest of the distance between them. With no particular attention to the well-being of the fragile negligee, his hands ripped it apart and forced it down her overripe flesh until it puddled about her ankles.

Her breasts popped up to greet him, quivering. They were large and once, years since, might even have been seductive, but they had lost any bounce or upward tilt. Thin blue veinlines crisscrossed their sag.

"Beautiful!" he murmured, not quite gagging on the lie.

She reached out, stubby fingers exploring. He watched the jewels on them shimmer. Zöe watched one rising jewel which held her mesmerized.

"Antoine! Oh, Antoine! Oh, Jesus!"

Awkwardly, she backed from him until her plump legs collided with the nearest library sofa. She half-sank, half-toppled onto the smooth green leather, staring up at him. And he stared down. The hag had not even troubled to shave where it mattered, nor to dye the matted hair to match her bonfire coronet.

"Please, Antoine?" She was babbling. "Please? Please?"

"Not here. Leather's too slippery for my liking. Get down on the floor, Zöe. That's where I mean to ride you. And not side-saddle either, my Arabian. Crawl on the floor."

There were surprisingly few in Boston willing to display much knowledge of Acadians. Roger had tramped the city for three weary days before he found any lead at all to the person he was seeking. But then it seemed a good one.

He had stopped on the edge of the snow-carpeted Common, vaguely wondering how much longer the moccasins his Penobscot friends had pressed on him as a parting gift might outlast winter punishment. Their leather was soaked through and ice cold to the touch. Skin inside what once had been a pair of home-spun stockings seemed to have congealed.

The acres of this public place stretched ermine white, serene and pretty as a painting. The streets had been trampled by horse and human traffic, however, until they were a sea of ugly, churned-up slush. The half-melted mess made going difficult, even on sidewalks, and God knew there were few enough of those. After all his long journey over frozen forest trails, which he had endured with determination rather than despair, this English city had all but done him in. Were there such indifferent folk anywhere else in the hemisphere?

All he had been able to discover this far was in the way of depressing generalities. Ships from Nova Scotia set to dump cargo here had arrived weeks earlier. Put ashore, the arriving Acadians had been treated like servants, or animals, or worse—in every sense regarded as uncaged prisoners.

From the numbers reported, Roger judged that a full quarter of his dispossessed old neighbors must have landed here. Since then they had been held under virtual house arrest, their every move under surveillance. Evidently, Governor Lawrence had convinced Boston that his refugees were a dangerous lot, close kin to criminals, and would breed trouble in Massachusetts if they could.

As expeditiously as possible, even distant kin had been separated one from another. They were swiftly scattered across the face of the colony—a few here, a few there, and all threatened with imprisonment if they tried to stir from their alloted communities. Shortly afterward, six more unwanted ships, bound for the Carolinas, had put in to discharge additional human sewage into the city. Contaminated water supplies meant the wretches could be ferried no further.

Those were the outlines of a story Roger encountered on every corner where he requested information. After scores of repetitions, his courage dwindled to the vanishing point. And he had as yet found no proof of whether Jules Despres or Rosalie had even come to Boston.

If at first you don't succeed, try, try again. Brave words, no doubt. But if you've slept three nights in wet alleys, eaten nothing but what could be salvaged from garbage heaps, you did begin to wonder. *If at the thirtieth time . . . the eighteenth. . . .*

So now, turning from the Common fence and the pleasant quietness beyond it, he felt hope guttering like the burnt final stub wick of a candle. He stepped out into the cross-street, feeling slush seep over his moccasins again, scarcely half looking where he was going. A farm cart trundling past sprayed him chin to knees with melted muck.

Dully, not even glancing up, Roger began to brush himself soggily clean. He paid no heed that someone was roaring "*Whoa!*" or that creaking wheels had halted. Not until the drayman on the high seat vaulted down did Roger really think of the driver at all.

"Here, then, I'm almighty sorry. Didn't mean to give you a bath, mister."

Brush, brush, brush. "I should have looked where I was going."

"You're a fine sight, that's for certain. I've got you soaking. Look, I'm on my way to a fireside and an ale. Come on along. At least I can see you dry, brother."

The mentioned fireside was that of a somewhat sleazy grogshop down on the quay. Not being a drinking man—indeed, refusing the ale part of the invitation in favor of a mug of spiced cider—Roger still found himself warming to the place. Its fire was cheery. Its clientele, if rough, seemed friendly. And he liked the hulking driver who was his self-appointed host. The drayman's name, it turned out, was Obediah Chatterly.

"And you'd be?" Obediah pressed, having first identified himself.

"I'm Roger Bernard. Just down from Canada."

Nearsighted eyes studied him owlishly. "Off one of them boats a bit back, are you?"

"Not off a boat. I came south with friends. Penobscot fishermen."

"Say what you want, I like the Indians. Known plenty of 'em I found bone-honest."

Almost by rote, almost as if it were ritual, Roger took a swig of his cider and began to ask the old, tired questions. "I'm looking for friends off a boat, though."

"Not help but to feel sorry for 'em. Threadbare lot. Which boat was they from?"

"I don't even know their boat headed for Massachusetts. Many didn't." There was little reason to go on, but he did. "You haven't heard of folk named Despres, I guess?"

"Now if that don't beat all!" Obediah whistled softly. "I most certainly did. Nice fellow with a girl in tow. Stood 'em a mug right here in this very ingle. Despres, for sure. Let's see. Yep, Jules Despres."

"And the girl?" Suddenly Roger's heart knocked his Adam's apple. "Named Rosalie?"

"Well, about the filly I don't rightly say. Can't recall he ever called her by a Christian name. Just family things, like 'Honey' and maybe 'Girl.' "

"At least you saw her? What was she like, Obediah?"

"Real pretty, in her way. Dark. Quiet, but lively. Flash in her eyes, if you know what I mean."

Roger knew very well exactly what Obediah meant. There hadn't been a girl with merrier eyes than Rosalie's in all Grand Pré. Dark? Real pretty? He had her to a tee.

"They're here in Boston! Can you tell me where?"

"Her, Roger, I can't more than guess. Him, yea, I can tell you."

"Where? Give me the address and I'll be off. I'm deeply, deeply obliged to you."

"No call to be obliged. Not if Jules Despres was a

friend of yours. His address is Pauper's Field. They laid him in a grave there maybe oh, three, four weeks ago."

Stunned, Roger stared back across the scarred tavern table.

"Died? Jules is dead? What took him, Obediah? Pneumonia? Starvation? He wasn't strong."

"Few fresh off those hell boats were what you'd call in the pink." Obviously, Obediah hated being a bearer of ill tidings. He peered down at his big hands disconsolately. "But this was a mite different. A knife in the back was what took Jules, see."

"A *knife?* Dear God, did he fall afoul of a footpad?"

"He fell afoul of a big six-footer who took what you'd call a real shine to the girl. Jules didn't cotton to that at all. Words led to words. It wasn't here but at some rooming house where places had been found for 'em. The fellow got disrespectful-like with the girl, Jules ordered him away, out came the knife, and well, there's the story."

"And they've buried my old neighbor. Can you direct me to his grave?"

Obediah grunted. "Folks in Pauper's Field don't get big marble monuments set over 'em. The city uses ditches. Many as can fit get crowded in, then dirt's shoveled over. That's how it was. I went to be witness, seeing he had no Boston friends. Me and the girl."

Roger took a deep breath. It didn't do much to settle his churning thoughts.

"You said you could guess where Rosalie has gone. Guess, will you?"

"Out of colony, that's all I know. Tagging along with the peddler."

"Peddler?" The tavern seemed to grow much too warm. "What peddler?"

"Why, the bloke that pulled the knife on Jules, of course. Didn't I say? It was in his bed Jules caught her making merry. She was as daft for him as he for her. She was after him like a cat in rut. That's what the whole fracas was over."

7

THE SLAP-SLAP-SLAP of dark waves against the little fishing skiff had a soothing sound to it, one to which Rosalie discovered restful words might almost be fitted. As poetry often mated with music and gave birth to a song, so this rippling cadence seemed a kind of counterpoint to hope and happiness she was feeling for almost the first time after five hard, anxious and uncertain years.

Squatting just ahead with others of their party of a baker's dozen, her father was looking eagerly about him—everywhere at once it seemed—at these coastal marshes which seemed to introduce the great fresh-water Mississippi to a salty Mexican Gulf.

Their stay in Baltimore appeared to have made Jules Despres younger rather than older, although

these days undeniable streaks of silver showed in his
thinning brown hair.

It was as if the period of lethargy following upon
Maman's sad death had been swept away by the sudden demands of The Great Expulsion, which was
what folk in Maryland had taken to calling the brutal
Nova Scotia uprooting of the Acadians. Before, he had
been sunk in some morass—not unlike this strange
place now drifting past the skiff as it nosed landward.
But a need to sustain himself and his daughter in an
alien city had reawakened him.

With his fine accumulation of book knowledge at
hand, Papa had set himself up as a private tutor to
children of wealthy Baltimorians. Within weeks of
their arrival, a heartening number of pupils had come
his way. Folk who at first hired him out of sympathy
or curiosity for his plight had quickly come to recognize his very real abilities. Within the first year, *École
Despres* (he had abandoned that assumed Sherrard
soubriquet, immediately upon quitting the *Katie O*)
was showing a modest profit. Instead of having to seek
servant work to support them, Rosalie was kept fully
occupied tending house for him and mothering the
youngest of the expanding flock in his classroom.

Baltimore had been good to them. They might have
remained there for the rest of their days, safe and
content. Various young men of the city had shown
budding interest in the attractive daughter of *Monsieur
le Professeur*, at least in the beginning. But Rosalie
had made clear to each of them her own intention. For
her, that sort of love was definitely over, burned away
in a tragic conflagration near Beauséjour. She would
remain for the rest of his lifespan as Papa's devoted
assistant. If she outlived him, why then there would be

a convent and whatever modest service she could render there.

What had uprooted them again at last was the increasing tales one was hearing, by 1760, of Acadian regrouping in the far distant land known as Louisiana.

Almost weekly, Baltimore's brisk seaport trade brought in some new vessel from that area, manned often by Frenchmen. On his constitutionals along the waterfront, Jules met with many of them. He brought home tales.

"The region still belongs to our old French King, Rosalie. They welcome Acadians there as blood brothers. Their New Orleans is said to be a second Paris."

"Do you hear any names, Papa? Have any of our old neighbors reached there?"

"Several, several. Last week I took coffee with a young ensign I met once before. Seems he's become friends with your old admirer, Antoine Rolande. The Rolandes are there in New Orleans, Etienne tells me. Antoine and Henri and Thais, all happily settled in together. Etienne has a funny story about Antoine."

"Antoine brought me word of Roger's death." She touched the fleur-de-lys on its almost invisible chain at her throat. "What was this funny story?"

"The Anglos shipped Antoine to Santo Domingo. The island Governor made him a common laborer. Henri and Thais, too. But you remember what a handsome scamp Antoine was. On the island, a very rich widow became enamored of him. Among her many possessions was a sea-going sloop maintained for her pleasure."

"One pictures Antoine lolling on a Cleopatra's barge, fanned by Nubians."

"Far more to the point, when the time was ripe he

stole it right from under her nose. He sailed it, with his parents and a crew of fugitive Acadians, clear to New Orleans. The bold wretch! I liked the lad, Rosalie."

"I liked him, too. I'm happy he is safe, Papa."

Their own sea journey had been no such picaresque adventure. Once a decision had been reached, the two Despreses had quit their modest rented lodgings and invested most of Jules's scrimped-together Baltimore hoard in passage to the Gulf of Mexico.

A sea run along the coasts of Virginia, the Carolinas, Georgia, and then (with some trepidation) around the great Spanish-held peninsula of Florida, had been almost without incident. Put ashore at a back bay called Biloxi, where Pierre Lemoyne had founded a frontier French colony sixty years ago, they joined other Acadians gathering to lease the fishing skiff and continue on. Now at last they were approaching Louisiana. Or had perhaps already reached it. In this strange watery world of reeds and swamps, it was hard to say whether or not one were still at sea.

In Nova Scotia, stark rocky crags reared belligerently from the grey Fundy waves, an instant barrier. Here, from all she could discern ahead, there was no high land to mark a difference. What one made out from the gliding skiff as shadows on the water were shadows at first, but gradually they became sandbars. The sandbars became land strips.

Their Bayougoula Indian pilot informed his party that newly arrived Acadians, whom he called Cajuns, already had given these strips a name—*cheniers,* from their *chene* for Oak. The *cheniers* poked just above water, like the carapaces of sunken turtles, and held back much of the salt Gulf. They reminded her of manmade Acadian dykes at home. Once one reached them, one was "ashore," although leagues of mud flats still lay ahead.

The skiff nosed onward, waves making love to its gunwale. Their Bayougoula seemed to have an almost supernatural talent for feeling out a channel, although at times Rosalie could not identify it at all. As he guided them along, he pointed out exotic Louisiana wonders they were passing; mangrove clumps, marsh grasses, oaks, stands of cypress and tupelo palms. Most fascinating of all to Rosalie were the freshwater back-swamps where tiny-flowered duckweed almost carpeted the shallow water. Here, the Bayougoula said, birds of a whole continent paused yearly on their eternal north-south migration. Sometimes ducks would cover the ponds until no water showed. The weed was their favorite delicacy, their caviar.

Not even as she trudged down the gangplank of the *Katie O* had Rosalie had such a sense of entering a world entirely cut off from anything she ever had known.

Jules left his forward position and worked back to where she was sitting.

"With every mile, *cherie*, one learns. Did you know there are already two kinds of "Cajun" to become? One may be *chapeau*, which means that one is a town-dweller. Or one may be more rustically *capuchon* and live along the bayous."

"What in heaven's name is a bayou, Papa?"

"As I understand, it's one of God-knows how many sidestreams branching off from the great Mississippi to pour its silt out into the Gulf. The richest topsoil

of the whole central continent is carried down by the
Mother River and deposited here. A Paradise indeed
for seasoned farmers like us Nova Scotians."

She laughed. "Be truthful. You never were an expert
farmer, Papa."

"Well, perhaps not. We may find new pupils need-
ful of a teacher in New Orleans. If not, we'll apply
for a ribbon farm further up the river."

"Papa! You're teasing. Ribbons don't grow on farms.
There's no such crop."

His turn to chuckle. "The term describes the land
itself, child."

"Land doesn't come in ribbons either, Papa."

"It does in Louisiana. Riverfront is prime property.
No farm grant may measure more than two to four
arpents of Mississippi frontage. But it can run forty
arpents back from the river. That's a mile or more of
fine farm terrain and bottomland hardwood."

"Surely such prizes don't drop into refugee hands?"

"On the contrary. Levees are vital to contain the
great stream at flood time. The skills of us so-called
Cajuns as dyke-builders are common knowledge. The
French authorities encourage our applying."

"So will you apply, Papa?" Rosalie shook her head
ruefully as the skiff edged along. "Jules Despres, the
great farmer, tilling a mile of fields shaped like a
ribbon?"

"We shall see," Jules countered mildly. "We shall
have to see."

There was some dispute between the two young
gentlemen as to which of them would mount the new
whore first.

She was called Henriette, and she was a choice

piece of woman flesh—small, active, sly, with dimples. Coming downriver from Natchez, she had signed for duty in Madame Sophie's elegant New Orleans bordello only the week before. Arriving tonight on Madame's marble doorstep at the same precise moment, indeed, in each other's company, they had sighted Henriette in the identical second. They'd made for her like a pair of homing pigeons.

"I gave way to you with last week's tart, Etienne. Tonight's my turn."

"But it's my name day, dash it! I deserve to be deferred to."

While she waited between them, waiting for the bicker to be resolved, Henriette made fascinating use of the dimples. It drove them both to hotter protests, back and forth. At last, with a laugh that began somewhere deep in her slim white throat, she resolved the matter with a light pat to each of their tensed jawlines.

"*Mes amoureux*, enough, enough! I don't want you both worn out before we even begin our frolic. There's enough of me to exhaust you both, and a dozen gents after you."

"I first!" Etienne snarled angrily.

"I first!" demanded Antoine, in an identical breath.

"What we'll do is this. Both pay Madame your fees. We'll go up to my room together, *à trois*. Flip a coin. Loser can look on while the other shows me he's a hero. And turn about."

In the bedroom, Etienne Blanchet won the toss—which was not at all to Antoine's liking. Perhaps, however, it could be best. The little kitten would be warmed up between her legs before he himself took over.

He sprawled on a red-velvet-and-gilt chaise lounge

in one corner and watched through narrowed green eyes, while Henriette giggled out of her spangles and Etienne dropped his britches and began to manipulate his quite average weapon for her pleasure.

On the whole, Antoine liked Etienne. They were indeed close friends, as much as Antoine permitted anyone really to be a friend. They had caroused together through many a night, in the two years since the sloop *Siberie* first dropped anchor in New Orleans water. As a naval ensign, Etienne was familiar with Louisiana's underworld and a valuable source of certain information. He even brought home from his official voyages occasional tidbits of true excitement. Such as the time a year ago, or almost that, when he had returned with an account of running into Jules Despres, no less, on the Baltimore promenade.

Careful, unhurried questions had amplified that bit of information. Yes, the professor had a daughter in Baltimore with him. Yes, her Christian name was Rosalie. Yes, the old man had seemed much interested in Etienne's stories of the increasing Acadian colony in lush Louisiana.

Antoine smiled quietly now as he recalled that conversation, and a sequel. Etienne's ship had put in at Baltimore a second time; and, because of their earlier discussion, Etienne had looked up Professor Despres for a small reunion. The name Rolande had been dropped into their talk. In all likelihood, Jules would have relayed it to Rosalie.

He felt sure that Rosalie thought reasonably often of Antoine Rolande. Girls usually did. Time would have blurred her memories of Roger Bernard by now. She would be ready to be kissed alive again, like the Sleeping Beauty of a fairytale. It seemed almost certain that, soon or late, Despres would drift toward New Orleans. Cajuns of a feather, one might say. Antoine would be ready when she came. More than ready.

He swerved attention now to the action on the ornate bed, making an evaluation.

Etienne displayed a pleasant bottom—narrow flanks, olive-hued buttocks with no hair on them, a smooth curve where they tucked back in. But, God's teeth, he didn't know how to use what he had. One couldn't sink a tack with a big hammer, as the saying went. He was too hot to climax, was Etienne, to pay attention to technique.

The girl pinned under his bare, sweat-polished belly was moaning slightly as she gave back thrust for thrust—rise, fall, rise, fall—but to Antoine the sound didn't seem like one of unalloyed ecstasy.

He reached for the cane he had leaned against one Cupid-infested arm of his chaise lounge. It was a copy of his father's, made by a master Dauphine Street silversmith a season ago, a gift to him by one of several rich elderly Creole ladies he had made it his business to charm, since arriving in their city. He much admired Henri's taste. He loved his cane.

Tapping its tip on polished floor planks, he established with it a more proper tempo for what was making the bedsprings creak. Did Etienne fancy himself a racehorse? Rise, hold, fall, thrust deeper, hold, rise, hold . . . That was the way it should be done. But Etienne, the clumsy, seemed not to be heeding him. The poor girl would be all bruises. She'd be whimpering for liniment before Antoine himself got to use her.

"That's right, you dolt," he muttered, "plow her!

She's a farm field, not a doxy. Run through her at a gallop! Rip the furrow open, don't ease it. Oh, *blast* you!"

In exasperation he jumped up from his seat and strode to stand over them, canetip still thumping the rhythm as it ought to be. Etienne kept on plunging with a frenzy. His naked back was lacquered with perspiration. A little puddle had collected in the hollow where spine met crack of division. Antoine's perfect nose wrinkled with disgust.

Henriette lay staring up at him, wide-eyed. Her mouth was open, red tongue tip darting from it like the tongue of some prey-seeking lizard. She groaned in desperation.

"In charity, Monsieur! Your friend will rip me like a melon!"

Antoine laughed. "You boasted of satisfying a dozen like us, Mam'selle."

"But how was I to know? He is an ox, Monsieur, a Percheron! I bleed already!"

"And my turn still to come. Are you sorry you ventured down the river, *petite*? Is the Natchez thrust more refined than ours here? Let us compare techniques."

"You mock me. Stop him, Monsieur! In Ste. Agnes's name, stop him!"

"Oh, very well." Antoine bent down and whispered. "The lady is bored, Etienne. She has had quite enough of you. She wishes me to replace you."

Still grinding, Etienne snarled back. "Shut up. Go away."

Antoine shrugged and smiled. He lifted the cane, positioned its ferrule exactly between the churning cheeks he had watched with dissatisfaction, and slowly pressed it home. With a howl of agony and rage Etienne flew up off the whore and made for him.

"You mother-raper, I'll murder you!"

Antoine backed away, hands upflung in imitation pleading, laughing all the while.

"Etienne, Etienne, I was thinking of you, my friend. Your performance is a disaster. I meant only to ring down the curtain while a suggestion or two still might help."

His comrade's face was scarlet.

"You smug bastard! Think you're the world's great lover, do you? Well, you couldn't even get into a simple farm girl back in your rube home town, could you? Her father hinted to me how hot you were after her. But she wouldn't have you!"

The smile drained slowly from Antoine's features, like water from a broken bowl. It left behind it only a gelled, expressionless hardness. Apollo in alabaster.

"You are speaking of Despres, I gather. And of Rosalie."

"Whom else? You wanted her like hell, Antoine. But you couldn't get her." Etienne was all but shouting, livid with vengeful triumph. "You don't even know that they're right here in New Orleans, do you? Their skiff tied up three days ago, and you don't even know. That's how eager the girl is to see the great lover again!"

"They are in New Orleans, Etienne? You have actually seen them?"

"Day before yesterday, on the street. The Professor was delighted to find an old friend. I spoke of you, gave them your address. They'd have made themselves

known—if Mademoiselle had any slight interest in
resuming relations with Grand Pré's fabulous Don
Juan."

For a moment, Antoine remained so still he seemed
almost to have stopped breathing. Then, abruptly, he
veered back toward the bed where the girl still
crouched.

"Thank you for letting them know where to find me,
Etienne. But that's scarcely the matter at hand. I am
about to show you how this thing should be done."

Unhurriedly, much as he once had made the same
gesture in a library at Siberie Plantation, he began to
remove his exquisitely tailored trousers. This time,
however, he did not kick the discarded garment aside.
He bent to retrieve it and folded it precisely and laid
it with equal precision on a windowledge.

"And now, *cher* Etienne, you will please observe."

Clutching a sheet about her nakedness, Henriette
stared up at what he just had exposed to her. He was
reminded, briefly, of Zöe Levi-Strauss's initial reaction at Siberie. But where Zöe's look had been all
dazed adoration, Henriette's showed only terror.

"You mean for me to take all that? *Twice* what
he . . .? No, no, Monsieur, no!"

"Yes, yes, *petite*, yes." He advanced on her slowly,
flexing.

"It would kill me. Please, if you have a drop of
mercy in you, sir—"

"I give lessons in how a real man makes love, Henriette. Once you open your portals, an angel will pass
between them. At the end, you will be imploring me
for more."

"Oh, God! No, I will not! I cannot!"

"You can. You will. I have paid Sophie well for

you. I shall get my money's worth. Observe, now, Etienne. Look closely."

He reached out a relentless hand and tore the rumpled sheet away from her.

Jules Despres returned just short of sunset from the over-two-nights trip that had taken him well upriver. He had earlier found places for himself and Rosalie in a respectable city rooming house, one where he need feel no qualms about leaving her during a brief absence. Their landlady, a Mme. Dominique Gilboy, was a pewter-haired, iron-spined epitome of all the sterner strengths and virtues. His first impression was that he had found in her the perfect dragon. Even in a town as lively as New Orleans, Jules need entertain few worries. Now, as he mounted the wooden steps to Mme. Dominique's door, Rosalie came skimming through it to prove him correct.

"Papa, you're back! Ah, how I've missed you!"

"And I've missed you, *cherie*. Many's the time I've wished I'd taken you along with me. But it seemed unwise. I had little idea what I might be getting myself into."

She hugged his arm, drawing him into the Gilboy parlor where they could talk.

"What *did* you find yourself into, Papa? Tell me everything!"

"Well, up around St. Jacques de Cabanocey, fine land is opening rapidly for settlers. Three years back, the local government legitimized what was already a good start on colonizing the area. Authorization's been given for building a new chapel there. Trekking down from St. Louis, more Acadians creep in from the woods every day. Shiploads of new 'Cajuns' turn up here in harbor with no advance notice, one after another."

"*Cajun*. Such a funny word. And it means us. Are we Cajuns?"

"So it seems. What matter what we're called, if the term is welcoming? This Louisiana is our refuge, Rosalie. Thank *le bon Dieu* we've found it."

"About St. Jacques, Papa? Is that where you mean to farm?"

The smile Jules bestowed upon her made his usually undistinguished face a veritable map of love. "Well, now, as to that. You yourself pointed out not long ago that I'm not exactly tailor cut to make a fortune with a handplow."

"But as you hinted just now—"

"I'm much taken with Cabanocey, no denying that. Even its name delights me. It's an Indian word, so trappers I chanced upon tell me. It translates to '*clearing where the ducks land*.' The migrant ducks, child. Like the migrant Acadians. It rings like poetry."

"It really does. But that's no cause for trying to make a farm there."

"A community will also be in the making. One already is. They'll want a schoolhouse, once prime needs are seen to. And a schoolmaster. I've made a few inquiries."

"So it will be Baltimore *redux*? But in our own little corner? Oh, Papa! We can begin to build *École Despres* all over again. And I'll take care of the house and—and—"

He reached out a gentle hand to find her. "Are you certain such a way of things could make you happy, *ma cherie*? A rough frontier? For decades to come it won't be the settled life of Grand Pré. You're so like your mother, Rosalie. I want the best for you."

"What is the Bible line, Papa? *Whither thou goest, I will go?*"

"As I recall, that had to do with dutiful daughters and mothers-in-law. A rare relationship. Still, if the *belle mère* is the right one. . . . You used to be very fond of Thais Rolande, as I recall. And she of you."

"Indeed yes. But what has that to do with now? She's not my *belle mère*."

Jules smiled vaguely. "On my way to the river boat day before yesterday, I chanced to meet young Etienne Blanchet. He's close to Antoine. He's the one who told me about Antoine's prank, stealing the sloop to fetch his family to Louisiana."

"Yes, I remember. But . . . Antoine?"

"He's always cared for you, Rosalie. He's such a handsome young devil he'd turn any heart. And a devoted son. Look how he turned himself in at the church in Grand Pré, just to comfort his father. Look how he plotted his sea adventure, mostly to rescue his parents."

"I *like* Antoine, Papa, yes. But if you're hinting about—"

"You respected Roger Bernard's opinions. Antoine was Roger's closest friend."

"I know. But marriage? I don't plan to marry, ever."

"It's a long life to lead by one's self, Rosalie. You can't grieve over Roger forever. It's the last thing Roger himself would want you to do."

"I still feel married to Roger, Papa. Even though we never were, not really."

Her father sighed. His mild eyes were unhappy. "At least, my darling, think about it. Don't close your heart. Antoine Rolande is a fine young man."

"And one who hasn't cast a glance toward me these past five years, Papa."

"He will, I think. According to Etienne, the Rolandes are living right here in New Orleans proper. Your paths are bound to cross. And when they do, *cherie*—well, a weight would lift from my old heart if you'd at least think on it."

8

THE RIVER, rolling brown and powerful beneath the planks of his raft, made a good companion. It carried him along on its shoulder as good St. Christopher was said to have borne the infant Jesus across a very different stream. Once mastering the trick of balancing against the pitching with wide-spread legs, Roger became almost fond of the raft's eccentricities.

He began to love the river itself, too. Healthy young settlements were strung out all along its banks on either side. No day passed that from his floating platform Roger failed to sight chimney smoke from a dozen prosperous farmhouses. Large flatboats hailed him in comradely style as they toted cargo down to cities on the Gulf. Once there, they'd be broken up for timber: no way to get them north again against the rush of the river. But for their brief day they were Tsarinas of the Mississippi. Waving back, Roger admired them.

Sometimes a stranger saluted him from the bank and Roger let him clamber aboard and hitch a day's ride. Mostly they were friendly folk, if a trifle rough and ready.

"Not much like the river used to be," a passenger might say. "Not like it was for your Quebec seminarian Robert La Salle when he first charted the stream. Him and them later priest fellows of yours, that Iberville and that Bienville."

"Why *my* La Salle and *my* Iberville and Bienville? Why *my* Quebec?"

"You're Canadian French, ain't you? Talk sounds that way. Nice country, Canada."

One of those to whom he gave a lift knew about other folk who had passed this way much more recently; Acadians. First of all, in '54, had come an uncle-and-nephew team.

"Skedaddled from Nova Scotia just before the British crunch began, I hear tell. That next summer, the Governor feller there pulled up all their kinfolk by the roots."

"You seem to know the river, friend. Who were this pair you mentioned?"

"Mouton by name. Salvador's the uncle, Jean's the younger feller. They walked trail along the Great Lakes all the way from Nova Scotia. Out of Illinois, they rafted. Ended up, I hear, in a Cajun river town called St. Jacques de Cabanocey up from New Orleans. Lots of Cajun people have followed since. Some by river, some by foot, some by sea."

"A Cajun town? What's a Cajun, Monsieur?"

"That's Louisiana talk for Acadian. Or maybe Canadian. Who's to say?"

Although he never had heard their names, Roger mightily respected those Moutons. They must have had visions of events to come, somewhat like the Biblical prophets.

Along a differing route though it was, he figured his own journey must have been just about as rugged. Back north in Boston, he had heard tales aplenty about this Louisiana. Rumors even reached him that his own father and brother were in the region and clearing acres on a farm the government had granted them. Even as the loner he had become since that grim winter night he'd shared with Obediah Chatterly in a rundown tavern, Roger continued to miss his blood kin. He had decided to somehow get himself to Louisiana. Nothing was left for him here, now he knew how Rosalie Despres had ended up.

Plenty of wagons were creaking westward nowadays, with new country for settling always opening up. An extra hand was usually welcome to tag along, herding livestock and standing night guard against uncordial Indians. The Iroquois were always a wagon train worry.

"You know about 'em, Bernard? Jealous of their hunting grounds, I hear."

"And ready to fight, the Penobscots say. You want an extra gun along, *monsieur?*"

Generally they did. Roger would travel as far as one party was going, then pause a bit and pick up with another. Raids? Rustler attacks? He had a bellyful of memories.

Once over the Appalachians and past most of Pennsylvania, which took two years, he had arrived with his latest wagon family at the confluence of rivers which spawned the mightier Ohio. Here the French had burned their own Fort Duquesne, two years before, to save it from the British. On this upland plateau Roger slept under open sky for a month before collecting enough timber and hardware to fashion his own raft.

Since then, it had all been down river.

The Mississippi soothed him at night like a mother rocking a baby. Tied up to some overhanging tree, he slept like a baby too. With his raft secured, he could make short trips inland to hunt and forage. At towns along the banks he could buy a few necessities.

"No way I know to get word ahead to Marius, though." That one thing did worry him.

So he came upon St. Jacques de Cabanocey without advance warning. It was a cloudless day, the sky overhead blue as a Madonna's robe. It was so hot he felt crawly even in shirtsleeves.

The little settlement was bustling, new cabins and cottages rising everywhere, people and hogs and chickens crowding the open squares, hammers ringing as men raised the walls of what evidently would soon become a village schoolhouse. Roger had to make inquiries to be certain he actually stood in the place which was his only point of reference.

"You're a bit off trail, friend," he was told. "Bernards live out along the Bayou Lafourche. But where it branches off lays upstream a fair parcel. You've overshot it."

"There's no way to raft upstream, is there? Not against the river?"

"Right. Thing to do, you'd best abandon ship and strike out across country. Bad area to tackle afoot,

though. Rattlers. Centipedes. You'll do yourself a favor
if you buy a mule. We got a few beasts around St.
Jacques that's available."

So Roger was astride—although scarcely in armor
and with banners, like the Spaniards who first discovered the river—as he arrived at last at his father's
property.

They already had raised a rough residence of sorts,
he observed, although it was scarcely prepossessing
and needed work. First labor, one could see, had been
on the tidy dyke holding back the bayou waters. That
barrier was already securely in place, built in the
efficient Acadian style. A newcomer had to build
dyke before he could obtain his land grant. As dyke
connected to neighbor dyke at either end, a strong
levee to guard the cropland had been completed in
less than a single generation.

In a muddy yard fronting the Bernard shack, a
spindly girl was mothering a corncob doll. She looked
up unwelcomingly as Roger reined in his mule at the
pieux fence.

"Hello," Roger said, and made a guess. His younger
brother Claude had a daughter, an infant in Grand
Pré. She'd be about this waif's age. "You're Sylvie,
aren't you?"

The girl neither denied nor admitted it. "I don't
know you."

"If you're Sylvie, I'm your Uncle Roger."

"That's a lie," the child said flatly. "*Oncle* Roger
died in a fire up north. My Pa told me. Word came
home with *Oncle*'s oldest friend, Antoine Rolande."

Something wrong there. "You mean the fire when
Grand Pré burned?"

"It was a church someplace. He was off fighting the dirty-damn Anglos."

Roger's dark eyebrows lifted. In Grand Pré, pennyworth small fry never had cursed dragoon captains. Claude must keep a very loose rein on his household. As for Marius—Roger tingled with impatience to see his father for the first time in near to six years.

"Is your *grandpère* anywhere about the house, Sylvie?"

"I won't tell you." With a savage glare, Sylvie turned her small back on him.

"Ah, now, that's rude treatment for a stranger. Why won't you tell me?"

"Because your voice sounds English. You may mean to do harm to him."

Roger blinked hard, adjusting to this. It had not occurred to him that his Boston years as an employee of a tea importer, and then his years of slow westward travel with a variety of Yankee families, might have altered his way of speaking. "Look here, Sylvie—"

He need not finish the sentence. Hearing voices, a woman stepped out of the shanty door and stood squinting at him and his mule in the raw sunlight. She had changed, put on twenty pounds since Nova Scotia and lost most of her rangy prettiness; but she was still Angelique, his brother's wife. Before she could recognize him, he spoke her name.

"Roger!" For her, at least, his voice had not changed. "*Nom de Dieu!* Back from the dead! But we were told—it has been so long, so many years!"

"It's a long story. I'll tell it later. Where are Claude and our father, Angelique?"

"In the far fields today. Almost a mile inland, Roger. We have all the farm two men can handle. Sylvie, run and fetch Papa and *Grandpère*. Tell them Roger is here."

With a panicked last glance at him—one obviously spawned by a sensible decision that anyone returned from the dead must be a ghost or otherwise unnatural revenant—the little girl was off like a forest fawn, still clutching the homemade dolly to her meager breast. Together, they watched her vanish; then Angelique recalled her hospitality.

"Come into the house to wait for the men, Roger. Tie your mule to the pickets, it will be quite safe here. Where's Rosalie? Did you leave her waiting in St. Jacques?"

Roger swung down from his saddle, keeping his back toward his sister-in-law so that she could not read the bleak look freezing his features at her question. Looping his reins around the nearest paling, he discovered that his hands were shaking.

After all these years, the mere thought of her sometimes could do this to him. Let her name be spoken (even silently, deep in his own mind) and the old wound reopened. He could feel the blood from it seeping through him, and the pain. They were like bile.

Through that first Boston year after meeting with Obediah Chatterly, he had thought he must go mad with it. Changes in the lives of all caught up in the outrage of the Great Expulsion, those were inevitable. But that Rosalie could have been so altered seemed incredible. The sweet, loyal girl he had been on the verge of marrying, their banns already published—how could she have disintegrated into the strumpet Obediah had described to him, flinging herself into an almost-stranger's bed, whoring with him even after the man had become guilty of her own father's murder? In one short year? *Rosalie?*

He had searched out city records, where "Jules Despres, deceased" was clearly inscribed in clerkish penmanship. That had led him to the mass grave where Obediah personally had seen Jules covered with earth. And Rosalie had been the only other mourner present. Oh, there could be no question of the facts. Yet they were so monstrous they had very near to killed him.

Gradually, with the passing years, scar tissue had formed. Gaunter now, a new hardness in his eyes and brain, Roger had driven himself to forgetting. Obviously, Rosalie had remained in Boston but briefly before larking away with her murderous peddler. So the streets of Boston were not particularly haunted for him by her. He had been able to endure the town. Her delicate phantom hovered in a place called Grand Pré which no longer existed.

Rumors of a new Acadian homeland in distant Louisiana, those had helped, too. Once set upon a plan to rejoin forces with Marius, he had a new purpose in life to keep him going. *The past is dead, Roger. Look ahead. Find your family. They're the future.* Most days, this now really worked for him. But then something, someone, would whisper, "*Rosalie . . .*"

His mule lines fast, Roger turned back quietly to where an ample Angelique stood.

"Rosalie is dead," he said. "Jules Despres also. In Boston, the year they were shipped there. I'd be grateful for a mug of cold water, sister. That's rough country to cross in mid-day sun, at least for so new a Cajun as this one."

* * *

Instruments in the musicians gallery overhanging the ballroom had begun to hum and twinkle again, and Antoine went off in search of Miss Amanda Wellington. It would be the third dance of the evening he had claimed from her, and with any luck at all he hoped to persuade her for a fourth. In the weeks since their first meeting at an assembly to honor Governor Ulloa he had lost no opportunity to see more of her.

When he and his parents first made port in the purloined *Siberie* he had been unnerved to discover that this famous French New Orleans was not in control of France at all, but under Spain. For a week or so of panic he had asked himself whether he had not pulled off his theft too hastily. Perhaps he should have remained with the detestable Zöe a while longer, servicing her bed and treating her like a slavey, until some safer refuge could be determined.

But in due time he had realized that politics were not a *bête noir* after all.

The one-time French stronghold was still a Creole bastion, its ways more gaily and elegantly of Paris than of somber Madrid. The official change dated back to the Treaty of Utrecht, when France had placed a Bourbon cousin on the Spanish throne.

Not long thereafter, France had secretly transferred Louisiana to Spanish hands in order to free itself for more important ventures elsewhere. Spain had accepted the "offer" grudgingly, and only to keep the Mississippi out of English hands. Antonio de Ulloa had been shipped over as first Spanish governor.

He was not at all popular in New Orleans, this Spaniard. But his arrival had timed roughly with that of the first Acadians; and greatly to Acadian advantage, as Henri and Antoine were shrewd enough to observe. Finding a sudden flood of refugees arriving on his doorstep, the dour Governor had established an "Acadian Coast" for them. He had ordered up-river forts erected to defend the newcomers and opened up a wide new region for them. The true purpose, of course, was to build a buffer between New Orleans and English-held country to the north. But it had given the "Cajuns" opportunity to flourish. A shrewd man, cozying up to Ulloa, could do himself much good under cover of pretenses at undermining the English.

Thus, the Rolandes, father and son, became frequent visitors at Government House. Thus, Antoine made the acquaintance of damask-cheeked Miss Amanda Wellington—whose father Sir Cedric Wellington was an eminent deputy of the British Crown in the Americas, and kin to the ultra-aristocratic Earl of Mornington, County Meath, Ireland. And thus, there had been frequent encounters at Government House thereafter.

It was just the sort of delicious double-handed game Antoine relished.

On the one hand, to please Amanda by lavishing praises of her father in her private ear. On the other, reporting to Governor Ulloa accounts of his spying out Wellington moves and intentions under a pretense of being a devoted friend of the family. Everyone on both sides of the political chess game felt obligated. Actually, he assisted nobody.

Great crystal chandeliers hanging over the heads of the dancers cast a shimmer like diamond confetti across the ballroom. Anyone who *was* anyone in Creole society was whirling to the fiddles, sampling the champagne and delicacies, flirting behind fans, or coaxing giggling debutantes deeper into magnolia shadows just beyond reach of the blazing *flambeaux* which lit the Governor's gardens. It was, Antoine silently conceded, indeed a *fête très pimpante*.

He came upon Miss Amanda on a corner sofa, being supplied with lemonade by a fat, perspiring young lieutenant whose father had purchased him a military commission. Her ennui had scarcely been concealed by a languid lace and seed pearl concoction, which she kept in constant motion to cool the rosepetal complexion. Her eyes glowed when she saw Antoine approaching. He noted this phenomenon with gratification. He was not unaccustomed to similar female reaction, but with Amanda it *mattered*. He intended to marry her.

"Miss Wellington! Our dance is next, I believe?"

"It is indeed, sir." She surged eagerly to her feet. "Such a pleasant little chat, Lieutenant Pomfret." As she turned, her abandoned alternate gallant was already forgotten. "And now, Mr. Rolande, let's see. What were we discussing during our last *courante*?"

Antoine tucked her small gloved hand neatly into the velvet crook of his sleeve as he veered her unobtrusively toward the gardens.

"We were discussing, Miss Wellington, the totally unjust effect of that delightful dimple of yours upon defenseless mortal men. And I was about to beseech you, as I now do, to allow me to speak with Sir Cedric."

"Speak to Father?" Her eyelashes fluttered. "But you often have long talks together!"

"You know quite well what I mean, minx! Surely you know I love you, Amanda."

"Mr. Rolande—no, I shall call you Antoine—we met scarcely a month ago!"

"We hadn't known each other an hour when I knew how I felt, Amanda."

In the light of a nearby *flambeau* he turned her gently to face him. Looking up into that face as handsome as a minor god's, she knew that Antoine meant exactly what he was saying. His fine emerald eyes burned with a tender glow of manly worship. Sincerity shone in them, making them flawless jewels. His whole beautiful body seemed suspended in longing.

As, to be sure, it was. Longing to have anything this exquisitely perfect hostessing the Rolande dinner table when profitable guests came to dine. Longing to show New Orleans that even its fairest social angel had not been able to resist him. Longing for the famous Wellington estate in Kent, England; the Wellington eminence in the best London circles. The dowry unquestionably accompanying Sir Cedric's only daughter would be generous.

With that fortune to invest, he and Papa could . . . But there must be a way of easing Henri out of the picture, when the time came. Splitting those profits would be moot.

Yes, it was sincerity, deep sincerity, that Amanda read in the green eyes.

After a moment, she blushed prettily and dropped her head like a modest flower. "I cannot deny I have entertained similar feelings, Antoine. You may speak to Father."

He caught her close. "If you knew the joy raging through me, Amanda!"

There was one bit of old business which still must be considered in this matter. He had small doubt, however, that he could take care of a dull trifle such as Rosalie Despres. Once (a trillion years ago?) he had really loved the girl. But that had been in rustic Grand Pré, where Rosalie was like a young queen. She could not compare for an instant with rare goods like Amanda Wellington.

Still, one bit of the Despres matter remained to be resolved.

On the Madame Sophie evening which unfortunately had terminated their friendship, Etienne Blanchet had challenged him before a witness that he, Antoine Rolande, had never been able to get inside a country girl he wanted. All this time later, that still dangled in the balance.

He had a score to settle with Etienne.

For Rosalie, the New Orleans years were much like the Baltimore ones—except that Papa, up-river in his new schoolhouse and mightily enjoying it, was no longer her daily companion.

Jules had felt strongly that the rude frontier was no place for a gentle young woman, who, if scarcely any longer a girl, still required protection. He had insisted that she remain in Dominique's respectable boarding house, with the ironclad Mme. Gilboy herself for a chaperone. Civilized New Orleans was a proper *métier*, and Jules himself would pay frequent visits whenever opportunity arose.

The separation caused them both unhappiness, in their separate ways. But Papa's new life in St. Jacques de Cabanocey was filled with the excitement of doing things, of creating a new school where there had been none before. Rosalie's own passing weeks and months were, by comparison, a dull parade.

When a year of this had limped away, an increasingly restless daughter finally persuaded Jules that she must find useful work or lose her mind.

The useful work turned out to be daily preparation of nourishing lunches for the smock-clad younger children in a convent school run by nuns in a neighboring block. It was not unlike the labors she had performed at *École Despres* in Baltimore, except that in Baltimore they had been under a roof she called home, and with Papa near at hand.

In Grand Pré, she had always known she was pretty; Roger had assured her of it, as had almost every other young man in the village, Antoine Rolande included. While the knowledge was pleasant, it had been of no great importance.

Nowadays, when she chanced to pass a mirror, she'd begin to wonder. Certainly the old look of eagerness and vivacity was fading. The more mature calmness which had replaced it was perhaps a poor trade. A hint that at any moment she might break into infectious laughter no longer played tag behind her eyes. Men on the street still smiled, yet not in the same way. (Which did not truly matter, since she never thought of marrying. But one did notice, just the same.)

Marriage would perhaps have faded from the Despres family vocabulary, had Papa not still pressed his idea about Antoine. On his visits, which were indeed as frequent as he'd promised, he was constantly easing the subject into their talks.

"I read in the *Bayou Livre-Journal* last week that Antoine has sold his *Siberie* at a handsome profit. He's making a fine future for himself, that young man."

Or: "What do you do here in your evenings, Rosalie? It must be dull, with only Mme. Dominique for company. What a difference it would make with a handsome, lively, amusing companion like, say, Antoine Rolande! Don't you ever think of that, Rosalie?"

Or: "Sometimes I worry myself sick over you, *ma cherie*. The years slip past so rapidly, one after another. May not a time come when you'll feel cheated because there are no little ones? What a sheltering father someone like Antoine would make!"

The worst of it was that, although Antoine had not exactly offered, and so could not be refused, he certainly had been making a point of returning himself to her life these recent days. Chance meetings on the avenues Rosalie could not believe were really by chance. Charming little nosegays appeared on her desk at the convent or on Mme. Dominique's doorstep. Increasingly occasional calls, with Mme. Gilboy seated hawklike in one corner, allowed Antoine to bring her a new book he thought she might enjoy, or to invite her to accompany him (and *cher* Madame, too, of course) to a new play at the theatre.

Most of all, there were the affectionate visits by his mother.

Madame Thais Rolande made no secret of her fondness for the girl from their old village. It was like a breath of home, she swore, to have an hour's conversation with dear Rosalie. If only Antoine—no longer living *chez* Rolande, alas, and actually quite mysterious about his new whereabouts—had the steady nest a girl like Rosalie would create for a man to come home to!

Sometimes Rosalie wondered whether Madame Thais and Papa were not forming some sort of league together, the purpose of which was to thrust Antoine's virtues upon her from every possible angle. Unlikely, since they themselves met so seldom in Louisiana. Yet certainly few facets of his charms were left unexplored. Papa fretted as the father of a too-quiet spinster. Madame fretted as the mother of a too-unsettled bachelor.

So long as Antoine made no such suggestion, what could she do or say to discourage him? It was thoroughly exasperating. But certainly it was not Antoine's fault.

It did seem odd that all these years he had remained unmarried. Certainly there were rumors in plenty about his many passing fancies. He was always seen at the opera with this one, at the races with that one, at the Governor's levee with yet another. Recently, the name of some girl named Amanda Wellington frequently had been whispered. Still, those polite and friendly little gestures, that impression of his unspoken affection, continued. Could Papa and Madame Thais both be entirely wrong?

No, much of it was right. Rosalie did grieve, sometimes, because there would be no children of her own to fuss over. Guilt because she robbed Papa of the joys of grandfatherhood kept building. The hollowness of endless boardinghouse years grew frightening.

"Roger?" she found herself saying aloud, more than once, in the privacy of her rather austere upstairs room, "Roger, what would you want me to do? What *should* I say, if Antoine ever asks me to marry him?"

9

Adjusting to life on the Bayou Lafourche was an easy matter for Roger, largely because very little about it was actually easy. Working the farm fields with Marius and Claude, he might almost be home again in Nova Scotia, except for the stifling heat which descended upon Louisiana at seemingly frequent intervals. To this he found accommodation difficult. But since it must be endured, he set himself to enduring it.

His father's chief crops were unfamiliar ones at first, though a farmer's fundamental approach would always be similar. Indigo sold well in New Orleans. So did sugar from cane set out by his father and brother. Rice flourished. It took time to learn the differences between growing seasons: in Louisiana they were doubled by the subtropical climate, so that a man worked his fields in a spring stretching into November or even December. One rearranged one's thinking.

"Isolated?" Marius had challenged his returned son, when Roger first brought up the matter. "You cannot be isolated on the Bayou. You move on the water, and the water connects you with everyone. More and more of us are moving in, *mon fils*. Soon a message can be transmitted for miles simply by shouting it from yard to yard. You'll see."

Roger had been on the farm for a year and more before he came to realize that this was an almost literal truth. But in any case, he did not miss neighbors such as they once had known in Grand Pré. The end of Rosalie had been, for him, the end of any deep need for communication with the rest of the human race, his own small family excepted.

Even here, the links were not of uniform strength. He was mildly fond of Angelique, appreciating her fundamental good horse sense and her easy-going tolerance of his presence, but they actually had very little in common. For his father he retained the same deep and loving respect as always. For Claude he felt the casual camaraderie of most long separated and never extremely close brothers, intermittent at best.

Little Sylvie was the real stumbling block upon which he was often tripped.

Even the passing months had not softened her first estimation of him. When he spoke to her, he was more apt to encounter a sour scowl than affection or even civility.

He came to understand that this might be because they were so much alike, himself and his scrap of a niece. As he had become, so she was starting out: a loner. For some reason he found himself determined to break through her barriers. But she had constructed them with much the same skill a Cajun used in erecting levee dykes.

At the innermost edge of the ribbon farm, far from the gradually improved shack which now seemed worthy to be called a house, lay the cypress fresh-water swamps which heralded the start of bayou-threaded wilderness. When he was not needed in the fields, Roger discovered they were a treasure trove for trappers. Furs provided an extra cash crop to help establish the little private kingdom of the Bernard acreage. He found the lonely hours deeply satisfactory. Marius had not been entirely right, after all, about isolation.

It occurred to him to invite Sylvie along on one of his expeditions. Surprisingly, she was still a stranger to the wilderness. Throughout their earlier years on the bayou her parents had kept her close within the farm yard. Rattlers and water moccasins and alligators still provided perils for the uninitiated. The menfolk were too busy setting up the fields to instruct her.

"Would you like to go with me to see how trapping's done, *petite*?"

Her stolid expression did not change. "Why would you want to take me?"

"For company, of course. It's no fun with only cypress trees to talk to."

"I don't talk very much."

"Perhaps my trap lines will give you things to talk about."

So they set out together, that first morning, before the sun had risen, both booted against hidden vermin. Trudging back through the fields, Roger accommodated his long strides to shorter legs beside him. Mov-

ing through a dawn coolness not yet dissipated, they
said almost nothing. Sylvie pushed aside the tall grass
like a tiny army marching on a somewhat disagreeable
foray.

Although the coming heat would make it uncomfortable, Roger wore a special sleeveless jacket Angelique
had stitched for him out of scraps of canvas. It had a
phalanx of outsized pockets all around it, depositories
for taken muskrats. In one of the pockets, wrapped
securely to guard against pollution from traces of previous occupants, he carried a packet of hearty sand-
wiches. At their backs, the sun crawled from bed. The
heat began to build.

When they reached the swamp, Roger indicated their
direction to the spot where his self-constructed *pirogue*
was dragged up onto solid land. Still in silence, Sylvie
watched him launch the craft and dump his discarded
jacket into the narrowest section of the prow. He
thought she might just go on standing there forever
and watch him paddle away alone.

"Well, *petite*, scamper in. You have to be aboard to
take a voyage."

She obeyed, scarcely glancing at him. Roger noticed
it was her left hand she used to steady herself as the
boat wobbled. He could not remember any left-handed
Bernards before her. The peculiarity certainly was
not inherited. Perhaps it came as part of her shut-away
childhood, although he could not think of a reason
why this should be.

The *pirogue* inched out into free water, cypress
trunks rising all around them and swamp grass wavering. Presently an egret soared overhead from branch
to branch, and he saw her almost colorless eyes lift to
follow the flight. For the first time, Sylvie half-smiled.

"They're beautiful, aren't they?" Roger commented quietly.

"Their feathers are as white as snow." She was still watching.

"You remember snow, do you?"

"I think I do. There was a big open place where it spread out like a blanket."

"A church called Saint Charles de Grand Pré stood there. Remember the church?"

She shook her head dumbly, retreating into her habitual silence. But as the *pirogue* slid along her eyes no longer seemed empty. They were darting everywhere, looking, seeing.

"We're near the start of my trap line," Roger said after a long while. "Now I'll start dropping the traps off." He began to slide his hands into a pair of gloves he had dredged up from the boat's shallow bowels. She watched this, scowling faintly.

"Why do you wear gloves? Papa never wears gloves when he's working."

"To keep the scent of a human off the traps, *petite*. The muskrats must not suspect that someone they mistrust has been at work."

"How do you know where to put the traps?"

"I drop them off along a place I've learned is a muskrat run. That's usually near where they come to wash food before eating it. They are very tidy creatures, are muskrats."

"Mama is tidy, isn't she? Why don't we wash our food?"

"Sometimes we do. But often our food comes to us cleaner than their edibles."

Roger knew she was watching closely as he planted the first steel trap, then others, each one on a chain with a ring he anchored to a cane pole back in the concealing grass. From many of the existing traps he retrieved motionless carcasses of 'rats taken during the night. He slid each carcass into a separate pocket of the vestlike jacket.

This, too, she watched. "Do you come here every morning to find them?"

"One must, times when one is trapping. Otherwise, a 'gator may get to them."

"How many traps will we set out today?"

"Oh, many. Two hundred, almost. This is a very long run we're following."

She was hooked now, her thin and rather plain face alive with questions behind it. He recognized an odd thing. Much as he relished his usual solitary days out here, with almost no sounds except these of birds and water, he was enjoying today more than any other. It was a kind of magic, how touchingly the break-up of her own stillness after so long broke also the swamp stillness.

They had been out an hour, maybe more, when he felt her tiny left hand steal into the brown leathery palm of his big one. It was something he had not anticipated.

"I love you, *Oncle*," said a voice not much above the merest whisper.

Roger sensed that it could break the spell if he so much as looked at her. So he kept bent above the trap he was cleaning. "And I love you, *petite*."

The rebellion shook New Orleans as only a choice nine-day scandal could. Seventeen sixty-eight, Antoine at first felt sure, would echo down the corridors of history because of it. Yet it turned out to be not such a very big rebellion after all, at least in so far as one carefully remote from it could tell.

Governor Ulloa had become increasingly more liverish because the Creoles supposedly under his sway continued to regard their city as a French colony—which was, in his view, exceedingly disrespectful to Spain. He took various steps to impress the citizenry with the truth. They did little more than laugh at him. So at last he pricked them where a Frenchman was most painfully pricked, in their purses. He issued a series of edicts inhibiting former free business trade with their damned beloved France.

Reaction to this was outraged and immediate. The colonial councilmen who represented the city's bourgeoisie organized an armed resistance, the more shocking because no other like it ever had been instigated in any American possession against any European government.

A force of several hundred additional armed rebels from upriver marched into New Orleans under cover of a tranquil night to aid the municipal uprising. Many came from the so-called Allemande Coast, settled by German farmers, who were stirred by His Excellency's failure to pay as agreed for delivered crops. There were even a smattering of Cajuns aroused by a notice, later found to be bogus, which had been mailed to the church door in St. Jacques to warn them that Ulloa plotted a new dispersal of them into more sterile farmland in Missouri.

This polyglot rabble took over the city with the utmost ease, since Ulloa had a force of less than a hundred men to guard it. Caught by surprise, the Governor had to flee to sanctuary aboard a ship at tether in the harbor. Cannon supposed to guard New

Orleans had been secretly spiked in advance. The ship lines were cut by ribald citizens. Ulloa floated out to the Gulf, thence eventually to Havana de Cuba. City streets were aboil with mongrel celebrations of a "great victory" achieved without the firing of a single shot.

This fiasco temporarily overturned Antoine's personal applecart, along with the government's.

His betrothal to Amanda had brought him still greater confidence on the part of Sir Cedric Wellington. Therefore he had been privy to even more secrets he could sell to the Governor. Now this lucrative sideline appeared to be scotched. It made funds needed to finance his public front as a highly successful young businessman, and future husband, far more tenuous than he liked. He itched to have the requisite period of engagement to his beloved ended. Once Amanda's fat dowry was firmly in hand, the thin times would be over.

Meanwhile, there were problems.

The scant outlay for his continuing campaign with Rosalie—of which he made certain no breath reached Amanda's ear—was no major difficulty. Flowers were cheap. An occasional volume of poems was scarcely a ruby. He had made amusing actor friends at the Theatre D'Orleans, and they furnished *gratis* the occasional tickets of admission which rendered Antoine's playhouse invitations paltry.

Now, at last, he was ready to pay off that insulting cub, Etienne Blanchet.

On the evening when he planned to bring matters to a head Antoine dressed, as usual, carefully. His plum-colored silk coat fit like a second skin. His shirt ruffles were a froth. His trousers hugged every flawless line of his lower body. His silver shoebuckles gleamed.

Halfway across town to Mme. Gilboy's rooming-house, he realized belatedly that he had not been quite so careful about another detail. But that was of such small importance that it did not merit his turning back. He had left his letter to Etienne open on his writing table.

"No matter," he told himself, keeping on his way.

The temporary status of his bank account had urged a recent return to Henri Rolande's roof, and the abandonment of his elegant bachelor flat where so many charming females had attended so many enjoyable little *rendezvous*. But Mama saw to it that he was plied with every comfort. Her servants were well warned that her son was to be pampered. It would occur to none of them to read those lines—if, indeed, they knew how to read at all.

He only wished he might be present when Etienne, who indeed could read, received the message. He had invested a truly delicious hour in composing the lines.

Blanchet:

You are able to call to mind, no doubt, an evening on which you were so rash as to challenge my ability to bed the little Cajun girl, Mlle. Despres. And the wager you set upon it. I should now appreciate payment in full.

Using the entertaining bijou of a marriage-in-pretense as bait—quite a frolic, really—I shall have Mademoiselle between my sheets before this hour next week. You may obtain verifications from my good friend the actor, Vermilion Guidry, at the

> *Theatre D'Orleans. He is to play the role of pre-
> siding priest at our little prank.*
>
> *He will accept your money for me and pass it
> along.*
>
> *As for yourself, Etienne, I can but hope that
> you profited from my illustration on that long ago
> evening. Do you now at last know how to pro-
> voke a lady to pleasure instead of (may I say)
> contempt? Are you still an ensign on the mat-
> tress? Or have you after so long been promoted to
> sub-lieutenant?*
>
>

*With compliments,
Antoine Rolande.*

"The clod should squirm at that!" He grinned as
he thought it. A pity Etienne could not acquire another lesson tonight, one in subtle maneuvers, from his
former friend Antoine. But the strategy afoot was
strictly to be played *à deux*. Rosalie had been so reluctant that at times even Antoine felt his confidence
waver. Ah, but tonight! Tonight things would be
different.

When he rapped on Madame Gilboy's unprepossess-
ing door, Despres's still-attractive daughter would be
at home to him. He had arranged it that she would be.
A note hand-delivered earlier by Mama's plumed and
uniformed negro pageboy had requested the pleasure.
Antoine wished to bring her a basketful of the truly
delicious bonbons his mother's cook had prepared the
day previous. If she were not there to receive them,
both he and Madame Thais would be desolated.

Rosalie herself answered his knock.

For the merest instant, as she stood bathed in lamplight from the hallway behind her, he felt an unex-

pected pang. She looked tonight almost as young as
the girl he suddenly remembered. That day when he
had found her by the lilac clump seemed far less long
ago than it usually did to him. He had wanted her then,
so sharply that it had hurt to have to restrain his need
and pass her Roger's retrieved trinket instead. An echo
of that yearning flicked him.

Then it was gone. He smiled down into her lifted
face, exuding sincere affection. And Rosalie smiled
back—not coquettishly, as his accomplished Amanda
might, but as though she were glad to see him.

"Antoine! I was so pleased to receive your word
this morning."

"As I've been all day, hoping that tonight I'd be
seeing you. Here, Rosalie, here, with *Maman*'s dear
affection. Our cook is supposed to be a true champion."

He passed the delicate little basket into her hands,
making sure that his own lingered to prolong the contact for just the proper instant. Mme. Gilboy herself
could not have called it overbold. Madame Thais
would have approved such evidence that her one-time
maternal lessons in propriety had been so obediently
heeded.

Rosalie gestured for him to precede her into the
parlor.

Past the door, he could glimpse her dragon squatted
by the fireplace with her interminable knitting. There
was nothing about the forthright *click-clack-click* of
needles to invoke romance and sentiment. He held
back, bending to Rosalie's ear and reducing his words
to a murmur.

"Must we? Aren't we at last, you and I, past an age
for chaperones?"

She set down the basket on a hall *tabouret*. "Papa would never say so."

"Perhaps he'd be right. You're certainly every bit as lovely as you were in Grand Pré, Rosalie. I have something special I came to say to you tonight."

"Can't you say it in the parlor, Antoine? Is it so horribly indelicate?"

"Not at all indelicate. Unless you think that of marriage."

He caught the change in her dark eyes. The sudden wariness. The glint of . . . was it alarm? Certainly, a drawing back. But so often women were like this if one took them by surprise. He must give her no chance to decide against him. That wasn't the plan.

"Surely you know I'm in love with you, Rosalie? It can't surprise you to hear me say I want you as my wife. All these years since we were young together, that's what I've wanted. If you'd ever given me one grain of encouragement—ah, Rosalie, give it now!"

"I don't know what to say, Antoine."

"Don't you care for me at all?"

"I'm fond of you, yes. Very fond. B-but—"

"We're grown up now, Rosalie. We're man and woman. Each of us has been so alone. If we miss happiness now, we may miss it forever." His green eyes begged humbly.

"Antoine, perhaps. I don't know. Papa seems to want it, and your darling mother, too. If you'll give me just a little more time to think it over—"

"Not a day, Rosalie. Not an hour. Oh, I love you so! Say yes!"

His hands were on her shoulders, drawing her to him. Careful hands, not greedy, but gentle and reverent. Vermilion Guidry himself could have given no more convincing a performance. She began to tremble. If Papa and Madame Thais so approved . . .

Antoine could read it all, there in the rapidly shifting confusions on her face. Rosalie never had been one to mask her feelings. That was how he always had known, in the old days, how utterly she belonged to Roger Bernard. That was why he had caught up a certain rock on a certain long-ago hilltop. And why he had brought back her fleur-de-lys.

Damn the wench, did he have to strangle the simple word "Yes" out of her?

"Please, Rosalie? Please?" He detested her for making him beg.

Her lips moved slowly in the lamplight, and Antoine struggled to read in advance the word they were about to form. But the word was never spoken. Outside in the night came a sudden clatter and rattle of approaching carriage wheels. They seemed to be racing far too fast over the cobblestones. A doctor racing to a deathbed? Who else would drive so insanely?

Like Antoine, Rosalie had tensed to listen. How could one not, when there was such a reckless urgency in the din of those wheels? Hoofbeats kept pace, frantic hoofbeats. Quite clearly in the night stillness came the crack of a whip, and a woman's cry.

"Rosalie!" it was shrilling, that voice. "Rosalie! Antoine!"

Around the corner and into Mme. Gilboy's narrow sidestreet the vehicle careened. The summons had been unmistakable. Rosalie already had jerked the front door open.

But she started through it too late. There came a

splintering crash as the light cariole, on two wheels as it made the turn, overtoppled. Sounds of destruction coupled with a second scream, one which cut off abruptly, as if shears had snipped it.

Off down the block galloped the terrified beast in the traces, trailing the ruin of a vehicle behind him. Limp against the curbstone, sprawled at a gruesome angle, a female form in cerise satin lay motionless. One had but to look to see her neck was broken.

Antoine shouldered past Rosalie's obstructing figure in the doorway and flung himself down the few porch steps. He was kneeling at the spot where the woman lay, what was left of her, before he even heard lighter footfalls behind him.

He gathered up the satin bundle against him, roaring protest.

"*Maman!* Speak to me, *Maman!*"

Cradled against his arm, her face was still the exquisite face of the belle of Quebec—not a year older, Antoine would have sworn, than when every officer in the garrison implored her slightest favor. Slowly, slowly, her eyes opened, as jewel-hued as his own.

"*Antoine* . . . " And he read awful contempt underlying the word, saw scorn in the look the green eyes gave him before they closed again as if deathly tired.

She was gone.

Rosalie bent down beside him, tears streaming down her cheeks. She was blind with them, crying the older woman's name over and over. She was a lost child weeping.

"Madame Thais . . . Madame Thais. . . ! No, no, no, Madame!"

Antoine set his jaw hard against the pain searing

him so unbearably. One of his dead mother's elegantly gloved hands had clutched the whip, and that had been wrenched from her. But crumpled tight in the other hand was a paper.

A paper he recognized.

Carefully, making sure Rosalie was too lost in grief to notice, he pried the knotted fingers apart. One corner of writing on the page unfolded. *Blanchet: You are able to call to mind, no doubt. . . .* He pocketed the note hastily, and slid a steadying arm about Rosalie's shoulders. To someone who could no longer hear, and who no longer cared, he murmured chidingly: "You should not read other people's letters, *Maman.* You know that's naughty. I am not a little boy any longer, to have my letters censored."

Huddled beside him, Rosalie stirred. "What did you say, Antoine?"

"I just said please don't cry, Rosalie. Please don't cry, dearest."

"I loved her very much, Antoine. She was almost a second mother. We were poor and she was rich, but that made no difference. Not once she had given me her heart."

"I know. She gave me her heart too, my darling." (*And took it away again, too, did you not, Maman? Setting yourself up to judge me? Looking down your handsome nose at me?*)

"Antoine, I just can't imagine any world without her."

"Nor I. Nor I. Rosalie, she was my precious mother. What shall I do now?"

He felt her move against him, slipping her arms around him, soothing his hair with gentle fingertips, drawing his head down onto her grey dimity breast.

"I was selfish, Antoine. I was thinking only of my own loss. How much worse for you!"

He caught at her. He crushed her close.

"Don't leave me, Rosalie. I'm so alone!"

"I won't leave you, Antoine. I'm right here, right here."

From adjoining houses, people attracted by the rending crash poured out into the night. If Mme. Gilboy were among them, which probably she was, what a shock this would be for the old harridan—her well-guarded pet down in a public gutter, hugging a man! It gave Antoine a vicious quirk of pleasure. Let Madame look her fill!

Voices were babbling all around them. Someone with oxlike arms was lifting up the limp bundle of satin and streaming yellow hair. Someone else was rushing off to summon medical assistance. As if all that mattered now! What mattered was over and done.

"*I'll miss you sometimes, Maman. I forgive you for rejecting me. . . .*" But all this he was saying in silence.

When he spoke aloud, it was to the slender woman to whom he still clung like a drowning man. He worked to make that pitiful message get across to her. *Like a drowning man, woman.*

"Come, Rosalie. I mustn't let you stay out here and suffer."

"It's you who matters, Antoine." She moved along beside him.

"And you'll marry me? You said you'd never leave me. That means yes?"

Rosalie answered almost as if in a trance. "Yes, Antoine."

"I don't dare to be alone, not even for one night.

Tonight would be the worst of all. Unless you're with me, Rosalie. Will you be, will you?"

He had a feeling she was only half-aware that she nodded in reply. But that was good enough. (*Comprende, Blanchet? Strike while the iron is hot!*)

"Then what I'll do, Rosalie, is this. I know a young priest, Father Vermilion is his name, who will come and read the blessing over us. In Mme. Gilboy's parlor, if that's all right. Not a fancy wedding, dearest. But I need you so."

"I know, I know. Call your friend, then, Antoine."

He left her just inside the hall, still dazed, and raced off on his errand. Vermilion Guidry was especially good in clerical roles. Antoine had applauded him once playing the great Cardinal Richelieu himself. And priestly robes were part of the theatre's costume rack. It would be a touching service. Even hardshelled Mme. Dominique might shed tears.

"So you see, *Maman?*" Antoine panted as he raced the streets. "Everything is turning out perfectly. I'll explain afterward that you were hastening to give us your blessing when the cariole upended. So you really helped me, didn't you, *Maman*, despite all your holier-than-thou horror at what you'd read? You helped your son, as a dutiful mother should."

10

FOLK IN THE CITY were far too engrossed with the arrival of a new Governor from Spain to much notice, even if she had been at all important, that one Cajun young woman among them was caught up in another arrival—that of a small, lusty-lunged male baby with hair so blond it seemed almost silver and the serious brown eyes of his grandfather.

In distant Europe, Louisiana's future had been passed back and forth between thrones like the proverbial hot potato. Spain had been outraged by the indignity to which its representative, Ulloa, had been subjected. France refused to take back her awkward colony, however much its aged and respected co-founder, Fra Bienville, might entreat King Louis. New

Orleans had behaved like a wayward child. It deserved a proper spanking.

A Spanish armada had swept in from the Gulf to administer punishment. It was under the firm hand of Don Alexander O'Reilly, an Irish mercenary who knew his business and proceeded to attend to it. The ringleaders of the late rebellion were rounded up and summarily executed. Having been careful to keep his skirts clean, at least in the public view, Antoine Rolande was not involved.

He continued to conspicuously improve the handsome town house he had built soon after his wedding to wealthy Miss Amanda Wellington. He made his usual graceful appearances at society's balls and galas. He was driven about in one of the city's handsomest carriages. He paid admirably filial visits to the private hospital where his father had been incarcerated since the death of the senior Madame Rolande in a tragic accident. Henri Rolande, once so capable, was said to have become a quite hopeless mental case.

One could look up to the younger Rolande as a model citizen, one of the city's most respected.

And of course he was prospering under the new O'Reilly regime. Having exacted proper punishment, astute Don Alexander then forgave the insurrection's minor participants and delighted the Creole population by rescinding Governor Ulloa's odious restrictions on free trade with France. With typical business acumen, Rolande had come into possession of several stout ships making fortunes in the commerce. The colony was once again happily sworn to allegiance.

At least there was peace in the streets. When Rosalie took little Christophe with her for a morning in the park, no rabble clotted the street intersections mut-

tering about distasteful politics. The worst she encountered were the chilly stares of other mamas airing their
progeny under the palmettos and live oaks. It had
somehow gotten about that her small son had no
father. If she ever had worn a wedding ring, even in
bold pretense, it no longer adorned her slim finger. In
such a state one would have expected a shameful creature such as Mademoiselle Despres to keep herself
out of the public view. It was an outrage that she displayed herself and her little bastard among their
superiors.

If she suffered from their icy snubs, however, Rosalie certainly did not permit it to show. Each sunny day,
when Christophe might benefit from an outing, she ran
the gauntlet of hostile eyes with serene dignity. She
sat a little removed from the other ladies in the park,
so there needed to be no overt gestures of rejection.
One would have thought, watching the creature engrossed in her book and cuddling her baby, that she
was actually decent.

What went on behind her stoical face, only Rosalie
knew.

"I can endure it for now," she kept assuring herself,
the thought coming between her and her printed page.
"But what about later? When Christophe is somewhat
older and wants to play with others and their mamas
forbid it? How can I explain to him then that it's no
fault of his own, poor mite, when they draw back
their skirts and lower their parasols to protect their
own offspring from contamination?"

This was the very fate of which dear Madame Thais,
becoming aware of her son's intention, had been frantically racing to warn her when the cariole overturned.
How ironically that well-intended mission had turned

out. Without her pity for the suffering she had imagined Antoine to be undergoing, without her own numbing grief, that "wedding" very probably never would have taken place. She had not really intended to accept Antoine.

Papa, still coming down from St. Jacques to be with her whenever he could, blamed only himself for her present plight. His self-reproaches were pitiable.

"If I had not urged it on you, if I had not praised the young *vilain* to Heaven—"

"Hush, Papa, hush. The decision was my own. I knew I did not love Antoine, but I believed he loved me and needed me and that I could comfort him. I made the choice."

"Believing him to be the honorable man I always took him for. You trusted him because I had pressed it upon you for so long that he was trustworthy."

"Not that alone, Papa. Much of it was because Madame Thaïs was his mother. I was so fond of her over the years that I never could have questioned her son. Then, too, it was Antoine who brought me word of Roger's death. That always made him special."

As she spoke, Rosalie lifted her hand to touch the silver fleur-de-lys dangling on its fine chain about her neck. It was the only bit of jewelry any of the park ladies ever had seen her wearing; and it was so simple, so discreet, that even they could find little to criticize about it. One day, when she was gone, it would belong to Christophe.

"At least," Jules sighed, "Thaïs never had to know of his infamy."

"At least that, Papa." Rosalie never had told her father the full tale of that night so terrible that even now she could not trust herself to look back at it. Papa believed, as Antoine just before betraying her still worse had told her, that Madame was rushing with fond congratulations when the accident happened. How quickly Rosalie herself had learned better! But there was no reason to stab Papa still deeper with that truth.

When word had reached him upriver and Papa had rushed to be with her, he had not even realized that Antoine only pretended to marry her, that their "priest" had been a sly actor from the D'Orleans, making sport along with the "bridegroom." Weeks later, Antoine had wed his true bride in the stately cathedral, with the aristocracy of New Orleans attending and Sir Cedric Wellington throwing open his doors for a great reception afterward.

"Do you, Antoine Rolande, take this woman . . . ?" The lines were the same. But when spoken by a secretly mocking imposter in the unadorned Gilboy parlor, how very different!

She still drew a veil over what happened after that.

The rented room to which he had hurried her for their "honeymoon" . . . the almost indecent speed with which he had removed her gown, not even a proper bridal one, and pressed her down upon the unfamiliar bed . . . the harsh bark of a laugh sounding in the dark as he mounted her . . . None of that did she dare, even now, to bring too clear in her memory. It was too shameful, considering what he had confessed to her at breakfast next morning. No, not confessed. Boasted.

Papa, when at last he did comprehend that part of the story, had hastened off at once to the Henri Rolande house where Henri's son was still temporarily living. He had meant to fetch back the young miscreant for a second ceremony, a legal one, a marriage in God's eye. But he had found the Rolande establishment in a furor.

Young Master Antoine had only that very morning committed his grieving father to a discreet hospital, having persuaded attendant doctors that his father was hopelessly deranged. He was off in the inner city now, or so a grim houseman informed Jules, attending to legalities concerning transfer of Henri Rolande's holdings to the devoted son who must now manage all Rolande affairs. No, this irate little man from St. Jacques could not have an audience with Master Antoine; neither now nor later.

Next morning, a curt note from lawyers arrived. If Jules Despres persisted in annoying Monsieur Rolande with nonsense, the true story of his daughter would have to be publicized with every means at the considerable Rolande command. Greedy eyes upon the family wealth, the girl had been attempting to seduce a too-credulous Antoine into marriage by first coaxing him into bed. The senior Madame Rolande, who knew the sly minx well and was outraged, had been whipping her carriage to halt an elopement when her sudden death occurred.

This story of a secret marriage? Sheer blackmail! It had happened in the home of Mme. Gilboy, the chit maintained? But Madame herself could not vouch for any such thing. She had been off to the morgue accompanying the corpse of Madame Rolande, at the time. She had not been a witness. Who had?

For once since their Grand Pré days, Jules crumbled. "What do we do, *cherie?*"

"The cards are all Antoine's, Papa. He will play them as he threatens."

"Is there no proof of your innocence? Not even a ring?"

"There was a ring. A man's ring with the Rolande falcon signet. When he told me what he did next morning, I ripped it off and threw it in his face. I haven't a notion what became of it then."

"But he can't be allowed to get away with ruining you!"

"If he does as his lawyers threaten, he will ruin more than my reputation. Very likely, Papa, I shall wind up a convicted criminal, guilty on all charges."

"Never! I'll take the stand in your support. I'll tell the whole ugly tale."

"And find yourself in the jail cell next to my own? No, Papa, no. Let it go. I was an utter fool, and now I must pay for it. The world will not come to an end."

Incredibly, her world indeed had not ended. Instead, in a very special sense, a new world had begun. Antoine had left her with a souvenir. Now she had Christophe.

The ever-increasing Cajun community upriver from New Orleans, and westward, too, considerably further than Bayou Lafourche, found themselves markedly content with the advent of Don Alexander O'Reilly. The program he instantly inaugurated suited them well.

In addition to the already established "Acadian Coast," more farmland was to be open to the Cajuns along each of the two major bayous, Lafourche and Manchac. Fanning out from protective Fort Gabriel, their farms would be spread clear to Galveztown on one side and French Settlement on the other. Already the region was coming to be known as the French Triangle. In Ascension Parish a second church would be established for the refugees (if they still could be considered such). The Chetimacha Indians in the area were friendly and thus no threat. The future seemed joyously empty of clouds.

"Our new governor bodes well," Marius approved in the Bernard field, pausing his labor to break off a sugar stalk and chew on it. "Never was one more different from Nova Scotia's Charles Lawrence."

"Thus far," his son Claude agreed, "everything he's done is to our advantage."

"Not to mention the fact that we're holding the English at bay for him," drawled Roger, his other son. "It isn't to be all give and no take, you realize."

"You!" grunted their father. "Sour as a pickle, these days. Comes a time when a man has to plow under all his old disappointments, *mon fils*. Comes a time to let a little happiness break in. What's dead and done with should be buried."

All highly sensible advice, of course. Roger would have been the last to deny it. Yet a man scarcely could turn on happiness like a spigot, nor shut out a quiet mistrust of wholehearted credulity by building a levee against it. He had seen something he once had believed in as he believed in God smashed to tinder. It had become second nature to him to answer enthusiastic babblings with a "Yes, but what if . . . ?" Life was confronted by a mountain of disappointments. Best not to count on anything overmuch.

Although he never raised the question when their father and Claude and even Angelique set out to argue him into a different way of thinking, Roger sometimes wondered if he and little Sylvie were not peas in a pod when it came to meeting life with a steadfast skepticism, never expecting too much of it. What could have undermined her confidence in goodness at so tender an age he could not imagine. But he could look back on their first words together and know that she saw things pretty much as her returned Uncle did.

"*I don't know you . . . I won't tell you . . . You may mean to do harm. . . .*" And those bitter young eyes glaring up at him. He should have known then, forking his mule by the Bernard fence, that he and Claude's daughter had much to share between them.

No denying it, they had come by now a long way toward sharing that, and more. Early expeditions they had made along his trap lines in the swamp had been a beginning. As time drifted past them, almost the only obvious changes had been those inevitable ones that lengthened her skinny frame and built breasts and a backside on it. Not yet a woman, she was not still a child. Uneasily, Roger could even see sometimes just what Sylvie would look like as an old grandmother, decades after he himself was dead.

She'd never turn pretty, that was for sure. Her complexion would always be muddy, her hair straight and lank, her yes aloof and never receptive to a stranger. Still, there was something about her he had cottoned to almost from the first day she'd trapped with him. He would have horsewhipped anyone who harmed her. It was a real love, however different it might be from the one he had felt for someone else a decade, two decades ago. He wanted Sylvie to be happy.

Yet happiness was built into her no more than it was a part of the Roger he had become—oh, so long ago that he couldn't remember how he had really been before. She was one of those who just didn't know how to look for rainbow ends. Maybe he could help her.

"Heading up to St. Jacques tomorrow," he said one night, after she'd helped her mother clear away the supper dishes. "Your *grandpère* has a mess of things he wants me to order at the store for him. Like to come along?'"

"It's a long hike." But her pale eyes had lit up for an instant, just the same.

"Didn't figure to hike. I'm taking the mule. Petunia's getting a bit long in the tooth, I grant you, but she still likes an outing. How about you?"

"I guess it would be all right." For Sylvie, that was gushing enthusiasm.

"First thing in the morning, then, the same as when we go trapping. St. Jacques isn't exactly in the Bernard back pasture, you know."

The sun was just an horizon glitter when they started off, Petunia stolidly plodding through the scrub grass, Sylvie straddling bareback behind Roger and clinging to his solid waist. Marshgrass and mangroves and moss-dripping oaks formed a sort of tapestry past which they rode almost in silence, each lost in separate thoughts. Yet the quiet was not uncompanionable. In a special way each was thoroughly aware of the other; enjoying the presence, cherishing a relationship which seemed to find small need of words.

"Red-breasted heron," Roger might point out, as one soared past.

"*Oui.*" Nothing more. But they had shared the beauty of the bird.

The *clump* of Petunia's unhurried hooves, the swish of wind in the tall grass, the lap of waves in shallow bayou backwaters, an occasional clamor from ponds where migrant ducks were feeding, that was all. To a stranger the trail might have seemed silent. To two content with it, a whole orchestra was playing its symphony. They rode. They listened.

"Can't have changed much since the *coureurs de bois* first came this way, exploring and trading," Roger murmured, not even turning his head.

"How long ago was that, *Oncle?*"

"First years of the century. You hadn't been thought of. Neither had I."

They came into St. Jacques past noon, afoot now so that Petunia could rest, one trudging to either side of the mule. It was no longer the raw enclosure Roger had arrived at on his rafting venture, years earlier. Street had been laid out. Wells had been dug. Stores, and the church of course, made a brave show along the few blocks of the chief thoroughfare.

The school he had seen rising was going full tilt now; had been for several winters. Lessons for the day were in the process of ending. Their schoolmaster, a frail looking oldish fellow with spectacles, stood in the doorway watching his class disperse.

Roger half noticed him, started to move on, stopped dead again, yanking on Petunia's guiderope. It wasn't possible. It certainly wasn't possible.

"Hold the line, Sylvia." His voice had a strangled sound. "I'll be back."

He loped up the schoolyard path, eyes still wide. The old man was turning back into the one-room building now, ready for the daily ritual of closing up shop. Before he quite disappeared into the shadows, Roger shouted after him. "Wait!"

Turning back, the spectacled figure peered down at

him. Roger halted on the bottom step of three. His gaze had never left the tired, somewhat wan older face above.

"But you're dead," he said. It didn't sound like his own voice, even to him. "You're dead in Boston, Massachusetts, in a ditch on Pauper's Field."

"You are mistaken, *monsieur*. I am alive, and I have never set foot in Boston."

"I know you, sir. Damn it, I *know* you. You're Jules Despres, from Grand Pré."

"I am." Behind their lenses, the brown eyes were straining for a like recognition. "School master of St. Jacques these several years. But once indeed of Grand Pré."

"I found your name in the Boston records. Jules Despres, deceased. Stabbed, sir. Murdered. And a man I met there told me he'd seen you buried. And-and your daughter—"

"Rosalie? She lives in New Orleans. But neither of us ever saw Massachusetts." Suddenly, the old face worked. Recognition struck Jules violently. "Blessed Virgin! It's *you* who are dead! You were—no, you must still be, somehow—the elder son of Marius Bernard!"

"Roger Bernard, sir. Certainly I'm not dead."

"You're older. But-yes, you are Roger. I'd remember your face no matter how much time had changed it. How can you be alive? Antoine Rolande"—Jules's lips seemed to thin bitterly at the name—"brought news of your death along with Rosalie's fleur-de-lys!"

"My death? Did Rosalie believe it?"

"How could she not? Over and over, she swore you'd never give up that trinket while there was a breath of life in you. You were off with Joseph Broussard, aiming to do what you could to fend off Lawrence's soldiers. A church was burning and you ran inside to rescue a nun."

Still dazed, Roger nodded. "Partly true. But I was still outside when the wall collapsed. I never reached her. If Antoine were about, he could explain why I remained behind when the others scattered. A certain stone. Antoine believed he had left me there for dead."

"Both of us were ill-advised to cherish Antoine as a friend, I think."

There was something in that sentence which required more probing. But Roger's reeling mind still centered on Boston.

"If you were never in Massachusetts, *monsieur*, how could you have been buried in Boston? I don't comprehend that at all. *C'est impossible!*"

"We were shipped out of the Fundy on a scow called *Katie O.* Her home port was Baltimore. We lived there for several years, I teaching school and Rosalie assisting. I was as alive then as I am now, I assure you. I can't understand, any more than you, how—"

Jules Despres's jaw worked convulsively.

"Ah, Roger! But perhaps I *do* begin to understand! If young Démocède Sherrard never got around to reclaiming his proper—you see, Roger, there was a trade of names. So that I could smuggle myself aboard the ship Rosalie was assigned to. I became Sherrard, he became Despres, to hoodwink the Anglos. Ah, it's confusing but I'll try to explain."

"You just said *young* Sherrard, sir. This man had a grown daughter with him. A daughter who fit Rosalie's

description like a skin. It was over her that Jules, or
Sherrard, or Gods knows who, fought with the peddler
fellow. And was stabbed dead for his pains."

Jules shook his head. "Poor Démocède. He was
scarcely twenty and had no family whatsoever. He
had a young woman with him? She was most certainly not Rosalie nor any other daughter. If he died,
as I fear from what you say he must have, their relationship was of a different sort. And it would have
begun after we both left Nova Scotia."

The schoolhouse, the steps, the whole bustling little
village, seemed to be spinning.

"It will take me the rest of my life, sir, to sort all
this out. I was so positive, through all these years
since, I've been so absolutely certain—"

One thing more than any other roared in his brain,
like a lion in a jungle.

The sound of it shook him. *Whoever had bedded
Obediah's peddler and run away with him, she was
not Rosalie!* Some nameless strumpet had larked from
one lover to the next, this Sherrard one week, the
peddler another. *But she had not been Rosalie.* Someone had blessed Sherrard-Despres' murderer with her
tawdry favors. *But she had not been Rosalie.*

Not Rosalie. Not Rosalie!

A hot mist was spilling out of his eyes. He dug at it
with clumsy knuckles, bitterly ashamed. Until he felt
a hand on his shoulder, he did not even realize that
Jules had reached out.

"There, lad, it's like an earthquake to both of us.
You'll feel better in a minute."

"I doubt I'll ever feel better, sir. What I've believed
of your daughter all this while, trying to hate her for
it, trying to forget her."

"It's been a long time, Roger. It's human to forget. Don't punish yourself."

The mist began to clear. Roger could see the old, lined face again. "I never forgot. At least believe that of me, Monsieur Despres. I never did forget her."

"Rosalie remembered, too, if that's any comfort."

Blindly, Roger reached up to close his hand over the one still on his shoulder. "Rosalie? Where is she? New Orleans, you just said. Married to someone else long since?"

"Married to no one." But he saw the gentle face harden above him, every line of it altering, until the only emotion one could identify there was a harsh hatred.

"*Monsieur!* Something's wrong? In pity's name, tell me!"

"I think she would not want me to tell you, Roger. You of all people."

"But I'll have to know. If there's something I can do to help her—"

"Very little. Our mutual friend Rolande has seen to that."

"They're married. But—no, you just said—it can't be that."

"Rosalie *believed* they were married. She had turned away all the other beaux, preferring to cherish you dead than accept any of the others living. But Antoine never gave her peace. And, God forgive us, his mother and I kept urging her. We thought it was for the best. We believed she'd find at least some consolation with a good husband."

"And?" Roger waited, but Jules said nothing. "And, *Monsieur?*"

"There was an accident. Thais Rolande was killed.

Antoine used his pretended grief to persuade my daughter that he needed her. Compassion undid her where nothing else had worked."

"Then you misspoke. They *are* married. And it is not a happy one."

"There was a marriage *service*, yes. One Rolande refuses to admit to now. The priest who presided was a playhouse actor in a theatre costume, no priest at all. I tried to face Rolande, the moment I heard of it. I was warned that Rosalie would be prosecuted as a black-mailer, and by the city's most capable lawyers, unless we yielded."

For a moment that seemed to stretch into eternity, utter stillness fell upon the schoolhouse steps. Then Roger managed to make a sound—raw, savage, terrible.

"Where in New Orleans can I find her, sir?"

"I doubt she'd want you to find her, lad. There's a reason—"

"*Where is Rosalie?*"

The address of Mme. Dominique Gilboy's rooming house had scarcely passed Jules Despres's trembling lips when Roger was off down the path, racing for his patient mule and the small, straight figure still faithfully holding Petunia's hemp line.

11

WHILE CHRISTOPHE TOTTERED about the park bench where she sat with her book on her knee, Rosalie looked out across the smooth green lawn—lost, as so often, in thoughts having little to do with a printed page. Occasionally, she reached out to touch the aureole of red-blond curls which for her made her small son one of the seraphim. But her dark eyes were fixed more upon a dreaded future than upon the scene about her.

It was beginning to happen. Now that Christophe could take a few unsteady baby steps without assistance, he was developing a curiosity about the world around him. Off he would suddenly scoot, in the direction of the nearest playing children. A dozen times a morning she would have to race after him before he

reached his goal and herd him back to the little seg-
ment of the square in which proper, pious families left
the two of them ostentatiously alone. They might as
well be wearing leper bells.

How would she ever find a way to bring Christophe
to terms with their world's realities? As of now, he
was still leading the life of a pigeon, merely wanting
to join a flock that circled together wherever crumbs
were thrown. But that would change, and frighteningly soon. Then questions would come.

"Why do the other people in the park never speak
to us, *Maman*?"

"Why did that lady catch her little boy's hand so
fast and hurry him away, when I went with my hobby-
horse to ask him to play?"

"Why did the nursemaid in the frilly cap call me
Little Bastard? What does Bastard mean, *Maman*?"

And what was she to tell her small adored one then?

"Because they think your mother is a fallen woman,
cherie. A *prostitute*."

"Because your mother did a certain thing that other
people don't forgive." She paused, tearfully.

"Because *Maman* was a stupid fool who let the wool
be pulled over her eyes."

A day was coming. Answers would have to be ready.
But how to couch them so that Christophe would be
hurt the least? Perhaps the poets who created these
volumes she always brought with her to their usual
bench would know how to say it. They had a way with
words. But she was no skilled *femme auteur*, only a
simple woman born and raised in a rural Nova Scotia
village. And Christophe was a bright child. He would
want to know.

The park today seemed somewhat less peaceful than

on most sunny mornings. Groups of citizens were constantly forming and reforming at its edges, babbling
about news just arrived from the Atlantic. Snatches of
talk reached her as they passed.

Something about rebellion against England in the
older colonies, Connecticut and Pennsylvania and the
rest. An armed battle near the Massachusetts town of
Lexington, was it? Had it to do with a Concord bridge?
Rosalie caught only fragments, but they seemed to
indicate real disaffection between the population and
its government. Old hat to New Orleans, where the
Ulloa affair was already history! Yet the passing men
seemed excited. As had been Roger, so long ago, rushing off to join Joseph Broussard's angry band.

Lost in reveries, she was only half aware of the tense
faces and the rush of voices. Automatically, her questing hand found Christophe's fair head again and drew
him closer. But she saw neither, except perfunctorily.
It was into a coming future she was staring.

"Rosalie?" a male voice asked, too close to be part
of the drifting crowd.

Rosalie looked up quickly, startled both by that use
of her name and by the fact that anyone hereabout
should speak to her at all. He was not a towering man,
but one tall enough to cast a substantial shadow across
the bench. He was staring down at her with a frightening intensity. She caught Christophe closer. Were they
at the mercy of a madman?

"Madame Gilboy told me where I'd find you. I
called at her house for you first."

No, it was she, not he, who was the crazy one.
Altered though he was, he still seemed so much like a
person he could never be that of course she had lost
her wits altogether. A silver thread here or there in

his brown locks, a line or two cut deeper than any she remembered, but still essentially so much the same! She shrank back, trembling.

He seemed to read the riot of confusion in her lifted face, for he spoke as if she had voiced a question. "Yes, Rosalie, yes. I'm Roger. And at last I've found you."

"You can't be Roger." She groped for her fleur-de-lys. "When Antoine returned—"

"Antoine, prince of liars. It's true he believed he'd done me in, though. Likely he still believes it. From what your father tells me, Antoine does cherish a lie."

"You've seen Papa"—and somehow she dared add the impossibility—"Roger?"

"In St. Jacques, a week ago. I'd have been here sooner, but I was on an errand for Marius that needed finishing. I couldn't just abandon Sylvie where she stood."

Rosalie looked away with an effort. "You're married, Roger? Her name's Sylvie?"

"Sylvie's my little niece, Claude's daughter. Think back to Grand Pré and you'll recall her as a baby. Even younger then than this fine big gentleman here."

As he spoke, he patted Christophe's curls. Her own hand still rested there and his met it almost as if by accident, closed over it, pressed hard.

"Your *grandpère* has been telling me about you, Christophe. He thinks you're the grandest fellow in all Louisiana. And who am I to argue with a professor?"

Rosalie's gaze clouded. "If you knew the truth, Roger—"

"I do know the truth, unless Jules is a member of

Antoine's liar club. Dear God, there's so much for me to make up to you. You're still my fiancée, aren't you? The church was ashes when I got back to Grand Pré. But no one's told me since that you revoked our intention to marry."

"Roger! You well know why I can never be any man's fiancée. If Papa's told you—"

"What I didn't hear from Jules, I can easily imagine." Standing erect by the bench, Roger was surveying the neighborhood. Several ladies nearby were staring back at them, scandalized and fascinated. A few of them sat close enough so that thoughts might be read on their indignant faces. *Why, the hussy's meeting her men right under our noses!*

"Study them, Roger." Rosalie spoke wearily. "That is your answer."

"That is *their* answer, *ma cherie*. This is *our* answer."

He bent quickly and swung Christophe up onto his shoulder.

"How would you like me for a papa, Monsieur Christophe? How would you like your name from now on to be Christophe Bernard? Bernard is my own name, Roger Bernard. I've always liked it, Christophe."

"Ro-ger Ber-naaar-d." Christophe seemed to have no great difficulty pronouncing the words. He considered what he had said well enough to say it over again.

Rosalie watched the sturdy man march off across the greensward, boy still on shoulder, until he reached the bench where the nearest startled mother sat. Here he paused. Ignoring the lady's sudden confusion, he beamed down upon her. It was the very smile which had melted Rosalie's heart every time she saw it, oh, centuries ago.

"*Bonjour, madame,*" he was saying, in a hearty voice which carried like a captain's giving sea orders. "Ah, it's a splendid morning, isn't it? A fine one for a man to get back to his family. Would you believe this is my first meeting with my son?"

The frosty face reddened visibly. "Your *son, monsieur?*"

"Whom I have never met till now. I hoisted ship's anchor before my wife and I knew he was coming."

"She is your *wife?*" The question faltered. "You mean that-that *you* are—"

"Her husband, but of course. Poor darling, what a wretched time she's had. We were boarded by pirates off Vera Cruz, you see. I was held for ransom and am only now free again. And I had left my little wife nothing to live on all those extra months. She's even had to pawn our gold ring. Now I am home to care for her. But what would she have done all this lonely while, if she had not had you kind ladies to befriend her?"

The woman's face was no more a study in amazement than was Rosalie's own.

"Why, you *liar*, Roger Bernard! You brazen liar!" she whispered unsteadily. "Not even Antoine could have dreamed up that shameless pack of falsehoods!"

It was only now that she began to weep.

The Rolande carriage rolled regally homeward along the fine avenues of New Orleans, uniformed driver spic-and-span on the box, uniformed footman behind.

Impeccably dressed, almost more handsome than in his youth with elegant maturity molding his features and thick, coppery hair paling toward vermeil, Antoine himself was the subject of several admiring glances

from strolling ladies to whom he bowed as he passed—
silver harness ornaments ajingle, up front the matched
chestnut pair like dancing satin.

He was a contented man, and contentment fitted
him well.

Having to pay weekly visits such as this one from
which he was returning was a bore, *certainement*. The
discreet mansion just outside town, where Papa and a
congress of his droolers and mumblers were kept out
of view at a scandalous cost, truly depressed him. The
public role of dutiful son, however, was one he had
long ago mastered. Dear Amanda would be shocked if
she dreamed he resented the wasted hours.

So many things shocked spoiled, pretty, rather bor-
ing Amanda. It was really no pleasure even to look at
her nowadays, swollen into monstrous shape as she
was with the babies she was carrying. (Twins, the doctor prophesied.) Any one of the smiling women scattered along his route might have been far more
amusing.

"Antoine Rolande, you know. The millionaire. . . ."

"Isn't he the most beautiful creature you ever saw?"

"His wife is English. Ah, what a lucky woman! I
could eat him with a spoon!"

The gratifying murmurs trailed after him, many of
them audible. Antoine smiled and saluted and pretended not to hear. He sat very erect and only a trifle
condescending, as royalty should. In New Orleans he
was royalty, wasn't he? He could think of no one who
outglistened him. The whole city admired him, fawned
over him, bless it.

At the pillared facade of the Rolande mansion, the
carriage came to a stop. The footman was down off his

perch and standing at attention before Antoine could
stir a muscle. He stepped down as exactly what he was,
monarch of all he surveyed.

Well-drilled servants were waiting. Doors opened
before him. Humble hands reached out to relieve him
of his yellow fringed gloves and lacquered hat. With
a passing glance in the long hall mirror as he passed it,
to make sure his immaculate cut-velvet coat and
breeches showed no marring wrinkle, he moved on
into the drawing room to kiss Amanda.

She sat somewhat uncomfortably, considering her
present bulk, in a favorite chair upholstered in heavy
pink satin. She turned up her damask cheek to accept
a brush of his solicitous lips.

"You're as lovely as usual, my dear." Antoine stifled
a yawn.

"I feel quite drained of animation. Will this waiting
never be over?"

"Be patient, dear heart. All our thoughts must be
of the little ones."

He did expend considerable thought on his as yet
unborn heirs. Please God the children would take after
their father, or even *Maman* or Amanda, in appearance. To have monkey replicas of Henri on hand would
be too disgusting. Yet until recently his father had been
forceful, vigorous. Perhaps his genes would be domi-
nant. What if Antoine Rolande spawned a pair of
gargoyles?

"I'd rather give thought to a ball," Amanda was
pouting. "How much longer before I fade away entirely and am socially forgotten?"

She sniffed a cobweb of handkerchief saturated in
toilet water.

"Speaking of society, Antoine, I believe your old crony is still waiting in your study. I had him shown there an hour ago."

A faint frown troubled Antoine's smooth forehead. "My crony?"

"That's how he styled himself. A ship's captain, I believe he said he is. Anyhow, he claims he's known you since boyhood. Do go and have your reunion."

As Antoine headed for his private sanctum, the frown deepened. Who now? Boyhood meant Grand Pré. There were precious few of those rustics he cared to acknowledge nowadays. They were off where they belonged, in the bayou backwaters, grubbing in black Mississippi silt.

He had kept up relationships with none of the old homespun neighbors since reaching New Orleans. Except for the Despres pair, of course, and there had been a reason for that. It had annoyed him during her lifetime that his mother was not of the same conviction. Beauty though she'd been, she had seemed to hold no class distinctions whatever. Her son had been more selective.

A ship's captain, eh? Who the devil?

The study was everything that a gentleman of means and taste could plan for himself: walls ivory and gold, draperies of rich canary brocade, rugs from the Orient, furniture of mahogany sumptuously carved and polished. The dark, solid figure who arose from one of those superb chairs as Antoine crossed the threshold seemed utterly out of character.

In fading light his features were somewhat indistinct. But he was not dressed in the *ton*, not by considerable. His suit was plain though serviceable, its cut

not fashionable and its goods not elegant. Even in
mufti, he did not suggest a naval officer. Had Antoine
been forced to guess, he would have thought the fellow
a farmer. Dash Amanda's stupidity! Having the oaf
shown in here, just because he claimed familiarity!

"Well? You wished to have a word with me?"

"Perhaps even two words, Antoine. Those would be
'You swine!' "

The shock was so staggering that Antoine actually
had to clutch at the edge of his mother-of-pearl en-
crusted desk for support.

"Good God! *Roger*! But-but—"

"But how did I get here? Why aren't my bones still
bleaching in a Nova Scotia meadow? We waste time on
trifles, old friend. You can see I *am* here, quite alive."

The voice coming out of the shadows was quite calm,
with no trace of anger in it. That was what made it so
terrifying. He had *killed* this man now facing him,
damn it. The devil should at least resent it, at least
show some flash of hatred. Instead of hatred: nothing.
An iceberg might be speaking. Antoine had to command his knees not to buckle.

"Well, Roger, well! And what brings you to New
Orleans?" He tried for a hearty touch, but the words
come out like sounds from a hollow drum.

"What brings me to New Orleans is my wife and
son, Antoine."

"You were married, then, somewhere along the years
since?" But no, that wouldn't do. The "since" led
them back to the very place he must now (please
God!) gloss over.

"I married Rosalie this afternoon. In a real church,
though it was only the chantry. By a real priest, although our abbé lacked the stirring voice of an actor.

Our only family witness was Christophe. Your son once. Mine now."

Antoine swallowed hard.

"Look here, old man, we have things to talk over, don't we? I sense from what you say that Rosalie's been feeding you a mass of deceptions. Let's set that story straight. You see, she'd been living in a dreary rooming house for years, nothing but drabness around her. I was obviously on the rise. So she took a notion—"

"Have you any idea, Antoine, how much you disgust me?"

"See here, now! No need to be offensive. As the old friends are—"

"We were never friends, Antoine. I only believed we were. I've taken the liberty of moving that pair of duelling pistols on the desk from your gun cabinet while I waited. They will say anything you and I need say to each other."

Antoine's glance slid sidewise.

Sure enough, his silver-handled pistols lay there on the surface beside him, neatly aligned. They were exquisite instruments. He kept them in flawless condition. If this crude barbarian actually believed he might stand up against Antoine Rolande, who had taken lessons from the finest pistol experts in New Orleans . . .

Then he remembered. When they had hunted together as boys, which of them had brought down the fleetest deer, invariably? Which of them had been able to shoot any quivering leaf from a distant tree branch, if a wager was down? Good God, never Antoine!

He felt the sweat begin to ooze from his pores and slither down inside his fine lace-ruffled linens. He felt fear rake along his spine, cold and remorseless. He could see the remembered face quite well now, even across the room. It was a death mask.

"Roger, you're jesting. A mere girl, a village flirt of no importance whatever—"

"I never jest, Antoine. I'm no longer much of a one for laughing."

There'd be no talking him out of it. There'd be no gambit to alter what this forest fanatic had in his vengeful mind. Antoine's hand shook only slightly. But he had to steady his voice, which was not as easy as he had expected.

"Roger, Roger, if there's no dissuading you . . . very well, come take your pick and we'll be off into the garden. It's your choice of weapons, challenger."

Standing braced as a cat beside his handsome desk, he watched Roger take that first forward step which meant the man was in dead earnest. To grant him a second step would be wild folly. Antoine swooped upon the nearer of the two matched pistols, scooped it up, aimed with lightning speed, and fired point blank.

The bark of the gun sounded less like a shot than the summons of a fox to his vixen on some frosty country hillside. Across a little curl of smoke, Antoine's eyes were nailed to the man who had dared presume upon him as an equal. Let the man drop. The servants could dispose of him without ado. Hopefully, there'd be little blood on the rug.

Instead, the man kept on coming. His left arm dangled limp, and wet redness was spreading from a small hole in the homespun sleeve. But he kept on coming. Suddenly wild with panic, Antoine pointed the slim muzzle again; jerked the trigger again.

Nothing. They were one-shot weapons, and he'd already fired his shot. The man was still coming. With a sob of terror, Antoine tossed his gun aside and dove for its mate. His hand closed over it, clawing.

On top of the hand, another crushed down.

"Still the cheat, Antoine? Some people never learn."

The hand—God! what a calloused hand, its palm like sandpaper—began to twist. It had sinews of steel wrapped up in the leather of it. Antoine had an agonized memory of Indian wrestling games they had played at in Grand Pré. The pistol dropped away.

"Roger! Don't kill me! Look, I'll pay Rosalie for everything I've—".

"That's the whole point, Antoine. I'm collecting for her. Now."

How it had shifted there so fast Antoine could not imagine, but the hand was at his throat. The pistol had been flung away like an unwanted toy. Those fingers were grappling hooks sinking pitilessly through snowy collar lace. Down and down. In and in.

"R-R-R-Roger!" It was more a rattle in his constricted throat than anything.

But the hooks only buried themselves deeper. Expressionless, Roger crouched over him. The emerald eyes women loved were bulging now. He could feel them popping. Dear God!

"Good-bye, Antoine."

It seemed to come to him from a great, great distance off.

She had been crouching in the moored dory for the best part of an hour, waiting. Bundled into a shawl, Christophe had fallen lightly asleep beside her. At their feet rested the single scuffed satchel into which

Roger had told her to pack everything she really needed. Mme. Gilboy was to store the rest.

The dark backwater stream had a sense of humor. It chuckled as it undulated past. Rosalie wondered what the joke was. Nothing as mordant, she begged an unseen Deity, as the thoughts which had pursued her all evening, almost since the three of them left church together.

"I'll have to leave you both for a few hours, Rosalie."

"Why, Roger, why? I don't want you to go. I feel so safe with you here."

"I'll be back soon, my darling. There's some business I must attend to."

He never had put a name to that business, never once. Yet she had known, just as she had known that, no matter how deeply Roger loved her, there was no point in trying to dissuade him from whatever he had in mind. The look in his eyes whenever she spoke Antoine's name had been all she'd needed to tell her that. All she could do now was wait where he had told her his boat would be tied up. Wait and hope. Wait and pray.

"I wonder," she thought, huddled there. "Was there ever another woman who had *two* such wedding nights? That awful room with Antoine? And now this boat?"

An owl hooted off in the darkness. Water like spilled ink heaved and mocked at her. A sough of wind in the live oaks came to her as the moan of a bayou banshee might. She hugged her threadbare cloak tighter about her, listening, listening.

News of him came before any living form was visible in the darkness.

Reeds crackled as someone shouldered through them. She caught the noise of boots wading the river muck and drawing closer. What if this were not Roger after all? There might be others roaming the desolate swamp on chores of their own. Chores dangerous to a lone woman.

She drew Christophe's small, sleeping figure closer, spreading the cloak to conceal it as best she might. Like many another mother creature in the night swamp, she tensed in readiness to battle for her cub. He was much closer now. And even closer.

Out of the blackness he came lurching, knowing the precise spot for which he was headed. A great, shapeless bulk at first. And then, blessedly—Roger!

He seemed to flop rather than climb across the high flaring side of the dory, awkward as Rosalie never had known Roger to be. For a moment his strong legs still dangled overside, water gushing off his hip-high boots and back into the wavelets left behind him. With an effort, he seemed to piece scraps of energy and will together. He moaned and finished his boarding. Slumped down on the flat bottom, he peered up at her weakly. But a grin curved his lips.

"Made it neat and proper." One arm reached up for her. "Hello, Rosalie."

She went down beside him, careful not to disturb Christophe. "Oh, love! Oh, Roger!"

"You missed me, then? I missed you, too. But I'm back for good now. We're off for the bayou. We're off to spend all those tomorrows-spend-spend—"

She bent still closer, eager to kiss him. The way he lay staring up at her—something was very wrong there. A dark, wet stain on his sleeve was not swamp muck at all.

"Roger! You've been hurt! Your arm! I should have known by the way you had to drag yourself from the water. Oh, my darling, what happened? A wild dog? A mink trap?"

"A pistol, *ma belle*. No matter. But as an oarsman I fear I'd be lacking tonight."

"You're not going to row at all, Roger Bernard. Here, let me look."

The wound all but made her gag when she had peeled a crusted sleeve away. The pistol must have been discharged at very close range. It was a miracle he'd survived.

"Rosalie? Another kiss like that last one—"

"Lie still and stop babbling. You've lost a lot of blood. Here, we'll rip the frill on my petticoat for a tourniquet. Stop trying to kiss me. Lie still."

"I don't want to lie still. This is our wedding night, Madame Bernard."

"You imagine I don't know it? I've waited for it twenty years. Now you just lie where I've put you, hear me, or I'll be a widow before I'm anything else."

Ten minutes later, the newest bride in New Orleans was bent to a pair of oars in the pitch-colored night, handling them with the remembered expertise of a girl brought up among the stalwart fishermen of Fundy.

Little Christophe slept on, pale hair a fuzz above the folds of his shawl. And on the floorplanks, stretched out as comfortably as she could arrange him, her husband was serenading her, however weakly, with a love ballade, one young folk had sung in Grand Pré, words and times away.

Each of them seemed to remember every word.

PART
TWO

12

THE TWO YOUNG MEN rowing their *pirogue* up the bayou were singing an old Cajun chanty as they dipped their oars. Neither one of them had a singing voice to rival the great opera stars who by now, in 1803, visited New Orleans with fair frequency. But both possessed sufficient lung power to make the flowing waters echo.

Except for velvety brown eyes they both had inherited from their dead mother, the brothers were as different as possible in appearance. A veteran of twenty-odd summers as a shrimp fisherman, Christophe was the taller and handsomer, as well as being by two years the older. His hair shimmered like pale fire in the shadows of the overhanging cypress trees. The younger one, Roger-Claude, was more like their father: shorter, heavier-set, a tanned brunette.

The song was a favorite in the Bernard family, one their father and Mama Rosalie had sung themselves as young folk back in Canada. With the senior Bernards proudly leading, it had graced many a family hearthside, the brothers' little sister Marie adding her delicate soprano. The tune was touched with a nostalgic sadness since the summer Mama Rosalie had succumbed to yellow fever. But her sons still loved the hearty rondel and the tune to which it had been set. They bellowed it now, sturdily rowing.

Around the next bend the familiar Bernard landing slid into view, the tin-roofed open boathouse Roger Bernard's sons had built for the *pirogue* awaiting them. Making fast to a jutting root of the cypress tree overhanging the crude structure, they walked together up the path leading to the log-and-clapboard cottage higher on the bank. Christophe, the contemplative one of the family, strolled along quietly. Roger-Claude, the athlete, was a bit inclined toward harmless swaggering. He whistled shrilly to announce their arrival.

At the first note of the whistle, Marie burst from the doorway ahead with a welcoming shout. She was small and delicate-boned, as Mama Rosalie had been, and she much resembled their mother too in her dark, appealing beauty. Sometimes, although he seldom spoke of it, they caught their father watching her and shaking his head, his eyes clouded over with sad rememberings. They'd know then that something in their sister's look or voice or movement must have brought Mama Rosalie too much into his mind again.

Marie flung herself at them, accompanying her arrival with a tomboy whoop.

"What present did you bring me from New Orleans, Christophe? Almond paste, Roger-Claude?"

Both brothers instantly and solemnly shook their heads. But she did not leave off her excited dancing in the pathway as she wheedled them. They never returned from one of their shrimp-selling expeditions to the city without bringing her a surprise.

"A hair ribbon, then? A new bandana? Oh, tell me, tell me, tell me!"

"You are a greedy child," growled Roger-Claude. "If we brought you anything, it would be a switch to keep you in order. Mama Rosalie wanted you to become a lady."

"I *am* a lady! Papa promised you'd take me to town with you next year, so I can see the city! He says I'll be old enough to go, with two brothers to watch over me!"

"Not until you leave off behaving like a brat. You'd shame us."

Marie had been circling them all the while, eagerly peering at the hands they both had thrust behind them the instant she burst from the cabin. To her dismay, she could see that both pairs were empty. For the first time ever had they brought her nothing? She left off dancing. Her great dark eyes became darker yet. Her wide smile began to falter.

"You're really angry with me, aren't you? But what have I done?"

Roger-Claude would have continued teasing her, but the sudden woe in her lifted face was more than Christophe could hold out against. He bent to gather her up in a bear hug that swung her clear off her feet.

"We are not angry with you at all, *petite*."

"But if you didn't want to bring me a surprise—"

"This time, we only brought it part way with us. If you look in the *pirogue* you may find something. In the prow. In a little reed basket."

"*Christophe! Roger-Claude!*" She was off down the bank like a fawn in flight.

Laughing with the sheer pleasure they always took in their mercurial sister, the brothers strode on indoors. Except for one iron-grey figure straddling the bench before the fireplace, whittling a small bird figure out of a bit of driftwood, the room was empty. After a quick glance about, Roger-Claude turned concernedly toward the carver.

"Where's Annette, Papa? I thought she'd be waiting."

Roger Bernard glanced up, in his eyes a smile which his mouth nowadays seldom echoed. "Annette baked fresh loaves this morning. She decided to take a couple to Cousin Sylvie. She's a thoughtful girl is your wife, Roger-Claude. Always kind to Sylvie."

"She took our other boat, then? I noticed it was missing."

"Don't fret, boy. She'll be home soon." Roger put down his weathered wood scrap on the bench surface among a litter of shavings. A special contraption of bent wires he had created to hold a block, so that he might work on it with his one remaining hand, was forgotten in favor of his returned sons. He sat looking them over with satisfaction.

But Roger-Claude still was scowling. "She shouldn't row. The baby's almost due."

"Ah, lad, she's no fool. She knows her limits. And at worst, with whom could she better be caught short?

Sylvie is the best *traiteur* on the bayou. Everyone knows that."

"Treater or not, Cousin Sylvie is no licensed doctor. And everyone *also* knows that she's a dotty old hermit and sees no one except those seeking her medical mumbo-jumbo. I want my wife in a good New Orleans hospital when her time comes, as Annette is well aware."

"Now," murmured Christophe at his brother's shoulder, "we become the stern husband."

Roger-Claude swung to face him. "A lot you know about a married man's anxieties! Sneaking up on thirty years and you've never worked up courage to ask a girl."

"There's still a week or two left for that." But Christophe's answer was gentle.

Well knowing the strong bond between the brothers, Roger was not unduly concerned. But he disliked even momentary friction between them. It always had upset Rosalie. It had been so important to her that their family be a tight, solid unit, although only he knew why.

"Annette will be back before dark. Let's get to important matters. How good a deal for our shrimps could you make today?"

"The market," Christophe said, "is up. Big news has come from Washington City."

"So what are they up to now, back east?"

"President Jefferson has purchased the whole Louisiana Territory from France, that's what! Lock, stock and barrel! All eight hundred thousand and more square miles, Papa!"

Roger whistled softly. "Talleyrand gave in to the Yankees at last, did he?"

"Only on orders from Emperor Napoleon. He underestimated Thomas Jefferson, did Napoleon, by sending a French army to Santo Domingo to put down the uprising of the Negros there. That sat very ill on our President. And then to withdraw the Right of Deposit, on the heels of the other! No wonder Jefferson shipped James Monroe to Paris to protest."

"I well understand that, son. The Right of Deposit is precious to the Americans. It's been *a* privilege of long standing. Being allowed to lay off goods at New Orleans pending transshipment was a vital spoke in the Yankee economy. So Monroe fared well, eh?"

"Very well indeed, Papa, after several ups and downs. The French liked none of the four American propositions. They didn't want to sell Florida and New Orleans. They didn't want to sell New Orleans alone. They didn't want to sell land of the Mississippi's east bank for construction of an American fort. And they didn't cotton at all to leasing perpetual rights of river navigation. But we've brought Paris to heel in the end."

One of Roger's grizzled eyebrows quirked. "Not by force of arms?"

"Oh, nothing warlike. It seems one-half of the French army in Santo Domingo was destroyed by the uprising, the other half by fever. Worse still, another war between France and England draws closer every day. That could mean English occupation of Louisiana."

"Very awkward for Napoleon."

"Very. So now he has about-faced with Mr. Monroe. The Americans have purchased all Louisiana for fifteen million dollars. The treaty is signed. Word just came in."

"I can imagine the city's in turmoil," Roger said. "I saw how excitement ran in the city when the colonies decided to be states and started nipping at the British heel. How long ago that seems!"

Roger-Claude had decided to drop the subject of Annette, at least for the moment. "You knew the city then. It's a pity you've refused to enter it ever since, Papa. You ought to come with us when we sell to the market. There's no excitement in this backwater."

"I've had excitement enough to last me the rest of my time, son."

"But you miss out on everything important that goes on in the world. This tremendous news today, for example. You'd get it all first hand."

"A man with only one hand keeps that hand quite busy enough on the bayou."

It was a useless challenge to try to persuade their father to visit New Orleans, as both Christophe and Roger-Claude well knew. Never within either of their memories had he set foot inside city limit. All through their growing years, they had begged, entreated, cajoled, to no good result whatever. As boys, they often had puzzled together over this strange aversion, and had come out with no clear answer. Why did Papa so hate the beautiful city? Or was it a fear? Yet why should anyone fear New Orleans?

Even by the most indirect questions, they had been unable to discover whether or not this phobia had any connection with the loss of Papa's left arm. Before either of them could remember, the arm had been amputated. But he would never tell them exactly why. On that subject, even Mama Rosalie always had maintained a mysterious silence.

"Was it cut off in battle, Mama?"

"Was it mangled by an alligator?"

"Did some laborer in the sugar fields wound him with a machete?"

To all their imagined explanations, the one their mother invariably had given shed none too much light. "Blood poisoning set in. It was lose the arm or lose your Papa."

"But what caused the blood poisoning? There'd have to be a reason, Mama."

"The reason needn't concern you boys. Get back to your chores now."

And that was the end of it. A blank wall. A barricade of silence. With time, the two of them had stopped asking. For some reason of his own, Papa considered the arm's loss to be exclusively his own business. Very well, he was entitled not to talk about it.

Once, Christophe had caught an unintended remark which persuaded him for awhile that the amputation had been performed by Cousin Sylvie, already a *traiteur* despite her tender years. But one never asked important questions of Cousin Sylvie. She'd only turn those pale, blank eyes on one with a creepy stare that made one feel she didn't know he was there at all.

Marie was enough younger never to ask questions. She accepted their father's handicap as though it were entirely normal. The arm that was left him was quite powerful enough to swing her up onto his shoulder and carry her through the shallow swamp, squealing with happiness. From her royal perch she could survey her bayou world like a queen, and adored Papa was her stalwart cavalier. She worshipped Papa even more than she did her brothers.

"World affairs are very grand," Roger was saying, altogether in the present. "But what about our own small concerns? You haven't told me yet about the market in shrimps."

Christophe answered at once. "Sorry, Papa. I thought I'd said it was flourishing."

"Enough," cut in Roger-Claude, "so we had a fine gentleman sniffing about with an eye to buying in on the bayou combine. He seemed to have heard our father heads it."

"Ah! Success on yet another market? Shrimps, and now potential dollars?"

"He offered us a *dix* just to carry his offer to you. We refused it, neither of us being messenger boys. I'd have refused it anyway. I didn't like him."

"Now, Roger-Claude, a man can't make business decisions on a basis of like or not like. If you sensed this offerer is a thief or a scalawag, that's something different."

"I don't know what his morals are. I just didn't like him."

Christophe eased in a more detailed observation. "He seemed to have ample funds behind him, Papa. It wasn't that. But his way of speaking to us was, well, so lordly. It put our backs up."

"Why should a man of such stylish cut want to get his hands on a few humble shrimp fisheries?" Roger-Claude growled. "You'd think we wouldn't be nearly grand enough to suit him."

"Who knows? Perhaps he has an ear to Washington City. Perhaps President Jefferson's fifteen million in Louisiana purchase money is expected to be dredged from the bayous." Roger had little interest in acquiring citified shrimping partners. But, like his sons, he did have a certain amount of curiosity. "You didn't by any chance inquire his name?"

"He readily volunteered it." Roger-Claude's answer was very like a sneer. "And asked us ours, which we didn't volunteer. He's called Roland, Papa. Anton Cedric Roland. I have his card for you. He pressed it on us. Insisted we take it. Much like this."

The young man's parody of their plush acquaintance at the fish market was so deft it brought a remembering grin to Christophe's lips. Except for the lack of elegant suede gloves, it was perfection. But Roger merely accepted the scrap of pasteboard.

His jaw set hard as he studied the engraving. His single hand closed to a fist. It hurled the crumpled card into the fireplace among the cinders. "Impertinent puppy!"

"What is it, Papa? You look like a rattler just bit you!"

"One just did. Or maybe he doesn't yet know whose flesh he fanged."

The door crashed open. Marie flung herself into the room like a small typhoon, clutching a tiny ball of fur to her young breasts.

"Papa! It's a kitten! Christophe and Roger-Claude brought me a *kitten* from the city. Oh, Papa, look, isn't she adorable? You're not going to say I can't keep her, are you? Oh, *Papa!*"

When night settled on the bayou, it descended through the silent trees like a dark veil. The dangling moss in a million branches faded slowly, grey lost to black. Moonrise sounds began; an owl's hoot, a trapped varmint's yelp, the twitter of insects, the *basso profundo* of bullfrogs. For mankind, it was a peaceful world.

But not, this particular night, at the Bernard cabin.

For Marie, yes, the world was peaceful. Having christened her kitten Moses with a fine disdain for gender—"Because Moses was found in the bullrushes, Papa, just the way I found her in the *pirogue!*"—Marie had fallen asleep quite early with tiny Moses curled up beside her on her pillow. Instant love on both sides, that was peaceful.

For the older members of the family, however, moods were wakeful.

Up overhead in the attic Christophe had shared with Roger-Claude until the younger brother's marriage, Rosalie's firstborn son lay staring wide-eyed at shadows on the underbelly of the cabin roof. Hands behind his head, cradling his mass of curls, he probed deep into the day's adventure. It was hard to connect the event with Papa's reaction.

There had been no adverse reaction until the name was mentioned and the card presented. Papa might have had no interest in the man's business offer, but it certainly had not angered him. So it must have been the name. The name meant something to Papa, something strong enough to stir a black hatred.

Anton Cedric Roland? It said nothing to Christophe. What could it say to Papa? This Roland was a New Orleans fop. Papa had not visited the city for as long as either of his sons could remember. Paths scarcely could have crossed, because Roland had seemed much Christophe's own age. Why, then, the violent gesture of rejection? Why the set jaw?

In the new side bedroom added last spring to the cabin by the brothers themselves, so that Roger-Claude might bring home his bride, Annette at last fell asleep after having convinced herself she would go mad

unless her husband quit his endless twisting and
turning. The bed had been filled for hours with Roger-
Claude's mutters and twitches. Generally this was a
happy bed. Annette simply could not fathom why it
no longer seemed so. Had he been more resentful than
she had guessed of today's visit to Cousin Sylvie? But
she had been moved by only the kindest of intentions.
Cousin Sylvie was so strange and, yes, so lonely. If
taking two loaves of home-baked bread to a poor
hermit—and Roger-Claude's own first cousin, at that—
were such a sin, how could one ever define virtue?

Long after her breathing changed rhythm, Roger-
Claude himself lay sleepless.

Roland, Roland, Anton Cedric Roland. It was like
a chant inside his skull like one of those Houma tribal
rituals he could call back from early childhood, maybe,
in days before the Indians had mostly headed west to
newer camping grounds. A war chant! Sure enough,
there in the livingroom tonight Papa had sounded like
a man declaring war. But why?

Outside the cabin, where the wild things of the
bayou usually had the night to themselves, Roger Bernard had hunkered down on the sloping bank with his
clay pipe clenched between teeth still strong enough
to hold the shaft unwaveringly. Down below, the
waves lapped secrets at the two tethered *pirogues*.
The whispers brought back a night so long ago that
sometimes Roger actually forgot it.

Rosalie had worked hard to make him forget it.
What had happened at the Rolande house was over
and done with. She'd understood that he had to do
what he'd done, and she'd never nursed any blame
against him. But she knew, too, that he was not a man

to whom murder came easy. She knew she was married to a haunted husband.

All his love for her, and hers for him, hadn't rubbed out the inner guilt. He'd been almost glad when Sylvie told him the bullet had poisoned him before curing and the arm had to go, if he were to live. He was paying his debt to God, although he'd owed none to Antoine.

And now, after so long, *this*. After the years of burying himself in the bayou, where Antoine's avengers couldn't trace him even with their bloodhounds. After all his dogged avoidance of the city, where he might be recognized and dragged to what most folk would call Justice. After raising the boys and the girl, and working like a coolie to set up a business so there'd be something left for them when he was gone. After all of it—now this.

Anton Cedric Roland. Even before his glance at the card Roger-Claude handed him, the three hateful words had burned their brand on him.

Anton, that would be Antoine turned English. The pregnant British wife would fancy that. Cedric was the name Jules had told him belonged to the titled father of the girl Antoine had *really* married. Roland, that was the old Rolande with the final "e" chopped off—again, to make it sound more like a London swell.

He wished Jules were still alive. Jules would have been about the only human being Roger could talk to now. Jules himself would have strangled Antoine, had he not feared those threats against Rosalie. Yes, Jules would have talked this new disaster out with his son-in-law and given sound advice. But he hadn't wanted to keep on going after Rosalie died. Within that same year, Jules too had been gone.

No one to talk with now but the bayou night. Well, the bayou had been his friend for more than two decades. It wouldn't turn against him in an hour of need. What had the night to say?

The lazy hum of after-dinner New Orleans was muted by drawn thick draperies. Street noise would have been an unwelcome guest in Amanda Roland's parlor. She waved a fan of dyed egret feathers languidly but beneath her modish breast ruffles she felt anything but languid.

"You did learn their name, Anton? We'll want to find them again."

"I asked. They wouldn't tell me, Mother."

"There are ways of finding out what one wants to know."

"Indeed there are. I've put out several feelers."

"The name will lead us to the location. Whoever this father of theirs may be, this bayou bumpkin, you've been told is key man of the shrimpers, we'll get to him. I find it odd that *no one* seems to know the young men's patronymic. In every other business I've gone into since taking charge at your father's death, the big fish don't remain anonymous."

"This is *real* fishing, Mother. Real fishing that smells of profits."

"Unquestionably. Otherwise, Roland money would not be interested. Seafood is a potential natural resource. Once we've developed means to ship and deliver a catch before it spoils, we'll have every city along the Atlantic coast for a market. There'll be the same money in it there is now in other natural resources—timber, or sugar."

"Both of which show black ink in our ledgers. You're a genius, Mother."

Several prominent New Orleans men who were not her sons had spoken that very word about Amanda Roland during the past quarter-century. Genius. It had a satisfying ring, although they could call her anything they chose as long as the family cash registers kept chiming.

She doubted many in the city still remembered her as a well-bred, cologne-and-roses debutante with an indulgent Sir Cedric Wellington at hand to satisfy her wildest whims. Even dear Papa would have been startled to know of her keen interest in the workings of the money behind her balls and gowns and carriages. Money had been Antoine's specialty, so *he* would have empathized.

Their marriage scarcely had become settled before she was able to read Antoine like a balance sheet. The romantic side of her still relished him. No matter how long she lived, she'd never again meet a male who was physically his equal. In bed he had been—ah, the only word for his abilities there was "fantastic."

Merely remembering him in her bed, so long afterward, could still make the fan's egret plumes quiver excitedly. The discovery that he had never really loved her did not lessen the feelings which surged through her whenever he mounted her. She had what she most wanted. And later, after that awful horror of his death, she'd had the twins. So she had not been cheated, at least, not by beautiful, clever, shallow Antoine. It was only an unknown sea captain waiting for him in his study on that unforgotten night who had cheated her.

Her resolution, as she'd stared into bulging green eyes with an awful fixed disbelief in them, had been Amanda Roland's one guiding star ever since: *No one will ever again take away from me anything I want.* And no one had. Business rivals who thought her only a silly society woman to be twisted about their practiced masculine fingers had discovered this fact to their sorrow.

She no longer kept track of the bankruptcies and suicides which seemed to lie like a well-marked path behind her. She reserved higher mathematics for the inexorable detail work of her next buy-in or near-swindle or take-over.

Anton was speaking. "Mother, if we were to hire a shrewd detective—"

"Who would be equally shrewd, Anton, at flimflaming me with preposterous bills. I'd rather have you undertake this search personally. I don't have to pay you salary."

"Whatever you think is best for the organization, Mother."

"That's my good boy. I know I can lean on you far more than on your brother Percy. You're much more aware than he will ever be of just how much will be waiting in the bank for you two to divide when I'm gone. You're really *much* more like your Papa than Percy."

"It's Percy who has Papa's handsomeness." For an instant, an unfamiliar wistful note crept into Anton's prosaic voice. "From the portrait in the library, Percy is all but his double. You yourself have often told us—"

"Yes. Your brother does have Antoine's poetic look.

But with Percy, alas, it's genuine. Percy is a darling, useless daydreamer."

Anton froze into himself again. "What exactly do you wish me to do, Mother?"

"I want you to find the man behind these shrimp gatherers. Who gets their catch to port? Who arranges their good prices? Once we know *that*, I'll make other plans."

13

THE THINGS ABOUT NEW ORLEANS that Percy Roland held most dear were things he doubted his mother even knew existed. The common street cries as humbler citizens went about their daily duties. The misty shapes of market stalls at sunrise, when the vendors were setting out vegetables and seafoods before their customers arrived. The jauntiness with which house-maids called well-meant insults back and forth to one another as they scrubbed front doorsteps. The early rush and bustle along the waterfront.

These might not be his aristocratic mother's city, but they were his. He dreamed of one day writing a book about them.

He wanted people he himself would never know, people who would not be born yet for a century, to feel how this gem among cities really had been in its glorious prime; not a fairytale of masked balls and glitter, but the New Orleans that sweated from useful work, laughed and made love in the byways, toted bales of goods off a forest of docked ships, gulped lusty ales at day's end. His might not be a romantic volume, if ever he learned enough about his subject to actually put it down in words. But at least generations still to come would know how these streets had smelled and sounded.

Sometimes Percy wondered how the father he never had seen would have regarded this real New Orleans. He knew (because Mother so often said so, and because of the revered painting hung almost like an icon in her distinguished townhouse) that in features he very much resembled the legendary Antoine Rolande. But were they at all alike *inside*? Somehow, he never felt he could have been close to the unreachable, untouchable subject of that magnificent portrait. It would have been impossible to live up to such elegance.

Lying in wait in their own house, that ruffian who had deprived him of ever knowing a flesh-and-blood father obviously had not been overwhelmed by The Great Presence.

Icy hatred in her tone, Mother often had told Anton and himself about that eventful night. How the fellow, in coarse seaman's clothing, had arrived at their door claiming to be Father's old friend, and had been shown to the study to await Antoine's homecoming. How Father had graciously gone in to greet the man. How, after a brief interval of silence, a single shot had shattered the house's regal dignity.

The servants had rushed in, Mother close after them, to find Father strangled by his handsome desk and his assailant leaping out an open garden window. The stranger's escape via a rear alley had been accomplished before pursuit could be mounted. In an odd way, Percy's lifelong picture of the murderer was the most genuine thing he knew about his father. Mother's "coarse seaman's clothing" suggested that at one time, at least, Antoine Rolande had been somewhat less remote than a god, had rubbed elbows with common, everyday folk and their world.

Other details of the family tragedy remained hazy. The pair of duelling pistols, for example, Why had they been out of the gun cabinet at all? Why had one of them been fired, the other not?

One could but suppose that Father somehow managed to reach a weapon and fire it desperately in self-defense before the strangler's brute grip closed on his windpipe. The intruder must have been wounded, too. A good deal of blood was spattered on the floor and later had been traced clear across the garden. Father himself bore no marks save those about his throat.

The actual picture never came entirely clear. One thing, though: Mother had been able, after months of relentless searching, to discover the name of Father's "old friend." He had been one Roger Bernard, and indeed he had known Father well back in their Nova Scotia years.

Bernard kinfolk now lived in the region out near St. Jacques. But when contacted they had denied any knowledge of Roger's whereabouts. He seemed to have dropped out of their world as if through some cosmic trapdoor. But likely these Bernards were lying. Mother had set spies on the Bernard farm. But after two costly years her men had no report to make and had been discharged. Since then, she had made no overt effort to trace the vanished killer. Yet Percy sometimes wondered if she'd really given up. That would not be at all like Mother.

This particular morning, Percy arose early and donned his modest everyday clothes and tiptoed from the house before even the staff was stirring. Through streets still deserted, past gardens wet with dew, past dark, silent, shuttered mansions, he made his way toward one of his favorite sections of New Orleans—the fish stalls.

Here, life was already at full gallop.

The boats of the shrimp fleet from the many surrounding bayous already were tied up, owners lugging bulging sacks of new-caught shrimp across the rough cobblestones. Percy paused to study the familiar scene. Two brothers he had noticed on various previous visits were deep in price haggling with veteran mongers along the line.

His interest was caught because, as Percy had noted before, one of them bore such a startling resemblance to himself. Although they'd never even spoken, you could all but take the shrimp man and himself for twins whereas he and his own real twin, Anton, bore no resemblance whatever.

Such a homely coincidence tended to spark Percy's curiosity. Almost unconsciously, he began to edge closer to the shrimpers so earnestly engaged in their bargaining.

"Now then, Christophe," the monger involved was protesting. "You'll be choking us to death, demanding such a figure. Ain't your father aware what a mere living costs us?"

"You'll resell for twice what you're paying us," the one who so resembled Percy, the one called Chris-

tophe, answered calmly. "Papa sets the price for all
the shrimpers, not just us alone. Our job is only to see
there's no undercutting. Do you buy or not?"

The monger moaned. "I buy. What do my customers
say, if I tell them no shrimp today? My best hotel
customers, my best private patrons, go elsewhere. But
you're choking me."

"You'll survive, Franco. And so will all of us up on
the bayous, whom you'd keep at starvation level if
Papa let you. How many pounds today, then? The
usual?"

This was the true heart of New Orleans. Eavesdrop-
ping happily, Percy only chanced to glance up. After
one startled look along the line of stalls, he ducked
instinctively for cover under a nearby archway.

What the devil was *Anton* doing out of bed so
early?

His twin would certainly tattle to Mother about encountering her other son on the market square, loiter-
ing amid the riffraff; and Mother, as usual, would issue
a stern reprimand. Her notion of how Percy should
spend his days—very much as Anton did—was in slav-
ish duty to the sacred cause of piling up more Roland
dollars in bank vaults. She had small patience with a
grown young man who merely (her word) *wandered*.
He, Percy, certainly would have been a disappoint-
ment to his super-perfect Father.

From his point of vantage, he could watch Anton
progressing along the stalls. At one after another,
Anton was pausing and engaging the vendors in whispered conversation.

It was evident to Percy that his twin was carrying a
fat handful of folded greenbacks. He appeared to be
offering money to man after man, in exchange for some

service. But the mongers did not seem eager. Heads
were shaken. Backs were turned coldly.

One or two of Anton's semi-secret gestures seemed
unquestionably to be in the direction of the blond
shrimper the others called Christophe. A possible explanation suggested itself. Anton, too, had somewhere
observed this tall blond fellow and noted his startling
resemblance to Percy (well, yes, and of course to
Father, too). He was out this early trying to buy information. He was curious to learn if this Christophe
might be some distant Roland relation.

It didn't seem likely, though, that Anton would interest himself in anything which bore no likelihood
of financial profit. In that, Anton was Mother all over
again. What else, then? Was Anton trying to purchase
a shrimp boat?

Percy chuckled. The fleeting image of his twin
becoming a shrimper was delightful. Wading boots instead of handmade leather? Homespun instead of
doeskin breeches? Hours in a rocking boat that reeked
of fish instead of the panelled offices, with secretaries
fawning and clerks making frightened obeisances?
That wasn't dear brother Anton. Yet how else could he
make yet another fortune here? So perhaps he was
becoming a little human. Perhaps, after all, he wanted
to investigate a possible blood-link on man-to-man
terms.

Whatever Anton's motive, his errand seemed to be
bearing no fruit. One after another, the mongers he
approached were refusing his generous remuneration.
After considerable time, Anton pocketed his roll of
greenbacks and stamped away, obviously disgruntled.

Free again, Percy eased from concealment and made

his way across the square to the docks. Here he climbed up on a handy piling and sat watching the morning pageant unfold.

Presently, popping up out of one of the nearest tethered shrimp boats, a slim girl with hair like a raven's wing sprang up onto the unloading platform. She moved with the lithe grace of a cat, Percy observed; and that was fitting, because draped about her shoulders almost like a boa rode a real cat, equally small, equally delicate.

"Christophe, hey! Roger-Claude, hey! I'm tired just sitting here and waiting!"

She made her way across the square to the two brothers. In motion, she seemed a poem incarnate. Although she couldn't be much older than sixteen at most, she was already a woman in everything that mattered. Evidently the brothers failed to recognize this, for they shouted back at her as she shortened the distance between them.

"We told you. You must be patient till we finish our business, Marie!"

"We told Papa you'd be a pest if he made us bring you!"

So they were obviously her brothers as well as brothers to each other. Percy watched the little sideshow interestedly. She had by now joined the pair in whom Anton recently displayed such interest. The darker one slapped her rump with careless affection.

"Go back to the boat. That's how it has to be."

"But the morning's half over, Roger-Claude!" the girl pouted. "I'll never see anything of New Orleans at all, and I've looked forward to today so long!"

"Back to the boat, Marie, or I'll paddle your bottom right here in public. Go on, now, do as you're told.

And take that blasted Moses with you or I'll chuck her overboard."

Scowling like a thundercloud, the dark little beauty turned rebelliously and began to stamp toward the dock. As she drew closer, her glance fell upon Percy where he perched on his piling. She stopped dead. Her brothers evidently hadn't told her it was rude to stare.

"Golly gee!" She studied him frankly. "You're the spit of Christophe!"

"If you mean that fellow yonder, I couldn't agree more. Amazing, isn't it?"

She drew closer, still gazing upward. "My name's Marie. This is Moses. Who are you?"

"I'm Percy. Your brothers do a great job as shrimp salesmen, don't they?"

"They ought to. Big as they are, Papa would tan them if they didn't. It's Papa who bosses the whole shrimp fleet. He wouldn't let his friends be short-changed."

Percy smiled down at her, amusement and admiration mixed in his green eyes.

"I couldn't help hearing. They're supposed to be showing you the town?"

"Those two! It'll be time to head back to the bayou before they're finished. I'll never see New Orleans at all. Moses won't either. And it's Moses' home city, where she was born."

"You live out along one of the bayous? Have you never come to town before?"

"Papa thought I wasn't grown-up enough. Not till today. Today's my birthday."

"I wish I had a present for you," Percy said, and meant it. "Hey, maybe I have! If your brothers don't mind, I could give you a little introductory tour while they're still busy."

"I doubt they'd let me. They just want me to wait on the boat and dangle my legs, like you're doing, until it's time to go. I love my brothers, but they're pigs."

"At least we could ask them."

He eeled down off the piling and led her back ashore. The cat around her neck glared at him, but Percy was unmoved. With Percy a step in the lead, they crossed the square together. The stalls were swarming. Morning was advanced enough so that customers were arriving. But her brothers were still at their task.

"I beg your pardon, sir." Instinctively, it was to Christophe, his duplicate, that Percy delivered the apology. "I've just been talking with your sister here. She tells me it's her birthday and she's come to celebrate by getting a look at New Orleans."

The tall young man turned from his haggle.

For a long minute the two stood facing each other like reflections in a mirror. (Except, thought Percy, that his eyes are as brown as Marie's and don't resemble my green ones at all.) Her brother looked the intruder on his business up and down and clearly there was an element of disbelief and surprise in the examination. Christophe, too, must be suffering a shock of recognition.

"What if all that's true?"

"You two are busy. I thought I might offer myself as a temporary stand-in. I could show her around the immediate area and bring her back whenever you think you'll be free."

The brown eyes never wavered. "We don't know you. Our sister doesn't go about with strangers."

"Let me introduce myself, then. I'm Percy Roland. My family is well-respected in New Orleans. My name should vouch for me."

To Perry's astonishment, anger flashed into this face so like his own.

"*Roland,* is it? Well, my brother and I will thank you not to speak again to our sister. Not ever. Not for any reason. Good day to you, Mr. Roland."

"Look here, I meant no offense. None ought to be taken. Marie and I—"

"Marie and you have nothing whatever to say to each other. Not now, not at any time in the future. Is that understood? Or must my brother and I make it clearer?"

"*Christophe!*" shrilled the girl, in astonishment and rising anger.

For an answer, the other one, Roger-Claude, caught his sister's arm and began to propel her forcibly across the cobblestones toward their anchored shrimp boat. And all that was left of Christophe to meet Percy's dumbfounded gaze was a broad back as the man turned away.

The shock of his brush with the two shrimpers cast a tarnish over the morning. Coupled with his unforeseen encounter with Anton, one-sided though it had been, it robbed Percy of any enjoyment of a day which had started well. Toward noon he gave up on his roamings and headed home.

It was Amanda Roland's custom to be driven home from the family company's offices each day for a private lunch and an hour's rest. The habit was a great revitalizer. It gave her the energy for an afternoon's decisions and maneuvers.

Today, as he re-entered the familiar house where in one sense he never had felt at home, Percy could hear voices from the dining room. Mother and Anton were already at the table. Reluctantly, Percy turned his footsteps in their direction.

"So I made a real inducement to one lump of scum after another," Anton was saying. They were evidently midway in some business discussion. "You'd have thought our dollars were counterfeit. Not a taker. Not even when I doubled the offer."

"Why is it that everyone is so mysteriously protective? It can't be that they fear the anger of this nameless, faceless King of the Shrimpers. Money always outbids fear. There has to be some other reason. Didn't you even get some inkling?"

"Well, yes, there I did have a little luck. Just a little. One bloke did mumble that 'The Boss'—that's what they call him—had once been in some kind of trouble. He's keeping his head down for the obvious reason. Let sleeping dogs lie. So, no thanks—he didn't want our cash."

As Percy slid quietly into his customary place across the table, Mother glanced over to acknowledge his arrival. She still was the handsomest dowager in the city, elegant and overbearing in her mauve velvet and her diamonds. She nodded vaguely and swung her attention right back to Anton.

"What about the other mongers? Did they bear out this impression you'd received of something illegal in the Boss's past?"

"Well, yes, at least an impression."

"That would explain why his name is so impossible to come by. Which would in turn suggest that he is liked and respected by men who do business with him. You'd only protect a man for genuine liking."

"To like him, they'd have to know him. Do you believe they do?"

"Well, let's review what we know. Evidently the man appears never, or seldom, in person. Yet his hold seems unshakable. They at least have an *image* of him, these people we can't bribe. Somehow, he has established confidence. And that will be much to our own advantage, Anton, once we've smoked him out. An honorable man lying low from the law. We can use that, come the time. We'll use it to twist him into line and let us buy in. How helpful to the Roland interests to have a man like that under our thumb!"

"You think of everything, dear Mother. No wonder we own a quarter of the city."

Amanda smiled gracious appreciation. She then, as if for duty's sake, turned to her other son. "And how have you spent *your* morning, Percy, darling? Taking a constitutional?"

"I was down at the shrimp market, Mother." Percy dragged back his attention which had wandered, during the dull business meeting, to pleasanter subjects. He had been thinking of the girl, how pretty and how vital she seemed. Despite her unfriendly relatives, he couldn't seem to get her out of his mind. "I saw Anton there, but he didn't notice me."

Anton glowered. "I had important affairs on my mind, Brother."

"I could see that. You were working very hard, Anton. I'd have helped you, if I realized you were there doing business for Mother. But I thought it was personal."

Anton only half-suppressed a sneer. "How could *you* have helped my work?"

"Why, by talking to people, the same as you were doing. I did talk to a few, actually. One girl in particular. Her name's Marie. Her brothers cut me short, though. They're that same two you were trying to check up on yourself, Anton."

Anton's somewhat plain face was a study. "You actually spoke with them? Well? What did you find out? What's their family name? Or hers? It'd be the same!"

Amanda leaned forward almost at the same instant, suddenly attentive.

"Do tell us all about it, darling. The girl must be charming to have attracted you."

"She is. But I can't say I much took to the brethen. They hated me on sight."

"The name, damn it! The *name!*" roared Anton. "If you got to know them—"

"I didn't, not very well. Christophe and Roger-Claude seem to take a power of interest in names, too. The minute they discovered mine is Roland, they all but threatened to beat me up."

Across the table, Amanda's eyes and Anton's met head on.

"So the family has a spite against the Rolands," Anton breathed. "I wonder why?"

Their mother was following a different tack.

"One of the two is called Roger-Claude, is he? How odd! My long-lost Bernard was a Roger. And his brother with a farm was called Claude. The combination there interests me. Yes, it intrigues me."

* * *

All the way back to the bayou, Marie sobbed desolately over the ruin of her birthday. It had started as such an exciting day, with Papa giving her permission to visit New Orleans at last with the boys and then, very tenderly, slipping the silver fleur-de-lys on a chain about her neck. She knew how he valued it, because it once had been Mama Rosalie's. Now he wanted her to have it as a token that she was indeed grown up. Annette had kissed her too, and promised to bake a birthday *gateau* for their return from town.

Even her brothers had seemed in a festive mood on the long trip to the wharf. Although they had teased her a lot about being a nuisance, each of them had outdone the other in thinking up sights for her entertainment. As soon as the day's trading was over, they'd give her such a tour as no Princess had ever been accorded. And buy her a fine gift, too.

Even at its almost-end, Marie had found the morning enchanting. As she was returning to the boat to wait awhile longer, after one protest at how time was passing, there on the dock had sat this handsome youth with green eyes. She had taken to him instantly, and not just because of his strange resemblance to Christophe, either. He had been really nice to her, as friendly as a puppy. He'd even offered to take her sightseeing.

Then the sky had fallen in.

The instant he made his polite offer, her brothers had turned absolutely savage. You'd have thought Percy had kicked their sister, instead of suggesting a thoughtful bit of fun while she waited for the real Grand Tour.

Huddled midway of the gliding *pirogue*, she hugged

Moses to her desolately and wept. She had done nothing, absolutely nothing, wrong. And their abominable behavior had smashed her lovely birthday to tinder.

"If you don't stop snivelling," growled Roger Claude, rowing behind her, "I'll throw you overboard, blasted cat and all."

She twisted to face him. "If you lay one hand on Moses, I'll kill you."

"Good riddance if I wring her neck. She's only a slut anyway. Three litters since we bought her for you. And that's not yet a year ago."

"Well, you needn't act jealous because Annette's only had one baby in all that same time. It's not her fault. People are different than cats. They can't produce as many."

"All right, all right, just stop *crying*, will you?"

Largely because this interchange informed her how much her tears were riling Roger-Claude, Marie let them flow. But they were genuine enough. Her whole beautiful day lay in ruins. After that short, ugly scene at the market they had bundled her back into the boat and taken off for home without so much as a backward glance.

For a long time, then, there was no sound on the bayou but the forlorn rasps of her breath and the rhythmic dip of their paddles. The world she had always known kept slipping past, mile by mile, grey and familiar. The world she had dreamed so long of someday exploring lay behind, still unknown, still a heaven of which she had been cheated.

"Marie?" murmured Christophe at least, still keeping up his rowing cadence.

"I'm right here behind you, as you very well know," she snapped. "What did you think? That I'd jumped over and swum back to New Orleans to celebrate my poor birthday?"

"We're sorry, *petite*, both of us. But you don't understand."

"I certainly don't understand. He was about the nicest young man I ever met, with such friendly manners and such a kind heart. And you two ruined everything!"

"He is Percy Roland, honey. *Roland.*"

"I think it's a pretty name. And I think he's absolutely gorgeous-looking. He does resemble you, Christophe, but he's much, much handsomer. *Much.*"

"Be that as it may, he's a Roland. Bernards don't mix with Rolands."

"For heaven's sake, why not!"

"There's a good and sufficient reason. Papa told us a little about it, a few days after Roger-Claude and I bought you Moses. He didn't give any detail, but once the Roland family did something cruel and vicious to Mama Rosalie. So it's impossible for any Roland to be our friend."

Marie rode on in silence for awhile, staring at the flowing water. Her fingers automatically busied themselves in Moses's fur. Moses responded with a loving growl.

"I don't think Percy had anything to do with whatever it was. About Mama Rosalie."

"No, probably not. But his *family* did. So it would be disloyal to accept him. Can you see that, honey? You wouldn't want to be disloyal to Papa."

"That's silly. Percy's just Percy, not a whole army of Rolands. I like him." She almost added that she liked him very much indeed. But the words wouldn't quite come out.

"Forget him, honey. You'll never see him again anyway."

"I may." Marie had her small chin in the air. "I very well may."

From behind her, Roger-Claude's deep snarl sent a sudden shiver up her back. For the first time in their lives, her brother really frightened her.

"You wouldn't like to see him dead, would you, this Roland? That's what will happen to him if you ever again speak a word to him. I'm making you a promise, Marie."

14

OFTEN THE SLOW turning of time's wheel exasperated Amanda Roland almost to the point of frenzy. Hatred of the man who had killed her husband seemed to grow with the years rather than ebb. Years of concentrated efforts to find the murderer and drag him to the bar of justice had congealed in her to a core of cold steel. To have that very man turn out to be the stumbling block of her plans for taking over the increasingly profitable shrimp fleet was a final galling frustration.

Once given her son Percy's innocent revelation as a starting point, she pressed her still-fruitless hunt for the fleet boss's identity and location. These problems were resolved with gratifying speed. She had only to hire private operatives to dress themselves as bayou denizens and follow the Bernard brothers on one homeward trip from selling in New Orleans.

Her men in their trailing *pirogue* were sufficiently expert to mask any indications of what they were up to. The Bernards tied up at their family landing without a flicker of suspicion that they had betrayed themselves, and thus their "criminal" father. The agents returned to the city with a detailed report. Amanda felt triumphantly certain that all the aces were at last in her hand.

"Now we have him where we want him," she gloated to her dependable Anton.

"You've won again, Mother. We've only to let Bernard know he has been tracked down. He'll have to knuckle under to any terms we lay down or face arrest for murder."

Amanda's mouth tightened to a bitter line. "You mean, my dear, let the man go free, provided he passes control of the shrimpers into our hands? I have something rather different in mind."

"Mother, we'll have to give him *quid* for *quo*. That's part of any deal."

"Not *this* deal, Anton. Roger Bernard will get nothing but a hangman's noose. He's the devil who strangled my husband, Son. Now the Law is going to strangle him."

Anton was frowning.

"Then we lose the shrimp fleet. Condemned, he'll not turn it over. Why should he? His men will close ranks and choose someone else as their leader. They'll all hate us for turning Bernard in."

"Think again, Anton. With their so-called Boss suddenly snatched away, they'll be in utter disarray.

Confused. Panicked. Easy to manipulate, if we pull the right strings. There's no reason why our names should appear at all in Bernard's arrest. Let the authorities do that. The bayou men need never discover we Rolands had a finger in the pie."

Flushed with victory, Amanda dressed in her finest silks and was driven to the offices of the *Sergeant de Ville* in the sumptuous Roland carriage. An hour later, she was returning along the same avenues in a towering rage.

Her documents of proof, sworn affidavits by responsible agents, detailed records of her long search for the murderer, all had been regarded by the dolts in charge of enforcing the law as virtual tinsel. Having newly taken over Louisiana Territory, the United States had little interest in events which had taken place there a quarter-century ago and under the flag of a different nation. They had no desire to take up matters both France and Spain long since had shelved. Surely Mrs. Roland could appreciate this position? They had many more pressing matters at hand than a dubious police raid on the bayous? There was no longer, properly speaking, even such a title as *Sergeant de Ville*. His successor had other concerns.

"They'll live to regret it!" she was muttering as she stormed back into her mansion. "I'll find the way to knock them off their high perches, if it takes a decade!"

But meanwhile there was Roger Bernard to be taken care of.

"I'll do it myself, if the police won't do their simple duty. I have some respect for justice, if they have none!"

Faced with her fury, Anton registered only alarm.

"Mother, be sensible! If we hire such a lynch party, the shrimpers will *certainly* discover who sent it. We'll lose the fleet for sure."

"Don't tell your mother to be sensible, boy. My sensibleness has tripled the estate your Wellington grandfather left to me. And improved on Antoine's shrewd deals, too."

"But now you're letting emotion run the show. It will trip you like a wire across your path. You'll only live to regret it."

"One more such word out of you, Anton Roland, and it's you who'll live to regret it. I have another son, please remember. I can always alter my will. Would you like to be cut out of it altogether?"

The occasional city newspapers brought home by Christophe and Roger-Claude remained a consolation to Marie. Because of the debacle in which her sixteenth birthday expedition had ended, she had yet to personally explore New Orleans. But printed accounts of city doings served to draw that imagined Xanadu at least somewhat into the realm of reality for her.

She read every line of them, although sometimes the process had to occupy several days because of the press of housework. Annette, of course, did as much in that department as was possible. But with her elder son René a toddler and her younger Gils beginning to creep and a third about due to be born, Roger-Claude's wife had enough on her hands. Most of the everyday load devolved upon Marie's young shoulders.

On the odd evening, however, or during one of those brief daytime intervals when a gumbo on the stove was cooking, she could lose herself in a page or two. It was one day while the boys were off at market that she came upon the week-old article, a brief paragraph only, buried among funeral reports on the very last page: PERCY ROLAND IS ACCORDED HONOR. Had a small-print heading not caught her eye, she might have missed it altogether.

Percy Roland . . . How often, although strictly in silence, she had remembered that name! Perhaps the loneliness of bayou life was partly responsible, but he had become an obsession to her.

Daily contact with Christophe would have made it impossible for Marie to forget Percy's physical image, in any event. More, she had her memory of a pleasant and kindly youth who really seemed to care about her—even more than her brothers, who were fond of her yet always put their shrimping first.

The Percy Roland so often in her thoughts was her surrogate knight in shining armor. Marie had totally believed, with a chill in her blood, the grim words Roger-Claude had spoken at her back in the *pirogue* heading home. *"You wouldn't like to see him dead, this Roland? If you ever again speak a word to him . . ."* Roger-Claude had been deeply in earnest. Never since that night had she dared even mention Percy Roland's name aloud; but neither had she ever again been able to love her younger brother in the wholehearted way she had loved him once.

The brief news item depicted what was for Marie a major world event. Percy, it seemed, had written a book about everyday life in his city. It had been published by a firm apparently well-thought-of, although such names all were foreign to her own limited experience. The book was receiving laudatory notices, and now some sort of literary prize had come its way. How proud Percy must be of that! And how proud she felt for him!

She ached to write him a brief message of congratulations. But the only way at hand to have such a thing delivered in the city was to entrust it to a brother. She well understood what their reaction would be. Instead of well-meant praise, the author would probably be awarded a challenge to a fist fight; or, if Roger-Claude called the tune, even worse.

Stifling her impulse, Marie instead carefully clipped out the paragraph and pinned it to the inner side of her bed's calico skirt ruffle. Here no one else in the household could dream it existed. Alone in her tiny room at night, she could take it out and pore over it in safety. As for the despoiled newspaper, it was an old one anyway. She wrapped fish guts in it and threw it away. The square hole in its final page was never noticed.

And, despite the rift with her brothers, loyal little Marie felt happy over the steadily increasing success of the shrimping combine. Papa had organized it and still headed it forcefully. Christophe and Roger-Claude, as his delegates, were doing splendid work at building up the fishing fleet. With every passing season, more of the shrimpers were joining. Praise for what the Bernard leadership was accomplishing for them spread through the parishes of the French Triangle like Saint Elmo's Fire, from Alexandria south to the Gulf, from Lake Ponchartrain west to the Cajun prairie and Texas.

Such news couldn't bring much pleasure to the Rolands in New Orleans, though, not if the Bernard brothers were to be believed. Their glee at word of

Roland pique on frequent visits to the city was reported to and fully shared by Papa.

Rocking on the high porch, making his endless guidelines for his neighbors' well-being, Papa Roger was (one had to admit it) guilty of the sin of gloating. His hearty laugh was every bit the equal of Christophe's or Roger-Claude's when they discussed some new discomfiture to those Rolands so set upon buying into the combine. Sweeping Roland plans such as one to construct a fine fleet of refrigerated ships, which would distribute Louisiana shrimp all up and down the coastline, were hooted down lustily in these family sessions.

"The little Princeling was at us again today, Papa."

"Was he indeed? What nonsense did he try to palm off on you this time?"

"A threat to press crippling new regulations on shrimp-taking through the next legislature, unless we accept a partnership."

"What did you say to the pompous little prig, sons?"

"We told him to take his regulations and shove 'em where nothing's meant by nature to be shoved, Papa. Little Lord Anton thought it was very crude of us. He like to exploded."

"And what about his Mama?"

Although no one seemed quite certain how, Roger seemed to be well acquainted with the true pecking order of the Roland clan. Supposedly, he never had laid eyes on Widow Amanda. Yet once, for some reason Marie now forgot, he had given a detailed description of the noted beauty while bloated with twins in her belly. It had the boys slapping their thighs. Another time, Papa had warned his sons, quite seriously, that the aging lady was the one really to be watched: the spider sitting at the center of the Roland web—and weaving a poisonous trap.

"Mrs. Roland just had to take our answer, too, Papa. Same as her whipping boy."

"Sometimes I kind of pity Anton Roland. I hear she's even set up a marriage for her obedient heir. Some snip of a debutante called Charlotte Vandtour. The girl's *grosse* already. At least Anton must have got her pregnant without Mama standing by the bed and telling 'em how."

"Maybe Anton mistook this Charlotte girl for a shrimp boat and boarded her unawares," Roger-Claude suggested.

A gale of merriment rang out along the porch.

Sitting quietly in her corner, Marie yearned to cry out a protest.

"Mrs. Roland has another heir, too! Why does everyone always forget about Percy? He's won a famous prize with a fine book, hasn't he? He's the son *I'd* be the proudest of!"

Of course she kept such words unspoken, bottled deep inside her. That aborted trip to New Orleans had made deep changes in her. She was no longer the impulsive, stubborn girl who once might have blurted out a rash opinion on anything under family discussion. Roger-Claude's remembered words had put an end to that.

"I'm making you a promise, Marie."

The two long *pirogues* streaked quickly through the bayou night, as silent as alligators on the prowl. Each carried five men in it, and each man carried a rifle. Since shortly after their departure from the Forbes levee, outside New Orleans, there had been little conversation among them.

Now there was none at all. They were a hard-faced crew, each man with eyes to which pity was a total stranger. These were the very qualities for which Amanda Roland had hired them. Their pay was tripled. That was all they had to know.

Although most of them were citybred even the eerie quality of the swamps at midnight held no particular fear for them. Almost literally, there was not a nerve to a boatload. Except for those throbbing now in Percy's body.

For Percy, the long evening had been one continued stretching of every fiber in him. In the first place, he had stumbled upon his mother's intentions for the Bernard family quite by accident. If Anton's excited protest had not been so loud that it lifted clear to the bedroom where Percy sat writing polite notes of gratitude to various critics who had spoken well of *My Own Queen City*, he might never have known what was afoot.

"Mother, it's madness! I've said it before. I say it again. It's madness!"

"You dare tell your mother she's a lunatic, boy?"

"Mother, please! I don't mean disrespect. You know how devotedly I've admired you. Always, all my life. But *this* is mass slaughter!"

"If the other Bernards keep out of range of the gunfire, they won't be hurt."

"You know that's not how it can possibly happen. They aren't just going to take cover and watch the old man ripped to ribbons. They'll go for their own guns. There'll be a battle royal. I know how little you care about any of them, even the womenfolk, but—"

"Why *should* I care, Anton? Which Bernard protested when my husband was assassinated?"

"As I've read in our agents' reports, most of the present family weren't even born when Father died. You can't blame an unborn generation."

"How humane you've suddenly become, my son! You'll soon go as soft as Percy."

"It isn't humaneness, Mother. It's business. I wouldn't care if every Bernard in shoeleather stretched out in a grave. But we Rolands mustn't bear the blame. Can't you see what such publicity can do to us? Every firm we deal with or run will turn against us. We'll be pariahs. Decent folk will no longer bow to us in the street."

"Folk will bow very pleasantly indeed, Anton, as long as Rolands stay in the saddle. Have I asked you to take any part in tonight's affair?"

"No, no, but I'm bound to be implicated."

"Go sit in your own drawing room and hold hands with Charlotte and coo about your coming infant. You'll have a perfect alibi. I will attend to the whole matter. My men are hired. They leave unnoticed from the Forbes levee at eleven, when no one's about. What happens to the Bernards is no concern of yours."

Appalled at what he just had heard, Percy sat rigid at his writing table for several moments after a door below slammed, cutting off the angry voices. Then he sprang desperately to his feet and rushed downstairs in what amounted to a frenzy.

He knew better than to reopen the study door and try to talk sense to his mother. Anton already had failed in that. Whatever was to be done must be done by himself. Who else was there?

From the family stable he led out and saddled his
own spirited chestnut riding mare, Antigone. Leading
her carefully, lest she arouse the household, he guided
her a half-block along the quiet avenue before he
dared swing atop her. Only now, as he headed her
toward the Forbes levee and telltale sound ceased to
be important, did he apply a whip to her.

A startled Antigone, entirely unfamiliar with whips,
leaped into action like an uncorked hurricane. Percy
had believed he knew his gentle four-footed riding
companion, but he found himself clinging aboard a
stranger. He was as glad for her runaway speed, however, as he was that he'd remembered to strap his
father's old duelling pistols to his waist, one at either
side.

The night rushed on while his heart stood still for
fear he was already too late. The thud of Antigone's
hoofbeats was a pounding of war drums gone wild.
He saw streets hurdle past in a sick blur, and then
open country.

Somewhere in the sleeping city the clock in a church
steeple began striking eleven doleful, measured strokes.
Eleven o'clock, Mother had said!

Up the landside of the Forbes embankment the
chestnut flung herself, still at a gallop. On murky water
below, two motionless craft were silently filling with
armed crews. Percy recognized their leader. He was
a Scot named Tom McAfee who before now had done
work for Amanda Roland, none of it particularly rep-
utable. Arm-breaking and bludgeoning, that was the
McAfee style.

"McAfee!" Percy shouted, as he vaulted from the
saddle and let Antigone race on.

The man at the water's edge glanced upward. "Ah! It's Master Percy."

"I'm glad I caught you in time," panted Percy, as he slid down the bank. "Mother has made a change in plan. She says one of us, Anton or me, is to go with you. There's a personal greeting of sorts she wants delivered by hand to the Bernards."

A cynical grin split McAfee's scarred lips.

"Wants family along to check that the job's done proper, does she? But there's no room in either boat for another man, Master Percy."

"One of the crew is to be sent back. He'll be paid at the office tomorrow, same wages as the rest. Which one of them can you best spare, McAfee?"

"Well, let's see. There's Legros yonder. He's oldest, and maybe slowest on the draw."

"Get him out of the boat, then, man. I'll take his seat."

Now, a good time later, the *pirogues* were well toward the end of their journey. In the place he had commandeered, Percy still hunched as immobilized as a carved Buddah. To him alone of all of them, the black water through which the two craft nosed was atremble with coming disaster.

Unsuspecting human beings were about to be ambushed and cut down like cattle in an abattoir, at his own mother's order. One of those people was Marie.

How often he had remembered that dark-eyed, eager, vivacious girl since that long-past day when they had met so fleetingly at the marketplace. He wouldn't have believed it possible that so brief an encounter could produce so enduring a memory. Yet he never had quite been able to banish the fetching picture of her from his mind. He could see her tonight, on his way with men bent on shooting her down, almost as vividly as if they just had parted.

How was he to stop the butchery? He had known at the Forbes levee that McAfee never would accept his own order to scrub the mission. That would take a direct personal command from Mother. McAfee was a crafty fox, and keen. He'd have seen through any such scheme in jig time. Probably he'd have knocked its perpetrator senseless and delivered him back home trussed up like a Christmas goose. The only plan Percy had been able to devise on the run was to stow away in person.

Now they were very near the Bernard dwelling. He didn't know the lay of this land himself but he could tell from silent signals McAfee was giving his men, and from their answer in readied rifles, that time had run out. All through the ghostly trip, he'd hit upon no answer.

High on the bank ahead, lamplight in a single window-square swung into view. A dark line of roof jutted above a porch and walls. Down by the water, huddled shadows suggested a boatshed. Ancient trees stood sentry along the stream's edge; useless sentries, tonight. Moss wavered on a faint breeze, like tattered lace.

The two *pirogues* veered noiselessly shoreward.

That anguished memory of Marie Bernard clicked into taunting place before Percy's eyes. Dark, happy eyes. Delicate hands, clutching a cat. A red mouth which could smile enchantingly, pout delightfully. A small, slender body with ripening curves. Ten minutes from now, she would be lying bleeding to death on her father's floor.

He felt a hot lump in his throat and feared he would

vomit. Such sounds would enrage McAfee. But they'd
not be loud enough to travel the remaining distance.
Those indoors would remain unwarned.

The lead *pirogue*, not Percy's own, dug its nose
gently into streambank mud.

Five almost shapeless forms arose from it and
stepped ashore, as quietly as ghosts might step. Even
with his gaze fixed on them in terror, Percy could
detect not the slightest crumb of betraying sound.
Still disembodied souls more than real men, the figures
separated to surround the house.

The Bernards were to be fallen upon from all sides
in one engulfing death wave, that was clear. In such
sordid business, McAfee was a master general. He had
it figured to the last gunshot, the last twitch and kick
of the last riddled body.

God, help me! Please!

Percy scarcely knew how one of his father's handsome duelling weapons found its way from belt to
hand. Its abrupt bark, spitting a lead pellet high
among the branches overhead, was his first conscious warning that he held a gun at all.

The sharp sound shattered silence as a bolt of lightning might. Cursing, McAfee whirled toward it.

"You son-of-a-bitch dunderhead!"

"It shot itself, McAfee. I was tugging it loose. It
just went off."

Whatever the cause, the low house above them was
no longer a haven of sleeping peace. To the rear of
the building, out of sight, a back door crashed open.
Someone—no, more than one—was bursting out into
open darkness, screened by crowding underbrush,
scattering.

Realization that he had indeed alerted the sleeping

household burst over Percy like the comprehension of a miracle. And what was he doing now? Why, he was sprinting up the slope like an antelope, shouting crazy words across a sudden blaze of gunfire.

"Stay away from windows, Marie! Don't show yourself! Get down on the floor!"

Behind him, McAfee howled like a maniac.

Wasps that were really molded bullets whizzed from those bushes bordering the house. One of the ghost forms half up the bank screamed and spun and crashed back toward the water. Another clutched at his waistline and crumpled where he stood. A third and a fourth fired back in fury. Whether or not either found a target in the inky murk, who was to say? There had been no wail up ahead, no cry.

The bullet ripping into Percy came not from the house but from the water's edge. McAfee's rifle still smoked as its target pitched forward onto his face in the grass.

"Damn little sneak traitor!" McAfee knew the total score. That crap about his pistol was a cowardly lie. It had been done a-purpose. He'd *meant* to wake the cabin before the encirclement could get in place.

Boss Lady's own brat had screwed her!

He was dead enough now; but she'd ought to have smothered the miscreant in his cradle and save herself all this. Look what was happening now! The whole clearing was a shambles.

"Are they gone, Roger-Claude?" Annette whimpered, where she lay by the stove.

"All that ain't pushing daisies, honey." Roger-Claude knelt alongside, studying her anxiously. "There's four corpses on the bank still to be coped with."

"But the second boat? There was two, weren't there?"

"It hadn't yet unloaded. It just turned back down the bayou and skedaddled. Faster than it sneaked in, I'll warrant."

"I wonder who fired the shot that wakened us all?" She stirred on the floor, moaning a little. "If not for that, we'd all be gone by now. The babies, too."

"One of the bastards was drunk, I guess. Or toted a faulty rifle. Who knows?"

"None of our family's been . . . ? I mean, Papa Roger? Christophe? Marie? The little ones?"

"All present and accounted for. The children are fine. Christophe took a slug in one shoulder, but Marie's working to patch up that. Papa hasn't a scratch."

"You—you went down the slope to look, didn't you? Are they really all dead?"

"Every man of 'em. Dead as their own tombstones. And guess who led the wolf pack against us? None less than the she-spider's spawn himself! Come to suck Bernard blood!"

"The man you and Christophe call Little Lord Anton?"

"Not him. The Roland brother leading them. The one that was such a spit for Christophe. Don't you fret, he won't be coming to do in any Bernard ever again. He's dead as a bullet can make a man."

She moaned again. "Which one—whose gun?"

"Might be Chris, might be me, might be Papa. Whoever got him, it was in the back. The varmint must have lost his nerve and turned to run. No other way for a back to be a target."

"Oooooh!" Annette clenched her lips desperately. "I hurt so! I hurt so!"

"Baby lamb, you weren't hit. I just looked you over. What's wrenching you so?"

"It's—nothing. I'll be all right in a minute. Roger-Claude, how are we going to tell Marie who it was brought those men here?"

"Just say the words, I reckon. Simple enough. No cause to grieve over a Roland."

She shook her head weakly. "Don't you know? Don't you even know that Marie's always, ever since that day in town, pinned on her bedskirt, to read over and over—" Suddenly she stiffened. "Roger-Claude, help me! Please! I hurt so, Roger-Claude!"

Her husband was on his feet in the instant, bellowing like a bull.

"Papa! Christophe! Somebody! Get out the *pirogue*. I'll carry her. We've got to get her to Cousin Sylvie almighty quick. Christ Jesus, Annette's baby's in trouble!"

a marauding
of course.
who dwelt
uced—in
be de-
urder-

uble
him.
her
d,

15

So FAR as Amanda Roland was concerned, the bayou failure amounted to a cataclysm. Although she would be the last person to admit she might be vulnerable, Percy's upsetting death very nearly had destroyed her. The whole horror of it was incredible. Percy had been safe up in his bedroom, diddling with silly verses or whatever. He hadn't even known the expedition was to be undertaken. How he had become part of it she could not imagine.

McAfee might have solved the riddle. But McAfee, like Percy, was no longer available to answer questions. The cursed Bernards had mowed him down along with several of his handpicked men. Summoned police had found him half in and half out of the bayou water, with a bullet in his head. Even more disgust-

ingly, sections of him had been lost to
alligator.

The police had identified Percy instantly
New Orleans people knew every Roland
within the city limits. It could only be ded
desperation, Amanda herself even helped it
duced—that her son had led a hired posse for n
ous purposes.

Poor, gentle Percy! But it scarcely would tr
him now to have blame for the attack laid on
She gave him a magnificent funeral, to show
motherly forbearance of a wayward son's misdee
no matter what it might be.

Then she proceeded to blacken his defenseless
reputation with every innuendo at hand.

"My son was an emotional young man," she told
the police captain, stately in her black crepe and her
mourning veil. "He aspired to become an author, you
know. Writing men are, I fear, apt to become unstable."

"You believe, then, that he alone inspired this
raid?"

"In some way, the dear boy's brain just snapped."

"Why should he lose his reason in this particular
fashion, ma'am? Going clear up the bayou like that
with two boatloads of paid killers? Clearly meaning
to wipe out a household of folks he didn't even know
by sight?"

How fortunate McAfee was no longer on hand to
be subpoenaed as a witness! "You make him sound
absolutely barbarous, Captain. My Percy was gentle,
the poor, poor boy."

"Nothing all that gentle about organizing nine hired

guns, if I may say so, Mrs. Roland. Four deaths. And one intended victim wounded."

"I wish you'd known my darling personally, Captain. He wouldn't have hurt a rabbit." And they were safely away from that one terrifying line on which the inquiry might all too easily have developed. They had not asked whether bad blood existed between Rolands and Bernards.

Should the Captain ever interest himself in *that* angle, too many mongers at the shrimp market might have come forward with damning testimony. It was well known there that Mrs. Antoine Roland had schemed for years to buy into the Bernard fleet interests. And it was no secret that the Bernard boys had frustrated her.

Through the funeral, and through the official investigation, Anton was a tower of strength. Not a single private reproach. Not a single I-told-you-so. And of course he had been quite right in their disagreement, she saw that clearly now. The family reputation *had* been put to dangerous risk. The chances of disaster *had* been too numerous. If she had been thinking clearly, she never would have committed company forces so recklessly.

But she had not been thinking clearly. Hatred for Roger Bernard had warped her reasoning. So the whole awful thing was Roger Bernard's fault, really.

How could she go on letting him live, that personification of evil? Yet there must be no second mass attack. It was enraging how every circumstance seemed to conspire to protect him. The loyalty of his shrimpers. Governmental changes involving an entire vast Territory. Even Percy.

For two weeks visiting cards inscribed "With Sympathy" kept pouring in. Then the flood dwindled. Sensational though the insane outburst of a Roland hitherto considered mild had been, other scandals arrived to elbow it out of the limelight.

Amanda began to relax a little. Her company was weathering disaster after all. The Roland ship of state still floated serenely, no stigma adhering to the bereaved mother at its helm.

This was when Anton found himself able to leave Charlotte and their adored little John alone for an evening and drive around to keep his mother company.

She was delighted to see him. That empty room upstairs which had been Percy's did weigh on Amanda. The servants moved about with such soft-footed consideration for her sorrow that often it seemed the whole big house was deserted, except for her own badly shaken self. Although one might realize that half Anton's filial concern was based on a healthy regard for the terms of her will, one could still be grateful for it. Amanda greeted him with uncommon warmth.

"How good of you, darling! I know you hate leaving your darlings."

"It's important for me to be with you, Mother. We have much to discuss."

She led the way to Antoine's study. "Sherry, son? Something stronger perhaps?"

"Nothing, thank you." He crossed to the liqueur cabinet. "Shall I pour for you?"

Seated in a favorite chair, facing the fireplace and thus the remembered countenance of the portrait above it, she accepted a *soupçon* of port in cut crystal. Turning it slowly between her ring-heavy fingers, she watched the ruby glint of the fine prisms. Her sigh at least approached contentment.

"I think we're really out of the woods, Anton. And let me admit that I know now I did a very foolish thing. I should have listened to you, instead of proceeding on my own."

"You should indeed, Mother. You very nearly scuttled our company."

She had not expected Anton to agree quite so flatly. She looked across at him in faint surprise. He stood before the brass grate, hands behind him, studying her.

"We all but went under because of your rash insistence," he was saying. It was not at all the tone of the subservient son and adjutant she believed she had raised.

"Anton!"

"If I had not taken the police off our necks, we might be facing bankruptcy. Not to mention a stiff prison sentence for yourself. What you did wasn't attempted murder. It was open warfare."

Amanda felt herself stiffening. Her diamonds glittered. "Don't take more credit than you deserve, Anton. It was I, remember, who handled the Captain."

"You really think so? He wasn't misled by your show of maternal grief for a single moment, dear Mother. He came around to quiz Charlotte and me direct from his interview with you. He may seem slow, but he's not an idiot. He'd already checked out the firm who published *My Own Queen City*. People there knew Percy well. What they had to say about him was at direct odds with the misdirection you tried to feed him."

A cold chill gripped her.

"What did he say to you, Anton? I'm sure I convinced him that no one else in our family had the least connection with the Bernard affair."

"What he said, Mother, was that the publishers had convinced him Percy was quite sane and entirely incapable of heading such an expedition. He wanted to know if we—if you, in particular—ever had formed any inimical connection with the Bernard family. He wanted to know why that one particular household had been picked out for elimination."

"Why should he imagine it was anything but chance?"

"During his not-at-all dimwitted investigations, he'd come across stories that Father and Roger Bernard came from the same village in Nova Scotia. Also, that you are on record as once having attempted to obtain Bernard's arrest for Father's murder. Disinterested though the present regime is in pursuing that, they do keep records of complaints."

Amanda's hand trembled uncontrollably. A bit of the port spilled over.

"My God! The bland little fellow was all 'ma'ams' and 'Mrs. Rolands,' as meek as a kitchen mouse. Why, he deliberately *led* me on to speak ill of Percy!"

"Indeed he did. And he was most interested in how easily Percy's mother could take the bait. In fact, the word he used to Charlotte and me was 'unnatural.' What he had begun wondering was whether there might be some undisclosed private reason for Percy's being on the bayou that night: such as that his mother had coerced him into leading the raiders as her deputy."

Eyes wide, she stared at her son.

"You know that's not true, Anton. How Percy discovered the men were going at all is beyond me. But it wasn't through me. I never told him."

"How did he know? Because you and I didn't shut the study door in time, earlier that evening. Our voices were loud. We were quarreling, remember. That's immaterial, though. What matters to the company is that I've sidetracked him. We're out of the woods, yes. But not because of you."

"You must have done something extraordinary. You've never mentioned it."

"What I did wouldn't have pleased you at all, Mother. I convinced him that you are suffering from frequent little mental breakdowns yourself. He now believes that for weeks before the attack Charlotte and I had been with you constantly, nursing you through one of those 'spells.' We could vouch that you'd had no opportunity to hire a crew of hoodlums, even if you were so inclined. He finally believed us because a pair of our own servants backed up our story of being here and away from our own home during the emergency. The bribes I had to pay those two made deep holes in my pocket."

"I must repay you, naturally. I'll draw you a bank draft tomorrow."

"That isn't quite the repayment I have in mind, Mother. I wasn't exactly lying to the Captain, was I? You *are* just a bit off-base mentally, aren't you? This obsession about Roger Bernard has truly impaired your reasoning. That's disastrous for the company. The time has come to protect it by a few basic changes in the management."

Amanda sensed the answer, but she spoke the question. "What changes, Anton?"

"You must turn over the chairmanship to me, immediately. For appearances sake, you may remain on the board in a nominal advisory capacity. But from today on, the decisions must be mine. As you can see, your own have all but wrecked us."

Her mouth opened, shut, opened again, before she could speak.

"You insolent puppy! We'll see who's in control once I change my will. Everything goes in trust for John."

"I'm sure my son would be flattered, Mother, if he were old enough to speak the word money or knew what it meant. But you won't alter your will. If you attempt to, I'll instigate a legal challenge to your sanity. I have persuasive witnesses on my side—my two housemaids, perhaps even the good Police Captain. How would you enjoy a public hearing?"

"Damn you, Anton Roland! Rather than hand over my life's work to you—"

"Please don't make wild threats, Mother. They're undignified and I've always been able to admire you for your regal presence. Then too, I have other arrows in my quiver. If by any chance a court declared you competent despite contrary evidence, I could then present tangible evidence that you alone had underwritten the bayou raid. Instead of remanding you to a silly farm, the law would send you to the gallows."

"What . . . tangible . . . evidence?"

"Why, the envelope, dearest Mother. Remember the money envelope? The one on which is written, in your own distinguished hand, *McAfee: To be distributed among men after completion of Bernard assignment, equal shares*"?

She surged to her feet, meeting his smirk with a blaze of hatred.

"How do you know about that envelope, you devil?
You had nothing to do with it! You never even saw it!"

"Not until quite recently, no. But having studied
your business methods over so many years, I guessed
there had to be one. So I paid a condolence call on
Tom McAfee's widow. She blames you for McAfee's
death, Mother. She's quite ready to testify to that in
court. And she was more than willing to sell me the
envelope, as long as I let her keep everything in it."

For considerable time after a departing Anton closed
the front door behind him, Amanda stood motionless
in the Roland mansion's superb hallway and glared at
the blank panel. Her son might have attacked her
physically and done less damage.

He was carrying away with him everything in her
world that she ever loved: the mighty family company she had built up with her own brain and hands,
on the modest foundation of Antoine's holdings. Even
those foundations had been financed by her dowry
from her father. The company was hers, hers, hers! His
tricks in wresting it from her were sheer blackmail.

In the stunned aftermath of his smug revelations,
she had been unable to withstand signing documents
of abdication he had forced upon her. He was carrying in his pocket, having obtained it through ugly
trickery, a legal hold on everything she valued. He
would be laughing in his carriage all the way home to
the treacherous Charlotte and their brat.

Charlotte! Means would have to be found to make
Charlotte suffer, too. Were it not for her mother-in-
law, Miss Charlotte Vandtour would never be sitting
so cozily in a Roland parlor which was almost an equal
of the one in the mansion itself. Only she, Amanda, had
brought about that socially desirable marriage in the

first place. Left to his own gross preferences, Anton would have followed his father's path to the whore-houses.

"I'll tend to you, Charlotte! And I'll tend to Anton as well!"

But the muttered threat held a hollow ring. Her precious son had left her hamstrung, cheated of the power of the company, utterly impotent. She'd not even been able to sign a bank draft at the office, unless Anton countersigned to make it valid. He might as well have clamped leg irons on her and locked her up in a dungeon cell.

There was still her personal bank account, true. That was separate from the company funds. It was not over-large, but it was adequate for a lone widow and a quietly run town house. Anton expected her to lead the rest of her life on that pittance.

Well, he'd find out, he'd find out. . . .

After a long while, still quivering with the new hate she felt against her most unnatural offspring, she began to climb the curving staircase. Earlier today, she would have swept up it like an Empress. Tonight she moved like a spent old drab, too tired to do anything but drag one foot after the other. She was exhausted and yearning for her bed.

Once that fine bed had been the sports field on which she and Antoine had played games she gloried to remember. Now, it was even more—a safe retreat. Even Anton could scarcely pursue her there with his obscene cleverness.

It was a wicked thing for a dutiful mother to have to face, ingratitude from her own tit-fed children. Antoine's twins were raised like the young kinglets she had sacrificed to make of them: every advantage at hand, every comfort or luxury provided. She had asked little in return. Only their loyalty. Only their reasonable assistance in her great adventure.

And what had they given her instead? Percy—a wishy-washy nothing, lost amid his silly writings. Anton—blackly treasonous, plotting cold-blooded self-aggrandizement.

Closing her sanctum door behind her, she moved heavily to the business of lighting lamps. For her, the lights of all the world had just spluttered out. Still, one must go through the motions. Where was that useless lady's maid Lucy? Never at hand when one required her!

She unhooked her brocade gown without assistance and let it puddle on the carpet where it slid from her. She jerked out restraining pins until her still thick and glossy hair uncoiled across her bare shoulders like Medusa's snakes. Lucy should be here to brush it out for her, to massage her shoulders.

Naked, she turned to face the gilt pier mirror sent over long ago as a wedding present from the cousinly Earl's London palace. Once she had admired the figure she saw reflected there. It still was erect and reasonably slender. Antoine would not have turned away from it in disgust. Yet it no longer stirred pride in her. Not tonight.

Who was left to care whether or not the mark of her early beauty was still strong on her? She was finished. She was dead. In a walking corpse, beauty was unimportant.

The figure in the long glass suddenly began to shake with laughter. A thought which just had occurred to her was so macabre it could make even a dead woman laugh.

This wasn't her own reflection here, staring back at her. This wasn't herself at all. Why, her *true* reflection had just closed the front door behind him downstairs in the hall. He was male, he was not particularly good-looking except in a serviceable, sturdy way, yet whenever she looked at him she was looking at herself. Until this minute she never had realized it, but what she saw in any looking glass was really Anton.

"Welcome back inside me, my fetus!" she mocked aloud. "You've been there right along, haven't you? Never born. Never set free on your own. You're me, always me, still me."

Understanding this seemed to make all the difference. She could feel strength and vigor flowing back into her. Good for Anton! She could have maneuvered his villainies no better herself. The thing to put her mind to now was how to checkmate him.

An hour short of noon next day, she was arriving on foot at the office of a modest but well-regarded auditor toward the far end of Bourbon Street.

She had walked here, in contradiction to her usual habits, because someone might have spotted the familiar Roland carriage waiting at a curb and have later mentioned it to Anton. Her son was to have no advance hint of what might soon be rising against him.

"So kind of you to arrange to see me on short notice, Mr. Rodrigue," she purred, having been gallantly seated across from the financial man's desk. She lifted her veil and threw it back, to give him full benefit of two eyes once widely compared to stars.

"An honor, Madam. We don't often receive a Roland in our premises."

"I'll come right to the point, Mr. Rodrique. I visit you after deep consideration, and only because I'm

assured you are the most trustworthy gentleman in
New Orleans."

"Too kind of you to say so."

"As you see, I am no longer a young woman, sir. I
have recently made a decision to retire from our family
business and pass along my crown to my able son
Anton."

"You've indeed raised remarkable sons, Madam. I
was much impressed by the literary kudos won recently by Mr. Percy Roland. But you must not consider
retirement. You're still a young and vigorous—"

She let a wan hand gesture.

"No flattery, please, Mr. Rodrigue. You must have
been a boy in pantaloons the season I was a debutante. I've now reached an age quite beyond compliments. I am determined to withdraw from business
affairs. But I do still care very much for the future of
the company I've brought to its present prosperity.
I must be quite *sure*."

"Sure, you mean, of the abilities of your successor?"

"Anton has never disappointed me. Not until just
lately. But a certain unpleasant rumor has recently
been brought to my attention which—well, although
it pains a mother to say so, it does raise some doubt.
That's why I've come to you. For confidential aid."

"Whatever Rodrigue and Associates can do, we are
at your entire service. What you wish, as I understand
it, is to have this rumor thoroughly investigated. Correct, Madam?"

"Oh, nothing quite so definite as that, dear Mr.
Rodrigue. Just a quiet probe into whatever Anton may
have been up to that would not meet the standards of
people like you or me. Anything you might uncover
I'd like to have brought to my attention. If he is not

worthy to head the honorable Roland interests, I shall find means to deal with that. The means, sir, would of course be much assisted by any concrete proofs of a misdoing."

"I entirely understand, dear Mrs. Roland. Let us hope your son is as high-minded as yourself. But if not, I promise you no stone will be left unturned."

Leaving the Rodrigue office, she had her veil again lowered to mask the smile of satisfaction curving her lips. If she knew Anton, there would be plenty for a competent investigator to lay bare. Fodder for counter-blackmail, although she fastidiously rejected that unpleasant word.

She felt completely confident. Anton was herself, after all, was he not? Her other self?

It was regrettable that the thoroughness of Casimir Rodrigue's investigations was not duplicated by any notable speed. She had received no word from Bourbon Street other than meticulous assurances that her man was steadily at work; those, and the expected bills for his retainers.

If Amanda were not quite sure of her man, she might almost have suspected she was being milked.

But that possibility she forced herself to dismiss as unworthy of her own sharp judgment. She'd had Rodrigue himself checked out by other sources. He came up lily-white, simon-pure.

So there was nothing to be done but to wait. Wait and chafe under the daily presence of Anton in possession. Wait and seethe and cover her true emotions like the proverbial light under the bushel. Wait and smile and pretend to have submitted to the inevitable.

Almost as difficult to bear were frequent evidences

around New Orleans of Roger Bernard's continuing successes.

The man seemed altogether incapable of making a false move. He himself now owned several of the boats of the shrimp fleet he represented. Each one was captained either by some Bernard relation or else by a far-too-well-paid employee. Turned loose upon the city with his notions as to how workers under one should be remunerated, her mortal foe well might bankrupt half the financial institutions in Louisiana. It was a God's mercy he seemed content to confine his radical activities to shrimping.

Payments to Rodrigue restricted her present modest personal finances. She found herself unable to underwrite more investigators, in the slim hope of catching out Bernard in a malfeasance. Her expenses in maintaining a suitable social facade were far too draining. But she was still able to keep some sort of loose track on the family McAfee had failed to eliminate. Informal reports did filter in to her from time to time.

The unmarried son, she learned, was no longer unmarried. And for this, her own ill-fated raid on the bayou seemed to be responsible. Young Christophe Bernard had been wounded in the fighting. Family members had rushed him to a female relative back somewhere in the swamps. This *traiteur*, known as Cousin Sylvie, the stories suggested, was some sort of a sorceress at her voodoo or whatever the pagan mumbo jumbo might be termed. Witch doctoress or no, she had cured her relation's wound in jig time. During his visits to her shack for treatment, beginning with the very first one, he had met a Cajun girl also under the *traiteur*'s care. She was called Dorothée, and was the daughter of an oyster fisherman named Trahan. There had been a proper courtship. More recently, there had been a modest wedding in the new church at Houma.

Follow-ups on the matter included reports on the appropriate arrivals of one baby, then another. This was a new cause of bitterness to Amanda. Why did those villainous Bernards flourish, while the meager Roland line either met untimely deaths or went rotten? Thank fortune there was still John!

He was turning out a really personable boy, was her grandson, with some pretension to looks, although he would never become a second Antoine, which she once had felt Percy might. As to character, she could only pray little John might escape the blight of his unscrupulous father!

Nothing presaged the long-awaited day of triumph when at last it came. Amanda was merely sitting in the study in idleness, which always irked her, when Wadham, the butler, announced a caller.

"A Mr. Casimir Rodrigue, Madam. Do you wish to receive him?"

"Show him in at once, Wadham." Suddenly, her heart was pounding. "Then close the door. We will be carrying on a private discussion. Keep the staff away, please."

And here he was, crossing the threshold, her expensive and discreet Mr. Rodrigue. Since he could not have come to dun her, wild hopes lit in her to set her blood racing.

"A very good day to you, Mrs. Roland."

He was as respectful as ever before.

"I trust it will prove a good day, Mr. Rodrigue. What have you brought me?"

From the somewhat battered leather *etui* he carried

with him, her accountant began producing neatly arranged papers. They made an encouraging little pile on his knee as he sat in the secondary chair to which she had waved him.

"I regret, Madam, that I must bring you bad news indeed. All carefully documented, as you requested should be done."

Her heart sank, then leaped again. Bad news for her, as he would term whatever those files might prove against Anton, was her idea of excellent news indeed. "Well, man?"

"Are you acquainted with the name Jean Lafitte, Madam?"

By now, who in New Orleans wasn't? But Amanda continued to present a placid face. It might be unwise to admit any personal knowledge of that daring pirate with headquarters somewhere on the Bayou, at a place called Barataria. Every tongue in the city gossiped about his blatant raids on Spanish shipping. All the *ton* jabbered over his thieves' market, where one might purchase almost any luxury at an appetizing discount. (It was widely known that Lafitte's renegades seemed seldom to be disturbed by police attention, which was odd indeed.)

Jean Lafitte, eh? But she kept her answer vague.

"I believe I've heard the name, sir."

"Then perhaps you have also heard that the ruffian operates under the protection of certain influential men in our own city? Men who share the profits of his piracy? It grieves me to upset you, Madam, but I have learned your son Anton is one of them."

She leaned forward eagerly. "And you bring me *proof* of this?"

"Undeniable proof, though I regret having to display it to an honorable mother. Now this first paper here, this is a signed and sworn affidavit from one member of the Lafitte gang—"

16

NEWS OF SUDDEN WAR between America and England was becoming almost daily fodder on the shrimping grounds. The Bernard brothers, taking over all but nominal leadership of the loose confederacy their now aged father had created, were bombarded with fresh reports by men aboard every boat that returned from delivering cargo to the New Orleans docks.

At first the trouble was only a matter of heated protest by Washington City over many English mid-ocean interceptions of American sea traffic; that, and the cavalier impressing of American sailors, literally kidnapped into forced service on British warships.

But London had ignored those increasingly angry complaints. A powder keg had been set to explode, and eventually it did. Repercussions echoed almost immediately throughout the bayous.

Ex-President Jefferson, before his term of office ended, had passed his Non-Importation Act. This boycotted all British-made goods from entry into America. Almost all business in the new states was scuttled, and smuggling was very shortly resorted to as a desperate antidote. Here in Louisiana, Jean Lafitte became instant king of that activity.

To Christophe and Roger-Claude, the skilled and brilliantly organized pirate was no worse than a good neighbor. His base camp at Barataria, called The Temple because its site was an old Indian burial ground, was as defendable as many a military fort. It lay on their own Bayou Lafourche, so that his impudent vessels passed the working shrimp boats frequently on their lawless expeditions. A wave from the gentleman pirate himself was no unusual event.

Fanned by the eloquence of orators such as Henry Clay and John Calhoun, both of them hawks in the tense situation with England, it was inevitable that sooner or later an armed conflict would break loose. Wanton British attacks could not be glossed over forever. Meanwhile, Lafitte's crew were defying the government like brash Robin Hoods, save that in this case the profits were not distributed to any worthy poor folk.

To men raised on the water as the Bernard brothers had been, the most fascinating feature of the war—once it was actually declared by President Madison in June of 1812—was the amount of the fighting which occurred in naval engagements. Those were for them the most exciting reports circulating in New Orleans, the ones they most eagerly carried back home.

"Hey, Christophe, there's been another one. Our *Constitution* against their *Guerrière*. We gunned 'em to a fare-ye-well. Left the Anglos wound-licking like whipped dogs."

"Word hit the market just before I left the city, Roger-Claude. The Americans under Oliver Perry launched a flotilla up yonder on the Great Lakes, nearby where Papa hails from. They've taken a whole English fleet just off Sandusky!"

It all made wonderful wake-up-and-listen reportage to spice long days of fishing. These shrimp they prized had inhabited Louisiana waters since before the arrivals of the earliest Cajuns. Roger Bernard, after his fatal encounter with Antoine Rolande, had been among the first of those who took to the waters. From Indians similarly occupied before him, Roger had quickly learned that shrimp could be scooped right out of his cruising *pirogue* and then dried in the sun. His own forebears in Nova Scotia had done much the same with Fundy cod on their rocky Canadian beaches.

First link in the chain of developments which now joined past to present, therefore, had been how to peddle dried shrimp to the wharves of New Orleans. They'd been known as "sea bob," Roger explained to Christophe and Roger-Claude in their childhoods, because the Cajuns called their catch *six barbe* for the sextet of little beards each shrimp displayed. The English had corrupted their terminology. Even the for-sale crop of sea bob had been small at first, though, because shrimp spoiled too readily with no ice at hand. It remained chiefly a catch for the Cajuns' own consumption.

Roger had brought together his handful of neighbors into an informal combine to try to combat this preservation problem. He taught them all he had learned, again from the natives. If a man packed a fresh seafood catch in spanish moss or palmetto leaves, thus protecting it from open air, it could be rushed to a market as close by as New Orleans without deteriorating. The *pirogue* fleet soon was scurrying to the city daily. And Roger Bernard was becoming widely recognized as its leader, its man who ran things.

Captaining their now much larger boats, Christophe and Roger-Claude still relished Papa's tales of those early shrimping days.

Study and experimentation had introduced many an improvement since then, of course. One side effect had been the creation of a brand new Cajun industry. Many of that ilk now supported themselves full time as moss-pickers. Flatboats upon which the overhanging grey masses could be gathered became a common sight anywhere along the bayous. Moss gins began to operate, processing the packing material.

These days, Roger's maturing sons were able to speed much larger cargos in far better condition of preservation to their New Orleans customers. They had brought haul nets into use for seining, vastly increasing a day's take. Moreover, they were beginning to spread out from the bayous to the brackish back bays that clustered all along their section of the Gulf coast. Perhaps most importantly, they were developing a method of catch which soon became standard procedure among most of their confederates, one increasingly favored by all in their business, save perhaps the "swampers" in the widespread Atchafalaya Basin who largely retained an earlier Bernard invention and employed burlap bags stuffed with bait of corn. So these were times of excitement and gratification, along with the hard work.

René, Roger-Claude's eldest boy, was pushing his teens now and old enough to be taken out with them to observe how the new Bernard system worked. It called for two men working in tandem. But in the Bernard family that was no problem. Soon René would have his younger brother Gils to team with him. If not, there'd be Christophe's youngsters, Denis and Baptiste, at the moment still too small.

"Now watch how it's done, René. Examine this net we've brought with us. It spreads almost a hundred and twenty feet long, and it's ten feet wide. The mesh is fine enough to hold shrimp, a half-inch weave."

"I'm looking, Uncle Christophe. But I know the nets already. Mama and Aunt Marie are always mending them, back home. Sometimes they let me help, and Gils, too."

"Now, your father and I take turns about. But today he'll be here aboard the lugger with you, and I'll take the little rowboat we drag behind us yonder. Pay attention to the pattern I'll be making as I row. That's the whole trick of it."

Bending to his oars, Christophe was as usual stripped to the waist. His still-plentiful blond hair was bleached almost white by weeks in the sun. He was tanned virtually the color of an Indian. Only the long scar on one shoulder, where Cousin Sylvie had sealed a bullet wound some years back, showed white, like a dash of paint.

Once well off from the lugger, he began his operation—careful to keep the rowboat moving so that René, observing, could master each maneuver.

He began to circle out and then return, indeed in a pattern, almost with the precision of a partner in a square dance. The net had been spread so smoothly that schools of shrimp alarmed by passage of an ominous boat shadow on the surface fled directly into them. Only then did Roger-Claude, aboard the lugger, begin to draw in the seine with its frantic prisoners caught fast.

Back aboard and with the rowboat fast behind, Christophe continued his lecture to the clan's youngest generation.

"This is the way it's now done in deep water, René. But in the shallows, where you can stand hip-deep at least while it's low tide, you can haul 'em in with a hand net. That's the way we'll start you out, comes the time."

On the whole, young René was disappointed. He had anticipated considerably more excitement.

"I thought you and Papa did dangerous work, Uncle Christophe. This looks easy."

"Spreading the net correctly takes long practice, boy. But you're right, there's little peril involved. That comes when a hard wind out of the north strikes suddenly. Let it hit our warm near-tropical waves and all hell can bust loose. Before you know what's happening, your lugger can be blown clean out to sea. Not one boat in twenty carries a compass."

"Why don't we buy us a compass, then?"

"Because unless you're driven far off shore it's no use whatever, hereabouts. A fog rolls in and. . . . But I reckon you already know about the fogs. You have to *listen* your way back home through one of 'em. Might as well be blind, for all the good eyes, or a compass, can do you."

Passing within yards of the spot where Roger-Claude still stood hauling net, a fellow shrimper bound in from New Orleans leaned far out across his rail and bellowed across the intervening water. His hands were cupped to form a crude megaphone.

"Ahoy there, Bernards! Hear the latest? William Henry Harrison's led our American army into Canada. One big battle's been fought on the Thames River, where he licked the Anglos and their Indians. Latest word in, he's set York to burning. And at sea our *Hornet*'s whipped their *Peacock*!"

Heartening though reported American victories might be to loyal Cajuns, who by now considered themselves as much citizens of the new Republic as anybody, they inspired few cheers within the dignified walls of the Roland mansion on its aristocratic avenue in New Orleans.

Over the decades Amanda had become sufficiently Americanized to outscheme and outsmart many of Louisiana's prominent business tycoons. But at each of England's recent humblings she found herself more and more retrogressing to the throne-proud girl Sir Cedric Wellington had brought from London with him long ago. It seemed unbelievable that Britain's invincible navy had its tail between its legs in a war against crude, raw colonials.

Home, she was discovering, still meant St. James's Palace and not Louisiana. Sitting on the sidelines of commerce—as she recently had done, while waiting for a perfect moment to use the delectable information Casimir Rodrigue had brought her—she had far too much leisure time in which to contemplate her homeland's humiliations.

To be sure, *all* the news arriving in New Orleans was not distressing.

When an England smarting under repeated embarrassments retaliated by augmenting its sea force in American waters, she actually applauded as if in her box at the D'Orleans. She cheered again when word reached her, via reports from a Charlotte still unaware that she sat on the edge of a precipice, that a strong army assembled at Bermuda had landed in the south and was rapidly advancing against Washington City. God had come to His senses at last. England was back where she belonged.

By year's end the British had reached the Potomac and Washington City was going up in flames—that ridiculous Presidential palace they called their White House included. President Madison was on the run and Dolley Madison had fled the capitol in a carriage loaded with as much of the governmental silverware as her horses could pull. Amanda's thin mouth curved with pleasure at that picture. No Queen of England she could recollect had been guilty of such craven flight—not since Charles I's wife, Henrietta Maria. And Henrietta Maria had been French, not British, so one need not really suffer over her.

But then again, something went wrong.

The army General Ross was leading so splendidly northward to wreak similar punishment upon Philadelphia and New York was halted dead in its tracks at Baltimore. Vaguely, Amanda recollected that Baltimore was a city which once had succored the refugee girl Roger Bernard married. It must be the very sinkhole of the Universe.

Whatever its other contemptible qualities might be, however, its crowning sin was that it shattered the

Ross advance. A broken English army reboarded its ships and made for Jamaica. The Colonials—well, whatever one called them nowadays, thirty-odd years after they shamed George III—seemed to be on the brink of winning yet again.

She decided to invite Anton and Charlotte to dinner. ("And do bring dearest John with you, my darlings, it's been so long since his doting Granny has seen him!")

The invitation was accepted with alacrity. Amanda Roland's cook was a back-scenes celebrity in social New Orleans, besides which Anton was becoming increasingly frugal with a dollar as his years advanced. Free gourmet fare served at Mother's table was not to be slighted.

They gathered in Amanda's parlor, civil and smiling even though one could not have described the wealthy Rolands as close and loving. They made small talk under the revered portrait of Antoine, which the mistress of the mansion had some time previously ordered moved from the study. The bitter defeat she had suffered in that study made her strongly dislike the room. She entered it these days as seldom as possible.

Their hostess felt reasonably certain that at least two of her three guests were puzzling over why the pleasure of their company had been requested. Amanda preferred to keep them on tenterhooks. Until an excellent dinner was chewed and chatted through, she dropped no clue. All black velvet and pearls at the head of the table, carefully coiffed by her expert maid Lucy, she kept the surface charming.

"How are you doing at school, John? I'm sure you are head-of-class?"

"No, not exactly, Gran. There's a scholarship boy from someplace near St. Jacques who beat me out last term. I wasn't even close. His scores in every subject were better."

"A *scholarship* boy? What is a fine school like yours doing, taking riffraff?"

"Almost all schools do, Gran. If boys are smart, they ought to be educated."

"I should think, John, that this country might breed sufficient *gentlemen* to lead it. Young men like yourself. The rest can make very worthy followers." Amanda smiled brilliantly and pushed back her chair. "Unless you'd like a second sherbet, any of you?"

There was a general, and sincere, murmur that anyone who ate another morsel would surely explode. The quartet headed back toward the parlor, Amanda sweeping ahead.

"Cordials for everyone? I can ring for Wadham, or perhaps your father will pour. Do your parents permit you an occasional brandy, John?"

"At Mardi Gras, and maybe at Christmas, Gran. That's just about all."

"We don't approve of currying our son to be a drunkard," Charlotte put in primly.

"Ah, my dear, so wise of you. Well then, John, I'm sure our dreary aged chatter would bore you out of reason. Those books that belonged to your Uncle Percy are still on their old shelf in his room upstairs. You know which door. Why don't you just run up and see if any of them appeals to you? I'd like you to have them."

"You mean it, Gran? I've spotted several, other times I was here."

"If you knew your old grandmother better, John, you'd know she never makes any promise, or threat, that she doesn't mean. Run on up now, darling."

As his tall son's footfalls faded on the stairs, Anton turned toward his mother uneasily.

"That last bit was meant for me, Mother, wasn't it?"

"Anton! But since I'm bragging of truthfulness, I'll have to confess I was hoping you'd grant me one special favor this evening. Are you in an agreeable mood?"

So now it came. Anton braced. The old woman—still quite an eyeful, really—had no power over him any longer. For years she had accepted defeat and meekly attended company meetings to vote whatever way he wanted on whatever matters the trustees were to consider. Yet this peaches-and-cream humility still made him nervous. He had suffered too long through his own years of subservience to quite believe they were over.

"You aren't short of money, Mother?"

"I've never asked you for a dollar, Anton, now have I? No, this is nothing for myself. This is for my country. It may amaze you, dear, but this is patriotism."

From a rapid blink of his eyes, it *did* amaze him. "You've never waved the flag before. You've never even seemed to like America, however well our family's done here."

"Goodness, you didn't fancy I meant America? *My* country is England."

"Well, it isn't mine. Nor Charlotte's. Every Roland dollar was earned on this side of the Atlantic. Our crumpets all are spread with American butter."

Amanda continued to smile serenely.

"There'd be no Roland dollars to vaunt, Anton, if your Wellington grandfather had not greased the wheels with good British pounds. Whether you feel personal gratitude or not, we owe everything we own to Britain."

"Not by a long shot!" Anton was reddening. "If you think I'd risk my bets on the English in this present disgusting imbroglio, you're much mistaken."

"Not your personal bets, Anton. Keep your money. I only ask your influence."

It must have been just about then, if Amanda read him aright, that Anton began to suspect he was hooked on some yet unseen barb. He patted his forehead dry.

"Only influence, Anton. It won't cost you a penny. All I want you to do is bring a friend of yours here to dinner, end of the week. The meal will be as good as tonight's."

Anton leaned forward. "What friend is this, Mother?"

"The pirate fellow, dear. Jean Lafitte. I'm told he's charming and has exquisite manners. I have a proposition I'd like to lay before him."

Redness mounted to Anton's cheeks again, but deeper, closer to true scarlet. "Invite a notorious pirate to a Roland dinner table? You're out of your mind!"

"You've expressed that opinion of me on previous occasions, Anton, so let it pass. This time, I'm being quite reasonable. He is a business man, as well you know. You've been in partnership with him, you and various others, for years."

"Of all the outrageous folderol! Why, to merely insinuate that I—that we—"

"Anton, I'm not making light talk. You're well aware I'm not. Nestled in my personal safe are a whole sheaf of legal documents that prove I'm not. Shall I mention a few names in them to convince you? Calcasiou. Vaughn. Olivier. Cassidy. Minden."

He stared at her as though she were a cobra. *"Where did you get that list?"*

"Isn't the important thing, Anton, that I have it? Now, I'd much enjoy a meeting with your *close* associate, Mr. Lafitte. Will Thursday be convenient? Can you bring him?"

"And if I don't?" snarled her son. But he wore a defeated look.

"You won't make answering that a necessity, will you, Anton? You've known Mother a long time. Ever since you were her darling little boy."

He sat facing her woodenly. "Damn! Whatever do you want of Lafitte, anyway?"

"He knows the Louisiana coast as I know the patterns on my table porcelains. Heaven knows, he's been despoiling its shipping long enough with help from others I've named, who arrange that he can sell his booty without interference."

"Mother—"

"Suppose Lafitte were asked to lead in to New Orleans a certain fleet that's even now on its way here from Jamaica? He could bring them in via his bayous so silently that they'd have the city under their guns before our defenders were even aware."

"*Treason!*" cried Charlotte, her tone that of a kicked mongrel dog.

Her husband glared at her. "Hold your tongue, Charlotte. What makes you imagine Lafitte would even listen to your nonsense, Mother?"

"I did mention I have a proposition for him, did I not? I should fancy that a legitimate transaction, with no risk whatever, might appeal to a hunted brigand."

"What have you in mind to use as your bribe? May I know that?"

"Of course you may, dear. It must already be obvious. All my own personal shares in the company you've been so busy making prosperous, these past few years. Every *dix*-worth of my Roland holdings. Wouldn't you enjoy having another unscrupulous pirate for a partner?"

René came panting up the path to the Bernard house as though he were on the last lap of a very long foot race. In a sense this was true. Most of it, however, actually had been undertaken on bayou water at the oars of the *pirogue* he had just now tied up with trembling speed.

"Grandpa! Uncle Christophe! Papa! Anybody! Everybody!"

They started spilling onto the high porch ahead while he was still bellowing. Aunt Marie was automatically tidying hair come loose over the kitchen dishpan. Gils had not left off gnawing on a stalk of sweet cane. Aunt Dorothée still clutched the baby jacket she had been knitting. Only Grandpa moved slowly, white head bent, single hand tight on a supportive brier stick.

"What in tarnation's got into you, boy? The house isn't on fire."

René paused below them, struggling to get back his voice. "There's to be a battle! The English are coming! They've beat a squadron of American gunboats off Lake Borgne and now they're closing in on New Orleans! Luis Mendez's father just got home with word!"

"Dear God!" breathed Aunt Dorothée. It was a prayer, not a curse.

"They'd have come in all unexpected, Mr. Mendez says, if Jean Lafitte had agreed to lead them. He was offered a big bribe, it's said, to do just that. But he threw back what was offered. He's an American, he

said, even if American soldiers do chase him and aim
to hang him."

"What double-dirty skunk made such an offer?" That
was Grandpa Roger's wavery voice.

"It isn't known. Only that the offer was made and
refused. Now General Andrew Jackson, him they call
Old Hickory, is in the city raising an army for defense.
Mr. Mendez says the volunteers look like they came
from the Tower of Babel in the Bible. Every breed,
every color. Indians. Negroes. Cajuns. Gulf pirates.
Militiamen from Kentucky and Tennessee. Mr. Mendez just came home to get his rifle. He's heading back."

Christophe loped down the porch steps to grab his
nephew by one shoulder.

"Where are the British now, René? What word did
Mendez have on their position?"

"He told Mrs. Mendez they'd landed eight thousand
soldiers at Lake Borgne, thirty miles from the city.
From there they came on by foot and by naval barges.
They'd got within ten miles before Jackson knew they
were coming. Rough weather's bogging them. But they
must be even closer in by now, mustn't they?"

The answer was so obvious that Christophe did not
bother making it. Instead, he looked up to where his
brother had appeared at the railing.

"I'm going, Roger-Claude. You'll have to look after
the family till I get back. Gils, fetch me my hunting
gun. You know where I keep it indoors. Dorothée, I'll
be home soon as we've tended to the Anglos."

Gathering up her skirts, Dorothée was already fol-
lowing him down the stairs, their three children—
Denis, Baptiste and Blanche—tottering in her wake.
"No, Chris, no!"

She flung protesting arms about him, but Christophe gently disengaged them.

"*La ville* has been good to us Bernards for a span of years, honey. It's bought our catch and let us prosper. It needs us now. It'll need every man it can muster."

"But think of the children! Think of me! If you never come home to us—"

"I'll be back. This is just another trip to the city, same as always."

"It's *war*! I've heard plenty about that army gathered at Jamaica, Chris Bernard. Most of its men are veterans who defeated Napoleon. Wellington's own brother-in-law, Sir Edward Pakenham, is their general. Jackson's ragtag will be wiped out, crushed!"

"Maybe not," Christophe replied quietly. "We're a tough young country, honey. Don't count us out before we're licked. Gils, where the hell's my gun? Fetch, boy!"

Roger-Claude, not his younger son, was the one who pelted down from the porch, however. In one hand he toted his brother's rifle. In the other he carried his own.

"You didn't think I'd stay behind like one of the womenfolk, did you, Gumbo-head? Jackson needs every Bernard he can net. Thing is, we've got to get word up the bayous to the rest of the clan. Likely, Uncle Claude's boys ain't had news yet."

Standing slim between them, René spoke so rapidly his words tripped over one another. "I'll tend to that, Pa, Uncle Chris. I can move a *pirogue* fast as any grown man."

For an instant Christophe stood motionless, hand lying gently on his young nephew's head. Then he grinned.

"Reckon you've heard about that Boston fellow, back at the start of the last war against England in '75. Paul Revere, his name was. He spread word the British were coming all over the countryside. Rode his horse to a lather."

"I've read about him, Uncle Chris. I can do the same by boat, if you'll trust me."

"Then why are you lollygagging here, René? Grab that oar! Get moving!"

René was off before the words were past his Uncle's lips. As the two Bernard brothers followed down the bank, toward where the second family *pirogue* lay tied up, a mixed domestic symphony rolled after them. Dorothée and Annette were sobbing. The flock of smaller children set up instant howls, too young yet to know why they were grieving. And clutching the railing with his single cracked-leather hand, leaning far out so his marred old voice would carry, white-haired Roger was shouting.

"Go get 'em, boys! Shoot the balls off 'em! Who the devil does Pakenham think he is, trying to take New Orleans away from us?"

17

A JANUARY DAWN FOG hugged the earth, stirring with the subtle undulations of a prone lover. The dank air picked up echoes. Thousands of marching feet were drumming the ground off toward the swamps where Pakenham had landed his army. The British came on now like the herd of a giant cattle run, except that with them the sound had a flawless rhythm, left, right, left, right, mechanical, unbroken, relentless.

Despite the chill, sweat streaked many faces among the men who crouched listening.

They had toiled all through the night, throwing up a protective earthen rampart and gouging out a ditch. The construction technique was one those among them who were Cajuns knew well. Dyke-building had been their specialty since Nova Scotia days, now lying so far astern that memories of them lingered only with a few oldsters.

From the sound, Pakenham's well-trained force was close to hand. Some of the rampart builders already had laid down their shovels and picked up their guns. But in the sector where the Bernard brothers were laboring, a few shovelfuls still needed pounding into place.

Bending to the task, Roger-Claude worked shoulder to shoulder with a stalwart husky to whom he had taken a real liking during the long and hectic night. The man was neither old nor young and his name, so Roger-Claude had learned, was Joe Wadham. From the zest with which Joe threw dirt, you'd have imagined him to be a stevedore. Actually, he turned out to be a butler employed in one of the city's most posh residences. His usual daily routines were carried out in elegant livery—velvet coat, powdered wig, satin kneebreeches.

But he was working his shovel tonight with undiminished vigor, although each man in the squad by now had aching muscles. "Sounds like the Anglos are on our doorstep, Bernard."

"Haven't knocked on our door yet, though, Joe. We've still a little time."

Wadham chuckled. "Let 'em knock when they've a mind to. They won't be let into the city. We'll inform 'em Madam is not receiving. I do that almost every day, back in town."

"With Andy Jackson for our 'Madam,' you can bank on that."

They grunted on without comment for several spadefuls more, flinging earth with a rhythm almost matching that of the unseen marching feet. The tramp-tramp-tramp was like approaching thunder now, rolling across the ground like part of the restless fog which still obscured its source. Wiping sweat off his eyebrows, Wadham dropped his shovel and reached for the weapon he had left propped up alongside. It was a breech-loading Ferguson, ornamented beyond the usual with fine brass designs, and Roger-Claude knew its reputation. It was a rapid-firer, a rarity in George Washington's war, but since then popular.

"Handsome firing piece you've got there, Joe Wadham."

His companion grinned. "Ought to be. My wife Lucy lifted it right out of the gun case in Madam's study. Belonged to her father, who was a British Sir."

"So your Lucy sent you out well-armed, did she? I reckon your Madam, whoever she is, won't much object. She'll be proud her gun is off to defend New Orleans with her blessing."

"Not our Mrs. Roland won't. She's English, like I said. All out for Pakenham."

Something tightened abruptly in Roger-Claude's throat. "Mrs. *Antoine* Roland? She's who you work for? If I'd known that before you and I got friendly—"

"You know my Madam?" Wadham looked surprised. "Say, I didn't figure that."

"Because my brother and I are from the bayous? Might seem unlikely, but we're no strangers to her. Papa thinks it was she who sent a posse to wipe us out, some years back."

Wadham's earnest face was a study.

"I remember, Bernard. Master Percy got all the blame, but my Lucy and I always sort of wondered.

There were big changes in Madam's way of living hard
after that. The staff couldn't help but puzzle. She was
never accused of wrongdoing, though."

"She's no friend to the Bernards," Roger-Claude
breathed grimly. "She tried hard to get Papa arrested
and hung. No fault of yours, though. You just make
sure this gun of hers gets in good use today."

Ahead of them, as he picked up his own Brown Bess,
the moving red mass which was the approaching enemy phalanx began to be visible as a wavering block
of color within the grey miasma. Individual marchers
could not yet be separated. They were not yet men.
But the hue of their uniforms was like a great blood-
stain across the forbidding morning.

Further along the line Roger-Claude could make
out his brother. Christophe, too, had replaced digging
pick with gun. Greying yellow hair still glowed, easily
visible despite the mists drifting between their positions. Christophe was handling his Pennsylvania rifle
with a practiced hand. He had carried it along on
many a hunt, the purpose for which some German gun-
smith up north undoubtedly had created it.

A sudden shift of wind caught the fog and rippled
it aside like a drawn curtain. Face to face with them,
and advancing inexorably, tramped the unconquerable
British army.

Lit by the wan first light, perfect lines of redcoats
rolled forward across the cane stubble. The whole
scene lay before him, thought Christophe, like a
painted picture. To his left a cypress swamp stretched
infinitely back into shadows still blurred by mist. To
his right rose the river levee, silent and high. Be-

tween these extremities, the picked troops of Sir
Edward Pakenham marched in scarcely-human serried
ranks. Their drummer boys were rat-a-tatting a death
knell.

They came on, did these veterans trained by the
great Wellington himself, as if they were on parade.
Dorothée or Marie well might knit a comforter in the
pattern the great force presented. Each individual
crimson square bore intersecting diagonals of white
lines that were cross bars; and each had sparks of glitter which would at closer range be military buttons.
Now and again the design was interrupted by a unit
of green-trimmed-in-black which denoted a Rifle
Brigade.

It was impossible to think of those squares as men.
They were parts of some flawless mechanism, some
terrible and splendid juggernaut.

At Christophe's side, second cousin Alphonse, eldest
of Uncle Claude's grandsons, barked a laugh like a
fox's. The moment seemed entirely devoid of humor.
Christophe turned in surprise.

"What's so funny, Alphonse? That out there is a
destruction machine."

"The Anglos have already cooked one goose, Cousin
Chris. I served a year in the militia up in Kentucky.
I've seen 'em in action. It's always the same drill. This
time someone's busted it."

Christophe looked back and could discover nothing awry.

"What's so wrong?"

"Someone's forgotten the scaling ladders. Not to
mention the facines to fill in our ditch. It's always
front-ranks equipment for taking an objective. Old

Pakenham will have somebody's skin for that. Unless it was himself who ordered a rocket to signal the advance fired off before they had their gear in position."

To Christophe, skillful with guns but totally unfamiliar with military procedures, it seemed impossible that these crack British veterans could make an error of any sort. If Cousin Alphonse knew what he was saying, such a breach should indeed prove important.

It had been a pure joy to recognize Bernard kinfolk from upriver as they swarmed into the American defense position somewhat after midnight. Cousin Alphonse was full of his account of young René's arrival at Uncle Claude's ribbon farm. René must have busted his lungs and pulled his arms from their sockets, rushing the news along. And the Bernards had wasted no more time replying than had he and Roger-Claude a few hours earlier.

All night, mounted on a white horse that seemed half mountain goat by the way it handled a levee or a defense ditch, Andrew Jackson had been riding up and down the American lines with crisp orders and explanations of his battle plan. Every man in the lot was well briefed. They were to hold all fire until Pakenham's soldiers were well within range, which meant, Christophe estimated, about two to three hundred yards. Most of the diverse mixture of weapons on the American side would be accurate then, though they were built for a wide variety of distances.

"Any second now, Cousin Chris," breathed Alphonse. "My trigger-finger's itching."

But as the whole line was aware, the first barrage would be laid down only when the marching English had crossed all but the final five hundred yards of stubble field. And it would be signalled by the cannon they had rope-dragged and hauled into position during the dark hours.

Expect it though he had, Christophe flinched as the artillery spat sudden thunder.

Without warning, the world of the mist-pocked field became a deadly bowling green. Doomed men advancing in ranks toward the ditch were blown in all directions. They seemed like game pins scattered by giant bowling balls. Yankee grape and canister was literally shredding them.

When the cannons' assault slowed, rifles from behind the long barricade took over. This was almost child's play, if a man knew his weapon. Safe with the earth wall to cover him, an American rifleman could pick a target almost at will. Then he could down it while the pulverized English lines were still reeling.

Like the others all about them, Christophe and Alphonse did fearful damage.

"This mist's a curse," Alphonse muttered presently. "Distorts the aim."

"Not so much as you'd notice." Christophe kept on firing. Englishmen kept on falling. The field was carpeted in crimson now, blood and uniforms mingling.

Somewhere along the embankment, in the direction where Roger-Claude would be serving, Christophe became aware of a slight disturbance.

For the most part, ill-trained though they were, the city's defenders were disciplined by Jackson's dominating personality. The line clung to his orders. But one raw volunteer apparently was unable to contain himself behind the barricade. Christophe sensed rather than actually saw a single figure vault across the top of the earthworks, descending upon the devastated field like a charging Indian.

Straight into the charnel the lone man sped, waving his rifle overhead and howling a yell of victory.

Among the fallen redcoats in the mud lay one who apparently was playing dead to save his own skin. In line with his running foe, he reared up suddenly on one elbow and fired point blank. Christophe saw the shouting figure spin and crash down. Before the sniper could flatten to earth again, Christophe's Pennsylvania rifle zeroed in on him and coughed. The Englishman crumpled. This time he did not have to play dead. Grim fact had caught up with him.

Beyond one quick glance, which had convinced Christophe the man breaking cover had not been Roger-Claude, he had little time to invest on the unlucky incident. It was over almost in the same breath that had begun it. He veered back to the battle line ahead. Only a handful of the decimated British were managing to reach the American barricade. These were mowed down as they struggled to climb it.

Along the line a ragged shout of enthusiasm ran like a wave up a beach. Someone had recognized General Pakenham himself as he was blasted dead out of his saddle. The exhilarating word set off a bonfire of emotion. The English themselves quickly read their fate.

Left leaderless, even Wellington's veterans cracked at the realization, and at the sight of butcher's meat sprawled everywhere about them. Automatons suddenly became human and frightened. What was left of shattered ranks broke and fled. Two thousand marching men would never stir again. Five hundred more, who had saved themselves by pitching prone, were staggering back to their feet and lifting their arms high in surrender. The rest were headed back for the swamps in wild disarray.

Flushed with his own awareness of a magnificent victory, Christophe turned down the embankment to find his brother. In all Andy Jackson's force only eight had been killed and not many more wounded. That contrast to the enemy's wholesale slaughter seemed a miracle. It was an hour for riotous celebration. He wanted to share it.

He reached the spot where he last had glimpsed Roger-Claude wielding pick and shovel, expecting to find the younger Bernard bathed in an equal effulgence. To his surprise, his brother was leaning against the barricade, gone ash white, and looking mortally ill.

"Roger-Claude! What in tarnation's the trouble? You ain't been hit?"

For a seemingly endless time, while cheers and shouts of victory kept ringing all about them, Roger-Claude merely stared back. Then he spoke only a single word. "*Wadham.*"

"Who's Wadham? You mean that chap who was digging alongside you?"

"He couldn't hold back, the damned sweet idiot. Had to bust over the top like some stupid brat at school games." There came a sound from Roger-Claude's throat which seemed very like a sob.

"You mean. . . . ?"

"He was the one picked off down the slope. I saw you get the Anglo who did it, lifting up like a crafty ghost from the dead. He's dead enough now himself, blast him. But so is Joe Wadham."

"It's bad, brother, bad. But it's battle luck. Some live, some don't."

"Joe had a wife, Chris. Name of Lucy. Lady's maid in the same *ville* mansion where Wadham was butler. She'll find out sometime that waiting for him to come home is time wasted. They loved each other."

"If you know where they worked in town, we ought to stop by and break the news. It'd come kindlier from someone his Lucy knew was fighting right beside him at the end."

Roger-Claude shook his head slowly.

"Any other house in New Orleans, I'd do just that. Not there, though. I'd be shot on the doorstep. The woman who hires them is Papa's She-Spider. The one who sent the raid against us. Amanda Roland, Chris."

The city had gone crazy well before darkness fell. Now full night had come. Barrels of tar had been set afire on almost every corner, making the streets virtually as light as day. Bands of celebrants roamed boisterously, waving bottles and singing at the tops of their lungs. Having spilled from their beds this morning to a terrifying serenade of cannon in the swamps, and having spent most of the intervening day in sick suspense awaiting reports of the battle, the citizenry were now in semi-hysterical reaction.

From hastily improvised platforms of crates, street orators shouted the praise of Andrew Jackson, hero of heroes. Musicians roamed everywhere, tootling exultantly on their flutes and pounding their drums to arouse the dead. Impromptu parades sprang up and wound along all the chief avenues.

Christophe made his difficult way through the crowds unsmilingly. His pride and relief at the stupendous Jackson victory were a full equal to that of any man or woman he passed. But he had a heavy errand weighing on his heart. It dulled the joy.

Cradled across one arm, he carried a rifle. Not his own modest but excellent Pennsylvania, which Roger-Claude was by now taking back to the bayou. This one was far more elegant, of the finest English make, a richly ornamented Ferguson breech-loader. Shortly after the shooting ceased, he had worked his way through a corpse-laden field to retrieve it.

That the weapon had been part of a gentleman's private arsenal, not the property of any servant, was abundantly clear. Roger-Claude's tale of how Lucy Wadham had secretly commandeered it for a departing husband wasn't needed at all. Christophe was sufficiently versed in the cost of firearms to know only wealth could afford what he toted now.

The murderous shrew who had attempted their father's assassination, that was who owned it.

Oh, she might not have been the original patron who ordered this fine workmanship. It could have belonged to her husband, or maybe her titled father. But it was her property now. And as a thorough-going British sympathizer, she would foam at how it had been used today.

To return Mrs. Roland's possession would not, alone, have detained him in the city after Roger-Claude's departure for home. But thoughts of a waiting Lucy had tipped the scale. He remembered now (although he didn't believe he ever before had been much aware of it) how Marie had waited—silent, hopeless—for another Roland, years ago.

Christophe knew his way to the Roland mansion without asking directions. He and his brother had

made it their business to check out the family, back
when Anton Roland first began pressing offers to buy
up shares in the shrimp combine. And if they had not
known the house then, they would have searched it
out after the bayou raid.

He anticipated every turn to take, walking from
the heart of the city. He marched along through the
flicker of the tar barrels almost as stolidly as one of
Pakenham's infantry on the road to Doomsday.

On another day, he might have been able to indulge
in admiration of handsome marble steps as he mounted
them; or the graceful curve of the ornamental iron
handrail. The heavy door knocker was a dolphin
shaped from polished brass. At any other time he
could have paused to admire it. Tonight, he was all
but unaware. His thoughts were elsewhere.

Dull reverberations of the knocker sounded through
whatever space lay behind the oak panel he stood
facing. They seemed not unlike the beat of English
drums this morning, leading the invaders to wholesale disaster. Christophe thought of the ranks of his
rugged Cajuns strung out through the American lines,
and felt pride stir in him.

The door opened.

Facing him stood a woman in maid's cap and apron,
her age just short of middle age. Her face showed
signs of tension. Behind her he caught a glimpse of
impressive hallway: rich carpet, framed portraits,
crystal prisms.

"My name is Bernard," Christophe began. "I've
come to bring—"

But she already had spied the rifle in the crook of
his arm. Her tired, haunted eyes fixed on it, widening

with recognition. One of her shaking hands flew to her lips, to press back a cry which seemed about to burst from them. She kept on staring.

"You're Lucy Wadham, aren't you?" he asked softly. "I'm sorry. I'm sorry, ma'am."

"When he didn't come back earlier, I knew," she breathed. "Joe is—"

She was unable to force out a final word, but it was obvious what that would have been. Christophe reached past her gently and leaned the rifle against polished wall paneling. Deep inside, he ached for her.

"Joe was a brave man, Mrs. Wadham. I reckon you already know that. He died helping save New Orleans. Andy Jackson would be right proud of him. So must you be."

He was turning on his heel to head back down the marble treads when, from somewhere behind her in the house, a male voice shouted.

"Who's that at the door, Lucy? Is Wadham back at last? High time, I must say! Kiting off without a word of permission, and with my mother ill."

From some room on beyond the entrance, a man with dark hair strode into view. He was dressed in expensive suiting, not the sort a dandy might affect, but the garb of a successful businessman. A heavy gold watch chain rested on what was already a more than ample stomach which bade fair to become even more so.

"Well, woman, well? If it's more details from my office on today's fiasco—"

He saw Christophe standing there, lit against darkness by the great chandelier overhead. He stopped as abruptly as a reined-in horse, fixed on the face of the caller in the doorway, his eyes narrowed to flint points. He sucked in breath, too audibly. (*He'll be suffering a stroke any minute now*, thought Christophe.)

If this were indeed to happen, the event was at least for the moment postponed. The man strode forward angrily. Had he carried a sword, Christophe would have expected to be run through and degutted. As things actually stood, even those furious eyes were a formidable weapon.

"By God, you have gall! Actually daring to show up on my mother's doorstep. You've come to gloat over her, have you? You bayou trash are incredible!"

Christophe stood meeting the violent outburst quietly. "Good evening, Mr. Roland."

"Ah, so you know me by sight!"

"You're Mr. Anton Roland. My brother and I used to see you in the fish market quite often, a few years back. Several times you approached us on money deals."

"Which you had the brass to turn down flat. Didn't know where the profits lay. That shrimp fleet of yours would be triple its size if you'd let us in."

"We find it big enough for our purposes, Mr. Roland. It was a fine gesture of our neighbor, Jean Lafitte, to join his crew up with Jackson's men this morning. But we'd have disliked seeing shrimp boats changed to ferries for pirate goods, none the less."

The reddened face before him darkened toward rich purple. "Get out of here, damn you!"

Before Christophe could accept the suggestion, which indeed would have pleased him mightily considering how he'd disliked coming to this house in the first place, a second voice—a woman's, this time—drifted to them from the rear of the hall.

Emerging out of shadows came a fantastic figure. Her hair was so white it would put a swan to shame, but it hung in untidy draggles about her gaunt face. She drifted toward them unsteadily, as if under the influence of opium or Lafitte-smuggled rum. The robe clutched loosely about her was of a rich material, with gold threads woven through it. But it was stained in several places and carelessly ripped. Not meaning to be rude, Christophe still stared.

She had spotted him already, standing in the door with full light falling over him. She headed for him directly. Anton Roland's muttered *"Damn!"* was ignored.

"Percy!" she trilled sweetly. "So you're back at last! Come in, come in!"

Roland laid a hand on her shoulder. "Go back to your room, Mother. This isn't Percy. Percy's been dead for years. You built his mausoleum yourself, remember?"

"Of course Percy's dead." She said it calmly, shaking off his touch with a shrug. "That's why he's come home, Anton. You know this house is haunted."

"Mother, you're talking nonsense. There are no ghosts."

"No? Look for yourself. There Percy stands. You recognize your own twin, don't you? The spit of your father. Handsome devils, both of them." The voice lost its sugar, took on a touch of vinegar. "A pity *you* didn't inherit Antoine's looks, I must say."

As if neither her surviving son nor a quietly sobbing maid existed, she kept on her wavering way toward the spot where Christophe waited. They stood very close now.

"Haven't you a kiss for Mother, Percy?"

"I'm sorry, ma'am, but I'm not Percy. My name is—"

"Ah, you're the cruel one! Still angry with me, Percy, because I had to use your name when they suspected me of sending those men out to kill Roger Bernard? That's ungenerous of you, darling. Ghosts ought to love their mothers."

"Be still, Mother!" hissed Anton Roland. "For God's sake, be still!"

"Tut, Anton. He already knows who sent out McAfee and the boats. No secrets from dead men. Of course dear Percy knows. But I thought he'd forgiven me. He *was* there with the others, after all. It was only natural to use that to cover up the true—"

"*Mother!*" Every vestige of dignity had abandoned Roland. Fear exploded from him.

"Did you know, Percy," the old woman continued, as if the man beside her did not exist, "that a pack of mongrels from New Orleans's sewers attacked dear General Pakenham today? I've been quite ill ever since news came. Our English rescuers all were killed."

"That's right. I was there fighting 'em, ma'am."

"Men trained by my own distant cousin, the Duke of Wellington, no less! How can such things happen, Percy? One begins to believe God must have abdicated."

Christophe swallowed uneasily. "Mrs. Roland, as I take it you are—"

"Now, now! Let's not grow formal with Mother, Percy. I didn't really think I much would, but I've missed you since you died. At least I could trust you. Anton is a common thief."

Anton laid hand on her again, and this time not lightly. "You babbling old fool! I told you to go back to your room, and you'll go if I have to drag you there!"

She slapped at her son viciously, and with more strength than Christophe would have imagined was in her. Across one skinny shoulder, as Roland began to manhandle her back toward the shadows, she shrilled like an outraged parrot.

"You see how he treats his mother, Percy? But I know why! It's his under-the-counter deals with that rascal Lafitte! It's all Lafitte's fault, the debacle today! If he'd accepted my generous offer to help the English surprise the city, we'd have seen glorious victory. But no, the scurvy pirate laughed in my face and went off to Jackson. Anton's secret connections with the man didn't help one bit. Did you know, Percy, that your precious brother—"

Somewhere to the rear of the house a door slammed and the screeching voice was cut off. In her corner, forgotten by everyone but Christophe, Lucy Wadham went on weeping softly, rifle clasped to her breast. After a moment's hesitation, he turned away. Her grief was hers alone. There was no way he could ease it.

Striding back past the splutter and glow of a hundred victory bonfires, the duplicate of Percy and Antoine shook his blond head. For all their money and comforts, for all their fine social position in *La Ville*, the Rolands were an unhappy lot. He wouldn't have been one of them for any number of prospering shrimp fleets.

18

HE WOULD HAVE FELT soiled by even a thought of using against them what he'd heard at the Roland mansion, on the night of Andy Jackson's great New Orleans triumph. The idea of that sort of vengeance, gouged out of personal tragedy, never crossed Christophe's mind. Their aborted raid on the bayou might be the Roland style, but it didn't fit the Bernards. As for anything beyond the attempts against Papa, let it go. They'd never been able to inflict real hurt.

He did miss Papa, though.

With the passing years, that empty place didn't much heal over; like a hollow place in a tree, it remained a hollow. Hopefully, Papa found himself at peace in the churchyard at St. Jacques where they had laid him to rest alongside Mama Rosalie and her own father, Jules Despres. It was for those left behind to do the grieving.

At least he didn't have to do the guilty kind of public grieving that Anton Roland, in the city, seemed committed to.

From his few contacts with the actual man, Christophe was inclined to doubt that grief was involved at all. But the public image was. Roland already had presented New Orleans with a small but beautiful public park overlooking the river. Now he was erecting a library as a gift to the city. Everyone was intended to know what a generous and public-spirited gentleman Mr. Anton Roland was. It must be made to seem altogether impossible for such a benefactor to ever have had any connection whatever with scoundrels like Jean Lafitte.

On the whole, Christophe felt far more sympathy for Lafitte than he ever could for any Roland—except one. Returning to the bayou that night after the battle, he'd found a chance to pass along some of what he'd heard in that fancy hallway to his sister Marie. There still were vacant spots in the truth, details he could not flesh out for her, but at least the confession Roland had tried so desperately to hush proved that Percy had not led the raid on the Bernards for any murderous reason. He trusted Marie to fill in the gaps, and felt certain she had.

Since the day of his return with the Percy story, melancholy had fallen from his dark sister like a discarded cloak. Aging with the rest of the clan, she had once again become the high-spirited Marie. he and Roger-Claude had known when the three of them were very young together.

As for the costly new library still rising on its dignified square in *La Ville*, he often pondered *that* true story, too.

Over the building's door, so René reported, they were setting a legend in stone letters. These spelled out: *In Loving Memory of Amanda Wellington Roland.* Maybe so. But certainly there had been small love on display at the Roland house, that night of the battle. Christophe would not have been surprised, thereafter, to have read in the headlines that son had strangled mother. No such open scandal had erupted. But in odd moments of brooding, he still wondered what had taken place once he left the doorstep.

Well, if you were born a Roland you were probably committed to your own private miseries. They were no concern of Christophe Bernard's, not as he could see it.

René saw it somewhat differently. They talked about it together, sometimes.

Roger-Claude's eldest was a pure pleasure to Christophe. When suddenly you found yourself head of a family, a patriarch sitting where Papa Roger always had sat, you developed a sense of time rushing past. Denis and Baptiste were still young men to be molded But you could see how René was turning out.

"Don't make any charitable mistakes about those Rolands, Uncle Chris," René would warn him. "That's a snake pit, no other way to describe it."

"Not many left of 'em nowadays. Only Mr. Anton."

"And his precious son. I see John Roland every so often when I'm uptown. His face is taking on that same hard look his Dad's is set in."

"Maybe the young man has a perpetual bellyache."

"It's their family code John's digesting. All cash, no vegetables. When we pass in the street, the look in his eyes tells me plenty. He's inherited the Roland hate for us."

"He believes that old nonsense about Papa having killed his grandfather?"

"Old Mrs. Roland believed it. She spent her life trying to get back at us, no matter how. John was in his teens when his grandmother died. She had plenty of time to rub her ideas off on him. They'd nail all us Bernards to a barn door, if they ever got the chance."

"But that they *won't* get. Not while your Pa and I head the fleet, with you and Gils coming up behind us to take over when the day comes. You'll have the education to fight off a dozen John Rolands. That's why we've sent you to classes in the city, to hone you."

"John would stick my head on a pike with the greatest of pleasure, Uncle Chris. He's resented me ever since I used to take away the prizes he wanted at day school. He'd sneer and call me Scholarship Trash, just loud enough for me to hear. We're not friends."

"No need to be friends. Just don't waste your time being enemies. You're good material, René. Too good to have any part of you wasted. Better to spend that energy in shaping up your own cousins. It worries me a mite about Denis and Baptiste, René. They just don't seem to be taking hold of the family trade the way I'd like to see."

The impressive new Roland library was opened to the citizens of its city with enough somber pomp to befit a medium-sized coronation.

Unfortunately, from Anton Roland's point of view, the times were somewhat unfavorable for the occasion. Too many other events were stirring the public's attention, usurping it from proper concentration on his own generosity. The first adaptation of the steam engine to sugar milling was brand new and causing a furor in cane fields investment. France's old Marquis de Lafayette was about to make a hero's visit to Louisiana, and would monopolize attention despite the decades that had rolled past since he was George Washington's dashing aide. Rumors flew that the state capitol was about to be moved from New Orleans to Donaldsville.

"They might have waited, John," he growled. "This library has cost the family a packet, as you're well aware. I'd like a little more public return on it."

"It won't be a waste," his far calmer son assured him. "You'll see. As I've already counseled you, a library becomes a vital cornerstone in any community where there's education. Every reader who becomes a member of ours will subconsciously think 'Roland' each time he borrows a book. The benefit to us will seem mild, but it will be cumulative. We'll be known for philanthropy."

"I'd like more applause, John. I can't taste 'subconscious.'"

"You're a lot more like Gran than you'd care to admit, aren't you, Dad?" His mature son smiled. "I remember her well. She was always one for fireworks."

"I'll thank you not to be comparing me to my mother, son. She had her brilliant moments, granted. But she was extremely unstable. She died in a room where we'd had to install window bars. I can't much relish hints that could be my own ending."

"You won't end like Gran. You'll die right here at your big mahogany office desk, yelling at someone who's disagreed with you. You know what the doctors warn about your blood pressure."

The world made it increasingly difficult for a man to ride herd on his blood pressure: of this Anton Roland was sadly convinced. The headlong rush and crash of civilization had begun disrupting every quiet bit of larceny on which a man ought to be able to count as his years grew more taxing. These modern 1830s sometimes resembled a spinning top.

For one example, take the cut-off just built by that man Shreve at the place where the Red and Mississippi flowed together. It had aided commerce in cities like Alexandria and Shreveport, even to a point of thus christening the new city after him. But it had flooded a host of Cajun farms in the process. How many of those displaced farmers owed stiff mortgages to the House of Roland? Of what value was collateral unexpectedly buried under water?

For another case, consider the complications involved in the state's switch-over to the Code Napoleon as a base for its legal system. Uprooted every one of the old-fashioned principles, it did. A man could scarcely figure how to out-trick a business rival, with the traps and gaps all different. Instead, one was all too often caught short one's self.

Even religion was crumbling. In Louisiana, Catholicism had shrivelled until there were only six active churches in the state; and only two priests to minister to those. A fine state of affairs! The Church was supposed to *be* there, a handy tool for teaching people submission to their superiors and trust in their betters.

Undermine that attitude and what did you have? A rabble who began to ask probing questions and doubt their money leaders.

Oh, it was a grey world for the most part—even though the House of Roland did somehow manage to keep advancing. Certain pockets of the community were still thorns in his side. In particular, that Bernard clan. The bayou scum never had moved one inch from their backward positions of years ago. They still resisted him at every turn. He despised them.

"We'll get them where we want them, Dad," John soothed. "Just be patient."

"Patient?" Anton all but screamed. "God in Heaven, how long am I expected to wait? You hadn't even been born, I hadn't even married your mother, when I started after them. And what good has any move I've made since done me? Do we own their shrimp fleet? No! They've only added profitable sidelines like oystering to it. And they're still the kings."

"They won't always be. Take it easy, Dad. Times are changing. And it's about some of those changes in particular that I dropped by to chat with you today."

"What now?" groaned Anton resignedly. "That word *change* gives me the ague."

"This isn't anything to worry you. Strictly speaking, it isn't connected with the company at all. But of course we'll profit from it eventually. I want to go into politics."

Anton looked much as though he'd bitten into a green persimmon. "Politics? Why?"

"That's where the big decisions really are made, isn't it? You know as well as I do that any truly worthwhile deal always winds up at the State House.

Now, I have no illusions about holding elective office myself. The public's seen too much Roland dirt swept under too many rugs to be exactly trustful of our name."

"My God, I've just given them a *library*! Without a dollar of public funds sucked into it! How public-spirited do they think a man can be?"

"A good many voters suspect that a Roland in office would steal the fillings out of their back teeth, I'm afraid. But becoming a power behind the throne, that's different."

"You imagine you have access to our present 'throne,' John?"

"Not the present one. But as I just said, times are changing. New parishes are forming. Lafayette Parish recently seceded from old St. Martin's Parish. St. Landry Parish bids fair to lose half of itself to a new one to be called Calcasieu. And there are Cajuns aplenty in all of them, just waiting to be politically organized."

"Plots and plans! You're beginning to sound like your Grandma at her craziest."

"Am I? I don't think so. It's time we ran a Cajun for Governor of Louisiana."

"Now I *know* you're crazy! The Creoles never would stand for it. They always scoop off the top cream for themselves. They're not going to let any immigrant Cajun run at that level."

"We'll see, Dad." John spoke with quiet certainty. "We'll see. What I want from the company is a reasonable amount of financial backing. A kitty for the game. Not too big a one."

* * *

At the invitation of second cousin Alphonse, Denis and Baptiste had been off for most of the autumn season "getting acquainted" with upriver Bernard relatives. November was closing in before they paddled back down the bayou again.

They found their tall father sitting on the porch high on its stilts over the bank. He was a welcome and revered sight to both sons as they tied up and strode to join him. The vermeil hair they remembered from childhood was edging toward snow now. But the brown eyes were still alert and vivid.

"So you're home at last," Christophe hailed. "We've missed you."

They hunkered down on the railing alongside him, pulled out their pipes, began to puff contentedly. "We've missed you, too, Pa. But wait till we tell you where we've been."

"Up at your great-grandfather Marius's farm is where you've been, isn't it?"

"Well, some. But not altogether. Cousin Alphonse is about to hoist anchor there. Since Uncle Claude died, he's had it in mind anyway. Now there's pressure on him to sell out to the big sugar plantation just next south of him."

Baptiste took over from Denis. "Sugar isn't like other crops, you know. A lot more land is needed. One planting has to take place before the previous harvest is in. Then there's ratoon crops to be considered. For all kinds of reasons, you have to have huge acreages to make big profits. All along the river, small farmers are being squeezed out."

"I know. I've seen a canefield or two myself." For an instant, a sadness brushed Christophe's eyes. "The

Acadians were forced out of their native homes in my father's younger day. Now it's kind of happening again. A second Great Expulsion."

"Could be," Denis agreed, although without any hint of a similar unhappiness. "The point is, this time there's an exciting place to go. Big things to do there."

"You don't think Louisiana holds opportunities enough?"

"Sure it does, Dad." Baptiste leaned forward. "It's still Louisiana we're talking about. But way, way west of here. It's the huge prairie stretching all the way to Texas. The Cajun Prairie, folks are beginning to call it. Displaced Cajuns, folks who've sold out to sugar, are pouring in there like flood waters from the Mississippi."

"And the opportunities are there!" Denis urged. "No limits to 'em!"

A faint scowl creased Christophe's forehead. "The shrimp don't know that, boys. They're going to keep on swimming right where they've always swum."

"We . . . well, we weren't thinking so much about shrimping, Dad. Out there, it's mostly going to be rice and cattle. Cousin Alphonse took us along for a look at the land he's bought there for a song."

"And Cousin Leon has bought right next to him. Leon's going into rice. Alphonse favors beef steers. Golly, it'll be a whole new world out there! New towns going up. New ranches being staked out. New fortunes to be made."

"What we Bernards know is the water," Christophe said slowly, trying to press the point without dampening their enthusiasm. Truthfully, he never had seen either of his two sons so enthusiastic.

"But on the Cajun prairie, Pa—"

"Let the Mexicans raise longhorns. Let the Chinese raise rice. We Cajuns are the shrimpers of the world. We're known and respected for our skill."

"Generation after generation?" There was something a trifle dark in Denis's usually sunny tone. "Do what your Dad does? He does it because *his* Dad did. And Dad's Dad—"

"I've wondered about something," Baptiste put in more mildly. "Bernard men always seem to expect to follow one pattern, Bernard womenfolk are as different as the designs on snowflakes, no two alike. There's Mama, the perfect homebody. There's Aunt Marie, anything for a laugh and always as ready to go as if she's still a youngster. Blanche is growing up to be a professional beauty; she thinks of nothing but how to rake the next beau into her net. Even somebody like old Cousin Sylvie, hermitting off there in the swamp, fits no family pattern. They're all, well, individuals. Shouldn't we men be, too?"

Christophe felt an iron weight at his dead center.

It never had occurred to him that his sons might not itch to step into the family occupation as he had done, as Roger-Claude had done, as René was showing every promise to take over. But these two, his own? They'd really never shown the same dedication. Granted, some of their feelings and inclinations must stem from their mother, Dorothée. He'd never until now wondered if Denis and Baptiste might be strangers.

This was *their* lives his boys were talking about. He'd have to get to know them better. Was there still time for that, amongst a trio bound together only by hot Bernard blood?

*   *   *

In the remote backwater where Sylvie Bernard had chosen to spend her life, the days were long and the silence profound. As she herself was well aware, folks thought she was on the dotty side. They came to her only when they needed help, the special kind of help she was able to give. Even she didn't know why the gift had been bestowed upon her. It just had come, this instinct for which herb would benefit what ailment.

Because the gift *was* a gift, she never charged any sort of fee for her services. What little she knew that was taught knowledge she had acquired from an old *traiteur* who'd treated Cajuns near her father's ribbon farm during her childhood years. *Mère* Therese had noted her left-handedness and received this as a sign of the girl's secret talent. All *traiteurs* were said to be left-handed, although Sylvie never had heard a satisfactory explanation of why this should be.

Much of the work she did lacked even makeshift explanations. Some of her neighbors, distant ones, all, thought she practiced voodoo or chanted incantations. Nothing of the sort. It was all in the herbs and her skill with them.

Nursing family illnesses, years ago, she had picked up increasing impulses which turned out to be correct. A few books on medicine and anatomy, obtained for her by Schoolmaster Despres at St. Jacques after Roger, during his teaching career, first introduced them, had helped.

And that was all.

One thing she would never make *any* explanation about. Not ever. And that was why she had crept away into the swamps while still a young woman, and almost never had left the wilderness since.

She maintained herself decently enough on a boggy garden patch and on the animals her traps caught for her. Her trap line was almost sacred to her. Every sunrise she followed it, she felt deep inside some eager vestige of the girl who once had made similar pilgrimages in the company of the only man who ever might have made her life different.

There never had been any chance whatever that this might happen; none at all.

For one thing, Roger Bernard was her own blood uncle, her father's brother. For another, despite a real affection for her, which Sylvie recognized and cherished, Roger never had entertained the slightest suspicion of how she felt. And for a third, she had always been certain there was some other woman to whom he deeply and permanently belonged. He never spoke of her, but Sylvie had sensed she was there. The ultimate barrier.

Then, one day, Roger had taken her along to St. Jacques with him on an errand run for Marius. At the bustling new settlement they had met Schoolmaster. Whatever Schoolmaster had told him, Roger was off to New Orleans next day like a pistol-shot.

Bearing the lead of a pistol shot in his arm, he was back within the week. And with him came the woman, Rosalie. Rosalie's tiny son Christophe was another addition. One look at Rosalie's radiant loveliness and Sylvie had all the extra proof she needed. Too often, she had seen her own thin, sallow, stark-featured little face peering down into a clear bayou pool.

The door closed. It would be closed always.

Yet she had been too wise to resent what could not be remedied. She was glad because of Roger's obvious, deep, soul-filling happiness. She was glad when, on that night the pellet in his arm seemed to be poisoning him past salvation, they hurried him to her cabin as a last resort. To cut away his rotten arm had all but killed her. But it would have killed her more certainly if she had not been able to save him, and to give him his future with his beautiful Rosalie.

Years didn't dim the memories. Sylvie merely set her lips a trifle tighter and outlived time. They'd had good years together, Roger and the girl he loved, before that first gravestone had to be set up in St. Jacques. Then he'd had more good years with his sons and girl child, before he too lay in the churchyard. She, Sylvie, had given him those. It was her repayment for the mornings he'd taken her trapping, way back when.

Even now, there were reminders to be treasured. There was Marie. His daughter.

Marie sat now, as she rather often did, on the thin platform of planks which made a sort of porch for Sylvie's cabin. She was a vital, forward-looking creature, who even in childhood had captured Sylvie's affection. Although she was feminine and pretty, her looks did stem from her father. Now threads of grey were beginning to wander through her dark mane, yet she still seemed young. She might have been Sylvie's own little one.

"So the chicks are flying the coop, are they?" Sylvie seldom smiled, as Roger could have remembered were he still alive. "It's right sudden, isn't it?"

Marie's lively laugh sounded magical there in the silent swamp.

"Hardly chicks, Cousin Sylvie. They're grown up young men, remember. Baptiste is keeping company."

"How can he figure to leave the country, if he's seriously intended?"

"He'll marry Elizabeth and take her along. Or he'll leave her behind and forget her. Denis is more sensible. Denis swears he won't get hitched until he has his ranch in top shape."

"And then, I suppose, marry one of his precious longhorn steers?"

They laughed at that notion together. Most of the kin would have been startled to discover that "weird old Cousin Sylvie" had a laugh in her. Even Roger had heard it very seldom.

"Baptiste isn't going in for animals, though, is he?"

"Rice, Cousin Sylvie. The million dollar crop of the future, so he assures me. Both boys have found land close by in the same new parish. They can keep tabs on one another."

"It will seem lonesome here without them."

"We're already well aware of that. Dorothée has a constant red nose these days from weeping."

"I wondered when Christophe first met her here in my shack how that joining would work out. She was a good girl and she had looks. But she was always a mite tearful."

"It's worked like a charm. Some men dote on women who'll weep on their shoulder and make them feel big-strong-manly. Haven't you ever noticed that?"

"I reckon I don't have much experience of men, Marie."

Sylvie observed that, despite her heartiness, the younger woman had colored faintly. Marie didn't have it in her to hurt another human being—not by intention anyway.

"Well, men can be studied even from a safe distance. I've never married myself, yet I'm really an expert. I've lived my whole life in a houseful of 'em."

"Some way, Marie, I've gotten to know swamp things better. They're my houseful."

The two of them sat silent for a while, then, looking out across the water. On a rope tied to a cypress pole at one corner of the shack, Marie's *pirogue* rode lazily and dipped to each wave. A heron flew over, arching from green to green. The ghostly mosses wavered.

"I'm glad you came today," Sylvie said gently.

"I sort of hankered to. You're restful to be with, Cousin Sylvie, when the house is too full of emotions. I don't want to wail for Denis and Baptiste. Since they're going, I want to send them off in happy style. But Dorothée does make that difficult."

"Perhaps she's right, like the chorus in one of those Greek tragedies. Who's to say? But this is sure enough the end of something for Bernards. Aren't we Cajuns ever to settle down anywhere for keeps? Is it always going to be a thing of 'Move along! Move along!'?"

"There must be roots for us somewhere. We weren't always nomads, were we?"

Silence again. Marie tilted back her head and stared up at the sky.

"I tell you what, Cousin Sylvie. Once the boys are settled out there on this Cajun Prairie they're so bound to get to, you and I will go out together and pay them a long visit. Maybe we'll catch Prairie Fever too and stake out our own new empire."

The thought of straying that far from the quiet churchyard in St. Jacques was something Sylvie could not even contemplate. He was there with his Rosalie again. But sometimes Roger might miss his Cousin Sylvie just a little.

"Empires are for the next generation, honey. I'd miss my trap line too sorely, were I ever to leave it. You go. I'll stay."

PART
THREE

19

HOMECOMINGS WERE ALWAYS occasions which, to John Roland, seemed balanced on a delicate scale: anticipation on one side, a sure knowledge of approaching boredom on the other. The house and his offspring weighted one side of the scale, his pleasure at reunion with the children and their stately mansion always glowing in him. The other hypothetical side of the scale held his wife Eleanor. Merely to think of her was apt to start him stifling yawns.

Despite her plainness, her prominent teeth and sallow skin and generally muddy coloring, their wedding had been the crowning social event of the New Orleans season three years earlier.

Eleanor Hadley was the only daughter of Senator Briggs Hadley. Guests had gathered in *La Ville* for

the ceremony from plantations as far up-river as
Memphis, Natchez and even St. Louis. The Senator
(perhaps in relief at disposing of an unattractive duckling) had spared no expense. Thirty houseguests had
put up at the Hadley plantation alone. Every important
townhouse in New Orleans had bulged with distinguished occupants. The bride's trousseau, to the last
stitch, was imported from Paris. Attendant balls and
fêtes, and the ceremony itself with an entire symphony
orchestra concealed among blossoming magnolias to
play the wedding march, had been the gossip of the
town for weeks beforehand, afterward and during.

Quite often, as these entertainments ran their course,
the groom had found himself wondering how much of
the talk centered on speculations about himself. How
had his bride ever acquired so presentable a husband-
to-be? Nobody really wondered. It was painfully obvious that only Briggs Hadley's money could have
brought about the miracle. Admittedly, the Rolands
were a highly respectable city family, having produced
three generations of leaders in New Orleans. But Anton
Roland must have fallen upon very evil financial times
to sacrifice his only son.

Actually, the whole connubial pageant had been of
John's own personal devising.

He fully intended to one day hold the reins of power
in Louisiana in his own practiced hands, no matter who
sat in the State House or traipsed off to Washington
City with Senatorial rank.

To achieve this, a man needed more financing than
John's own parsimonious father was willing to risk in
the political arena. Being himself a politician, and a
shrewd one, Senator Hadley became John's logical
target. If swinging Briggs Hadley into line behind him

required gulping down a deep breath and marrying the ugly duckling who would never become a swan, so be it. He would have done even worse things to achieve his purpose.

The house and the children—not to mention Briggs' checkbook and canny advice—were his compensations. The "old Roland place" had been left him in his grandmother's will, the last will among many which a judge had considered to be lucid. His father and mother, being already handsomely housed on a nearby street, were agreeable. So John had suitable quarters to which to return with the scarecrow bride.

He genuinely loved the proud place, which to him meant Amanda Roland. Since babyhood, he had idolized his majestic Gran.

Mounting the marble steps on this particular late afternoon, he remembered as he often did to be grateful. At least he never had been required to present to Gran the newest Mrs. Roland. The contrast between them would have been too cruel.

The sour-visaged butler who had replaced the Joe Wadham of John's schoolboy years replied to John's knock and subserviently accepted his master's beaver, cane and gloves. Stepping into the almost regal reception hall, Amanda's heir glanced about himself proudly.

"Have the children been well during my absence, Hull?"

"The two young gentlemen have been teething, sir. It has made them at times a trifle restless. Miss Glenda has been her usual uncomplaining self, so Mrs. Wadham reports."

"Excellent. And"—John paused in some distaste—"Mrs. Roland?"

"Waiting for you in the parlor, sir. In the hope you'd arrive in time for dinner."

John headed for the parlor, more with the stride of a condemned hero than of a joyous spouse. As he entered a room still elegant with furnishings and mementos of an earlier mistress, Eleanor looked up from her novel to pucker her lips for the necessary kiss of duty. John delivered it with eyes half shut. Those teeth! Facing such a ceremony, he always half-expected to be bitten.

"We waited for you last night, John, until dinner grew tombstone cold. You might at least have sent word you'd be detained on that dreary prairie."

"How distressing, my love. Alexander Mouton had an extra campaign speech at Lafayette jammed into his schedule. Naturally, I had to remain alongside. I've become his right hand of late, and we're taking no chances on his becoming the first Cajun Governor."

"You politicians lead such wretched lives. It's always the same with Daddy. Miss a good dinner and kiss a hundred grimy Cajun babies. Ugh!"

Plentiful experience had taught John that dinners at the Roland house no longer approached what they had been in Amanda Roland's day. The famed cook had departed in a huff during poor Gran's final illness, unwilling to remain in a household where guests no longer came to praise her soufflés and *poutine râpure*. A string of replacements had been mediocre at best. In any event, to face those rabbit fangs while eating would ruin the finest meal in Christendom.

"We mustn't complain," John said, as he had said many dozen times before on similar homecoming evenings. "Louisiana deserves the finest we can give her."

"What does a neglected wife deserve?"

"Alexander and I are proud to sacrifice even our firesides for our duty. I'm going up to kiss the children."

Mounting the gracious stairs he so often had watched Gran descending in his youth, he felt the stone in his chest lighten with every step. Uncle Percy's old room had been redone for the thriving twins. He looked in there first. Apparently the tiny pearls along their small pink gums had subsided for the night, because they both slept like angels. In one crib Bruce hugged a rag tarbaby. In the other Gareth dangled one hand appealingly between the bars.

John tiptoed out and went along the hall to Glenda's door.

As he entered here the old woman rocking in a far corner creaked to her feet and curtsied. Lucy Wadham had been with the family as long as John could remember, long ago as Gran's personal maid, later as poor little Glenda's attendant nurse. She was deaf now, and semi-blind. But her loyalty still made her invaluable. Despite Eleanor's complaints, John flatly refused to discharge the old retainer.

"How's she been while I was off in the parishes, Lucy? Everything all right?"

"Not much change, Mr. John. No worse anyway, not as I can see."

Just why his small crippled daughter held the spot she did in his heart, John might have found it difficult to say. The two boys had inherited the looks in the family. Little Glenda took after her mother in every unfortunate feature. The birth accident which had twisted her spine, shortened one leg and doomed her to a life of unceasing pain seemed to him an unforgivable tragedy. God must have been out of His mind to per-

mit it. Just to watch Glenda's uncomplaining endur-
ance of her fate shredded his heart.

He crossed to the dainty spool bed where she lay
looking up at him, gladness in her unremarkable brown
eyes. He took her hand, and as he did so slipped a tiny
package into it. He never returned from one of his
campaign tours without some evidence that he had
thought of her.

"I'm glad you're home, Daddy. We all missed you."
And he knew that by this at least, he truly had been
missed.

Presently, because he didn't want to tire her, he
slipped out of her room and went downstairs again.
Hull was just striking the Chinese gong which served
as a summons to dinner. But John turned instead to
pick up his hat and gloves from the gilt side table.

"Tell Mrs. Roland I couldn't delay for the meal,
Hull. I have business to discuss with my father." He
was out the front door before his message could be
delivered and Eleanor's whines of protest could com-
mence. How did he manage never to strike the
woman?

Only a few blocks separated the two Roland houses.
The distance did not merit ordering out the carriage.
John walked it, framing in his mind what he wanted to
say to the man who was still titular head of the House
of Roland, but who nowadays leaned on him so
heavily.

Both his parents were seated by their discreet fire
when their uniformed maid—John never quite could
remember the hag's name—showed him in. Anton
arose to offer a pompous handshake. Charlotte put
aside her *petit point* as if resenting an interruption.

Nothing but needlework seemed to interest her in the slightest, these days; not even her lone son.

"The tour with Mouton was successful, John? Vote looks hopeful for him?"

"He'll carry all the new Cajun parishes like a tidal wave, Father. It's New Orleans that could trip him. You know how the Creoles are about advancing their own."

"Would it were true of Cajuns! We Rolands never had great success with 'em."

"Alexander Mouton is of a different cut, Father. His family's never been accused of sharp practice, or any other malfeasance. People still remember that two men of the Mouton name were first to venture down the river to start Cajun settlements here."

"Did Mouton return to the city with you?"

"Of course. It wouldn't do to leave him out in the hutments alone. He might get some absurd idea that he could run this campaign without me. Besides, we both have a meeting scheduled for tomorrow. Plans for the new westward railroad are under discussion."

"That railroad is a pipe dream. It'll never be built, John."

"It will be, it will be. If Mouton wins the Governorship, we'll have surveyors out in those new prairie parishes in jig time. Ten years from now, rail should run as far toward Texas as Lafayette. Western Louisiana will open up like a book."

"I'll never see the day. Neither will you. That's wilderness, son."

"Give it a decade and it won't be. Not once our plans get moving. I found those new border parishes very interesting, Father. In the open country beyond

St. Martinville one feature interested me particularly. Two ranches out there belong to—wouldn't you know it?—Bernard spawn. One's in cattle, the other in rice."

"Bernard?" Anton's face darkened. "The *same* Bernards that always stand against us?"

"I checked them in town. They're both sons of Bayou Lafourche Christophe, the one who looks like Uncle Percy. And they're both flourishing like the green bay tree in the Bible, curse them."

"While we Rolands largely missed out on the Prairie," Anton grated.

"Perhaps it's not too late in that quarter, Father. I've been mulling over some thoughts I'd like your views on. I boil to see Bernard riffraff lapping up the richest cream."

Denis Bernard stood on the porch of his solid ranch house with his sons Hosea and Daniel beside him and stared out across his acreage with the good feeling this wide view never failed to give him.

This far west of the Bayou Teche, where he and Baptiste had chosen to settle, the world seemed to stretch from horizon to horizon with little manmade interruption. Innumerable small bayous and streams cut up the land like veinings in a slab of marble to give this new country a touch of the familiar. It was just enough like the shrimping grounds where he and his brother had grown up to help allay any occasional homesickness.

The fringe of live oaks was familiar, too, although the cottonwoods were less so. And the area was filling up with Cajuns ousted from earlier farms for the sake of sugar. One of those immigrant families had brought him his wife, Hermione. Where he stood, Denis could hear the clatter of her kitchen pans as she readied dinner for her menfolk.

It was a good world. He loved it.

"Hey, Pa," nudged the elder boy, Hosea, fetching his father back out of his random reverie. "Why didn't you take me with you to St. Martinville like you're always saying you will? I could help hustle back our new beef stock. I'd save you wages on one driver."

Denis reached over to muss up Hosea's thatch of unruly hair, as flame-red as Hermione's. "You're still a mite small to handle a steer that didn't want to head where you head it, son. Pretty long hours in the saddle, too, all the way from St. Martinville."

Daniel was still too small to entertain personal dreams of grown-up activities. Going after crayfish in the shallow ponds where cypress grew was the height of his present ambition. But he was a boy with a healthy bump of curiosity. "What's St. Martinville like, Pa? Is it big?"

"Well, not so big as New Orleans, where Uncle Baptiste and I used to be taken sometimes when we were your age. But pretty big just the same. It's the most prosperous steamboat port along the Teche. Folks call it *Le Petit Paris*. Reckon it's not quite *that* grand, though."

"What made it so grand, Pa? The steamboats?"

"The steamboats brought the people, sure enough. But it's the people that really matter. Cajuns like us, first off. Then, later, a lot of other French-speaking folk. Refugees from the bloody revolution in France. Followers of Napoleon, after he'd been exiled to Elba. It makes a good mix of neighbors, same as the things your Ma puts in her gumbo."

"I'd admire to see St. Martinville, same as Hosea.

Except I wouldn't pester you to let me drive cattle with the hands, like Hosea does. I'd keep out of the way, Pa. I'd just look."

"There's plenty to look at, Danny. There's a big church, named after St. Martin of Tours, facing on the fine old square shaded by big oaks. There's rows of stores and such, overhung with galeries. You'd bear as much French as American being gabbled."

Hosea cut in. "Why do you have to go to St. Martinville so often, Pa?"

"I go on business. When it's not to collect new stock shipped to me up-bayou, it's to check question answers in the brand book. That's kept in St. Martinville, and it's been the legal decider on cattle ownership disputes for almost a century. The first recorded Cajun brands in the book go back to the 1760s. The way our stocks roam open range, *au large*, there'd likely be warfare among the *vacheries* if the brand book didn't keep claims straight."

Smiling and buxom, her hair on fire like her son Hosea's, Hermione appeared in the doorway behind them to announce the evening meal was on the table. As they trooped indoors behind her, kitchen smells told them what to be expecting: a jambalaya of crawfish, vegetables and rice, homebaked bread, a pecan pie. The pie was special, prepared in celebration of Denis's return from a long session on the trail.

"Golly-gee!" Daniel applauded. "We haven't had pecan pie since Aunt Blanche came here to visit, back last year! Ma did all her fanciest cooking then to make a big impression."

"It wasn't to impress Aunt Blanche," Hosea scoffed. "It was to impress all the cowboys that started buzzing 'round the minute they sighted her. Ma likely figured to catch a husband for her, so Aunt Blanche would stay on here and not head back home."

Hermione laughed. It was a hearty sound that rang through the whole comfortable kitchen.

"The husband your Aunt Blanche would marry hasn't crossed her vision yet. It's only admirers she hankers for, the pretty thing. She loved having every bachelor on the prairie making oogle eyes at her. But just let any man try to rope and hog-tie her!"

"Blanche's way since she was a baby," grinned Denis. "She hadn't changed a hair."

"Which reminds me," said his wife. "There was a nice long letter came for us while you were on the trail. I stuck it up there on the dish shelf for you and plumb forgot it."

As she made a move to rise, Denis interrupted.

"Don't bother now, honey. Time enough to read it after we've tended to this choice grub. Just fill me in on the main points."

"Well, let's see." Hermione settled back. "Two more men have proposed to her and both been turned down. She's considering taking employment in the city. Aunt Marie's had the fever, but she's safely over it."

Denis spooned up more jambalaya. "My sister Blanche actually considered *working?*"

"It's in a new government office. They're organizing to survey westward for some railroad the Governor plans. Blanche thinks there'll be lots of young men hired, I reckon. What they want her for is to be an office receptionist. With that smile and those green eyes, they must figure she could dazzle any enemy who happened by."

"Likely she could. I'd hate to be the unsuspecting

male my sister went to work on. Did you figure from the letter that she might actually take up this work offer?"

"It didn't sound impossible. She was even trying it out the week she wrote. At least one male caller seemed really to impress her. What was his name now? Roland, John Roland."

Denis's chair crashed over backward from the violence with which he pushed it back from the table. "God Almighty! Not those bastard Rolands in our hair again?"

"Denis Bernard, don't you cuss before the boys like that. Sit and eat your dinner."

"John son-of-a-bitch Roland!" Denis seemed not even to have heard her. "Blanche ought to know what bad blood lies there. She ought to *know*. Does Papa have any idea what's up with her? Does Aunt Marie suspect Blanche would pass the time of day with a Roland?"

"How should I know such things, Denis? The old feud's way before my time. Blanche's letter is right there on the shelf for you. She certainly doesn't sound like she holds any grudge against this fellow."

"She damn well should! Papa and Aunt Marie would flay the hide off her if they sniffed any part of this. And I'm sure as Hell going to write and warn 'em. Rolands once tried to wipe out our whole family, Hermione, in a mass murder!"

The Surveying Office was hot enough to bake cookies in. Every window in the place stood wide to catch any fragment of a breeze. Overhead "coolers" revolved lazily, disturbing even lazier flies. None of it did much to make the central room bearable. Blanche Bernard

sat limp at the reception desk and daintily manipu-
lated a palmetto fan.

"If I had one wish granted me," she murmured to
the girl filing blueprints beside her, "it would be to
live my next life as an Eskimo. That's just plain
truth."

"Lordy, why an *Eskimo*? They bundle up in furs
and gnaw on whale blubber."

"They also live in little houses built of ice and float
around on icebergs. Not a drop of perspiration to
annoy them. A girl can at least stay presentable."

"I never noticed you had trouble looking presentable, honey." The file clerk had been hired for effi-
ciency, not beauty. She tended to be a trifle waspish.
"*He* never seems to notice, either. And here he comes
again right now. Get that smile ready, peaches."

Blanche sensed his arrival without actually looking
up, made aware by her fellow employee's tactful sidewise move out of hearing range. She allowed almost
a full minute to pass, conscious that he stood before
her desk with eyes fixed hungrily upon her yellow
curls and the cleft between breasts which open buttons of her shirtwaist half exposed. Then, slowly, she
raised her head. Long eyelashes lifted to reveal twin
jade eyes.

"Why, Mr. Roland! Good afternoon, sir. How may
I help you?"

"Actually, Miss Blanche, it was you I was thinking
of. Such a hot afternoon. It's not fit for a lady to set
foot on the pavement. I just happened to be passing
in my pony cart, and thought perhaps you'd like a
drive to your ferry wharf."

"How very considerate of you, Mr. Roland. But I
mustn't impose on your kindness."

"No imposition at all. The kindness would be yours, Miss Blanche."

"Then I thank you and I do accept. Our office closes in a very few minutes."

All politeness, all formal courtesy, they presently walked out the office door together and down the flight of stairs leading to an almost steaming sidewalk. The file clerk peered after them with a sour grimace. Why did everything good have to happen to blondes? She, Aggie Amos, would have to drag herself home through the fire of Hell itself, no man to her rescue.

The pony cart set out smartly enough from the curb where John Roland had left it. But its direction was not toward the ferry wharf where one would embark for a crossing to Algiers. Instead, it veered into the old French Quarter. Gaze fixed on the lovely figure beside him, John seemed to let his dapple grey find her own way. His look glowed with naked hunger.

"Aggie knew perfectly well we weren't mere passing strangers, John. She kept hinting all afternoon. That witch possesses supernatural powers, I swear."

"I wouldn't care if the whole world knew about us, darling."

But that, of course, fell considerably short of the truth. Mad as he was for this enchantress, crazy though he was to have her beside him always, he would not have sacrificed Briggs Hadley's support for anything as ephemeral as love. It tortured him to remember that someday a free spirit like Blanche might meet some other man and drift away from him. But business was business.

When they reached the small house on a quiet courtyard, the one John had purchased the day after his first glimpse of this vision at her desk in the survey office, the gray pony did indeed turn in under the archway through force of habit. John handed Blanche down with the gallantry of a cavalier, feeling younger at the mere touch of her hand. He fumbled for the key to unlock an inconspicuous blue door.

Only when the door had closed behind them did he turn to her and sweep her into his impatient embrace. The feel of her against him, all softness and smoothness, all ripeness so different from scrawny Eleanor, set hammers inside him to pounding insanely.

Not even waiting to paw her thin clothing off her, he dragged her down onto the waiting bed.

20

NEW ORLEANS was booming by the year which hinged the century in its middle.

Although the State Capital just had been moved up-river to Baton Rouge, the older and more elegant city had grown until it was rated fourth-largest in the entire Union. Plans for an ambitious railroad westward now were definite. Everyone was saying that by the decade's end tracks would be laid as far as Brashear City and Berwick Bay.

That this would spell a vast opening up of the Cajun prairie (within foreseeable years, clear to the Texas border!) was predicted on every hand. Half the state's territory was still uncharted, and Governor Alexander Mouton's successor was remedying this. The Survey

Office hummed almost audibly with increased business.

To many in the city such growth and expansion seemed progress at breakneck speed. To the present ruler of the House of Roland, time dragged its feet. Old Anton, nearly retired now, might simply shake his head and struggle to hang onto the coattails of catapulting events. John, handsome and increasingly dignified as he passed into his middle years, had been developing his patience and urging progress along at every opportunity. He had been waiting patiently for the day when a certain long-cherished plan could ripen.

Now, that awaited point in time at last had arrived. With the railroad no longer a mere pipe dream, even people far out on the prairie were accepting the most fantastic prophecies as to growth in the west. Every cattleman from the Teche to Texas anticipated tripling his herds against a day when beef could be transported to New Orleans by rail. Rice forsaw an equal sales increase.

So it was time to bait the trap.

He had summoned the man to an office which had been his father's and grandfather's before him. Behind his impressive desk, he sat studying his visitor critically.

"You are doubtless somewhat puzzled, Mr. Deane, as to why a business office such as ours has suggested it might interest an actor to call on me. We produce no dramas."

"Precisely why I have arrived at the time you appointed, sir."

The voice which answered him was one of the most mellifluous John ever had heard. And so fastidiously

English that Gran, in her day as a *doyenne*, would have welcomed him to her exclusive soirées with open arms.

"How could one not be piqued by the payment of one's round-trip journey from Baltimore, Mr. Roland, when the payer is a gentleman entirely unknown to him?"

"I trust your long trip will not prove idle. You were born in England, Deane?"

"In Brighton. I was full grown when I left there for London and the theatre."

"Since when, I believe, you have specialized in high society roles? Dukes and the like? I have already admired you on stage during my business trips to northern cities. You have a genius, Deane, for portraying the *ton*. You are flawless in your roles."

Roderick Deane permitted himself a gracious smile, framed by perfectly barbered Dundreary side-whiskers. "How extraordinarily flattering of you. My thanks, Mr. Roland."

"Not flattery. Merely fact. I've studied your work very closely, you see."

"Ah? I regret your having had to trek such distances. Alas, I have never as yet had the pleasure of performing in Louisiana."

"If you'd ever before acted here, sir, I should have not sent for you now. The role I hope to interest you in is one for which no actor known to New Orleans would be appropriate. A fresh face is absolutely requisite. As is your special talent, sir."

"You do intrigue me, Mr. Roland. You are opening a new theatre?"

"It might be put that way. But one with a very wide proscenium. My stage, Deane, is to be the whole

Cajun Prairie—an enormous area. It will concentrate on a special area of that giant expanse, of course. The plot deals with one rice plantation in particular."

A wary glint lit Roderick Deane's limpid eyes. "I begin to suspect that this play is not yet written? And that the role you offer me would require considerable *ad lib?*"

"You'd play a very wealthy English Lordship, Deane. One planning to buy up considerable tracts of land. It's your intention to build whole new towns once the railroad goes through. Being an international financier as well as nobility, you will make tempting offers for such specific areas as interest you."

"Mr. Roland, what you say hints at the . . . may I say, criminal?"

"Would crime offend you, Deane? Considering your original reason for fleeing from the Bristol police? Or your ingenious adventure with those diamonds in Chelsea?"

For a single instant, Deane's well-disciplined face registered stark terror. "How the blazes did you ever uncover—"

"As a businessman, I customarily do my homework. I've had agents in London check out your whole history, sir. The moment I settled on you as ideal for what I have in mind, I set out to discover everything about you. It was as I'd hoped. The lawmen of four cities in Britain and one in Canada have warrants sworn against you."

"I was not guilty of those charges in Liverpool, I swear!"

"No matter. The warrants are all in the name of Rudolph Daitch, which of course is what you were born. You'll remain quite safe here in the States as

Roderick Deane. Unless, sir, someone should reveal
your true identity."

"What do you want of me?" The accent was still
flawless. The eyes submitted.

"Splendid! I hoped you'd be interested. Your character's name will be Lord Chisholm. I will furnish all
the wardrobe necessary, and backing. At the end of
the run you'll be generously compensated. For obvious
reasons, there will be no written contract. And it will
not be known in New Orleans, Deane, that you and
any Roland ever met."

John watched the actor's back as it vanished through
his open office door minutes later. A small package of
untraceable bank notes, which he just had taken from
a desk drawer and passed to Deane to cover temporary
expenses, made no visible bulge whatever in Lord
Chisholm's well-tailored coat pocket.

Face-up in the open drawer lay a worn old account
book which had belonged to his grandfather.

The entry there which had first sparked John's daring plan when he came upon it still intrigued him now.
What could old Antoine Rolande have been up to, way
back then three-quarters of a century ago?

He leafed the pages until a neatly penned record
stared up at him, refusing still to bare its secret: *To
Vermilion Guidry, actor, for private services rendered. . . .*

Progress! Expansion! The Railroad! They were fa-
vorite words all across the Cajun Prairie, these days.
Land prices were climbing steadily as more displaced
Cajuns arrived each week to put down roots in the
Promised Land. Those already in residence were

greatly increasing their former holdings. Only Good Times could be coming!

As with most of their neighbors, the boom was a favorite topic whenever members of the Bernard clan foregathered. When Baptiste and his wife Elizabeth and their little daughter Mimi drove over to Denis's ranch for a family dinner, no other subject of conversation seemed of comparable interest. Even Hosea was mature enough by now to dip a paddle wholeheartedly in the inevitable debates.

Younger Daniel was still content to play host to his smaller cousin Mimi, and keep her entertained with tours of the corral. There they could watch Pa's cowboys at the dangerous chores of roping and bronco busting. But his elders derived more excitement from speculations as to the golden times bound to come.

"I finally did it, Denis," Baptiste said proudly. "Rode up to Opelousas and had my talk with Silas Eagleton. His bank's ready to grant me the mortgage money."

"You'd have to put up the land you already own as security, Baptiste."

"That's only a formality. I can add those south acres to my paddies and double my rice yield in a few years' time. By then the railroad should be well on its way out to us. I can ship at a fraction of present costs."

"It looks so, brother, it certainly does. But I can't help holding back just a pinch, not adding to my own land yet. Sure, the open range will shut down as populations grow. But I still see a few stumbling blocks. Maybe caution's called for."

"What can go wrong, once the railroad comes through?"

Denis chewed thoughtfully on his pipestem. "Well,

for one thing, suppose they re-survey their route and decide to switch it somewhat? That could throw the whole present plan out of kilter. Rail is certain to run somewhere. But what if it's laid too far off from us?"

"They're *bound* to come through Crawley. It'd be folly to route trains elsewhere. And once rail hits Crawley we're home free. Take a few chances, Denis!"

"Another thing," Denis brooded. "All this northern anti-slave feeling busting out in the Congress up in Washington City. Folks seemed to be getting more riled every session about people owning other people. We're an agricultural state. What happens to big plantations if suddenly our labor's gone? Our whole economy would bust. What then?"

"You don't own slaves, Denis. It's no concern of yours."

"No, I don't. Don't need 'em. Don't even much cotton to the whole idea. But I'm not Louisiana as a whole. Come Emancipation, this state would go broke. There might be no funds to build railroads. Then where would all plans to expand end up?"

Baptiste shook a tolerant head. "Silas Eagleton wouldn't let us down. His advice to me was to buy up even more property. Offered me a bigger loan than I asked for. He's had private recommendations in that direction from New Orleans. Everybody's riding the wave of buy, buy, buy."

"Remember how storm waves on the Gulf used to swamp some of Pa's shrimp luggers, Baptiste? That's what a wave can do, if it takes a mind to. Sink everything in sight."

The prairie spread about them, flat as a great green platter, as they sat in the shade of the cottonwoods and watched the sun go down. Almost too far away to identify, a Bernard herd grazed placidly. Hermione and Elizabeth kept their knitting needles clicking as they listened to their men. Hosea turned raptly from Uncle to Father as the conversation shifted, head moving as if he were watching a contest at battledore-and-shuttlecock.

"You heard anything new from back home, Denis?"

"Aunt Marie writes that Papa shows signs of failing. Cousin René's doing fine, with cousin Gils to help him, keeping the fleet running. But Papa seems just to have lost interest since his falling out with Blanche. It's been most of two years since those two have even spoken. Mama's still crying up a storm over that, I reckon. She always was a champion weeper, Mama was."

"Witness how she carried on when you and I first told her we planned to pull up stakes. But the business about Blanche has been even worse. For a Bernard to take up with a Roland, a *married* Roland at that—it still seems unthinkable."

A moment passed before Denis answered.

He still felt a weight of guilt over what he had written home in the white heat of anger. The rupture had therefore been his doing. Yet certainly affairs in New Orleans would have come to their father's awareness in some other way, if he had not written.

Uncle Roger-Claude had paid them a visit shortly after the explosion, coming out to the prairie to check on possibilities for setting up a crawfish sideline to fleet operations. He had related the whole ruckus grimly.

Like an avenging prophet out of the Old Testament, his brother Christophe had swept down upon *La Ville* armed with the letter from Denis. He had

marched his daughter out of her place in the Survey
Office, not quite literally by force. On a bench in the
nearest park, he had plumped her down and demanded an explanation of the impossible.

Blanche might easily have sidestepped the issue by
claiming John Roland was only an unwelcome office
superior to whom she was compelled to exhibit ordinary politeness. That evasion would have been her
usual approach to a storm. She'd always disliked bad
tempers and sought only peace and masculine admiration.

Instead, she had boldly faced her father with a
statement that she loved the man, Roland or not, married elsewhere or not. That in itself had been a bomb-
shell. So far as anyone in the family ever had been
aware, Blanche had never loved anyone but herself.
To act the family Juliet was a stunner.

According to Uncle Roger-Claude, Christophe had
threatened to go after John Roland with a horsewhip—
mighty melodramatic, considering the difference in
the two men's ages. Blanche had replied by threaten-
ing to spread the truth of her goings-on with Roland
and create a scandal. She claimed defiantly that Roland had been the seduced, not her seducer. With his
deep concern for family respectability and his shame
for Blanche's misconduct choking him, Christophe
had returned to the bayou and an ever deepening
withdrawal from all that had animated him before.
His silence and Dorothée's incessant weeping had
made life at the family homestead difficult thereafter—especially for Marie, who remembered her own
past dreams of a Roland and tended to sympathize
with Blanche.

The memory did not sit well on Denis's conscience. He sighed deeply.

"Bad enough our sister'd do what she did. I can't believe it's made her happy."

"It's gone on a matter of years now. Beyond reason why she'd settle on a Roland, after leading half the males in the state such a merry chase and never taking one of 'em seriously. But that's how it is. We can't change it."

"Maybe we could have, if we'd stayed on the bayou. She's our sister, after all."

"But we didn't stay there, Denis. Our roots are down in the prairie now. We've got our own worries. Mine today is whether maybe I should have listened to Eagleton and taken him up on his offer for a bigger loan to buy even more land. Maybe I'm missing the boat."

The house with the little blue door, facing as it did upon its quiet courtyard shaded by old magnolias, had been built decades earlier by some Creole gentleman creating a nest for his Octoroon mistress. Whatever the love story that had been enacted behind its matching blue shutters, the romance was long over and its lovers doubtless mouldering in separate New Orleans graveyards. Sometimes Blanche found herself wondering about them.

It still amazed her occasionally that she had given herself over so entirely to one man, especially to one several years her senior.

The old days of fan-flirting with each new swain as he came along had been great fun. There had been a seemingly endless line of admirers to dangle. That she was breathcatchingly beautiful had never been exactly a secret from Blanche herself. She had been well aware, always, of what to do with those emerald eyes, so unlike any other Bernard's. Her creamy complexion and truly golden hair had been treasures she'd loved to flaunt and always took painstaking care to nurture.

Then John had come along.

The first thing about him to catch her attention, there in the Survey Office reception room where she was already bored after two weeks of work, had been his eyes. They were as green as her own and marvelously alive. Looking up into them was almost like looking into a mirror. No Bernard before her ever had green eyes. Hers were duplicates of John's. The resemblance was unsettling.

A second thing was the aura of raw power which he exuded: a power like that of a flood released by a breaking dam.

Despite the sophistication and culture which underwrote every catlike motion he made, every word he drawled so charmingly, one felt a little quiver of fear at what he might do to one were he so minded. New Orleans in every sleek line, he was still a savage underneath. He intrigued her from the very instant their glances chanced to lock across the busy bustle of the office.

Afterward, he had told her that the same electric thing happened to him. Even before they actually talked together, he had gone out searching the French Quarter for a place he could take her. He had bought the small house on the courtyard before they so much as touched hands. He knew he had to have her, and

being John Roland, it had not occurred to him that
he might not get what he wanted. That was part of
his fascination.

Now almost three years had passed, and for her the
blue door spelled home. The crude, eager young men
who had panted over her on the Bayou Fourche, or
out west on the prairie when she'd gone there to visit
Denis and Hermione, were vanished as if they never
existed.

The Survey Office he visited so often on business
connected with Governor Mouton, whose aide in matters related to this great railroad project John was,
had to become a thing of the past. Employees there
such as ditchwater-plain Aggie Amos were all too
sharp-eyed to remain ignorant of what was going on.

But there had been no real need for her to work,
even after Papa's devastating visit to the city disowned her. Upkeep on the pretty house tucked away
so discreetly out of public view was a bagatelle for
a man of John Roland's financial resources. So were
the lovely dresses and geegaws he delighted in show-
ering upon her; and Gemma, the mulatto house
servant; and the smart little phaeton with liveried
Rufe, Gemma's husband, to drive it.

In exchange, his mistress gave her lover everything
his marriage to that gargoyle wife denied him. He
never unlocked her blue door without finding Blanche
waiting—bathed, perfumed, coiffed, soft-fleshed, ready
for the canopied bed he had ordered for them shortly
after their first visit to the little house. She satisfied
his body with skills which seemed to somehow burst
instinctively from deep in her own loins.

"I must have been a whore in some previous in-
carnation," Blanche sometimes told John, both amused

and surprised by her own talents. "Delilah? Cleopatra? Who knows?"

But more than catering to his lust, she was also the woman to whom he could talk. The wife to whom he had to make ritual returns on many an evening, leaving Blanche with no company but a book or embroidery, had neither the intelligence nor the interest to listen to his ambitious schemes. Eleanor Roland was the daughter of Briggs Hadley, millionaire and senator. You'd have thought she would be bred to cotton to business and politics. Not so. She moped over each difficulty created by their crippled daughter. She whined at every problem connected with their growing twin sons. She bored her husband excruciatingly.

Blanche felt well acquainted with John's family, even though she knew them only from a distance. He brought every domestic problem straight to her blue door, and relieved himself of them in her sympathetic ear just as he relieved himself elsewise in her willing body.

The twins, whom she had glimpsed on several occasions, Blanche found charming. They were growing up like young weeds; handsome weeds, too, who would one day be the spits of their father.

For the ugly, misshapen girl, whom John obviously adored, she knew she should feel compassion, but didn't quite know how. That a man could dote on such an ill-begotten female, even though he'd sired her, was a mystery. Beauty had always been Blanche's altar and she worshipped at it devoutly, well aware how her own kept John beside her.

"How is the dear little thing coming along?" she would murmur dutifully to her lover as he lay naked beside her in the exhausted aftermath of release she had brought him. "Does the old nurse you've told me about—Lucy, is it?—really nurse her well?"

"Lucy cares about Glenda as much as I. Far more than the poor mite's own mother does. To Eleanor she's a guilt, I suppose. The doctors told my wife to leave off riding during the pregnancy. But Eleanor kept on. Galloped to the country daily. God knows what was happening to the jolted child she carried. But the delivery was a nightmare and Glenda—as she is."

"Small wonder your wife feels guilty, then, *cheri*. Her baby should have had a more solicitous mother." This was as close as Blanche ever dared approach the matter dearest to her heart. She yearned to be the legal Mrs. John Roland, but the barrier was unsurmountable. A gold locket John gave her, engraved with the rampant falcon of the Roland crest, had to substitute for a wedding ring.

"If only Eleanor weren't such a shrew and so unsightly!" John's hand on her breast tightened as he teased her nipple. He was hungry again. She pressed against him, ready.

"I'm glad she's both those things, John. Is that wicked of me? I want you to want *me*, no other. If I didn't have you, I think I should die."

"Not of loneliness. A thousand men would rejoice to take my place." John was now astride her. He thrust deep into her, and she arched her back to take his entry.

"You're the only man who ever will. Does that please you, John?"

"If I didn't have you," John gasped, pumping harder, "I'd have nothing to live for."

This, Blanche knew, was a vast overstatement. No woman alive, not even herself, could fill every need in John Roland's power-oriented life.

Every evening he came to her, he brought excitement over some new venture to share with her. It might be his new vision of creating commercial orange groves in Louisiana, it might be the sulphur mine he was cosseting toward actual production. If such matters did not burn white hot in him, she doubted she ever could have loved him so much. They were his essence.

One vacuum in that passion of his, however, did somewhat puzzle her.

"John, everyone who'll still speak to me seems these days to talk only opportunities for profit out west on the prairie, once the railroad comes. Aren't you the least bit interested in those? I should think you'd be wading in up to your hips."

A wary gleam seemed to take over his eyes. "Plans for the railroad itself are all I can handle in that department. Let others make the land grabs."

"I spent many weeks out there once, visiting my brother Denis. He's into cattle. Our brother Baptiste is developing a rice plantation. Everything seems to be booming." What did this odd look of John's mean? "Aren't you at all intrigued?"

"A man can spread himself only so far before he'd rupture."

"You know best. But so many are rushing into prairie speculation. I've even heard about some fabulously rich English nobleman—Lord Chisholm, I believe he's called—who is out there buying everything in sight, convinced there's a fortune to be had."

John actually scowled at her, a thing almost un-heard of.

"Let's drop it, Blanche. I need no lessons from the English. I've heard of this Lordship somewhere. He sounds like a fop."

"And certainly no one to make you frown, my *homme celeste.* Kiss me, John. Long, deep, as only you can." But behind her soft smile, she kept on wondering.

21

SUCH AS IT WAS, prairie society was stirred to its heels by a new British arrival. When he and his valet and his secretary and his investment advisor checked into the most spacious and luxurious accommodations in the one really fine hotel in Opelousas, word spread like a brush fire.

Certainly the impeccable elegance of Lord Chrisholm and his retinue bore out every rumor which had preceded His Lordship.

Cajun prairie towns were not yet accustomed to entertaining virtual royalty. But in short order every citizen of the area was struggling to discover how one did it. Frantic pleas for grand recipes were being rushed back to New Orleans' great hostelries. Volumes on etiquette were being written east for. Wardrobes were spruced up. Family *parures* and other gems were being retrieved from bank vaults, cleaned until they sparkled.

Certainly no such fine gentleman had taken up residence among them since the earliest Acadians drifted in from the bayous. Somehow it became known that Lord Chisholm was a distant cousin to Queen Victoria herself. His appearance and carriage well supported the rumor. At a time when such adornments were not familiar, his immaculately barbered Dundrearies alone lent him striking distinction. His manners were impeccable, although as one might expect a trifle lofty. His costumes, of course, were all Saville Row.

Almost His Lordship's first visit in town was to Silas Eagleton's bank.

Here, after making an impressive cash deposit, he also rented vault space in which to file the elaborately sealed envelopes which contained, so he explained to banker Eagleton, deeds to American lands already purchased. They also enclosed various London bank drafts which he would employ to acquire prairie properties, if he found any to meet his needs. Those needs included the founding of whole towns to house the work forces he intended to import. Impressed as never before in his career, Silas Eagleton spread the word.

"One thing's for real," Hermione Bernard smiled relievedly. "Our ranch house is far too humble for the likes of royalty. So we're home free, praises be."

Young Hosea was disappointed. "Gee, Ma, he might really relish a good barbecue. If he's so interested in America, maybe he'd like to see how life's really lived here."

"That's all *you* know about grand society, son," his

mother chided. "His Lordship probably never sat down in the whole of his life to a table that wasn't served by a dozen footmen. Can you fancy him dripping sauce from a sparerib onto that splendid waistcoat?"

"You could just ask him to a picnic then. No drippy foods."

"And how would I be togging myself out in the way of diamonds? Could you rig me up a tiara out of the tin kitchen forks? We're not His Lordship's fancy breed, Hosea. Ask your Pa to let you ride in to Opelousas next time he goes. You'd likely catch a glimpse of the great man on the street there, if that means so much to you."

It certainly meant much to the prairie citizenry at large. People a generation older than Hosea felt that same hankering to gawk at a real Queen's cousin. A man in the habit of weekending at Windsor Castle seemed more celestial than human. Although much too refined for vulgar boasting, Lord Chisholm did drop a provocative reference to Kensington or Buckingham now and again. Palaces were so usual to him, of course, that he could not suspect what ripples such mentions sent through his avid listeners.

Invitations poured in at the Opelousas House. Even the untitled gentlemen in His Lordship's suite were being lionized, although they proved to be disappointingly discreet concerning any discussion of Chisholm's real estate intentions. Every silver spoon in the surrounding parishes were polished until it gleamed. Table linens were laundered to perfection.

Various promoters in Opelousas organized a tour of inspection for His Lordship, and picked up the tab. The Opelousas House imported special fruits from

Mexico for its exalted guest. Montezuma himself could have been no more kowtowed to. Chisholm responded in noble style by drawing up a shuddering list of prairie acres he intended to purchase at top prices.

"Wow!" breathed a dazzled Silas Eagleton, summing up reaction for the entire area. "This is about the biggest thing ever to hit west of the Teche! Almost as big as the railroad itself."

Denis and Baptiste wrote glowing accounts of the lordly visitation back home to their Aunt Marie on the bayou; and Marie relayed them enthusiastically to her niece Blanche, on visits she occasionally made to New Orleans just to span the breach Christophe had created.

"Your brothers say it's a miracle what Lord Chisholm is bringing to the prairie. Everyone worships the man. There's actually society of a sort beginning to blossom out there."

Blanche was puzzled. "I've heard about Lord Chisholm from John, Aunt Marie. He never met the man. But he's heard plenty. John isn't impressed at all."

"Most likely because he's after the same lands Chisholm is gobbling up."

"No-oo-oo, I don't think it's that. John doesn't seem to want to get involved out west at all. He has a dozen irons in other fires, but he lets the prairie boom alone. I've tried to figure why he feels this way, but I can't. Denis and Baptiste are right there on the ground. If *they* think this expansion must pay off, they should know."

"They're both bright men. But I never heard that John Roland bypassed a penny."

At the usual time on such visits, an hour before

John could be expected in from his office, Blanche
ordered Rufe to bring the phaeton around and
escorted Marie back to the waterfront where a ferry
home to the Fourche would await her. It was an un-
written rule that Aunt Marie was not expected to act
friendly with John Roland. Aunt and lover were to
be kept in separate compartments of Blanche's affairs.

As they kissed to part on the wharf, Marie patted
her grey hair back into its sensible chignon. "If the
prairie subject ever comes up with your gentleman
friend, do ask him."

"I don't think I'd better, Aunt Marie. The subject
seems to annoy him. I can't think why. There's your
boat whistle. Come back soon again to see me. I love
you very much."

On the drive back to the French Quarter, however,
what they had discussed was much on Blanche's mind.
It *was* mysterious, John's attitude in the matter. He
evaded any mention of it almost as though it held
some guilty secrets. Probably dozens of those existed
of which she had no knowledge whatever. But this
particular one at least tangentially affected her own
two brothers. If John smelled some sort of rat, she
wanted Denis and Baptiste aware of it, too.

She stepped down from the vehicle in the courtyard and Gemma opened the blue door for her.

"Gen'man in the parlor, Miss Blanche. Brought a
dee-spatch for Mr. John."

"I'll speak to him, Gemma. Perhaps I can help him."

As she entered the small but charming parlor, the
messenger seated there scrambled to his feet politely.
"Good evening, ma'am. I'm from Opelousas with a
letter for your husband."

"If I may have it, I'll see that he receives it as soon as he returns."

"That'll be just fine, ma'am. Lord Chisholm wants it to get to him direct, and I guess there's no directer way than by his own lady. I'm obliged to you, Mrs. Roland."

The young man bowed again and took himself off. Still standing with the envelope in hand, Blanche scarcely heard the door when Gemma closed it behind the messenger. Her heart, having skipped a long beat, was pumping now at double pace.

Lord Chisholm!

But John had assured her that he did not even *know* the man. He had made serious, even angry, protestations to that effect—which meant that he had deliberately lied to her.

Which in turn very likely meant that he had some scheme afoot that could adversely affect her own brothers, and therefore did not want her to know about it.

Add to that the fact that this sealed message had been sent to him here in the French Quarter, rather than to his House of Roland offices or to the fine townhouse, which was presided over by a very different "Mrs. Roland." It could only mean that Lord Chisholm was in very close contact indeed with John; otherwise, the Englishman could not have had this address.

His message would have been sent here only because it held very secret contents indeed. And Lord Chisholm was currently stirring up a great dust in the very region where her brothers lived.

Blanche was not altogether a novice at the private

unsealing of letters. On several occasions in her younger days, it had helped along whatever current romance was afoot to know the contents of a *billet-doux* without letting its author know she had read it. She called for hot tea, and when Gemma brought it was ready to make use of the pot's steaming spout.

A few moments later, the resealed missive was neatly propped up on the writing desk where John could not fail to notice it. And leaning against it was a second note, this one on her own scented notepaper.

Darling: A sudden message just now. Papa is very ill. I'm off to help take care of him. Return soon. Despite our ill feelings, I'd never survive it if he died without a reconciliation. She paused for a long moment, pen in hand, before she added the final line she knew he would expect. *I love you, my darling. Blanche.*

As always when His Lordship deigned to cross the bank's threshold, a cathedral hush fell over the counters where minions toiled. Nodding his vague, condescending greeting to each employee as he passed, he was shown immediately into Mr. Eagleton's private office. Several clerks all but curtsied to his erect, perfectly tailored backside.

Silas Eagleton was only slightly less reverent, gesturing his caller to a seat.

"Delightful to see you again this morning. How may I assist Your Lordship?"

Lord Chisholm smiled, reservedly but graciously. "I have decided upon my first land purchase here, Eagleton. As you've offered to handle my acquisitions, I'm here to close the deal."

"Excellent, excellent! If you'll just name the properties you want?"

"The only one I've settled upon thus far is the south acreage just adjoining a rice plantation belonging, I believe, to someone named Bernard. Baptiste Bernard, is it? That unoccupied stretch of country would do me very nicely. So you'll draw up the deeds, Eagleton, eh?"

The banker's eager expression stiffened by a visible trifle.

"Ah, now, what a pity! Bernard himself has taken an option on that particular property. He plans to expand his paddies in that direction."

"I plan to construct my first specimen settlement there."

"If only you'd put in your bid a few weeks sooner, Your Lordship—"

"I have put it in now, Eagleton. As you know, I have been shown over everything in the area that's obtainable. Those are the only acres I could presently consider."

A sick grimace twitched the banker's lips.

"But surely, in this whole fertile land—"

"The *only* acres in which I am interested. If I cannot start my development there, I shall simply cancel all further plans. I trust this will not disappoint your fellow townsmen."

His Lordship made a dignified motion to arise. Silas Eagleton was beside him instantly.

"Something must be arranged. I mean, to lose your promised patronage—"

"*Promised*, Eagleton? I made no specific promise, did I? I need hardly point out that my word is my bond. But I made no promise. Everything has always been contingent upon my decision to buy. That decision is made. You have chosen to reject it."

The banker was all but on his knees. "Please, Your Lordship—"

"My mind is made up, Eagleton. I shall be leaving Opelousas in the morning, with my staff. I regret our acquaintance has not ended more pleasantly. Good day to you, sir."

Lather foamed Denis's big quarter-horse as he reined it in before Baptiste's wide-spreading farm house. Whatever the message from Elizabeth meant, it had to be serious. Baptiste was too young a man to undergo a stroke. Yet that was the word scared little Mimi used when she galloped up to the Denis Bernard spread. Surely some lesser one would apply?

He loose-hitched his reins and strode into the house. His sister-in-law was huddled by the fireplace; and although Elizabeth was no weeper like their mother, she had been crying.

"What the devil's happened? Mimi scarcely could get out sensible syllables."

"I think he's dying, Denis." She stood up like an old woman, which she certainly was not. "He read the letter and just keeled over where he stood. We got him to bed, Mimi and I. But he doesn't even seem to understand who we are or where he is."

Denis was into the double bedroom while she was still speaking. On the broad cypress bed, Baptiste lay staring at the ceiling. His eyes were wide. So was his mouth. A trickle of saliva seeped from one corner of it. His breathing came irregularly, raspingly.

After he had spoken his brother's name twice without receiving the slightest hint that he had been

heard or recognized, Denis took Baptiste's hand in
his. It felt deathly cold. Finger pressure drew no
response. Presently, Denis returned to the parlor.

"You've sent for the doctor, Elizabeth?"

"Mimi was to ride on for him as soon as she'd
alerted you."

Denis set his jaw hard. "This letter? What about
that? It's what hit him."

"It's from the bank. They're foreclosing, Denis.
They're taking everything."

He stared at her, assuming she had gone daffy.
"Foreclose? Silas? On a *Bernard*?"

"Here's their letter. Read it. The loan to buy the
new land was guaranteed by a mortgage, although
Mr. Eagleton assured Baptiste that was a mere formality. When Baptiste was late two payments because of the new equipment needed to expand, Mr.
Eagleton told him not to worry a bit. And now, out of
the blue, they're taking everything."

"That can't happen! I'll see Silas in the morning.
I'll cover whatever's due."

"It won't be any use, Denis." If the dead ever
spoke, they would probably speak like Elizabeth. "The
bank has already resold all our acreage. To Lord
Chisholm, the letter says."

"Impossible! A man of Chisholm's fine reputation
would never—"

"But he has. It's all sealed and delivered. We've lost
everything. Even Baptiste."

Blanche was all but collapsing in her wagonseat,
the last few miles out of the town where she had
rented shay and horse with money obtained by pawn-

ing several jewels John had given her. Those endless days while she hid away under a false name in a New Orleans hotel, shut out of view while she waited for return news from New York City, had dug a great hole in her purse. Subsequent travel, by back bayous John would have difficulty tracing, had taken most of the rest. This shay and nag had stripped her completely.

She felt a thousand years old, and heartsick.

"Lord Chisholm," the young messenger had said, obviously in all sincerity.

But the name on the letter bearing regal seals had not been Chisholm. It had been Roderick Deane. The message itself was clear enough. John Roland had hired an imposter to convince the new prairie parishes that he was a nobleman on a land-buying mission. But the only property he was actually to purchase, and with John's funds, was whatever belonged to Denis or Baptiste Bernard. The rest was to be rejected, on one pretext or another.

Along the back rail she had vomited twice. Her plain black travel cloak was stained with it. She *was* sick, in truth. But the cause of it was shame. Every time she remembered how she had lain under John, returning his kisses avidly, giving back pelvic thrust with eager thrust, the bile in her threatened to surge past her throat again. The man she loved. The man who had bought—yes, bought—her body. Oh, dear God!

From New York, a reply had come at last. This Roderick Deane was a fairly well-known stage performer, specializing in what they called "society business." Although he never had acted in New Orleans, managers of various theatres there could provide Madam with written substantiation and even professional photographs.

She had thanked the police very kindly for their trouble in replying. It seemed to her vaguely that her initial request had carried some excuse about hiring the man. She was too tired now to remember more than bits of what she had said.

When the lights of the Bernard ranch swung into view at last, far ahead, she turned the horse's head toward the yellow pinpoints and sank back into her numb lethargy. The trail behind her stretched endlessly. She had long ago half-forgotten why she had to reach her brothers. They were not even friends. Denis had set Papa against her. Yet the same blood flowed inside them. They were Bernards. Their enemies were called Rolands.

A lifetime later, the shay was turning in between sturdy gateposts. She was almost unaware of stumbling down from her seat and tottering across a simple covered porch and pounding at a panel with fists which seemed as weak and futile as beating moth wings.

"*Blanche!*" The door opened before her, pouring light across her like water from a heaved bucket. She stared back blankly, numbly, into Hermione's startled eyes.

"Denis . . . Baptiste . . . must see. . . ." Her dry lips quavered.

"Come inside, my dear." A strong yet kindly arm drew her across the threshold. "Denis is over at the farm. Baptiste has had a stroke. What in the world are *you* doing here?"

Guided gently to a chair, Blanche collapsed into it.

Because she once had spent pleasant weeks here, the room itself seemed familiar. But it kept dipping and twisting about her.

"You look about ready for a stroke yourself, dear. Hosea, fetch black coffee. Dan, go outside and see to your Aunt Blanche's horse. Now, then. What's all this about?"

"John," said Blanche. It came out as a rasping sob. "My John . . . to rob the boys of everything . . . hates Bernards, always hates . . . hates me, too. I'm one, a Bernard. . . ."

"I can't imagine what you're talking about. Perhaps you'd best not try, just yet."

Others were moving in the lit room, so she and Hermione were not alone together. Hosea? Daniel? But they were too big to be the little boys she'd known. A mug of scalding coffee had been thrust into her hand. Someone had just mumbled that the horse was fine.

She took a deep gulp from the mug, almost searing her throat. The restless walls seemed to settle. She closed her eyes for an instant, then sat more erectly.

"I'm all right now, thank you, Hermione. But I've got to tell my brothers."

"Tell them what, Blanche? In his present state, Baptiste wouldn't understand."

A word wriggled about her brain like a pollywog and came back. "You said . . . *stroke?*"

"He got news from the bank in Opelousas. They're foreclosing on him, taking everything. Denis talked to Silas Eagleton, but it did no good. Denis says the man looked as shamefaced as a boy who'd just wet his pants. But he was still set to do it. Otherwise, he kept whining, Lord Chisholm would withdraw his entire offer. And for His Lordship only the Bernard farm would do."

"His Lordship? There *is* no Lordship, Hermione. He's a fraud, a fake."

"Dear, you're overtired. It's confused you. Why, he's Queen Victoria's own cousin. Everyone hereabouts knows that. He's one of the richest peers in England."

"I'm overtired, I guess, but I'm not confused. If you think I'm crazy, let one of your sons go fetch my portmanteau from the shay. The papers are all there. Signed letters from the theatre managers. Even the lobby display photographs. It's a distinguished face, I guess. At least, it couldn't be mistaken."

"Theatres? Photographs?" Hermione was looking uneasy now, as if she believed she were alone in the house with a maniac while Denis was miles away across-prairie.

Hosea, however, seemed to detect some possible grain of reason in what his disheveled aunt was babbling. Quietly, he eased out the front door—on his way, Blanche sensed, to fetch the portmanteau.

She sat rigid in her chair, awaiting his return. The filth staining her cloak sickened her anew, suddenly an overpowering stench. With shaking hands she undid its fastenings and threw the garment open. Against a breast ruffle of the rumpled gown beneath, the locket John had given her shone like a golden star.

John . . . John . . . John . . . And the room was swaying again. She forced it steady.

"Look in the portmanteau, Hosea. Under the folded clothing. There's a packet of papers, tied up with a green ribbon. Find it. Undo it. Look at what's there."

For a good while, then, the rough but friendly room

lay in silence, except for an occasional soft crackle which sounded more like unfolding paper than a fire's low spitting.

"Crickety Wacket, Ma!" Hosea exploded abruptly. "Hey, it's all like Aunt Blanche was saying, all right here! This picture *is* His Lordship, sure as shooting. Only down below the name printed is Roderick Deane, not Chisholm!"

"You can't be right, boy! Why the whole parish has been—"

"Look for yourself, Ma. Here. And here. And here."

Blanche stirred heavily. "Denis has to see this. Baptiste has to see. It's proof of fraud that would convince any court. I knew I'd have to bring strong legal proof."

"Uncle Baptiste couldn't recognize the picture if we held it in front of him." Hosea grated.

She looked up into the face above her. Why, he wasn't a boy at all any more. He was a full-grown young man, hard-eyed at the moment, cold with fury, as he glared at the golden locket and its crest.

"You must be sweet on John Roland, Aunt Blanche. Anyways that's what I've heard said. I'm sorry about that, for your sake. Because the next Roland that sets foot in this parish, I'm going to kill him dead. Before Almighty God, I'll kill him!"

22

PUBLIC FURY ERUPTED all across the prairie over the exposure of the Chisholm Fraud. Rage would have reached even vaster proportions were it not for even more staggering events which immediately followed it. Realization of the chicanery practiced upon it could not quite match the population's awareness that Louisiana had suddenly ceased to be a state of the Union. She was instead at war with former friendly sister states.

Angry repercussions of the fraud affair still rolled across the great plains like echoes of irate thunder when first word came to the settlements that South Carolina, beyond patience with the North's intrusions upon her slave holdings, had seceded from the United States. This was closely followed by reports that every

other southern member of the American federation
was hastening to follow suit.

Louisiana itself summoned a hasty convention to
vote similar action. Presided over by the much-re-
spected Cajun ex-Governor, Alexander Mouton, the
decision to secede was swiftly reached. Louisiana was
now one of eleven commonwealth members of the
Confederate States of America, a brand new political
nation. The South was about to set up an independent
government of its own.

Still, despite the uproar generated by this stunning
news, local talk about the Chisholm Affair was slow
in dying.

When rancher Denis Bernard first made charges
that His Lordship was a mere imposter endeavoring
to swindle fellow Cajuns of their hardwon land, the
first general reaction was hooting disbelief. Good old
solid Denis must be looney. But the papers Bernard
presented to the Court in Opelousas proved to be
beyond contravention. Queen Victoria's "cousin" was
only a skillful rogue with a history of confidence
schemes behind him in his native England.

In the dock and struggling to extricate himself, this
Roderick Deane—unless his true name were Rudolph
Something Else, as was now being broadcast—did
his cringing best to involve the well-known Roland
family in New Orleans.

John Roland, he swore on the stand, had hired him
for his impersonation, the object being to so over-
whelm Silas Eagleton and others in control that means
would be found to strip the Bernard brothers of their
holdings. It was rumored to be a matter of pure personal Roland spite. Stories circulated underground

about bad blood between the families in previous generations, and these carried an aura of truth.

Legal proof of any such connection proved a different matter from public credence. John Roland stoutly denied that he ever had met this Roderick Deane, or known anything whatever about him save what was printed in the newspapers. Deane's claim of a letter inviting him to Louisiana, a letter enclosing a rail ticket, could not be substantiated. The rascal's hotel room had been burglarized, it developed. Any such paper (had it once existed) had vanished into thin air. Not one scrap of writing could be introduced by the unhappy lawyer appointed to act as Deane's Defense. His client hadn't a leg to stand on.

Evidence against him, on the other hand, was damning.

Theatrical photographs proved him to be indeed Roderick Deane. Comparisons of "Lord Chisholm"'s signatures at Eagleton's bank with autographs of the actor showed identical handwriting. The chief concern of the law was not the criminal's guilt but how to transport Deane to a New Orleans jail to serve a maximum sentence without having attendant guards furiously ambushed on the trail and their prisoner lynched.

After prolonged litigation, the rice plantation created by Baptiste Bernard was returned to its proper owner. The debts used criminally against it were paid off by public subscription. The Bernard daughter Mimi kept assuring sympathetic neighbors that her father was slowly recovering from the stroke Deane's villainy had caused, although still walking and talking with difficulty.

Mimi's New Orleans aunt, Miss Blanche Bernard—briefly prominent during the trial as a Prosecution witness—had gone back east and entered the Convent of the Sacred Heart in Grand Coteau to become a lay worker in some menial capacity.

Reports on John Roland himself was somewhat confusing.

His departure from Louisiana was well established. But the reason for it seemed ambiguous. Some versions had it that he was living in London, on a protracted visit to English relatives of his genuinely titled great-grandfather, Sir Cedric Wellington. Others held that, having escorted his twin sons north to Boston to enter them in Harvard University, he was now travelling in Canada on a protracted vacation. Either way, he was out of the country and well out of reach of investigators, until the storm blew over. While nothing whatever had been proven against him, a mass of unsavory shadows did linger.

Such shadows would have taken far longer to dissipate were it not for the sudden bitter war which swooped upon southern and northern states alike. All else was swept from the public's attention. In the face of the shattering, bloody conflict nothing else could stand.

Repercussions of more distant battles almost immediately had their effect upon the prairies. In 1862, Union forces crushed the defenses of New Orleans and were pressing upriver toward the fortress town of Vicksburg. The Confederate government hastily removed its operations to Opelousas, well out on the Cajun prairie, where a Union assault would be far more difficult. New and unanticipated importance drew all surrounding citizenry into a more intimate contact with the conflagration.

Of course the younger menfolk were involved from the outset. Denis Bernard's two sons, Hosea and Daniel, were off with their neighbor youths to join the Louisiana volunteers almost as soon as the war's first far-away shots were fired.

From the defense of *La Ville* before it fell, Hosea sent home contemptuous reports of the Roland family there. These were of much interest to prairie Cajuns, who still connected the name with the recent Chisholm outrage.

"Hosea writes," his mother Hermione related to the group of neighbor women now meeting daily at the Denis Bernard ranch to sew grey cloth into uniforms and assemble surgical dressings, "that John Roland is still prudently among the missing. Since the city fell, the Yankee military government has taken over the famous Roland mansion as an officers' billet. The lady of the house, she who was a prominent Senator's daughter, has left the city with a crippled daughter and their servants. Hiding out at some family plantation, it's said."

Hetty Eagleton, who even now was a bit timid about speaking up in public after her husband's well-known cowardly submission in the fraud, ventured a question. "Weren't there two sons of the family, also? In college up north when war broke out? What about them?"

"That's part of what Hosea discovered. One of the Roland twins, the one named Bruce, seems to have defected to the North. He's serving in Yankee uniform. The other, Gareth, has just disappeared. Like father, like son, one would imagine."

"The old gentleman who heads the family, Mr. Anton Roland, must be disgusted."

"Not any longer, Hetty. He's beyond all disappointments. Hosea says it was a fatal stroke, worse than Baptiste's, brought on by the complete collapse of their New Orleans commerce. But I wonder if my boy is quite fair. He hates those Rolands so, for what they did to poor Baptiste. I think he ought to give the old gentleman more credit."

Amelie Bourdeaux, the Opelousas hostess who had proudly staged the most ostentatious of all the entertainments for Lord Chisholm and therefore felt the bitterest shame, sniffed audibly.

"What other reason could there be? Whether or not John Roland was behind the bilking, men of his line have always been money-grabbers. Everyone knows that."

"How would you feel, Amelie, if your only son were a virtual fugitive and your grandsons had behaved like traitors? Even Hosea doesn't deny grief could have caused the stroke."

"It was dollars, believe me. I'd bet my last one they hired Roderick Deane."

"In one of his letters my boy mentions that before his death Anton Roland disinherited the grandson, Bruce, and warned him never to come back to face Louisiana folk he's betraying. If Gareth is too cowardly to fight, his grandfather must have been just about as heartsick over that. There's only so much that human self-respect can take before it cracks."

"You can make all the excuses you like, Hermione. That family was always a nest of vultures, no matter how high-and-mighty they always rode in the city."

* * *

As war blazed hotter in Louisiana, it became a more immediate affair to every citizen on the prairie.

Sometimes the fighting came so close to Bernard family holdings that distant echoings of cannon fire could actually be heard on the range or in the rice paddies. Although the only direct family contact with war was via letters from Hosea or Daniel, resistance to the Yankee invasion still linked to places well within Cajun territory. Denis and Hermione prayed often and worried oftener about their absent offspring.

Both boys were fighting with the 18th Louisiana Regiment, of which young Alfred Mouton, son of their former great Cajun Governor, had become Colonel. All three of them saw action together at Pittsburgh Landing in '62 and again in the bloody encounter at Shiloh in April of '63. During that latter battle Mouton was severely wounded. Afterward, although still in his early thirties, the hero was promoted to Brigadier General. When either of the Bernard sons wrote home, he poured out adulation on their leader. To his men, Mouton was a near god.

At the Battle of Labadieville, on Bayou Lafourche, Daniel took a bullet in the leg and another in the hip. But by sheer providence, his brother Hosea was able to boat him to the tumbled-down swamp retreat of their ancient Cousin Sylvie. Her art as a *traiteur* had long been family legend, and in the face of Daniel's imminent death—field doctors and other medical personnel were all but unobtainable then, on the bayou— Hosea had been worried sick. Cousin Sylvie took over, however, as if she herself were a brigadier.

"She's as old as Methuselah, Ma," Hosea wrote afterward. "But she must be some kind of white witch, the way she worked on Danny. He's coming along right smartly now. The poisoned flesh is all clear of pus and the fever is gone. We're told he'll be sent home on furlough as soon as he can travel. Meanwhile, I head to Brashear City with the General's force. A Yankee contingent in that area is asking for a good Confederate licking. . . ."

Their pretty young Cousin Mimi, a real *mademoiselle* now, rode over from Baptiste's place every time she heard a new letter had arrived from either of her soldier cousins.

She was still somewhat in awe of Hosea, was Mimi, because of his greater age; he had seemed "one of the grown-ups" to her, throughout her own very recent childhood. But for Daniel, her dear companion always, she felt a sisterly and comfortable devotion. She was always eager for news from either source. It was her great sadness that she, too, had not been born a boy. She might then have written the figure eighteen on a slip of paper and slipped it into one boot and taken an oath that she was "over eighteen" and thus of the required age for military service.

Deprived of such a chance to fight for the Confederacy, Mimi was still as deep into war work as they'd let a girl become.

In addition to the burdens she carried at the farm, where she and her mother bore the brunt of managing the paddies while Baptiste still recovered from his disaster, she was sewing for the army with the most loyal of her elders. She was also attending nursing classes being organized in Opelousas, in an urgent effort to fill that need in Southern field hospitals.

In this project, Elizabeth gave her determined child scant support. A female of such tender years facing the horrors of so bloody a duty? Elizabeth rejected the very notion. Until recently, such gruesome tasks had been reserved for men. To her maternal belief, they still ought to be, or at least relegated to older women, better seasoned to grim physical realities.

"You, darling? A *nurse*, dealing with death and amputations, surrounded by the moans and sweat of men torn to ribbons?"

"The men may need me, Mother."

"I shan't permit it! It's quite unthinkable!"

In her sweetly stubborn fashion, Mimi refused to quit her courses. A silent truce evolved between mother and daughter. Elizabeth developed a pretense that Mimi's regular absences from the farm were all for the sake of sewing bees. Mimi in return avoided every possible reference to medical matters she might be studying.

Word that Cousin Danny had arrived home at Uncle Denis's ranch delighted Baptiste's young heiress. It had shaken Mimi badly to hear that he was wounded. More recent accounts telling of miracles wrought by the legendary Cousin Sylvie had not cheered her as much as it seemed to have done the rest of the family.

Her very recent instruction in care for the injured led her to suppose, someewhat toploftily, that Cousin Sylvie's vaunted skills were only old wive's tales. She hungered to see for herself that Danny was really recovering, home as he now was to be on leave.

One afternoon she saddled her own filly, Cinderella, and rode over immediately to Uncle Denis's spread. As always when called away by some unforeseen happening, she left a proper note on the kitchen table to prevent parental worries: *Danny back. Gone to ranch. Home late.*

The miles between farm and ranch were so familiar that she scarcely noticed the land through which she was passing. Cinderella took the route as a matter of habit, keeping at a brisk trot and requiring no direction. Shadows already had begun to lengthen across her father's rice fields, and shallow water flooding them glistened with the dull patina of half-rusting steel.

When the rice fields fell behind and rangeland opened up ahead, it was still terrain which for her had been home since as early as she could remember. It required no attention. She could still think her own thoughts, just as she always did.

Today, those thoughts ran a shuttle between her two cousins.

Danny occupied the foreground of them because of her present position. But Hosea had his share, too. From latest reports, Brashear City had fallen back into greatly reinforced Yankee hands. The enemy were now pursuing General Mouton's men back along the Bayou Teche, fighting to take each bend as they reached it. Mouton's regiment—and this meant Hosea, too—were adept at guerilla tactics. They would strike by surprise and then melt into mist, each time that Northern force attempted to engage elusive Louisianans in battle. How was Hosea faring with such evasive combat? As well as earlier in orthodox conflicts?

She began a small prayer for the absent Bernard brother.

"Dear God, if my Cousin Hosea needs special care from you—" That was as far as the prayer had progressed when, without warning, Cinderella reared back violently.

It happened so quickly that Mimi had no chance to

prepare for it. The reins she had been holding lightly jerked from her startled grasp before she could grab to retrieve them. Cinderella danced in panic and went back up on her hind legs in some waltz of terror.

Mimi felt herself sliding from her saddle into the tall, rippling prairie grass through which, only a moment later, they had been serenely cantering.

"Cinderella!" But the filly was already fleeing in panic. "*Cinderella!*"

Mimi had landed jarringly, but so far as she could determine she was not injured beyond a shake-up. She struggled upward, stumbling back onto her feet and glaring in impotent fury at the rapidly diminishing little mare. What in tarnation had caused the beast to carry on like this, she who was generally so steady? *Now* what could be done?

Her first thought was a rattlesnake in the undergrowth. Horses dreaded them. Truth to tell, Mimi herself was not notably courageous about reptiles. If she had to make it back home or ahead to the ranch afoot, tramping through snake country, it wasn't a happy proposition.

Gazing down to search the grass for some hint of shimmering scales or slithering coils, she caught her first glimpse of something visibly more substantial hidden by the hip-deep herbage. Its shape, its solidity, its unthreatening motionlessness, all breathed to her, "*No snake!*"

Why, it was a man! A dead man, sprawled here miles from anywhere!

She inched forward, parting the grass as she did so, until she could look down at him. A surge of pity went over her as she stood alongside, studying him.

He was a young man. Handsome. And *very* young.

At a guess, not many years older than herself. His copper blond hair, thick and curling, was matted with a crust her class instruction taught her was dried blood.

How could he have gotten here? And in such appalling condition? She could not imagine. If he'd come from the west, it was miles and miles to the last settlement before uninhabited wilderness and Texas. If he'd come from the east, he never would have made such a trek afoot. There was no indication of a horse, or that one had been here.

"The only possibility," she heard herself saying, softly yet aloud, "is that he was driven here in a wagon and dumped. Whoever murdered him figured he wouldn't be found. Not until he was a skeleton, and maybe couldn't be identified."

Pity for the handsome stranger who had met so sad and lonely an end engulfed her.

She went down beside him on her knees and reached out hesitantly to touch him. Under her questing fingertips his flesh felt cold as marble. But was that the barest flutter of a pulse at the base of his tanned throat? Was he not quite dead, after all?

Mimi bent closer, her face mere inches above his own, eager to catch any hint of breathing. If only she had a scrap of mirror with her! They said in class that a way to detect breath was to hold glass above the source. If breath existed, the glass would cloud over.

But she had no mirror. A struggling new rice plantation, well out from even the smallest town, was scarcely a place to breed female vanity. Back home, a serviceable wall glass hung above the washbasin. Nothing more was necessary. But even that was miles away. Hours away, unless it came into Cinderella's head to wander back in this direction.

Perhaps she could force breath back into him. That feeble pulse hinted it might not yet be too late. Mimi struggled to remember the text pamphlet's directions. You put your own mouth against the patient's mouth and then— Well, at least she'd have to try.

In the very act of trying to remember, she became aware of some minute motion.

Those eyelids with their thick tangle of lashes had rolled back slowly. Inches from her own, enormous eyes so green-blue she could liken them only to peacock feathers were staring up at her.

The retreat up the Teche had been slow and tricky. General Mouton led his retreating troops with a skill amounting to genius. With every mile they coaxed their pursuers deeper into trackless country. And all the way they tormented exhausted Yankees unmercifully.

Although it was they who seemed to be fleeing, the Cajuns were well aware that what appeared to be flight was actually strategy. The pitiless heat, the torments of trying to overtake an enemy as unsubstantial as a horde of bayou banshees, a developing dread of shadows which might or might not be armed ambushers, was telling unerringly on the supposedly victorious pursuers.

It was an exercise in artfully induced exhaustion.

Alfred Mouton played out the enemy deftly, until he was quite sure they were too spent to hit back with any vigor. Then at last, when he had lured his reeling prey as far north as Mansfield, the General

ordered a swift attack. The Yankees staggered back
from it in stunned confusion. Many were mowed down
in the first fusillade. Others turned and ran, scattering
through the inimical swamp like wasps from a broken
hive. The Union troops were broken beyond reassem-
bly.

Mouton was not a conqueror without pity. He signalled to his regiment to take prisoners and leave off
killing.

It was his own death he had signalled.

One tenacious Yankee sniper had taken to a tree
overhanging the stagnant Teche waters. He took aim
on the victorious General as he rode along the bank,
issuing merciful orders. A rifle barked like a brief
scrap of grim laughter. Mouton stiffened and began
to slide out of his saddle. He had not yet hit earth
before avenging Cajuns were blasting the sniper from
treelimb to Eternity.

A goodly portion of the Regiment could be reassem-
bled by subordinate officers and turned southward
again, bearing their dead leader with them. But others
had deployed deeply into the swamps in pursuit of
fugitives, and were hours from base when decamp-
ment orders were issued. They returned only to discover that the main body of their comrades already
had marched out.

To guerillas now leaderless, the proper course of
action was obvious. *Follow and catch up. Don't be left
behind.*

Hosea and a neighbor volunteer from out Opelousas
way, Valex Boudreaux, were together as they started
on their way toward reunion, seeking those departed
ranks still under orders.

"Nothing for it but to backtrack down the Teche,"

Hosea advised, and Valex agreed. "They're bound to stick close to water on their way. We'll pick up news of them."

Whatever the route the junior officers had decided upon, it did not seem to have been the one two stragglers trying to overtake them had elected. The pair toiled down-bayou day after day without encountering a sign that troops had passed before them. The only hints of war they came upon were souvenirs of former abortive battles, left to moulder in the silent swamps.

"Hey, here's something!" Hosea paused on the trail to gaze down upon what was left of a Union officer. The man had fallen at one ambushed bend, perhaps a month before.

Weather and animal visitations had just about done for the flesh of the Union casualty. His blue uniform was tattered like a clump of fallen tree moss. But evidently no vandals had followed the tide of battle along this particular bank. Amazingly, the dead man's sword and sheath still clung alongside his decayed ribcage, shining as brightly as they must have done on the last day their owner polished them.

Hosea bent over and detached the weapon from a rotting sash.

"Yankee steel," he said quietly, his eyes meeting his friend's. There was no triumph in the glance. A soldier didn't exult over another soldier fallen in the discharge of duty. "It will be something to show my kids, providing I live out this war to sire any."

"The Yanks are on the run," Valex replied. "We'll be back on the prairie this time next year, trying to snuggle up to all those Lafayette and Opelousas pretties. You got your eye on anything in skirts for when we get there, Hosea?"

"No time to think about that. Pa still needs all the help he can get on the range."

"Damn, but I can't keep my thoughts on work these days. I'd sure like a little roll in you-know-what before we're back in the front lines again. I just now was wondering—"

"I know you, Boudreaux. I know what you was pondering."

"It wouldn't take us more than a couple of hours to stop off, when next we hit a town that looks big enough to have a whorehouse in it," Valex mused. "How's about it, Hosea?"

"You go ahead and play your games, neighbor. I'll just keep moving. I remember a shortcut through the swamps ahead that ought to catch me up to our main force sooner."

23

NIGHT HAD CLOSED IN while Mimi clung beside the stranger fallen in the tall range grass. As it could when it took a mind to, darkness had brought a deepening chill along with it. Some time back she had lain down alongside the badly injured man whose unexpected presence in the grass had caused Cinderella to bolt. The heat of her own body was all she could offer to protect him. He had precious little heat of his own.

She still was afraid he might be dying.

For the most part, during the hours they had lain here in such queer intimacy, he had slept with his battered head against her breast and his breathing frighteningly slow and shallow. But sometimes, for a brief stretch, those incredibly beautiful eyes would open. He would even attempt a few sometimes disjointed words.

"Are you really an angel?" he murmured, the first of those times.

"Of course not. I'm a rice farmer's daughter. Our plantation's ten-odd miles from here."

"That's funny. Bending over me, you looked like an angel. I thought I must have died."

"This isn't Heaven, Mr. Whatever-Your-Name-Is. It's the Cajun prairie."

"Name?" The eyes were already closing. "Mine is Gareth. What's yours?"

"Mimi Bernard," she said. But she wasn't at all certain he understood.

That was along about sunset. More than an hour must have passed before he stirred again and she realized he was once more watching her. Her pillowing arm had gone to sleep under his bloodied head. She eased his weight and flexed to lessen the cramp ache.

"We must have been here a long time," he sighed. "How did you get here with me?"

"My filly shied when she came on you in the grass. I was on my way to see a cousin. The great mystery is, how did *you* get here? At first, I thought you were dead."

"So did I. They must have tossed me out of their wagon. I was coming on foot from Texas."

"*Texas?*" Her dark eyes widened. "But that's, why, practically over the edge of the world away! Who tossed you out of a wagon?"

"I never knew what they were called. Gamblers, they were. On their way to New Orleans to milk the Yankee soldiers. They offered me a ride when I told them I was headed there too. I reckon they'd seen my poke in the saloon where we met. I'd stopped off there for food. Anyway, I can't feel any lump in my pocket. That's where my money was."

"So they robbed you too! The miserable varmints!"

"In the wagon, I was up front with the driver. The other two sat behind. I never even knew the one with the gold tooth was moving, not until his billy hit my head."

A sudden look of alarm flashed across the white face at her bosom.

"Oh, God! Mimi—did you say your name is Mimi?— would you do me a favor? I can't seem to move very well. Would you look down inside my left boot, please?"

She laid him back on the grass as gently as possible and did as he'd requested. The boots she could not very well fail to examine told her a little more about this Gareth. They had obviously been costly equipment, the best footgear obtainable. But he must have walked them clear across the continent. They were warped and split now, their heels practically nonexistent.

She tugged off the left one and plunged a hand into it. What she brought up out of a neat slit in the lining, where it had been carefully concealed, was a man's gold ring.

He saw metal glint between her fingers and choked with relief.

"They didn't find it, then!"

As he reached unsteadily to take the circlet, Mimi blinked. It was a distinctive crest ring, adorned with a rampant falcon. But the hand which now weakly clutched what she had handed over was adorned with the ring's exact duplicate. She couldn't help staring.

"I know." He seemed to sense her confusion. "They're twins. Like Bruce and me."

"I've never before in my life heard of twin rings."

"The idea was Grandpa Anton's. He had them made when we went north together to college. Then, when the war began, and when Bruce decided he owed more loyalty to America than to Louisiana, Grandpa disowned him. The rings are a family crest, you see. Bruce peeled off his when Grandpa's letter came and made me swear to fetch it back home and put it into Grandpa's own hand."

Mimi tried to absorb what he was saying.

"So you weren't staying up North wtih your twin?"

"We look at the country's split-up differently, Bruce and I. To me, it's our home state I owe the most. I wanted to get home and enlist where I was born."

"And now you're here," she said, instinctively smoothing his crusted hair.

"Not quite. Not yet. If this is the prairie, I still have a way to go. Were you ever in New Orleans, Mimi? I'd love to show you around there, once the Yanks are driven out."

"You must have been a long time getting here from Boston."

"Like our Cajun ancestors, I reckon. My great-grandfather came from Grand Pré, a village in Acadia. After the British expelled them, he was three years getting here."

"Imagine! *My* great-grandfather was driven out of Grand Pré, too!"

He was tiring fast. With a vague, lovely smile, he looked back at her. "Coincidence?" he whispered.

"Beautiful. . . ." He was asleep before her arms could slip around him.

Several times more during the night hours he awakened, more clearly conscious and more aware of her each time. Between awakenings, she lay quietly and held him close. It seemed likely by now that he wasn't dying. The gashes in his head did not reopen, as she'd feared they might. When he did briefly rouse, there were snatches of words between them.

"What time is it, Mimi? Oh, but a girl doesn't wear a pocket watch."

"I can tell time by the stars, pretty much. It's an hour past midnight."

Or: "What will your family think? They must be wild with worry."

"They'll think I stayed over at Uncle Denis's and Aunt Hermione's."

"But what about morning? They'll know then you're missing."

"Cinderella may have wandered back this way before that. I'll just ride home."

Or: "Are you absolutely positive you're not an angel, Mimi?"

"Of course I'm not an angel. Don't be silly, Gareth."

"Was that being silly? Some way, it didn't seem so. Hold me closer, please."

Just when the nurse-feeling of protective duty began to change to something else, Mimi never afterward could have said. But somewhere during these long hours, while a crescent moon rose from the direction of far-off New Orleans and rode the sky like a silver *pirogue* and sank again toward the Texas Gareth had limped through on his long detour to avoid the Yankees cutting off himself from home—somewhere during these starry, silent hours, she fell in love with him.

It was a different feeling entirely. It was like sipping too much heady wine, which she had done at the ranch the night the boys went off to war and the whole family—even Cousin Alphonse and his brood, from far upstate—gathered for a sendoff.

Gazing down at his sleeping face, so beautiful and so trusting, she ached with what she was feeling for him. So short a time! Yet her whole life seemed changed by just holding him. There wasn't the slightest reason to suppose Gareth was even aware of that. Much less felt in any degree the same.

But if he didn't, very likely it would be she who faded away to brittle bones because of what those robbers with a wagon had done.

Advance hints of morning began to inch their way into the stillness. Gareth stirred against her and threw one arm about her to hold her as she was holding him. The movement was instinctive, Mimi knew. He was not yet fully awake and only on the rim of knowing.

Forewarned, she could be braced and watching him when the blue-green eyes did open. Yet when it happened, she felt the prairie tremble. They lay, eyes to eyes, so close that his now normal breath brushed at her cheek. And he was anything but a dead man, anything but.

"You know too, don't you, Mimi?"

Suddenly the world was singing; and it wasn't just those distant birds in the cottonwoods, greeting an impending sunrise.

"I'm not sure what you mean. But I think so, Gareth."

"All this was meant to happen to us, wasn't it? We

had to find out we belong together. You'll marry me, won't you, my darling? You'll be my wife for always?"

"If you want me, Gareth. I know that I want you."

He began to work the signet ring off his finger. "This is for you. To say I'll come back as soon as the war is over. Here, take it. It's my sacred promise."

"But it's *your* ring. You may feel lost, not wearing it."

"I'll wear Bruce's, until I can hand it over to Grandpa. I'll wear it on my finger instead of inside a boot. But it's my own ring I want you to have. Until I can come back for you with a proper wedding ring, and carry you away with me."

Mimi sat reverently turning the signet to catch first light. "The Roland falcon!"

"You recognize it?" Gareth regarded her in astonishment.

"My whole family would recognize a Roland signet. Didn't it mean anything to you when I said my name is Mimi Bernard? Don't you know our families are sworn enemies?"

"Oh, Mimi!" Gareth moaned it, catching her close. "If you ever hated me—"

"I couldn't. I never will. When our time comes, the others will understand."

War seldom touched quiet Grand Coteau directly, although echoes of war often quivered in the air like a beating of wings. They impinged upon the peace which Blanche had somehow patched together. But the peacefulness itself remained inviolate. Here with the sweet, pious Sisters she felt that she had at last begun the only life she ever should have lived.

Going about her simple duties, mending the convent linens, tending to arrangements of modest garden flowers, she knew the old restlessness was gone for good. The old febrile hunger, the old shallow egotism, might never have existed. Devout and gentle nuns had opened for her a vista of service to others to which, until now, she had been blind.

At present the order's talent for giving was symbolized, for Blanche, in the tender care the Sisters were bestowing upon an ailing *religieuse* recently arrived from St. Louis. This young woman had stopped in the great river city while on her way down the Mississippi from still further north, in Canada. There she had become a convert. The Fathers had sent her on toward Louisiana to enter St. Michael's as a novice.

But on the river boat she had boarded for her extended journey, an agonizing pain in her side had attacked the poor candidate for the order. Unable to diagnose any source of trouble, the steamboat's medical officer had landed her as near to Grand Coteau as possible and she had been rushed to the convent. Solicitous nursing by the Sisters had gradually eased the anguish. The girl was now able to again take up preparation for donning the habit.

Blanche had played her own small part in this recovery, toting trays from the kitchen and helping with sickroom cleanups. The joy she found in these menial tasks had been for her a revelation. Watching the gradual ebbing of their patient's torment was a tonic for herself as well. Sometimes she had to suppress an instinct to go about the convent halls with a song on her lips; not a *Te Deum*, for she did not yet consider herself worthy, but a simple Cajun carol of happiness Aunt Marie had taught her years ago.

The Blanche Bernard who once had flirted with every callow youth on the bayou, the lover-besotted young adventuress of the house with the blue door, might never have existed. Looking back on them now, the woman who once had been both those people scarcely could recognize them. Their vanities and passions were as alien as if they belonged to characters in a novel.

Sometimes, as she went about her work, she did think of John Roland. But when she did so it was only with a murmured prayer that she might one day cleanse herself of her disgust. Wherever he was, hiding behind those lies he had built up for a screen around himself, he could not be a happy man. Perhaps he never had been happy, even in the embrace of a stranger–mistress who once, incredibly, had been herself.

She still must find a way to pray for him and truly mean the good for which she would be asking. For John, for his two fine sons, for the pathetic daughter, and for the wife she had once sorely wronged, she must make what amends she could on her knees.

Gareth had improved so rapidly that Mimi, far from Grand Coteau on the spreading prairie, also felt strong impulses toward prayer; prayers of earnest thanksgiving.

If her mother were only aware of it, surely she'd have to admit that things her daughter had learned in those disapproved-of nursing classes had proven a Godsend. In the early morning following that first night with her husband—yes, in Heaven's sight already her *husband*—in their bed of grass, Cinderella came frisking back across the range as if she never had bolted in terror. Despite his protests, Mimi helped her wounded love into the saddle, and herself took the lead afoot. Hand on the filly's bridle, she knew exactly where she was leading them.

On a remote corner of the Denis Bernard acreage there stood a disused cabin originally erected as a bunkhouse for temporary extra hands hired on for cattle runs. Now, with war bringing such treks to a standstill and most of the drifter cowboys off fighting for the Confederacy, the building was no longer in service. Uncle Denis nowadays would never attempt to move his herds. No market for them could be reached except the Union force in military possession of *La Ville.* A Bernard would never sell supplies to the Yankees. Destroying a herd would be better.

"Here you are, my darling of darlings," she told Gareth, as she ushered him proudly into the place where he could hide in safety while his strength crept back. "It's not a splendid castle, but no one will discover you here. I'll smuggle you supplies any way I can. In no time, you'll be yourself."

"Not my old self." He took her into his arms. "My old self didn't have you."

"You have me now. I'd wait for you forever and ever, Gareth."

When she left him, glancing back over her shoulder longingly and too often, she headed Cinderella directly toward the ranch house. The cousins were at breakfast when she cantered in. Danny, rising, seemed somewhat thinner and paler than she remembered. Otherwise, so far as she could tell, he was in prime condition. Uncle Denis and Aunt Hermione fussed over him like mother hens.

They welcomed her happily. A few discreet ques-

tions quickly established that there had as yet been
no concerned queries about her overnight absence.
As Mimi had hoped, her unsuspecting parents trust-
ingly assumed she had decided to sleep over at her
Uncle's place. In the free-and-easy style of the prairie,
this was quite ordinary.

"So my only worry," she told herself silently, accepting Aunt Hermione's offer of a shared morning meal,
"is keeping Gareth out of sight until he can move on.
Oh, Gareth dear, if you only knew how my folks react
to that word *Roland!* You can't quite grasp that you're
in danger here, even among loyal Louisianans. You
just don't hate very well, I guess."

At least Hosea wasn't anywhere about. Of all the
clan, Hosea was the worst. She never until now had
blamed him much for that. It was her father's stroke,
brought on by John Roland's unproven villainies, that
had hardened Cousin Hosea and lay behind his oath
to kill the first Roland who ever entered the region.
Hosea had admired his stricken Uncle Baptiste almost
as much as he did his own father. Before war service
claimed him, he'd thirsted for reprisals.

"But he's nowhere near here now, thank God. I
don't have to worry about Hosea. And Danny never
nursed that same black fury. Even our two sets of
parents didn't."

The crumbling bunkhouse would be safe enough.
So, if she took care not to be caught at it, would be
transportation of the few necessities she must provide
for Gareth.

Theft was a new experience for Mimi, but she found
herself swiftly becoming adept at it. The knife and
fork from the kitchen, the small ham from the smoke-
house, the bar of soap and the bandages from her own

sturdy kit, all found their ways craftily into Cinderella's saddlebag. To Elizabeth's mild surprise, her daughter suddenly formed a habit of long solo rides.

"Where in the world do you go these mornings, Mimi? I'd think you were too used to the same old rangeland to find much to enjoy riding out there alone."

"It's therapy, Mama. Sometimes I get to fretting about this endless old war until I most want to scream. The peace and quiet out yonder just sort of soothes me."

Fortunately, her mother's curiosity was diverted. "Therapy? There's an odd word to crop up in a healthy young girl's vocabulary. Not that I can't guess where you got it!"

On the third day, Mimi had to face up to her most complex problem.

It worried her that Gareth had no weapon whatever in his possession. He had carried a pistol all through his foot journey in and out of Texas; but the robbers had stolen that. The thought of him making the rest of his journey to the Confederate lines barehanded was insupportable.

So today she was taking him the sword. This presented new difficulties. Not that the family was apt to notice their weapon was missing; neither of her parents ever bothered to look upstairs in the crawl space, where it had lain wrapped in old towels since Mimi herself was a toddler. But a sword could not be camouflaged in a saddlebag. Its long, rigid outline could only be concealed by her flowing calico skirts themselves.

She had to wait until no one was watching before riding out. The stiffness of her posture in the saddle could not have passed unnoted. Today's was by long odds the most thoroughly uncomfortable canter she ever had taken. Yet never for an instant did she regret it. When he moved on (the mere thought of that was an agony) he must not face the trail defenseless.

Gareth himself was startled when he saw the donation she had brought him. "What the deuce?"

"It's a sword, darling, as you can very well see."

"What am I to do with it? Cut up my jerky?"

"I couldn't bear to think of you back on the trail with no means of defense but two bare hands. Next time, robbers might club you just a little bit harder." A sudden doubt flashed through her mind. "Gareth! You do know how to use a sword, don't you?"

"Oh, magnificently." He bent to kiss her. "Bruce and I were drilled in *escrime* almost from the cradle. Our father considered it a requisite for gentlemen. But I don't think a sword will do me much good if I run face to face with a patrol of Yankees."

"I couldn't very well have scavanged you a cannon. It might be noticed."

He sensed her pique and held her closer. "Bless you, my own angel. I was only teasing." With one fingertip he traced the line of her lifted lips. "Tell me about my Excalibur."

"It's an old weapon. It's been in the family for generations. I think Great-grandfather Roger brought it with him when he migrated from New England. Wagon routes were dangerous in those days. You never knew when footpads might descend."

"So you're entrusting a Bernard heirloom to a detested Roland?"

"I'm entrusting it to the man I love. Oh, how much I do love you, Gareth!"

* * *

The Gulfward trail was lonelier, once he parted
company from Valex Boudreaux. Hosea sometimes
even half regretted not having fallen in with his lifelong neighbor's grinning suggestion that they stop for
sport with whores together. Sloshing through the
backwater swamps alone was a dismal business. Valex
would have made a sight more cheerful company than
the occasional muskrat or wild mink. The basso booming of alligators at night did not sound nearly far
enough away for comfort.

But Denis Bernard's elder son had been raised with
a strong sense of duty.

At the moment, that duty was to find his regiment
and report back for service. So he slogged along
through the muck and slimy waters, mile after mile,
the weapon he had taken from a dead Yankee slapping
at his side. More than once he found himself on the
verge of throwing his souvenir away. It did impede
his progress in this dank terrain. But somehow he kept
it, regardless.

Country along the bayou was vastly different from
open prairie where he'd been brought up. This swamp
world closed in on a man. The stands of cypress towering up out of rancid ponds had a funereal look. Grey
moss strung overhead in curtains half-obliterated the
sky.

He was glad poor Danny was back on the ranch, at
least for a respite. Homesickness clawed at him. Once
this war was finished, God help him, he'd never stir
again from the home parish.

A swamp, Hosea long since had decided, was his
sworn enemy. It caught at his booted ankles with
submerged roots bent on tripping him. It dangled

water moccasins from overhead branches, so a man had always to keep a wary eye Heavenward for dropping peril. A Cajun had to be mad to settle in so gaunt a place. No wonder Pa and Uncle Baptiste had fled it. The wonder was that other Bernards had stayed behind.

The lapping of water in sluggish motion had become a familiar counterpoint to his own wading steps. He paused now alongside a fallen tree to close his eyes and listen.

The eyes flew open again, suddenly alert. Someone was coming!

As he ducked low, concealing himself by the great horizontal trunk and its shadow, the sounds grew steadily nearer. A Yankee patrol? No, the sloshing noise was made by only one pair of feet. But they still could be Yankee feet. Crouched down, he waited.

After a moment there was vague movement behind the swaying mosses. The man came on, almost directly toward him, thrusting aside hanging foliage which delayed him. The dim outline became a man. Young. With red-gold hair which made the brightest splotch of color in the picture.

The stranger wasn't wearing any formal uniform, but the same sort of casual gear favored by Hosea himself. General Mouton's guerillas, most of them, had dressed this way for their trip up the Teche. You weren't on parade while on such a mission. You dressed for concealment and for swift free movement during a lightning sortie.

This was one of Mouton's men?

No, he decided after a quick examination. The fellow had a trail-weary look about him and moved with much the same doggedness that Hosea felt in his own bones. But the face, poster-handsome, at that, lacked the special, detectable look that spelled an aftermath of battle. The stranger, if tired indeed, was drained from some other source.

Hosea rose slowly into view, hand hovering at his sword hilt.

The man saw him at once and halted. Across the slime-scabbed shallows still separating them, he grinned with an engaging friendliness. He lofted a hand.

"Hey, there! Am I glad to find somebody else alive in this forsaken sink! I think I'm lost!"

"Maybe you are. What way are you headed?"

"Trying to locate the Confederate line nearest to New Orleans. It's got to be around here somewhere. I have something I must deliver to my Grandfather before I enlist. But it shouldn't be hard to slip in and out of the city, since I'm still in mufti."

"New Orleans lies that way." Hosea pointed. "Come on. I'm headed in that direction myself."

They converged in mid-pool, each smiling. The stranger held out his hand.

"This is my lucky day, I guess. I've had a couple of *very* lucky days, just lately."

In the very act of accepting the handclasp, Hosea froze. His eyes had taken in the ring on one extended finger. He'd have known that rampant falcon at the gates of Hell.

"Who are you?" he grated. "What's your name, mister?"

The stranger looked surprised. "I'm Gareth Roland. Is something the matter?"

Nothing was the matter. Nothing at all. Hosea's slow, deliberate gaze swept over this Roland bastard

from bright crown to submerged ankles. He drew
back his hand half-offered in response to an offer of
comradeship.

This Roland carried a sword, so they were an even
match in the essential department. No reason to diddle
with fine points or formalities.

"I'm Hosea Bernard, Roland. Reckon you've heard
of my family."

Roland merely looked confused. "Why, sure. Actually, just two days ago—"

"Rolands and Bernards don't swap gab, mister. I'm
going to kill you. Defend yourself!"

"Hey, wait! If you're Hosea, you must be the cousin
she—"

"*Draw!*" And the Yankee sword already flashed
naked in Hosea's own grip.

He started forward, circling, stalking. His eyes
were deadly. Roland read their intention and dropped
his right hand to his own hilt. A sad look of regret
showed in eyes which Hosea could at this close range
detect as being a remarkable blue-green.

The two blades struck together with a crash which
set echoes shuddering back into the cypress forest.
Whatever he had assumed about a Roland, Hosea
swiftly recognized that he had been overconfident in
one particular. His unwilling opponent was a drilled
expert in fencing, no clod.

This was no moment of melodramatic cousinly vengeance. This was a moment to remember every detail
the regiment had drilled into him concerning the
science of swordplay; the measuring eye, the awareness of every tiniest flicker in the enemy he faced.
This was *now*.

As their swords struck, and struck again, each man measured the other skillfully.

They kept moving counterclockwise in the malodorous water like figures in some stately dance. Roland made a sudden lunge. Hosea parried. Roland was thrusting for his thigh, he could see, and the flurry of clicking swordtips which followed struck bits of light in the gloom.

Roland's tip made for him, cutting low, and Hosea had to deflect it with a swift, sidewise twist. They both were panting now. Sweat streaked their foreheads.

They drew apart for an instant, sucking rotten air. Hosea's lips curled back, exposing strong white teeth. Devil-bred Roland! He leaped forward like a jungle cat, hate burning his throat. He slashed the swordblade as though it were a wand capable of magic.

Roland parried, then parried again. But the third time was not quite quick enough. It left a sliver of an opening, and Hosea lunged straight for that.

With every ounce of strength in his shoulder he drove the weapon's slim edge forward. It buried itself a good several inches into tardily guarded flesh. Out of Roland's grasp the other weapon slid away as though its owner were suddenly weary of it.

"Cousin . . . Hosea . . ." the man sighed, and pitched forward with his face in the water.

24

WITH THE SURRENDER by General Lee of the Army of Northern Virginia, the dreadful fighting at last was at an end. In the north, bells rang and bonfires blazed and homecoming heroes paraded; crowds cheered, bands played, flags flaunted. In Louisiana, as everywhere in the Southland, broken losers licked their wounds and wept.

Opelousas was no exception. The aftermath of hard fighting to maintain a treasured way of life demanded that the Cajun population now transform themselves into a race of Phoenixes and struggle up out of the ashes. Crushing terms of surrender had been forced upon them by their conquerors.

Folk were saying all across the prairie that the peace terms would have been far more generous had that actor John Wilkes Booth not assassinated Abraham Lincoln. Many local residents had their own old reasons to detest an actor, be he a Booth or a Deane.

For Mimi, all meaning in the long struggle's end ceased to exist.

Only a few months earlier, she would have welcomed this peace with joyful thanksgiving. Defeat or not, it would have meant Gareth's return. The end of the great Southern dream could only have spelled the beginning of her own. They would be together, she and Gareth. Nothing beyond this one great central truth could really have mattered.

The return of the Bernard sword had written *Finis* to that. The day Hosea walked into her father's plantation house, bearing the easily recognized relic, ended everything.

"I brought this from the Teche, Mimi." His once familiar voice was almost a stranger's. "I think it's yours."

Her eyes, wide with apprehension, met his. "You and Gareth met?"

"Briefly. I didn't recognize our family relic until it fell from his hand. But I recognized who was carrying it. His Roland signet was on his hand."

All too clearly, she comprehended what he meant.

Everything inside her seemed to contort violently as if at the epicenter of a gigantic tremor. Her world splintered into bits and shuddered away. She could barely force incredible words.

"You killed him, didn't you?"

"He was a Roland." Hosea's eyes were like flint.

"He never did a thing to harm you or any Bernard. Yet you *killed* him."

"He was a Roland. That's all that was necessary."

"The kindest, gentlest person I ever knew. And you killed him."

"Damn it, Mimi, he was a *Roland*. Don't you remember what Rolands did to your own father? Don't you remember hearing what Rolands tried to do to the whole Bernard family on the Bayou Lafourche, years ago? Christ, of course I killed him. He was a Roland.

"And now you stand in front of me and gloat about it. I hate you, Hosea."

"Never mind hating *me* for doing what any man with guts would do. What the hell were *you* doing, turning over our Bernard sword to scum like that? It had to be you that did it. Uncle Baptiste wouldn't. Aunt Elizabeth wouldn't. And the sword was kept here."

"I did it, of course," Mimi said steadily. "There was always a chance he'd run into some unspeakable monster like you on his way. I wanted him armed."

"By God, I ought to crack you one. A Bernard giving aid to a Roland!"

"Wrong. A Roland gave aid to a Roland. You murdered my husband, Hosea."

The expression in Hosea's dark eyes was a whole volume on astonishment. "Your *what*? You're actually low enough, contemptible enough, to . . . Ah, but you're lying. It isn't possible. How the devil could you have met the man? He *stole* the sword."

"He was trying to reach our Confederate line and enlist. Near here, three assassins much like you set on him and left him for dead. I found him. I nursed him. And the day he left to do his duty, I rode with him as far as the first town that has a preacher. That wasn't *his* ring you saw on his hand. It was his brother's. Here is Gareth Roland's ring."

She pulled it out from between her small, compact breasts on the slender ribbon where she had strung it. It glittered icily in the afternoon light. The engraved falcon seemed almost to beat tiny wings. Hosea had a chilled feeling that even the ring detested him.

For a moment of rigid silence they both stood staring down at the golden geegaw, each of them thinking starkly separate thoughts. Hosea actually trembled with his anger.

"Bitch! You did lie with him. A Roland! You took him inside you. If he left you with child, Cousin Mimi Roland, let me warn you now. I'll do the same with the brat I did with its father."

"No you won't, Hosea." She said it so evenly she might have been commenting on the weather. "You won't be alive to harm my baby. I'm going to kill you before then, Hosea. You may be a soldier, I may be only a female, but I'll find a way. You won't be here for the christening."

The months limped past, one and another and another, while various units of the Bernard family accustomed themselves to life at the vortex of a savage feud.

That one of the involved parties was steady and dutiful Hosea, while the other was a once-lively slip of a girl who only last year had hero-worshipped him, made the whole sad situation even sadder. What lay between the young cousins tinged every other family matter with its dark dye.

Mimi had grown too cumbersome to ride Cinderella across the range as recently she had loved to do. She would not have ventured far from Baptiste's doorstep in any event. Whatever the nowadays perpetually scowling Hosea might be planning, she had no intention of letting it befall her.

Bearing the son or daughter whom Gareth never would see had become her one purpose in living. She spent long hours ensconced on the plantation porch overlooking rice fields which shimmered like silk under their shallow water; and her sole thoughts were of the baby stirring actively inside her. Hosea already had carried out one hateful vow to its terrible finale. She wouldn't allow him to achieve the same satisfaction with another.

Of course she had spoken beyond her normal abilities when she matched his grim threat with one of her own. Looked at in practical terms, what she had vowed to do was mere fantasy. The sword safely back in the crawl space was too heavy a weapon for her to wield, even were she not pregnant. Baptiste never had taught his daughter the proper use of firearms. Poisons were not available, and she actually knew little about their uses. Beyond these obvious death tools, what ones had she within reach? Hosea probably would survive.

Hosea on the other hand, had means to harm her expected baby at every turn.

Let her drive past her father's gates and he could be lying in wait for her anywhere. A wire across the road might halt her horse. A rope noose might drop over her shoulders. A pistol? Hosea was expert at pistols. A rattler tossed into her pony cart. A scorpion. A poisonous spider. Whatever he did to her, there would be no proof against him afterward. The Bernards would merely have suffered one more regrettable family tragedy.

Mimi had always until she was made a widow been a logical, clear-thinking girl. But now, brooding the certainly not imaginary dangers Hosea represented, she could feel the balance of her reason shifting. If she did nothing to check it, she might well be a lunatic before she produced Gareth's child. She was still too sensible to let that happen.

What she did was write a letter to Great-Aunt Marie on the Bayou Lafourche.

Arriving at her nephew Baptiste's once-again prospering rice plantation on a sunny day some two weeks later, Marie Bernard brought her usual vigor and good cheer through its welcoming door along with her.

Elizabeth greeted her on the steps with outflung arms.

"We were happier than you'll ever know when your letter came, Aunt Marie. We felt blessed just knowing you were arriving for a visit. You're the tonic every one of us stands in need of."

"Pills or syrups, powders or lotions, I never fail. What's got you all so in the dumps, my dear? Spring fever? Malaria? An epidemic of ingrown bad dispositions?"

Marie untied her bonnet ribbons and removed the straw concoction to which they were attached. Her hair had gone almost totally white since Elizabeth last saw her, but her pink face seemed not an hour older. You never thought of age or other ills in Marie's upbeat presence. Elizabeth had heard that once Aunt Marie was the vortex of a tragic love affair. Yet her placid surface certainly revealed no chronic sorrowing.

It would be a blessing to have the jolly old lady

about the house for awhile. It might even raise Mimi out of her worrisome doldrums. She, Elizabeth, was on the verge of collapse with worry over the child. So often lately, Mimi seemed even less connected with the life around her than had Baptiste been in the first few weeks following his stroke.

"Well!" beamed Marie, when tea and lemon-rice biscuits had made an appearance and the two women were seated outdoors under the shading cottonwoods. "What's all this I've heard back home about my favorite greatniece? She's having a troublesome confinement?"

"Not physically, no. Doctor says she's in splendid condition. But something's gnawing away at the dear girl's spirit, or mind, or something. She often seems actually *terrified*."

"Does she tell you why, Elizabeth?"

"Not a peep. And there's certainly nothing to be frightened of, here safe in her very own home. It's nothing either Baptiste or I has done. Despite the original shock when we knew she'd run off and married, and then that a baby is coming. we've *tried* to help."

"Is it perhaps because you resented the lad's being a Roland?"

Elizabeth pursed her lips. "That angle didn't make us rejoice. We couldn't imagine why she'd done it. But we didn't punish her. When she learned he had died—in the final week of the war, I believe—we tried to pamper her."

We didn't punish her, Marie thought silently, sipping her tea. *Old enough to be a widow and a mother, but still thought of in terms of punishing. I remember just how you sounded in the boat, Roger-Claude, on*

*our way back from New Orleans. So that's what has my
baby lamb tied up in knots! They can't acknowledge
hers is grown-up grieving.*

Later, with Elizabeth safely working in the kitchen,
the new arrival moved back to the porch which surrounded Baptiste's substantial house on three sides,
rather like a spread fan. Mimi sat here almost immo-
bile, after one wan smile in her Great-Aunt's direction.
She looked like a wax doll.

"It isn't easy, honey, is it? Falling in love with a
Roland man?"

Mimi kept on looking out across the flooded rice
fields. "They hate him. Gareth never even thought a
thought against them. But they all hate him."

"They all hated Percy, too, and he was just as innocent. Of course, in his case they had cause to suspect
him of black things right at first. But even before then,
they hated him. Not for any reason on earth but that
his name was Roland."

Now, Mimi did turn.

"Percy? Percy Roland? Was he . . . Weren't you—"

"It seems so far back I can hardly believe it myself.
But yes, that's how it was. We seem to be Roland-
jinxed, we Bernard women. Me with Percy. Blanche
with John. Now you."

"Tell me, Aunt Marie. Tell me how it happened with
you. Please tell me."

A thread of desperation wove through the younger
voice. It had not escaped Marie. Yet she answered
placidly. "Why, very suddenly. One morning in the
New Orleans fish market, when I was just about as
young as you are now. I saw him sitting there and it
just happened."

"What did he look like? Can you remember, after so long?"

"As if it were yesterday, honey. Handsome as Apollo. Folks said Percy took after his dead father in that. His hair looked like it was all the gold in the world set on fire. But he was a quiet young man. Gentle as my kitten Moses. And deep, under the quietness."

"But-but that's my Gareth you're describing! Every word the same!"

"Our brothers and fathers and cousins would hoot me, Marie, but do you know something? I do believe Roland men are blessed. Look at how their women go on and on remembering them!"

"So do Bernard men," Mimi whispered sickly. "Hosea says he'll murder my baby."

"He says *what*? Now look here at me, young Mrs. Gareth Roland—"

"We were alone in the house. Nobody else heard. But he *said* it, Aunt Marie.'.'

A moment of silence then. "I'd expect better of Hosea. Hate does surely twist a man. You're positive he meant it? Wasn't it just bluster?"

"I think he means it. That's what I can't get out of my mind."

"Then do you know what I'd suggest, honey? Don't have your little one here, with all that worry pressing on you. Go off somewhere else. Ask Baptiste and Elizabeth to take you."

"They'd never leave the rice crop. They'd never believe in any danger."

"All right, honey, then it's up to Great-Auntie to take charge, I reckon. And I think I know just the spot for us to go. The convent at Grand Coteau, if they've got space to take us. Blanche is so happy there. She'd be a great help to have at hand. Tomorrow you and I are packing you a valise. I'll be making the shortest prairie visit on record."

The walls of the convent seemed to breathe peace as the carriage turned in from the roadway. Mimi looked along the driveway with a sigh that was half yearning, half moan.

These past several jolting miles had stirred pains in her until sometimes she all but screamed with them. Only Great-Aunt Marie's unshakable presence at her side convinced her that she was not actually dying, as doubtless Cousin Hosea devoutly wished she would.

In the doorway Aunt Blanche was waiting for them, waving as they first caught sight of her. Although Papa's sister looked older than Mimi remembered, from that time when she came out to Opelousas to testify in court against an actor man related to no Queen whatever, she still seemed radiant, the Bernard family beauty beyond question. As the carriage halted she ran down the steps as lightly as a girl to take over their valises.

"Welcome, both of you, to Grand Coteau!" Blanche's warm smile embraced them both. "I'm afraid we're a bit short-handed at the moment. But I'll make you cozy."

"Where are all the others?" Marie demanded. "Why, this place was a dignified beehive, last time I came to see you here. Today it seems so quiet."

"There's a novena going on, Aunt Marie. You remember I told you when you were here about our young novice sent down from St. Louis? The one who contracted a pain no one could diagnose?"

"Of course I do. How is the dear girl now?"

"She was so much better for a while. But then the progress reversed itself. Her agonies came back tenfold. It's not in her side alone. It's been spreading through until lately it concentrated in her poor mouth. She can't swallow, can't speak."

Marie sighed. "Can nothing at all be done for her?"

"The doctors hold no hope whatever. Her tongue is swollen hideously. And it's turned hard as leather."

They were indoors now. Along the corridor as they followed it a faint murmur of praying voices filtered. Instinctively, the three women dropped their own to whispers.

"They're praying for help to Blessed John Berchmans," murmured Blanche.

Marie nodded soberly, as if well acquainted with the name. But Mimi never had heard it. "And who is Blessed John, Aunt Blanche?"

"A young Belgian, dear, who was born in Diest almost three centuries ago. The son of a humble shoemaker on Beaver Street. Before he died in 1621, his holy works were many. The decree for his Beatification was promulgated by His Holiness, Pope Pius IX, only two springs ago."

Mimi grabbed for her side, to ride out a passing tremor. "What an exceptional man he must have been. Will he intercede for your poor novice, do you think?"

"We pray. The rest is up to him. Exceptional he was, indeed. Just a few months ago, after his beatification, his relics were deposited beneath the altar of the Blessed Virgin in the magnificent San Ignazio

Church in Rome. If anyone can help our poor young lady in her distress, surely it will be Blessed John."

As they all but tiptoed along the corridor, Mimi gasped suddenly and crumpled back against a wall. If Marie had not caught her, she might have fallen. "OOO-oo-ooh!"

"Darling! What is it, child? You're white as a ghost!"

"I—I think—the baby's coming, Aunt Marie. I can't —go on—"

Between them, the two older women supported her and half-carried her into the clean, spare little room which had been prepared for her at Blanche's plea. As she lay on the simple bed, her agony receding slowly, Mimi still could hear that distant murmur of beseeching voices.

It did her good to remember that within the convent someone else was enduring even greater pain than her own. Under the circumstances, she could regard the unknown young *religieuse* as a companion in arms. The thought diminished Mimi's frightening loneliness wonderfully.

"Blessed John," she moaned, "please help her if you can. Please help me, too."

The bells began pealing, a joyous clamor, midway of the long tapestry of stabbing anguish and alternating relief which this fading day had become for her.

Mimi stirred on her bed, aware that Great-Aunt Marie had been wiping her damp forehead with a cloth saturated in lavender water. Aunt Blanche seemed to have vanished. She and Marie were alone together.

"What are the bells for? They sound so happy!"

"I don't know, darling. Probably Blanche will tell

us when she returns. She's gone to fetch one of the doctors. It's almost time."

"Wouldn't it be beautiful to have Gareth's son arrive while the bells are still singing? I guess our boy wouldn't remember, but I'd love to have that the very first sound he hears."

"Just lie still, Mimi. The doctor will come. It will all be over soon."

"I wish I could have other children for Gareth, Aunt Marie. Lots of other children. Do you think this one will mind being my only. . . . *Oooo-oo-h!*"

Marie's firm, wise hands were holding her.

"Quiet, Mimi, quiet. The pain will pass. Who ever heard of a girl saying she wanted *more* babies while she's in the midst of labor? You're truly one of a kind, Mimi Bernard. No wonder I love you."

"Mimi *Roland*," the girl on the bed corrected. "Will the family all really hate my baby because of that?"

The plain door across from her opened smartly. Aunt Blanche rustled through it, with a man bearing a surgical kit just behind her. Between spasms, Mimi watched them as they bent above her. The doctor was all concern. But Aunt Blanche was beaming.

"Are the bells ringing for my baby, Aunt Blanche? It's too soon yet."

"No, darling. They're for the miracle. *Our* Miracle of Grand Coteau."

Mimi frowned, trying to understand. "What's happened? If it isn't Gareth's son—"

"It's the young novice for whom we're rejoicing. The miracle we all were praying for has actually happened! A vision of Blessed John Berchmans appeared at her bedside. He reached out and laid a finger on her swollen, twisted tongue and immediately she was cured. There's no question of it. He was seen, the lady is already well, and our Sister in charge is already writing a report to His Holiness in Rome. It will be Blessed John's third qualified miracle. It ought to assure him of Sainthood. One day, a shrine will be built here—Louisiana's first! Small wonder the bells are singing."

A fresh spasm wrenched her, but despite her gasp of agony Mimi kept on contentedly smiling. "What a wonderful, wonderful day for my child to be born!"

Hours later, when the long ordeal was over and indeed half forgotten by a resting young mother, bells still spread their reverent message over the treetops of Grand Coteau.

She lay listening to them contentedly, her scrap of a son held lovingly against her. He was so tiny she feared he might break, although a bustling Great-Aunt Marie kept assuring her that he was a veritable wonder of sturdiness. His eyes were still screwed tight shut. She prayed that when they opened they would be peacock blue-green.

The plain door across from her already stood wide, so air might circulate. Past it swept Aunt Blanche, and with her a young man in Federal uniform.

Her breath caught. *Gareth!*

No, of course not Gareth. Who would dare pray for three such miracles in a single day? Yet he looked so much like that handsome youth she had found in the range grass that suddenly the small room seemed to be spinning.

"Mimi?" Aunt Blanche stood between them. "This is Lieutenant Bruce Roland."

"And you are my new sister." The tall Lieutenant's smile was so identical a twin of another smile she cherished that Mimi could not help returning it weakly. "I've known about you for quite a long while now. Gareth wrote me about his new wife from the trail."

"D-did you mind much, Lieutenant? When Gareth married a Bernard?"

"Mind? When the girl who saved his life was the bride? How could I?"

"Another Bernard, soon afterward, ended Gareth's journey. Did you know that, too?"

"I was told. But I think I grasp why. Our families have been enemies so long. The hate had to crystallize. Perhaps it will be over now."

"Too late, for Gareth and me."

"But maybe not for your son. In the waiting room outside, I've just been talking with a couple of fellows from your part of the country—your cousins Daniel and Hosea. They'd ridden here as soon as they learned where you were, both worried sick about your well-being. They'll be brought in to see you soon."

Mimi stiffened in panic. "*Hosea* is here? But he's the reason I left home!"

"Don't look so frightened, sister-in-law. He's in an anguish of remorse out there, realizing how your fear of him endangered you. That's why he's come. To beg forgiveness."

Her words seemed to stumble. "Do you know Hosea, that he and Gareth—"

"I know. But Gareth felt no hatred for anyone. He'd have understood. So I'll have to try to understand, too. Can you, as well, Mimi? Knowing Gareth would want it?"

Deep inside, Mimi knew the answer to that. It was as if a great stone had been rolled clear of her. Had

Blessed John accomplished this feat also? She'd have to think that over. But she knew that, however achieved, the result was unmistakably Blessed.

"Do you really believe after all that's passed between our two families . . ."

"It has to happen, doesn't it? For my new nephew's sake? It may be hard for our older folk to adjust. But our own young generation can manage it, if we have the will."

Happiness was washing over her. "I'm glad you've come, Bruce."

"As soon as I heard you were here, and why you were," Bruce nodded.

"We're going to be friends, aren't we? You look so much like Gareth he almost seems here in the room with me now."

She moved slightly to push a scrap of blue blanket from the cherubic face of the infant slumbering beside her.

"I'd like you to meet Gareth's son, Bruce. This is Master Bernard Roland."

THE END

*TWENTY-SECOND IN THE
BESTSELLING SERIES,
THE MAKING OF AMERICA!*

THE
GUNFIGHTERS

by Lee Davis Willoughby

Young Wes Cardigan meets Wild Bill Hickok, town marshal of Abilene, while helping him stand off a murderous band of outlaws. Under the legendary gunfighters tutelage, he learns the art of the fast-draw, and falls in love with Wild Bill's cousin, the beautiful Helen Butler.

But as Cardigan's star rises, Wild Bill's declines, as his incomparable skills fade and he gains one enemy too many. Jack McCall, a relentlessly evil man, plots a final showdown for Cardigan and Hickok, with all the cards stacked against them.

BE SURE TO READ
THE GUNFIGHTERS
ON SALE NOW FROM DELL/BRYANS

THE DONNER PEOPLE

by Lee Davis Willoughby

From the moment in 1846 when the Donner-Reed wagon train set out from Springfield, Illinois, the men, women and children of the party suffered from a plague of bad luck. There was illness, inept leadership and bitter feuding.

By the time they reached a certain storm-battered pass in the high Sierras, all the ingredients of horrifying tragedy were in place. There were heroes, such as the patriarch, George Donner, and the bold young mountain man, Thornbird. There were heroines, such as tiny, spirited Tamsen Donner, and the bewitching Liza Williams.

But there was also among them a madman, a murderer—and those accursed ones who, when disaster, starvation and death struck, would break the last human taboo.